The Book of Mormon Sleuth

C. B. ANDERSEN

D1468553

BOOKCRAFT

SALT LAKE CITY, UTAH

For Chloe

Library of Congress Cataloging-in-Publication Data

Andersen, C.B. (Carl Blaine), 1961-

The Book of Mormon sleuth / C.B. Andersen.

p. cm.

Summary: Great Aunt Ella gives twelve-year-old Brandon her rare edition of the Book of Mormon, expecting him to follow its teachings and keep it safe from the menacing thief who is determined to take it from her Iowa farm.

ISBN 1-57345-664-0 (pbk.)

[1. Mormons–Fiction. 2. Book of Mormon–Fiction. 3. Farm life–Iowa–Fiction. 4. Great-aunts–Fiction. 5. Iowa–Fiction] I. Title.

PZ7.A51887 Bo 2000

[Fic]–dc21   00-025616

Printed in the United States of America   18961-300238
R. R. Donnelley and Sons, Portland, OR

10   9   8   7   6   5   4

Contents

Chapter 1   DON'T BET ON THE WEATHER   1

Chapter 2   PREPARATION   13

Chapter 3   MORONI'S VISIT   31

Chapter 4   NAUVOO   46

Chapter 5   THE GREAT SALT LAKE VALLEY   65

Chapter 6   MY 116 PAGES GET LOST   83

Chapter 7   SEEK AND YE SHALL FIND   99

Chapter 8   THE LIAHONA   115

Chapter 9   A THIEF IN THE NIGHT   126

Chapter 10   THE ANSWER TO MY PRAYER   141

Chapter 11   INDEPENDENCE   152

Chapter 12   HANNAH   168

Chapter 13   A LITTLE CHILD SHALL LEAD THEM   179

Chapter 14   TRAIL OF TEARS   196

Chapter 15   YOUR PRAYER IS IN VAIN   208

Chapter 16   THE MARTYRS   224

Chapter 17   THE CAVITY OF A ROCK   236

Chapter 18   LED BY THE SPIRIT   254

Chapter 19   THE PROMISED LAND   269

Preface

The purpose of this book is to introduce principles taught in the Book of Mormon through a medium that will keep young readers (or listeners) interested and involved—a work of fiction, filled with excitement and adventure. The intent is that the principles will remain firmly embedded in the reader's mind after the book has been put away. Obviously, the principles need to be applied to real life for them to be viable, but one must first *know* the principle before it can be applied.

This book will be most fun for those readers who already have some understanding and familiarity with the Book of Mormon and for those willing to keep a copy of the Book of Mormon nearby as they read; but the book can be easily enjoyed by any and all. Some Book of Mormon references are never actually quoted, leaving it to the reader to find and read them.

CHAPTER 1

Don't Bet on the Weather

April in Utah usually isn't too hard to figure out, but this year it was. We'd had a lot of snow in March, but just a week later it was way too hot to even wear a jacket to school. At least that's what I argued to Mom. I was standing on the porch with the front door open.

"If I wear a coat today, I'll be the only one of my friends who does! It's *hot* out here—come *feel* it!"

She's always worried about me getting picked on, so I usually win the argument when I use the "only one of my friends" trick. Luckily, we live less than a block from the school. In fact, you can see it from our front yard. She didn't end up making me wear my coat, but she did stand on the sidewalk and watch me all the way around the corner of the school building. I guess she was worried that I would suddenly get hit by a blast of cold, Alaskan air and fall over frozen in the sixty seconds it took me to get from our house to the school.

It turned out I was about the only one of my friends who *didn't* have a coat. The coat hooks for the sixth graders were completely full. Gabe's mom had told him that a big storm was coming and convinced him he'd need a coat on the way home. By afternoon recess time, it was starting to get a little cold, but after a few minutes of running around, it didn't feel too bad.

I hit the crash bar on the school door at a dead run about ten seconds after Miss Cook told us we were "dismissed for the day." By the time I got to the bottom of the four stairs, I realized it was far too cold outside for any *living* creature that wanted to stay that way.

1

So I spun around and headed right back up the stairs into the school. I stood just inside the glass doors staring at huge, fluffy snowflakes that were falling so thick you could barely see to the corner of the building. There was already about an inch on the ground. Gabe came running down the hall. He gave me a weird look and asked, "What's wrong with you?"

"It's *cold!*" I whined. My arms and shoulders gave a little shudder just thinking about it.

"I told you it was going to snow today," he said with a goofy look.

I watched him run out the door and down the stairs, then slip on the last step and land right on his backside. A couple of kids laughed at him as he slopped around in the snow trying to get up, then limped around the corner toward home.

"If you're so smart, why didn't you wear your boots?" I yelled after him, but he was already long gone.

It took only about half a minute of people saying, "What are you doing, Brandon?" and "Why aren't you going home?" and "Did you forget something?" before I decided I had better just run as fast as I could and hope my mom wouldn't give me too much grief for refusing to wear a coat.

I came flying around the corner of the school faster than I ever had before. I usually wait for the crossing guard to hold up her cute little "stop" sign before charging into the street, but she's learned that there are certain times when I'm willing to take my life into my own hands, and if she wants to keep me safe she'd better be ready. This was one of those times. Luckily, even with the big snowflakes, she saw me coming and managed to get pretty close to the middle of the road with her sign held up high before my foot left the sidewalk. I always try to be polite, so I yelled, "Thanks!" as I ran past her. She yelled something, too, about a hospital or an asylum, but I didn't catch the whole thing.

Whenever I do something pretty dumb Mom always says that

I'd "better learn this" or "better learn that" before the next time. Well, today I was trying to figure out how to avoid her lecture when I saw Dad's car parked in the driveway. *What's going on?* I wondered. He's *never* there when I get home from school. Usually I'm over at Gabe's house till dinnertime, and he picks me up on his way home from work. When I tromped into the house, I was surprised to see him standing in the kitchen talking to Mom.

"I think we ought to do it," Dad was saying.

Mom looked annoyed and said, "Craig, we don't have anything arranged!"

"We don't have anything arranged for what?" I asked.

"We can take care of things before we need to leave, and besides, this is a perfect opportunity," Dad answered.

"Perfect opportunity for what?" I asked again, but neither of them seemed to notice me.

Mom asked Dad, "Well, what are we going to do with the house for the next two months?"

"Why aren't *we* going to be in our house for the next two months?" I asked, giving them another opportunity to include me in the conversation.

I was starting to get worried. Mom and Dad had told us we probably wouldn't get a vacation this summer. Dad always teaches the summer term at the state college beginning the last part of June. We usually take a family trip the first half of June, but this year he was trying to put together a new class or something. He had told us he was going to be busy doing research, so we probably wouldn't be going anywhere. But now it was starting to sound like things might be changing. It always got scary when Dad had big plans.

"It's a perfect setup, Sarah. The farm is only about forty miles from Waterloo. I can do my research there, as long as I'm back at my office by the first part of June. You know," Dad continued, "this will be the only chance the kids have for a vacation this year."

"What farm?" I asked, slightly perturbed that they were still ignoring me.

"There is only a week before we'd have to be gone! That's not enough time to make arrangements for someone to watch the house," Mom protested, "and the kids are still in school and . . . and . . . and they have music lessons and . . . and . . ."

"Gone where?" I said a little louder, getting more and more worried. "Don't tell me I'm going to miss soccer!"

My competition soccer team had been practicing for the last month, and the spring season was about to start, followed by a tournament in May. My team took second place last year. I had friends on the team that beat us in that championship game, and I'd been waiting all year for the chance to get even.

Dad laughed, continuing to pretend that I didn't exist. "It's not like Lehi getting commanded to leave everything he owns and march his family into the wilderness. Oh, I'll bet we can get all that worked out in just a day or two! I'm going to make some phone calls."

Mom didn't have even a trace of a smile on her face when she said, "Yes, but even Lehi had to pitch a tent a few miles outside of town and send Nephi back *twice* to get something else."

Dad laughed again as he left the room.

Mom looked at me with her mouth twisted to one side, shook her head, and said, "I guess he's serious."

"About *what?*" I asked, trying to sound as exasperated as possible.

Mom sighed. "You remember my Aunt Ella. She's my mother's sister. You know, she lives on a dairy farm in Iowa."

"Iowa?"

"Well, she called today and practically insisted that we come stay with her on the farm for a few weeks."

"Did you say *dairy* farm?"

"Dad and I were planning on visiting her next fall," Mom went

4

on, "but she said that she needs the whole family there for a while. I tried to get her to explain, but she said she couldn't. It's apparently just a strong feeling she has. Anyway, Dad had already arranged with the college to use most of April and May as research time, and now I guess he thinks he can do it in Iowa as well as here. So he wants to go."

"So are you telling me that we're not going to be living at home?"

"It would be only for a couple of months," Mom said, without sounding too convinced.

"And I'm gonna miss the *entire* spring soccer season?"

"I'm sorry, Brandon. Your dad seems determined, and if he can work things out, we'll have to leave a week from today. But there are so many arrangements we need to make . . . I don't think you need to worry about it."

I thought to myself, *I'll just bet Dad will con Mom into thinking he has everything worked out and then we'll find out that nothing really is. It's going to be a disaster.*

The front door banged shut. It was my older sister, Shauna. She rides the bus to school and gets home a few minutes after I do. She's in tenth grade.

"Brandon doesn't have to worry about what?" Shauna asked.

"Dad's making us go to Iowa to live on a dairy farm for *two months!*" I blurted out.

Mom smiled. "You had a great time when we were there before. You remember Aunt Ella's farm, don't you, Shauna?"

Shauna had a horrified look on her face. "What farm?" she said softly, her lips barely moving. "And you're not serious about Dad making us live on one, are you?"

"You really enjoyed it when we went there! We stayed for almost a week, and none of you wanted to come home!"

Mom usually remembered things a lot better than they really

were, and I had a feeling that we were probably all *begging* to leave by the time Mom and Dad got around to taking us home.

"Besides that," Mom continued, "I'm sure we won't be able to get it arranged."

Dad walked into the kitchen with an envelope in his hand. He was writing on it with a pen and saying things like "call my boss about doing research in Iowa, . . . call the university library in Waterloo, . . . get a substitute for my Sunday School class." He always uses the back of a used envelope to make lists on. It seemed to me that envelopes were pretty easy to lose; anyway, he always seemed to lose his lists. At least once a week he'd walk around the house asking, "Has anybody seen a long envelope from the Ford dealer that had my shopping list on the back?"

Mom looked at what he was doing and added, "Don't forget to make a note to contact the schools about the kids being gone for two months."

Shauna almost screamed. "Dad! Tell me you're not going to make me miss school and live in Iowa for two months!" Then she looked at Mom and said, "I don't remember *ever* being on Aunt Ella's farm!"

Dad laughed. He obviously had no clue that we were ready to start stomping on his toes and kicking him in the shins. "I didn't realize you liked school so much, Shauna!" he smiled. "Come on, you guys, it was only three and a half years ago that we were there! You mean you don't remember the cows and the pigs and all the big fields of corn? We went out walking in the corn, and it was twice as tall as any of you!"

Shauna's eyes got big. Then she spoke very slowly, "Do you mean the place where Meg went out by the pigs for the first time and threw up because it stunk so bad—and she gagged every time she even thought about it after that?"

"Y-e-e-s-s-s!" Mom and Dad had the silliest grins on their faces.

I suddenly had a vision of terror. "You mean the place with the

100-mile dirt road before you ever get to the house and nobody else lives even close?! That place that stunk really bad?"

Meg wasn't the only one who threw up. You didn't even have to go outside to smell the pigs and cows and everything else that stunk! You couldn't get away from it. I remembered covering my face with a pillow so that I could hardly breathe when I tried to go to sleep at night. It was disgusting! And anytime somebody would drive past the house, they'd go flying by at 90 miles an hour, and it would kick up dust all over the place.

Dad tried to calm me down by saying, "Aunt Ella told me that the county just recently covered the dirt road with gravel! Besides that, it's only about two miles from the main highway."

"But what about the smell?" I gasped.

"Oh, it's not so bad. Don't worry; you get used to it!"

Something is seriously wrong with my dad because he smiled like what he was saying made perfect sense.

"Oh, that's great, Dad," I complained. "We're all used to air pollution, too, but it still kills our brain cells." I thought for sure Dad had lost about a hundred brain cells too many.

Meg, who had been standing there listening to all of this, didn't remember throwing up three and a half years ago because she was only four at the time. She just looked at Dad and said, "What's gravel?"

Right then and there I knew this whole thing was a big mistake, but Dad just didn't seem to get it.

"I bet I don't throw up this time," Meg said, without waiting for the "gravel" answer, " 'cause I'm a lot older now."

Shauna had sort of fallen backward into a chair at the kitchen table and was staring at the wall. She was almost whimpering when she said, "Just today I got my first date with Tom, and it's for the junior prom in May. He said he asked me early before anyone else had a chance to ask me. Excuse me, but I'm going to be in Iowa? I'll bet they're all hicks and they wear cowboy boots and stuff."

I think that was the most depressed I'd ever seen her.

Jeff came walking into the house just then. He's in seventh grade and gets out of school the same time I do, but he always takes a while getting home. He looked around at everybody as he was taking off his coat and gloves. "What's going on?" he asked slowly. "I'll bet I don't want to know."

"Well . . . ," Dad started, but I interrupted him.

"Excuse me. I don't really want to hear all this again," I stated sadly, "but before I go to my room and get sick, Jeff, will you please tell me how come you took your coat and gloves to school today?"

"I've been reading the weather report in the newspaper every day this week for school," he said with a shrug. "Last night I read that a big storm was coming today."

"Thanks for the warning," I said as I twisted up my face.

"I was going to tell you this morning," he said, "but since today's April Fool's Day, I didn't think you'd believe me."

I just stared at him. "Hello-o-o, Jeff!" I said. "That was yesterday."

"Oh, yeah!" he laughed and continued pulling off his coat. I turned and went to our bedroom to stare out the window.

When I came out a while later, everyone except for Dad was in the kitchen. Mom was cooking something and talking about all that would have to be done if we really did go to Iowa.

Jeff looked at me and said, "Hey, Brandon, guess what?" As usual he didn't wait for a response before going on. "Just this week we started talking about consumer goods at school, and I have to do a ten-page research paper on some product that's made in the United States. Since we're going to be living on a dairy farm for two months, I can do milk as my product really easy!"

I just stared at him while I tried to think of something nice to say. Mom looked over at me. My mouth was open, but my tongue wasn't moving.

"You're supposed to say something like 'That's great, Jeff!' or 'Cool!' or something equally polite," she suggested.

I said, "Cool, Jeff" as enthusiastically as possible, which wasn't very at the moment.

Just then Granny came in the front door with her arms full of shopping bags. I always thought we were pretty lucky to have Granny living with us. Granny is Mom's mom. Mom and Dad moved in with her when they were first married and didn't have any money, and I guess they just never bothered moving out. Either that, or Dad still wasn't making any money. Anyway, Aunt Ella is Granny's oldest sister. I guess that really makes Aunt Ella my great-aunt. Granny always went with us on all our vacations and came to our soccer games and recitals and stuff, and Mom was quick to say that Granny loved the farm.

Mom's dad died when Mom was only two, so Granny and Mom lived alone together while Mom was growing up. Granny used to be a nurse, but she retired when I was in fourth grade. We always went running to her when we got hurt. She always had lots more sympathy, more Band-Aids, and more medicine to offer than either Mom or Dad. It was a lot more fun to howl when Granny was there because she'd always rush to the rescue. Dad would just say something really helpful like, "Oh, come on, it doesn't hurt that bad."

Anyway, I always thought she was great to have around, but she certainly didn't help with this situation. It turns out that Dad had gotten everything arranged while I had been in my room. He'd also called our schools and found out it would be "no problem" for us all to get our homework ahead of time, as long as we mailed our finished assignments back to the school once a week while we were gone. Dad's envelope was on the kitchen table, and all the things on the list had big check marks by them except one. The only thing left on the list was what to do with the house while we were gone. I noticed that soccer was *not* on his list of "items-to-take-care-of-before-I-abuse-my-family-by-taking-them-to-Iowa-for-two-months."

As soon as Granny appeared in the doorway, Mom said, "Have we got news for you!" You can always tell when Granny has been out buying gifts. She hurries through the kitchen with her bags, before taking off her coat or even dropping her purse. If anybody says anything to her she replies with, "I'll talk to you in a minute. I have to go hide this stuff first." And she would always do a good job of hiding it, too. We always got Christmas presents from her for a couple months after Christmas because she could never remember where she'd hidden them all. Her bedroom wasn't very big, but it sure had lots of stuff in it.

She must be shopping for Easter, I thought. Her load was so wide that the bags rubbed along both walls down the hallway. I was sure hoping that we wouldn't be able to find anyone to live in our house while we were gone so we wouldn't be able to go. That's where Granny failed me. When she came back to the kitchen after hiding her treasures, Mom gave her the whole story. There's a door from our kitchen that goes right into the garage. We could hear Dad in there moving things around and whistling. He always whistles when he thinks things are going great.

"I figured you'd want to come, too," Mom said.

"It sounds really fun to me," Granny replied, "and the kids will have a blast."

"Then the only problem," Mom continued, "is what to do with the house while we're gone."

"I bet I know someone who'd do a great job taking care of the house for a couple of months," Granny said with a smile, and she jumped up to make a phone call to whomever she was thinking of.

It took only about thirty seconds of listening to Granny's half of the phone call to figure out that she knew someone who needed a place to stay. The last thing I heard Granny say was, "That's wonderful. Why don't you plan on staying here for a couple of months."

I'll have to think twice about running to her the next time I get a bloody knee, I thought. *Thanks a bunch, Granny.*

I went back to my room and started thinking about all that had happened. It's amazing how fast things can change. "Sunny and warm before school," I said out loud, "cold and miserable after."

Well, it seemed like everybody was willing to "bet this" or "bet that" about this "vacation." In fact, it sounded to me like the whole thing was going to be a gamble. Hadn't Dad just given us a family night lesson about the evils of "games of chance"? I sat on my bed just quietly shaking my head, thinking about how unfair the whole thing was. I lay back on my pillow, but my head hit something hard. Without looking, I reached around and pulled my Scout handbook out from under my head.

I stared at the book, but my mind was still somewhere else. After a couple of minutes I started thumbing through it and thinking about what Brother Davis had worked on with us the day before. He'd given us an assignment to start keeping a journal. He said it was one of the requirements for the personal progress merit badge.

I took a deep breath. I couldn't believe I was going to have to miss my soccer tournament, but if I was going to have to go to Iowa, I decided I might as well keep a journal for those two months. That way, something good might come of the whole rotten deal. I could also keep track of all the bets that were being made about why it was a good idea or a bad idea to go to Aunt Ella's.

I opened the bottom drawer of my desk and found a spiral notebook. Only the first few pages had anything written on them. It looked like my science notebook from third grade, so I ripped out the used pages and threw them away. Then I wrote these notes on the first page.

Thursday, April 2. Andrews Family Bets about Dad's Crazy Vacation:

DAD: Bet that he could get everything worked out in a day or two. Dad says that he has it done already—need to wait until later to see if it's true.

MOM: *Bet that Dad wouldn't be able to work things out. See note above about waiting until later.*

ME: *Bet that Dad would make Mom believe that he had everything worked out, but he really wouldn't. We'll see.*

MEG: *Bet that she wouldn't throw up this time.*

SHAUNA: *Bet that all the kids would be hicks and wear cowboy boots.*

JEFF: *Bet that he wouldn't want to know what we were talking about.*

GRANNY: *Bet that she knew someone who'd do a great job taking care of the house.*

As I looked over my notes I just shook my head slowly back and forth. After staring at the list for another minute I added this:

Andrews Family's Betting Results:

JEFF: *(Lost) Judging from his reaction about his milk research paper, he probably did want to know what we were talking about.*

I was sort of hoping that keeping track of all this stuff might make the time go by a little faster. But when I tried to imagine my whole family on a dairy farm for two months, I had serious doubts that anything could make this "vacation" bearable.

CHAPTER 2

Preparation

The following Monday after school I heard the phone ring.

"Brandon, phone's for you!" Shauna called.

"Who is it?" I asked.

"I didn't ask. Sorry!"

I picked up the phone and said, "Hello?"

"Brandon, is that you?" came a woman's voice.

"Uh-huh. Who's this?"

"It's Aunt Ella."

"Oh, hi! Umm, did you want to talk to my dad or my mom?" I asked, thinking Shauna must have heard wrong when she thought the phone was for me.

"No. As a matter of fact, you are the one I wanted to talk to, Brandon. Let me ask you something. How old are you now?"

"Uh, twelve," I answered, wondering why she wanted to know.

"You have actually turned twelve?" Aunt Ella said.

I didn't know she was going to be so exact. My birthday was in June, so technically I wasn't twelve yet—but almost.

"Well, no, not really. My birthday is June third," I said. "I'll *be* twelve."

"Then you have not received the Aaronic Priesthood yet, is that correct?"

Aunt Ella sounded like a lawyer or something, the way she asked the questions.

"No, not yet," I admitted.

"Very well," she said. "I suppose you will want to prepare yourself for that important event, correct?"

"Yes, ma'am."

"I am very glad that you are coming to see me," Aunt Ella continued, "because I have something very special for you."

"For my family?" I asked.

"No, just for you, Brandon. That is why I phoned you. This is a special time in your life, and I have something very important to give you. That's why it is so timely that you are coming for a visit."

"What is it?" I asked slowly. This was sounding a little strange.

"There'll be time enough for that when you arrive," she answered.

"Okay," I said, "is that all you wanted?"

"Yes, it is. But just make certain that you are ready."

"Okay," I said again. After pausing for a moment I asked, "How do I get ready if I don't know what it is?"

"Alma and Amulek knew," she responded quickly.

"What?" I asked. I wasn't sure that I'd heard her right.

"In chapter 16 of the book of Alma we learn that Alma and Amulek knew about being prepared."

"Alma in the *Book of Mormon?*" I questioned slowly.

"That is correct," she replied. "And the sons of Mosiah knew, too. We read about that in the next chapter."

"You mean the next chapter in Alma?" I asked.

"Yes. I am very excited to see you, Brandon. We will start working as soon as you arrive."

"Start working on what?" I asked. I was *way* confused.

"I'll explain everything to you after you arrive, but just make certain that you are prepared. I would bet that you will have *no* trouble with that."

As she said this, the words *I bet* stuck in my head, and I thought about the list I had started a few days earlier in my spiral notebook. I thought maybe I should write down Aunt Ella's bet in there, too.

"How soon will you be leaving?" she asked.

"Thursday," I answered. "We get out of school Thursday and Friday for spring break, so we're leaving early Thursday morning."

"Tell your parents that I will expect to see them Friday night unless they call. And you and I can begin working first thing Saturday morning."

"Okay, I'll tell them," I said, still wondering what we would be "working" on but not brave enough to ask again. Neither of us said anything for a moment.

"Remember that before you can accomplish *anything*, you have to know what you want and then go after it with all your might," she said. The way she said it, it sounded kind of like a lecture.

"O-Okay" was all I could manage to get out.

"Good-bye," she said.

" 'Bye," I answered.

After hanging up the phone, I stood there thinking. I tried to remember everything that she'd said, but it was all too confusing. Dad wasn't the only one being weird about this. Then I remembered that I was going to write something down in my notebook about Aunt Ella, so I headed for my room.

It took a minute to find the notebook because it had been a few days since I wrote my first notes about this vacation. Once I found it, I read over what I'd written before. I decided to write Aunt Ella's stuff on a new page:

Monday, April 6. More Andrews Family Bets about Dad's Crazy Vacation:

AUNT ELLA: Bet that I would have no trouble being prepared.

I stared at what I had written.

"Be prepared for what?" I asked myself out loud. I wasn't sure I remembered the chapter I was supposed to read. I grabbed my Book of Mormon and found Alma 16 and read the whole thing while I was lying on my bed. That part of Alma was about the Lamanites killing a bunch of people and the Nephites coming back and driving the Lamanites out. But so many people had been killed that they just piled up all the dead bodies, and the place stunk so bad that nobody could stand to live around there for years. Then Alma and Amulek started preaching, telling the people that the Son of God would appear in this land after his resurrection.

I didn't get it. How could any of this possibly prepare me for *anything?* And what did she want me to prepare *for?* The only thing in the chapter that seemed to have anything to do with Aunt Ella and the farm was the horrible smell. But I knew *that* couldn't be it. I couldn't see any connection between wars or Christ appearing in America, either. I had no idea what to think about any of this.

Just then Shauna stuck her head into my room.

"Mom told me to find out if you got all your homework for the trip," she said.

"No, Miss Cook promised she'd have it all ready tomorrow," I responded without looking up. I was still staring at my notebook.

"Remember, Mom wants to look over everything before your last day so that she can ask questions if she needs to," Shauna continued.

"I know," I said absently. "I'll be sure to get it tomorrow."

Shauna didn't leave. She stood there in the doorway for a moment and then asked, "Whatcha doin'?"

"Well . . . ," I hesitated. I didn't really know where to start. "Aunt Ella just called me and told me she had something to give me and so I'd better be sure I was prepared."

"What is it?" Shauna asked.

"I don't know."

"Then how are you supposed to prepare for it?"

"That's what *I* asked!" I almost shouted. "But she just said I should have *no* trouble figuring it out."

"That's weird," Shauna said as she walked over and sat on the floor next to my bed. "What are you reading?"

"Well, Aunt Ella said something about Alma and Amulek knowing about preparation, so I was trying to figure out what she meant. I thought she said it was in Alma, chapter 16, but it doesn't make any sense to me."

"What's the notebook for?" Shauna asked.

"I've been making notes about our trip," I said.

"So did you write down the chapter she told you to read?"

"No," I confessed, "I just wrote down that she thought I'd have no trouble figuring out how to be prepared."

"Huh?" Shauna looked at me funny. "Why didn't you write down what she told you to read? It sounds like she's giving you clues or something. If you had written down what she said, you might have a chance to figure it out."

"Well, it's not going to do me any good now because I don't think I remembered the right chapter. And besides, I didn't have my notebook with me when she called."

"Did you look up *prepare* in the index?" she asked, with a look that said she thought I really might have done it!

"Uhh, no," I answered.

She took my Book of Mormon and started thumbing through the pages. "If we look up 'preparation,' " she said slowly, as she was searching in the back of the book, "we might be able to find something close to Alma 16."

Good idea, I thought, but I didn't bother saying it aloud. Shauna had always been the smart one in our family, and sometimes she made me feel stupid.

"Okay," she said, "here's the section for *prepare, preparation, preparatory.* Let's see now. . . . Here's First Nephi, Second Nephi. Okay! Here's Alma chapter 5, 12, . . . 12, . . . 13, 16! Hold on. There *is* something in Alma 16—chapter 16, verse 16."

"There is?" I asked, not really believing it. "What does it say?"

"The Lord pours out his Spirit to prepare men's minds and hearts to receive the word," she read. "Let's look it up and read the whole verse."

She quickly flipped the pages and read the verse out loud.

"Looks like we already read the important part," she said. "Write it down."

"Write what down?" I asked, still not sure what this had to do with me.

"Write down the reference and what it says about preparation!"

"It says something about *preparation?*" I asked.

"Yes!" she smiled. "It says that the Spirit prepares people's minds and hearts to receive the word."

I thought it was nice of her to repeat it for me without making any comments about my missing the point the first two times. This is what I wrote down:

PREPARATION:
Alma 16:16: The Lord pours out his Spirit to prepare your mind and heart to receive the word.

"So is this a Church thing that she's going to give you?" Shauna asked.

"I wish I knew," I said thoughtfully. "It must be, if I need the Spirit to prepare my mind and heart."

"Is that all that she told you?"

"I think so," I sighed. "No, wait, she said something about the sons of Mosiah in the next chapter."

"Was that about preparation, too?" Shauna asked.

"Yeah, but I forgot to read it," I admitted. "Not that it matters much, since I didn't find anything when I read the first chapter!"

Shauna looked in the index again, but she couldn't find anything about "preparation" in Alma 17.

"Let's just read it," she suggested.

Again she read out loud until she got to verse four.

"Wait!" I said. "It says, they had 'much success in bringing the Lamanites to the knowledge of the truth.' Isn't that what Alma and Amulek were talking about?"

"Oh, yeah!" Shauna said.

I felt pretty smug about finally contributing *something* to this discussion.

"But what does that have to do with preparation?" she asked, as if I might actually have figured something out.

I hadn't.

"I don't know," I confessed.

"Oh, *I* know," she smiled. "We already read about what they did to prepare themselves so that they could have success!"

"We did?"

"*Yes!*" she said with excitement. "It says . . . now write this down . . ."

"I'm writing! I'm writing!" I said. "Tell me the reference again."

"Alma chapter 17, verses two through four!" she said. "And it says that they were strong in the knowledge of the truth, and they had sound understanding, and they had searched the scriptures diligently and . . ."

"Slow down!" I yelled. "Verses two through *what?*"

Well, we managed to get her over her little "frantic time" there, and this is what I wrote in my notebook:

Alma 17:2–4: Strong in the knowledge of the truth

Had sound understanding

Searched the scriptures diligently

Much prayer and fasting

I looked at what I had written.

"So what does it mean?"

It sounded like a dumb question, I guess, but I couldn't see what any of this had to do with what Aunt Ella was expecting me to do. Was I supposed to spend the next four days searching for truth and sound understanding? Did she expect me to show up at her house having fasted for the last four days?

"Was that all she said?" Shauna asked again.

"I hope so!" I practically yelled at her. "I think it will take me a little longer than four days to develop sound understanding and become strong in the knowledge of the truth."

"Chill, Bran." Shauna was not overly impressed by my dramatic outburst. "Did she say anything else?"

"No, that was it," I said much more quietly.

"Okay, well, let's figure out what you need to do then," she said with a smile.

That didn't sound particularly fun to me.

She stared at me and then asked, "Do you want to do this or not? I'm happy to help."

"I don't know *what* I want," I said lamely. "Wait! She *did* say something else. Something like, you have to know what you want before you can have it. And you have to 'go for it' or something like that."

"Aunt Ella said 'Go for it'?" Shauna looked a little surprised.

"Well, something like that," I said.

"Okay," she thought for a moment, "so what do you want out of this vacation?"

"Huh?" I responded, showing off my clear understanding of this entire conversation.

"You have to know what you want and 'go for it.' You're stuck with this vacation, so what do you want to get out of it?" she explained.

"I want it to end a month early so I can be back in time for my *soccer* tournament," I said with a smirk. I half expected her to respond with something like "you know that's not what I mean," but instead she was quiet for a moment before simply offering, "I know. Me too."

After another pause she said, "You know, Bran, the only thing keeping us in Iowa for two months is Dad's research. So, if what we want is to come home early, then why don't we fast and pray for Dad to complete his work in half the time?"

"Are you *serious?*" I questioned.

She shrugged her shoulders. "Why not? Mom said she was sorry that I couldn't go to the dance with Tom 'cause she thinks he's nice. And you know Dad likes coming to watch you play soccer. Just think how ecstatic Dad would be if he got finished in half the time."

"You're right," I said, thinking I was *finally* starting to understand.

"So let's do everything we can to help make that happen," she smiled triumphantly.

"It sounds like you're telling me I'm going to be fasting a lot—more than I think I want to."

"No, I think just the normal fast Sunday is fine," she said, "but there are lots of *other* things we can do to help."

"Like what?" I asked.

"Like making sure he gets out of the house early every day and that he has a good breakfast before he leaves and takes a sack lunch with him so he doesn't have *any* reason to leave the library once he's there."

"He'll think there's something wrong with us if we do all that," I laughed. "Let's do it!"

Shauna smiled mischievously and said, "Don't you mean, 'Let's go for it'?"

This is what I wrote in my notebook:

MY GOAL FOR THIS VACATION:

Help Dad in every way to get his research done in half the time so we can come home early.

Fast and pray for him to get it done as quickly as possible.

Get him up early every day.

Make sure he has a big breakfast before he leaves.

Make him a sack lunch every day.

Four days later I was awakened by the sound of gravel under the tires of our family's van as we turned off the main highway. I was pleased to be awake so I could see for myself if it really was only two miles from the highway to the farm, like Dad had said, and not closer to about 100, the way I remembered it.

I was glad I had slept for the last couple of hours. After two days straight in the van, I was more than ready to get out. Though I was worried about how my nose would react, the rest of my body hurt from sitting, lying, and basically being bounced around for the last two days. It's no use complaining to Dad, though, because that just launches him into some big lecture about how tough it *really* was "back when he was a kid."

I must admit Dad had tried to make traveling a little easier. The van *is* pretty big, and a couple of years ago he bought one of those little TV/VCR combos that he hooks up so everybody on the back two seats can watch videotapes as we travel.

The only problem is that our family's pretty big, too. I haven't mentioned Chelsea and Daniel before now. Chelsea's five and Danny is three. That makes six kids and three adults, counting Granny. Even with one of those luggage bins on top of the van, by the time we got everybody's junk in with all the people, there wasn't much room left in our 12-seater MAV. (That's what we call it—the Mormon Assault Vehicle.) And the rule with the TV in the van is this: If either Chelsea or Danny is unhappy in any way, then we have to watch something that they like to watch. I think it's also part of the rule that if they happen to *like* a certain video, then we have to watch it at least *twelve* times before we can go to another tape.

Supposedly, the older kids get to take turns choosing movies when Chelsea and Danny are asleep or happy with something else, but it's not hard for anyone to imagine just how often *that* happens. I'm not sure if I've *ever* had a turn choosing the movie. It seems like we always take turns by starting with the oldest or the youngest, neither of which is me, and then the next person never gets a turn. We have to keep popping the tapes in and out every time Danny starts to cry or somebody happens to notice that both Danny and

Chelsea are asleep and we can continue watching *our* movie again. Using this method, a two-day trip is almost exactly enough time to watch a single hour-and-a-half-long movie like *Star Wars*, broken up every fifteen minutes by two or three hours of Tweety and Sylvester cartoons.

Anyway, the gravel road wound down into a valley between two long hills that were covered with trees and underbrush. The road was high enough on one side that we could look out over the valley, which was covered with tons of small green plants growing in long rows. The crop started near the edge of the road and went clear to the other side of the valley. The huge field looked wide enough to fit at least five or six soccer fields end to end. As we came around a bend in the road, I noticed the valley getting wider and the hills on each side stretching out for as far as I could see.

Dad called back, "There's Aunt Ella's farm!" I saw several buildings not too far ahead. There was a two-story, white farmhouse on the right, facing the road. Just past the house was a big, brownish-red barn. Next to the barn was a silo that was probably twice as tall as the barn. Back behind the house was a large blue metal shed that Dad said was used to store the tractors and other large farm equipment. As we got closer I could see a long narrow building on the other side of the barn, near the road.

"What's that big, round tower?" Meg asked.

"That's the grain silo," Mom explained. "All this corn that Aunt Ella is growing will be put into the silo next fall for the animals to eat all winter long."

We pulled up in front of the farmhouse about five minutes after the gravel woke me up, which means Dad was probably right when he said it was only two miles from the main highway. Or maybe I was still a little groggy and just couldn't judge time very well. The doors of the van opened, and the "sweet aroma" rushed in to greet us. Meg started gagging almost immediately.

"If you're going to throw up," Mom whirled around, "*don't* do it in the van," she warned.

Meg kept her nose and mouth covered with her hand as she got quickly out of the van and down onto the dirt driveway. Her eyes were big and round above the hand on her face, but she managed to keep her lunch (which, by the way, had since been followed by three cans of Shasta and half a bag of potato chips) under control. If I had eaten everything *she* had in the last four hours, I would have thrown up *long* before I smelled the farm.

We all made our way up to the house and got some pretty hefty hugs from Aunt Ella, who came out on the porch to greet us. Then Dad sent me, Jeff, and Shauna back to unload the suitcases and take them up to the bedrooms in the loft. The house wasn't very big, but it was probably more than enough for Aunt Ella. Her husband had died a few years before, and they had never had any children.

Aunt Ella poured us all some lemonade, and we sat around the kitchen trying to relax for a few minutes. There was a large round table, which took up most of the space in the kitchen. There were only eight chairs, though, so Jeff and I took our drinks into the room that Aunt Ella called the "sitting room." Mom, of course, made us promise that we'd willingly submit ourselves to death and torture (hopefully in that order) if we happened to spill any of our lemonade. Aunt Ella didn't seem all that concerned, but Dad had this intense look on his face that I interpreted as, "I've been in a confined space with six children *way* too long."

After just a couple of minutes we began to hear cows mooing outside. I hopped up and looked through the lace curtains. A large herd of black and white cows was being driven from the pasture toward the barn. There was a big kid about Shauna's age yelling at them and shooing them through an open gate into the barnyard.

"Let's go see what's going on," Jeff said, leaning over my shoulder. As we went back through the kitchen to deposit our lemonade glasses, Meg was asking anyone who'd listen, "What's that sound?"

"I believe that is the sound of the cows moving into the barn," Aunt Ella smiled. "It must be milking time."

"Can I go watch?" Meg almost bubbled out of her seat.

"Sure," we heard Aunt Ella, Dad, and Mom all reply at once. I'm sure they were all wondering just how long she'd be able to stand the smell, but I didn't hear anything else that was said because Jeff and I were already through the screen door at the back of the house.

We turned left and headed for the barnyard on the north side of the house where the cows were moving inside a white wooden rail fence that kept them from coming into Aunt Ella's backyard. Jeff and I climbed up on the fence and watched as the cows made their way past us. The boy we'd seen through the window didn't seem to notice us as he walked around the outside of the herd and urged them in the right direction. But after a minute or so he turned and said, "Ya can come in if ya want. Just be sure t' stay 'long the fence 'r barn."

Jeff and I looked at each other, then back at the boy. He pointed to the side of the barn next to the large door where all the cows were moving and added, "Why don't ya stand over there."

The cows were pretty well stacked up on the opposite side of the yard from where we were as they moved into the barn, so we had a clear path to the outside wall of the barn where the boy had pointed.

Meg was standing slightly away from the fence, holding her hand over her mouth and nose.

"Are you coming?" I asked.

Her eyes got big, and she stumbled back a step as she shook her head quickly back and forth. Her hand never left her face.

Jeff and I climbed through the fence and made our way along it, until we came to the corner of the barn. Then we followed the wall of the barn till we came to the door where the cows were going in. We climbed up on a concrete ledge that was about a foot high. As the cows moved past us, they were close enough that we could have reached out and touched them, but standing on the ledge, we felt pretty safe.

I never realized how big cows are. They were huge! Most of them were about as tall as me before I got up on the ledge. We watched them lumber through the doorway and begin to take a place in the milking stalls that filled the lower level of the barn. As one cow started into a stall near the door the boy put his hand up and said, "No! C'mon, that's not yers!" The cow immediately reared her head back, moved away from the stall, and went deeper into the barn.

"Do they each have their own place?" I asked, astonished at the thought.

"Oh, yeah!" said the boy. "Each cow has 'er own milkin' stall. The milkers are set up and fitted for the cow in that stall. Each one knows where she's supposed t' be. That one just got greedy and thought she could steal some hay before goin' back to 'er reg'lar place."

"Wow!" said Jeff, glancing over at me. "I never knew cows were so *smart!*"

"What did you say about milkers being set up for the cows?" I asked, not sure what he was talking about.

The boy pointed to the low ceiling, and for the first time I noticed a maze of metal tubes running from each stall to a large pipe in the middle of the ceiling that ran the length of the barn. Each stall had a rubber hose with four connectors at the end.

"Those are the milkers," said the boy. "They hook onto the cow's udder an' milk 'em dry in just a few minutes."

I had no idea they used machines to milk cows. I just stared up at the tubes and hoses in amazement and didn't notice the boy come over to where Jeff and I were standing.

"Name's Clyde!" he practically yelled. I jumped because I didn't know he was standing so close.

26

Jeff laughed, "Hi. I'm Jeff and this is Brandon."

Clyde had his arm stretched out toward us, so we each shook his hand. The skin was rough, and his hand was hard.

"You here to do research on milk production, or are ya related t' one of them cows?" Clyde asked with a smile.

Jeff looked slightly confused by the question, so I answered for him. "We're here visiting our Aunt Ella for a few weeks."

"A few weeks? Wow, you boys must really like dairy farms," he said.

"Uh . . . yeah," was all I could manage after a short pause. It didn't matter though because Clyde was already busy, using a rag and a bucket full of some kind of liquid to wash each cow's udder before attaching the milker. The connectors made a loud sucking sound as they glommed onto the cow, but they didn't seem to mind or even notice what he was up to. They were each chomping away on the hay at the front of their stall.

Cows are not only smart, they're also efficient. They were eating, giving milk, and depositing something out the back all at the same time. Clyde didn't even seem to notice the stuff piling up behind most of the cows. He was wearing a pair of rubber boots, and he just kicked right through the mounds as he went about his work. He was also wearing a well-shaped and well-worn cowboy hat that never fell off his head, no matter *how* far he leaned over attaching the milkers under each cow.

Once Clyde had all the cows doing their thing, he invited us back outside the barn and took us around the corner of the barn to a door that I hadn't noticed before, even though we had obviously walked right past it. Meg was still standing outside the fence, but now she had her hands to her sides and her mouth partway open. I think she'd figured out that she did better with the smell when she breathed through her mouth instead of her nose.

Clyde opened the door, and we went into a room where there was a huge, open-topped metal tub that was probably ten feet across and almost as tall as I am. The large pipe that I had seen running the length of the barn ran into this room and was dumping milk into the tub.

"All the milk comes in here," Clyde explained, "where we keep it 'til the milk truck comes t' collect it."

"How often does the truck come?" I asked, as I watched huge white bubbles forming around the bottom of the tub.

"Twice a day—after each milking. He'll be comin' 'long in 'bout an hour."

Clyde stepped up onto a wooden stool and reached for a lever mounted to the metal pipe that was dumping milk into the big tub. "This valve has t' be open when the milk's comin' in," he said. "It's open when the handle's parallel with the pipe like this."

"Why would you ever want it closed?" asked Jeff.

"Well, I hafta sterilize all the equipment after each time, an' sometimes I start workin' on the piping before the milk truck's hauled off the milk. So I close the valve t' keep the soap and water from dumpin' into the tank with the milk."

Clyde opened the door and stood there waiting for us to follow him back out and then walked quickly back inside the barn to where the cows were getting milked.

"What's that over there?" Meg asked Jeff and me while we were climbing back through the fence.

Meg was looking past the front of the barn to the long, narrow building we had seen when we drove up to the farm. It was only about eight feet high and open all along the top of the outside wall.

"I think that's where the pigs are," Jeff answered. I watched closely to see how Meg would react. "It's called a pigsty," he added.

She stared at it for a moment.

"Does it stink?" she finally asked.

"Probably not any more than it does right here," Jeff offered.

"Will you guys go over there with me?" She asked the question as though she were trying to muster the courage to face the biggest fear in her life.

"Sure," I said and started in that direction.

As we got closer, we could hear the pigs snorting and snuffling around, and I noticed that the smell seemed to get a little stronger. There were a couple of logs lying by the wall of the pigsty, and Jeff and I climbed up on them so we could look through the opening along the top of the wall. The smell was pretty strong, and it was so dark in the shed we couldn't see much.

"What's in there?" Meg asked. She was standing back a few feet, looking up at us. Her voice sounded funny because she was using her finger and thumb to keep her nostrils pinched closed.

"Pigs!" Jeff and I both blurted out at the same time. "What did you think?" I added.

"Will you help me see?" she asked.

After we explained to her that she would have to come a *little* closer before she'd be able to get on the log and look inside, she moved slowly toward us, her grip on her nose getting tighter with each step. When she finally got to the log where we were waiting, we helped her up so she wouldn't have to take her hand away from her face. She wasn't quite tall enough to see in, so Jeff and I had to boost her up higher.

"I can't see anything," she mumbled through her hand. "It's too dark."

"Wait a sec," Jeff grunted. "Let your eyes get used to the dark."

"Oh, I see the pigs now!" She was so excited that she accidentally took her hand away from her face and took a big breath. As soon as she realized what she had done, she jerked her hand back up to her face, but it was too late.

Meg was gagging violently as Jeff and I tried to get her down as fast as possible. We discovered the quickest way to get her down was just to let go and allow gravity to do all the work. Meg went sprawling and pretty much took Jeff out as well. As she was falling, she pulled her hands away from her face and threw them behind her to break her fall, but she hit the ground so hard it made her gasp. That was all it took to make her launch her lemonade, her lunch, and everything else. Jeff and I tried *gently* to encourage her to move *away* from the pigsty between heaves.

"Move!" we yelled at the top of our lungs, but it was too late. She left a trail of barf all the way back to the farmhouse.

When Meg burst into the kitchen, she was wailing, and everyone wanted to know what had happened. After she blubbered that she had thrown up, Aunt Ella handed Meg a wet towel to wipe off her mouth while Shauna got her a cup of water. After a minute Meg quit crying, but she was kind of whimpering as she stood next to Mom and rested her head on Mom's shoulder.

"Well, supper will be ready in half an hour," Aunt Ella smiled, "and now you should have plenty of room to enjoy it."

Meg didn't even look up. As usual, Dad offered some real helpful advice. "Maybe you better stay away from the pigs for a while," he suggested.

I went outside, climbed into the van, and pulled my backpack out from under one of the benches. Here's what I wrote in my spiral notebook:

Friday, April 10. More Andrews Family Betting Results:
MEG: (Lost) She threw up at the pigsty.

CHAPTER 3

Moroni's Visit

"Brandon!" The voice sounded far away.

"Brandon! Wake up!" I realized that this was probably the third or fourth time I'd heard my name.

"What's wrong?" I asked, but the words barely made it to the end of my tongue. I managed to open one eye far enough to see Aunt Ella leaning over me.

"I will wait for you in the sitting room," she whispered, and then she disappeared past the end of the bed.

I pulled the quilt off the bed and wrapped it around my shoulders. I tried to walk quietly across the floor, but it seemed like every step I made was announced to the rest of the house by a loud creaking or groaning sound. The stairs were even noisier than the rest of the floor. I wondered how Aunt Ella had made it all the way back downstairs without me hearing anything.

The door at the bottom of the stairs opened directly into the sitting room. Aunt Ella was sitting in a rocking chair. The reading lamp behind her was on. I shuffled across the floor and sat beside her on the sofa, which she referred to as a "davenport."

"I am glad you are here," she smiled.

You're lucky *I'm here*, I thought.

I glanced back at the door that led to the loft and noticed the fireplace next to it. The lack of warmth or light coming out of the fireplace was *extremely* obvious. I shivered as I wondered if the missing fire was due to the season or the fact that morning was still several *years* away. The room was lighted only by two small lamps, the one behind Aunt Ella and one against the wall opposite the fireplace.

I squinted at the clock on the mantel over the fireplace. It was a fancy kind with a double butterfly-looking mechanism spinning slowly back and forth at the bottom and a glass jar covering the whole thing. It looked more like a container for a school bug collection than something that would be useful for telling time. There was no way I was going to be able to read that thing from across the room.

"What time is it?" I managed to croak.

"A little past five," she said, like that was some kind of normal time of day.

I wondered if she got up that early every morning. It wasn't like she had to. She'd already told us she hired out all the work done on the farm.

"I am glad you are here," she said again. "I hope that you have prepared."

"I read the scriptures you told me about on the phone," I said, hoping that was what she was talking about.

"What did you learn about preparation?" she asked.

"Well, the only thing it said about preparation in Alma 16 was that the people were prepared to receive the word because the Lord poured out his Spirit."

"What did you learn about the sons of Mosiah?" she asked without saying whether I got the stuff about Alma and Amulek right.

"Well, the sons of Mosiah were filled with the spirit of . . ." I was trying to remember what it was. "There were two things, I think. . . . But I can't remember what they are." I managed a weak laugh.

"Then how about just reading it to me," she suggested. "No doubt you have your scriptures under that quilt somewhere."

Who was she kidding? She wakes me up at five in the morning the first day we're here, drags me down to the sitting room with no fire in the fireplace, and I'm supposed to have my scriptures clutched between my frozen fingers?

"Uh, I think they're still in the van," I offered, hoping this would not make me look so bad.

"Does this mean that you did not read them last night before going to bed?" she asked. I think she was *serious*. My excuse obviously made me look worse—not better.

"No, ma'am, I didn't," I admitted. "Sorry."

"There is a set on the mantel you may use for now," she said with a smile.

It seemed likely that this would be the last time she would smile about it. I walked over to the mantel and picked up the set of scriptures. I noticed the clock said about ten minutes after five. The scriptures were wellworn. I almost dropped them because I was having trouble keeping my precious quilt around my shoulders as I moved back to the sofa.

As quickly as possible, I opened up the Book of Mormon to the book of Alma. Luckily it's the biggest one in there, so I was able to find it pretty quickly.

"They had the spirit of prophecy, and the spirit of revelation," I read aloud.

"That is right!" she said with an excited voice that surprised me. "And how did they prepare for these great gifts?"

I tried to remember everything I had read so I could answer her without reading it.

"Prayer and fasting," I said, "and it also says that they searched the scriptures."

"And have you been doing these things?" she wanted to know.

"Well . . . like I said, I've been searching the scriptures about preparation that you told me about, and I've been praying."

"What have you been praying for?" she asked.

Now how was I supposed to answer that? I couldn't think of any way to say I've been praying that I wouldn't have to be here so long without it sounding bad.

"Well, you said that I needed to know what I wanted to get out of this and go for it. So I decided what I wanted, and I've been praying for it," I said sincerely. "At least twice a day," I added, hoping she wouldn't probe for details.

"Have you been fasting, also?"

"Not yet. I was waiting for fast Sunday."

"Fast Sunday is tomorrow," she said with a smile, "since general conference was last Sunday."

"I thought we just skipped fast Sunday when something else got in the way," I said hopefully.

She just smiled, and I knew that wasn't how it was going to be.

"We will begin our fast right after dinner this afternoon," she continued. "It will be ready at five o'clock. Right now it is time to talk about why you are here. But first will you offer a prayer and ask the Lord to bless us with his Spirit during our discussion?"

We did the same thing at home when Dad got us together for family scripture study, so this seemed like a good idea. I said the prayer.

"Thank you," she whispered, sounding almost relieved. "Now, will you please go to the mantel and fetch me the leather pouch next to the clock?"

Aunt Ella always said "fetch me this" or "fetch me that." I never knew anyone else who used that word when referring to humans. It always made me feel sort of like a dog.

Setting the borrowed scriptures on the sofa, I got up once again and crossed the room to the fireplace. Next to the clock was an old-looking, brown leather pouch about the same size and shape as the Bible I had borrowed. I had not noticed it during my first trip to the mantel. The pouch had an opening along one edge that was covered by a large flap of leather. The flap narrowed to two straps that were tucked through slits near the opposite edge and tied to each other.

I handed Aunt Ella the pouch and returned to the sofa. I watched as she untied the straps, pulled them from the slits, and gently opened the pouch. Slowly she removed an old book that fit tightly inside. The book had a plain brown leather cover on it, somewhat lighter than the color of the pouch. There was nothing printed anywhere on the outside of the book. The pages along the edge of the book were slightly uneven and wellworn. She laid the book and the pouch very gently in her lap, then placed both of her hands on top.

"This is for you," she said simply.

"What is it?"

"This is a copy of the very first printing of the Book of Mormon."

"Wow," I breathed. "Thanks."

She stared deep into me, but I'm not sure what she was looking for. I began to feel a little nervous, so I said, "This is really cool, but why are you giving it to me?"

"I am in my 80s, and I am not going to live forever," she said frankly, "and this book is very valuable. I want to give it to you because I believe you will make the best use of it. Now, when I say that it is valuable I mean that in two ways. Historically, it is valuable because it is over 150 years old. There were only 5,000 original copies, and many of them contained differences. Apparently, corrections were being made during the time of printing, but pages were not discarded even after errors were discovered. Some of the copies have some corrections, while others have different corrections. There have been several historians who have shown an interest in this book, and some have come to see it. One gentleman spent several days here last summer, carefully reading it and making notes. I did not allow him to take it from the house, though I am sure he would have preferred that."

Her hands never left the book on her lap as she talked.

"There has been another man here lately," her face darkened slightly. "A Mr. Anthony, he said his name is. I do not feel that he is trustworthy. He has been to the farm twice now and tried to per-suade me to let him borrow the book. He does not seem to show any interest in actually looking inside of it, he just wants it. I decided it was time to keep it in a safer place. That is why you are here."

"I'm a safer place?" I asked. I wasn't sure I wanted something in my possession that needed to be kept safe—especially if there was some "untrustworthy" guy who was so interested in it. "What makes you think I'm a safer place?" I asked.

"The book's real value is not simply the fact that it is a piece of history over 150 years old," she continued, conveniently ignoring my question. "Open up to Joseph Smith's history, and I will show you what I mean."

She had to help me find Joseph Smith—History in the Pearl of Great Price. Once we got there, it seemed like we ended up read-ing most of it. Well, actually, *I'm* the one who did all the reading. Her hands never left the leather book in her lap as she would tell me which verses to read. Then she asked questions to make sure I had understood correctly. Sometimes she would even correct a word I'd read, but she couldn't see what I was reading, so I think she must have had the whole thing memorized or something.

We spent close to an hour doing this. Then, without warning, she said, "That is enough for today, Brandon. I would like to plan on meeting with you at this same time each Saturday for the next month. Will you please return this book to the mantel until then?" She began to put the book carefully back inside its leather pouch.

"I thought you were giving it to me," I exclaimed, completely forgetting the fear I'd felt when she first told me about the man, Mr. Anthony.

She smiled and slowly raised her eyebrows. "We've already discussed that."

"We . . . have?" I asked, trying to remember when we did that.

"After you spend some time reviewing our discussion, I feel confident you will see what I mean." I guess I had a perplexed look on my face when she said, "Think about Moroni's visit to Joseph Smith." She was holding the book out, so I stood and took it from her and laid it carefully on the mantel.

"Will you please say another prayer for us now and thank the Lord for permitting his Spirit to be with us during our discussion?" Her head was already bowed as she finished the question. I was still walking back across the room and wasn't sure for a moment if I should sit down again or stay standing. I decided to stand.

"Thank you for that prayer," she smiled when I finished, "and the discussion. I do believe that you have made good preparation. I am going to make some breakfast for your family now."

The room was lighter now. I walked back over to the mantel to replace the scriptures I'd borrowed and noticed the butterfly clock said it was almost 6:15. I went back up the stairs to return my early morning friend, the quilt, to its bed.

The loft had three bedrooms in it. The largest room contained two double beds, and the other rooms had one double bed each. The stairs came up at the south end of the bedroom in the middle, where Mom and Dad were sleeping. Our portable crib, which we always took with us on trips for Danny to sleep in, was set up in one corner. There was a door at each end of the room which led to the other two rooms. Granny slept in a small room at the north end. The door near the top of the stairs led to the room with two beds where the rest of the kids slept: Shauna and Meg in one bed, Jeff and me in the other. Chelsea was in a sleeping bag on some cushions on the floor.

"Shauna," I whispered, "Shauna, wake up!"

"What time is it?" she mumbled.

"It's 6:15. Don't we need to wake up Dad and get him to the library?"

She blinked her eyes several times before answering, "Yeah, let's get him moving!"

We made our way back into Mom and Dad's bedroom. Shauna stumbled so much that I wondered how anyone else was staying asleep. Had I made that much noise an hour and fifteen minutes ago?

"Dad," we whispered, as we were shaking him. "The library's waiting."

"What are you guys doing?" he grunted as he fought to open his eyes.

"You've got to get to the library," I explained. "You've got research to do."

"I wasn't planning to start until Monday," he mumbled, snuggling back into his pillow.

"What?" Shauna said out loud. "Why?" we both asked at the same time.

"Well," he sighed, "I guess I really don't have anything else going on today. There's no reason I couldn't . . ."

We didn't even wait for him to finish his sentence.

"I'll go get the shower started for you," I called as I hopped down the stairs two at a time. Shauna was already getting Dad's bathrobe from a chair near the foot of the bed.

"Here's your robe, Dad. Can I get anything else for you?"

All the noise we were making apparently woke Jeff up because just a few seconds after I got the water warming in the shower he came into the bathroom.

"Excuse me, Bran," he mumbled.

"What?" I asked.

"I need to use the bathroom," he smirked.

"*You're* not using the bathroom," I said, shaking my head back and forth. "Dad needs to take a shower."

"I'll hurry," Jeff promised.

"You can wait," I insisted, "Dad takes fast showers, and he needs to get to the library."

"But it's the only bathroom." Jeff acted like he was in pain.

Just then Dad appeared in the doorway.

"Shower's warm now, Dad," I smiled. "C'mon, Jeff, let's let Dad take his shower." I turned my head so Dad couldn't see my face and glared at Jeff as hard as I could. Jeff just stared at me for a second. I think if Dad had been any more awake he definitely would have caught on, but he just shuffled to the cabinet and pulled out a bath towel. Since his back was turned I took the opportunity to point violently at the door. Jeff just glared back at me as he slowly followed me out.

"What is your *problem?*" he almost yelled after I'd shut the door behind us.

We were standing in a narrow hallway that joined Aunt Ella's bedroom, the bathroom, and the kitchen. There was also a door to the cellar. We could hear Aunt Ella humming as she prepared breakfast.

"Do you want to stay here for two whole months?" I asked as quietly as I could, hoping she couldn't hear me.

"What?"

"Shauna and I are doing everything we can to help Dad spend as much time as possible at the library so maybe we can go home sooner!" I whispered.

"Oh," Jeff said. He forgot to close his mouth.

"So come help me make him a sack lunch to take with him," I continued.

We told Aunt Ella what we were doing, and she helped us find some homemade bread and lunch meat for sandwiches. She offered some fresh fruit and cookies to go along with it. I got two cans of Fresca from the cooler we had brought with us in the van. We made three sandwiches to go with a bunch of grapes, two oranges, and about eight cookies. We had so much food that we had to get a bigger sack than the one Aunt Ella first got out for us. Shauna came down and said she had laid out some clothes for Dad to wear. Then she started helping Aunt Ella with breakfast. Dad showers pretty fast, but by the time he walked back through the kitchen on his way upstairs, both his breakfast and lunch were ready and waiting. Jeff almost knocked him over trying to get into the bathroom.

"Wow," Dad said, "something smells great!"

Aunt Ella had prepared bacon, eggs, orange juice, and wheat toast from homemade bread. It really did smell good, but we'd all been too frantic to notice.

"Hurry, Dad," I said as I pushed him out of the kitchen toward the stairs. "You don't want it to get cold."

He didn't have time to answer before Shauna called, "I laid some clothes out for you. It was no bother. Happy to do it!"

"Uhh, thanks," Dad said as he forced a smile.

He took way too long getting dressed. It was probably four or five *minutes* before he returned. I think it was because he wasted time waking up the rest of the family for breakfast. Meg and Chelsea came romping down the stairs and headed straight for the bathroom. Mom and Granny looked like they needed more time to recover from the trip as they slumped at the table. But we managed to get Dad out of the house by seven o'clock. Every time he tried to make conversation, either Shauna, Jeff, or I would remind him about the library or ask him if we could get anything else for him before he left.

Once Dad was finally out the door we were able to relax a little. We started joking around and laughing as we sat at the table. Mom brought this to a quick halt by asking, "So, since Dad is working today, does that mean it's a school day for you?"

We all just stared at her.

"Tell you what," she smiled, "anyone who's still where I can see or hear them ten seconds from now does homework this morning."

"But, Mom!" I cried, "we still have to get dressed, and the only way to get outside is through the kitchen!"

"You may come back through the kitchen after you're dressed, but only if you don't make a sound," she threatened.

We all just sat there looking at each other.

"Can it be a school day for me?" asked Chelsea, her eyes sparkling. Chelsea wouldn't be starting kindergarten till the fall, so she still thought school was something fun.

"I've got some things that we can do together," Mom said to Chelsea. "I'm just talking about the older kids for now."

"Oh," Chelsea said as she returned to her scrambled eggs.

"Five!" Mom called out without warning. "Four!" Chairs started falling over, knees banged into cabinets, toes got stepped on, but all four of us were out of the kitchen and at least partway up the stairs before we heard the number "one" being called. Chelsea completely ignored the whole thing and just kept eating her eggs and humming softly to herself.

Ten minutes later we were all dressed and moving as quickly and quietly as possible through the kitchen. Mom, Granny, and Aunt Ella were chattering away. Meg was the last one out, and we all jumped when she let the screen door slam. We were frozen with the fear of homework as we waited for Mom to call us back into the kitchen because we'd made noise. After about five seconds of silence we sneaked away. We were smart enough to wait until we'd reached the corner of the house before all yelling, "Meg!" at the same time.

"Sorry!" she giggled, "but luckily they didn't hear it!"

Jeff laughed as he shook his head back and forth, "Meg! They heard it fine. They were just nice enough to ignore it!"

"Oh!" she giggled again.

We wandered over to the barnyard, where Clyde and a man were working.

"Where are the cows?" asked Meg.

"Back in the pasture," Clyde said as he pointed off in the distance. "We graze 'em all day between milkin' times." Then he nodded at us and said, "How ya all doin' this mornin'?"

"Fine, thanks."

"This is my pa." Clyde gestured to the man working with him.

"Mornin,' boys." Then the man nodded his head toward Shauna and Meg and said, "Ladies."

Meg giggled and Shauna smiled.

"Good morning," we all responded.

Clyde had already returned to his shoveling. There was a tractor in the barnyard with a weird-looking trailer hitched on the back of it. Clyde and his father were shoveling up manure from the barnyard and loading it into the trailer.

"How often do you have to do this?" Jeff asked.

"Every mornin'," Clyde grunted as he tossed another shovelful onto the trailer. "This here is a spreader," he said, pointing to the trailer. "We use it to fertilize the fields."

"Where did those piles of mud come from?" Meg asked. She seemed to be doing okay with the smell this morning. I thought maybe she was getting used to it.

"It's not mud," I laughed. "It's manure."

"What's manure?" she asked.

"Cows don't have a bathroom they can use," Shauna said as she tilted her head to one side.

Meg just stared at Shauna for a minute. Then she pulled her hand up to her nose as she looked over at where Clyde and his dad were working.

"Meg!" I yelled. "Don't throw up again!"

"I'm not!" she mumbled. "I'm okay!"

"Good!" I said, watching carefully. I wasn't completely sure I believed her.

Clyde's dad chuckled as he leaned his shovel against the fence.

"You finish here," he said to Clyde. "I'm gonna check on them geese in the barn."

"When's the hay comin'?" Clyde called after him.

"Thursd'y or Frid'y, if we're ready for it."

We all watched him step through the fence and head up the slope to the front of the barn.

"We're gettin' some new hay, but we still got nests in the barn that are in the way of where we need to stack the new bales," Clyde explained. "We might have to wait longer if them eggs don't hatch in time."

Jeff and I followed Clyde's dad around the front of the barn to see the nests, while Shauna walked Meg quickly back to the house. Meg obviously had absolutely no interest in getting any closer to the hogs than she already was.

There were two levels in the barn. The lower level, where the cows were milked, had a low ceiling, but above that was a large, open second floor, where hay was stored. The huge barn doors were open, and Jeff and I walked in. We found Clyde's dad on the lower floor inspecting a nest in a pile of loose hay. It had five eggs in it.

"Might have a chance if the bird would stay on the nest," he muttered to himself.

"I still got two nests that ain't hatched," he told us. "One here on the floor and one up on top there." He was pointing to the loft above us, where some bales of hay were stacked.

We followed him up a set of stairs to the loft. It still had a few bales of hay stacked on one end but was mostly empty. Hanging from the rafters above us were several really thick ropes that were looped through some large blocks of wood and huge wooden pulleys. Hanging at the end of it all was a heavy metal hook bigger than my head.

"Jeff," I gasped, "look at the size of that thing!"

"Whoa!" Jeff answered.

"Ain't you never seen one of them before?" Clyde's dad asked.

"That there is a block an' tackle system we use t' lift them bales up an' down, as well as anythin' else heavy we need t' move 'round in here. See them tracks up there?" he asked, pointing to a set of metal rails mounted to the ceiling. "That's how we move it 'round t' where we need it. Gotta be careful with it though," he cautioned us. "That block 'n' tackle there packs more weight than I do." He paused for a moment and then added, "An' it shouldn't be jus' hangin' there like that, neither." He climbed up a ladder mounted to the front wall of the barn. "Looks like somebody forgot t' put it away," he muttered.

Jeff and I watched as he used the ropes and pulleys to pull the hook up to the rafters and then hang it on a metal hoop mounted on the wall next to the top of the ladder. He also took the end of the main rope he'd been pulling on and tied it to the same hoop.

"Tying off that rope keeps the hook from fallin' all the way t' the floor when ya unhook it," he explained as he came back down the ladder. Once he was back down, we all climbed down to the main floor, to where we had seen the nest. "Now *what* am I gonna do 'bout this?" he shook his head. "I ain't even sure them eggs is still warm. Don't never see no bird sittin' on 'em." He walked over closer and stood staring down at the nest for a few moments.

"Them eggs prob'ly ain't even 'live no more," he muttered to himself. "Well, there's one way t' find out," he said with determination. He leaned down to the nest and carefully picked up one of the eggs without touching the nest or any of the other eggs. He held the egg between his hands for a few seconds.

"Don't feel warm t' me," he said as he held the egg out to me. I touched it gently with the back of my hand. I had to admit, it did feel cool. He pulled the egg back, then walked past Jeff and me out to the front of the barn. Without even slowing down he tossed the egg in the air and then walked over to where it had landed. Jeff and I followed.

"What in the world! I ain't *never* . . . !" He didn't finish what he was saying. He just stood there shaking his head. I looked down where the egg had landed and saw a skinny, wet baby bird about four inches long wiggling around on top of the shattered egg shell. It was slowly kicking its feet, flapping its stubby wings, and stretching its head back. It was covered with some thick, sticky goop that looked like white honey. We all just stared at the baby bird for about a minute until it quit moving. I was really glad Meg had gone back into the house; she would have been asking all sorts of questions—either that or just *gagging* all over the place.

"Fetch me that shovel I left by the fence," Clyde's dad said without looking up. Jeff ran to get the shovel and brought it back. We just watched as Clyde's dad scooped up the egg shell and the dead bird and carried it down to where Clyde had just finished loading the spreader. He tossed the tiny bird's body onto the pile of manure and kept walking, still shaking his head until he disappeared through the door of the big blue shed in back of the farmhouse.

CHAPTER 4

Nauvoo

I woke up Sunday morning just as it was beginning to get light. My mouth was dry and my stomach growling. I hadn't eaten since five o'clock the day before because I was fasting. I must admit that even though I wasn't too excited about the idea of fasting, I'd been very sincere in my prayer as I began the fast. After everyone had finished dessert, Aunt Ella "invited" Shauna, Jeff, and me to go up to our bedroom and begin our fast with a prayer. "Take time to determine the purpose of your fast before you kneel down to pray," she counseled. Shauna and I knew exactly what we were fasting for, and we strongly encouraged Jeff to join us. He agreed. Next time I'll try to remember to ask nicely before I threaten him. We said a prayer together, and then each of us said our own.

Before going to sleep the night before, I'd read Joseph Smith—History again. I kept thinking about the old Book of Mormon Aunt Ella was giving to me. Why did I have to wait a month before getting it? She said that we had already talked about the reason, but I was sure we hadn't. She also said that reviewing the discussion about Moroni's visit would help me figure it out, but reading Joseph Smith—History again hadn't helped at all.

I got out of bed and sat down at the desk. I pulled my notebook out of my backpack and made this entry:

Sunday, April 12. Review of first discussion with Aunt Ella yesterday:

Joseph Smith—History 1:30–35: Moroni first appears to Joseph Smith in his room and tells him about the gold plates.

J.S.—H. 1:42: Joseph sees a vision of where the plates are buried.

J.S.—H. 1:50: Tells his father about Moroni and goes to find the plates.

J.S.—H. 1:53: Moroni tells Joseph to come back every year for four years.

J.S.—H. 1:54: Goes back every year and gets instruction.

J.S.—H. 1:59: Gets the plates and the Urim and Thummim and breastplate.

Moroni tells Joseph to take good care of the plates.

After a moment I added this:

More Andrews Family Betting Results:

AUNT ELLA: (Lost) *I had a little trouble being prepared.*

I read through what I had written. "What does this have to do with me?" I asked out loud. "Why do I have to talk to Aunt Ella every week for four . . . ?" Before I finished the question, I slapped myself on the forehead and dropped my elbow to the desk with a loud crack. Shaking my head I said to myself, "I have to wait for four weeks to get the book, just like Joseph Smith had to wait for four years to get the gold plates."

All my noise woke up Shauna. "What are you doing, Bran?" she mumbled.

I sighed. "I'm just writing down what Aunt Ella talked to me about yesterday."

"Oh. Well, it's a good thing she got you up early," Shauna said, "so we could get Dad off to the library."

"Especially since he came home at five o'clock for dinner," I agreed.

We talked for a while about Aunt Ella and the Book of Mormon that I was going to be given, and I let Shauna read what I had written about Joseph Smith's history.

In the afternoon we all went with Aunt Ella into Waterloo for church. I looked around carefully, but I didn't see one single person wearing cowboy boots or looking like a "hick" in any way. That night I made this entry in my journal:

Sunday, April 12. More Andrews Family Betting Results:

SHAUNA: *(Lost) Nobody at church looked like a hick or wore cowboy boots.*

We got into a pretty regular routine the rest of the week. Aunt Ella gave us an alarm clock to keep in our bedroom so we could get Dad up at 6:00 A.M. every day. She helped out also by having breakfast ready every morning by 6:30. She's a great cook and would prepare waffles or pancakes or French toast along with bacon, eggs, or sausage. I don't think she's ever even heard of cold cereal. Dad never left the house later than seven o'clock, and we made sure he always had a huge sack lunch to take with him. He really got into his research and began spending more and more time at the library. Toward the end of the week he wasn't getting home till 6:30 or 7:00 at night. It looked like there was a good chance we would get our wish and that he would be through with his project within a month.

After Dad left for the library each day we all got busy on our homework. Once in a while Aunt Ella helped us a little, and it was fun to get to know her better. I was getting to know Clyde pretty well, too. He went to school in town during the day but came out to the farm every morning and evening to milk the cows. His dad was there all day, doing chores and taking care of the farm equipment. Most evenings I helped Clyde bring the cows in for milking. He even let me hook up some of them to the milkers, and he'd send me in to close the valve above the big milk tub when he was ready to start sterilizing the pipes.

At 5:00 on Saturday morning, Aunt Ella greeted me once again. I didn't have nearly as much trouble waking up this time as I had the first week. Probably because I'd been getting up at 6:00 A.M. all week and was used to Iowa time by now.

"Do you have any questions about our discussion last week?" she began.

"I don't think so," I answered. "But I figured out why I don't get the book for four weeks."

"Why is that?" Her eyes sparkled in the lamplight.

"Because you have some things you want me to learn before I'll be prepared to take care of it properly—just like Joseph Smith."

"I felt certain that you would understand waiting four weeks, just as Joseph waited four years," she smiled, "but I wondered if you would understand *why* I wanted you to wait. I am pleased that you do."

"I brought my scriptures with me this morning," I said, poking my hand out from underneath the quilt to show her. "And I brought a notebook so I can remember what scriptures we read."

"That is absolutely wonderful," she replied. "Would you fetch me the book from the mantel now, please?"

Just like the week before, she carefully removed the book from the pouch, placed it on her lap, and then left both hands on top of it during the entire discussion. And just like the week before, she asked me to offer a prayer to invite the Spirit of the Lord to join us.

"Last week we talked about the monetary value of this book," she began, "as well as the circumstances surrounding Joseph Smith actually obtaining the gold plates. Today I would like to talk about the spiritual value of the Book of Mormon. And, of course, this applies to your copy of the book as well as to the copy here in my lap. When Mormon put this book together, he wrote about the importance of the book."

We read several scriptures together and talked a lot about what the different writers in the book said about what they had written. I wrote the references down in my spiral notebook. That turned out to be a really good thing because what happened right after breakfast would have made it almost impossible for me to remember much of our discussion. Here's what I wrote sometime before six o'clock that morning:

Saturday, April 18. Second discussion with Aunt Ella:

1 Nephi 9:3: Nephi is commanded to make plates and keep a record.
1 Nephi 19:3: Nephi is commanded to write precious things.
Records are for instruction and other wise purposes.
Jacob 1:2: Jacob writes what is most precious on the plates.
Enos 1:13: Enos prays that a record will be preserved.
Words of Mormon 1:7: Records are kept for a wise purpose.
The Spirit tells Mormon which records to save.
Words of Mormon 1:11: Mormon knows his record will be preserved and that his people will be judged out of it.
4 Nephi 1:48: Ammaron is told by the Spirit to hide the records.
Ether 4:5: Moroni is commanded to write and seal up record of the brother of Jared.

Our discussion ended about 5:45 A.M. I thought about waking up Dad a little earlier than usual, but I didn't dare push my luck on a Saturday. I got dressed and made his lunch instead. Before I'd finished making his sandwiches, though, he came walking through the kitchen on his way to the shower.

"Good morning, Brandon!" He sounded wide awake. It wasn't even quite six o'clock yet, so I figured he must have gotten up on his own. Maybe we wouldn't have to keep waking him all month. I was getting so confident in what we were doing that I kept thinking about this trip being only a month long now. "Thanks for making my lunch," he called as the bathroom door closed.

A couple of minutes later Shauna came into the kitchen with a surprised look on her face. We could hear Dad whistling in the shower. "Is Dad in there already?" she asked, even though it was obvious. Nobody else whistles like that.

"Cool, huh?" I smiled back at her.

Dad was actually out of the house and on his way by just a little after 6:30 A.M. This was all going far better than expected. "Maybe our plan's going to work," Shauna whispered to me as we sat at the table. Aunt Ella looked at us and smiled, but I'm sure her hearing wasn't good enough to catch what Shauna had said. At least that's what I hoped.

I finished my breakfast just a few minutes later. "I'm going to go see if I can help Clyde finish up the milking," I said to Mom. "We're not doing homework today, are we?"

"No," she smiled, "I need a break. Did your father take the envelopes with him to mail to your schools today? He said there's a mailbox at the library."

"I put them in his lunch sack," I said. Then I added, "And you know he'll be into that sack long before noon."

When I got to the barn, Clyde had taken most of the cows off of the milkers and they were moving out into the barnyard. He always cleaned up the barn before taking the cows out to graze for the day.

"Will you go shut the valve above the milk tub?" he asked. I'd been doing this for him every evening for the last week, but I'd never done it in the morning. The back of the barn faced east, and the sun was just visible above the top of the hill. So when I opened the door the sun hit those metal pipes and tub and glared right back into my eyes. I was squinting as I stepped through the door, and I tripped on the ledge because my eyes were mostly shut. I reached for the door jamb but couldn't catch myself. Instead, I scraped the underside of my arm against the rough wood. Then I landed on the cement floor—hard!

"Ouch!" I grunted as I hit the floor. I rolled over and sat looking at my arm. There were two or three large slivers and a bunch of small ones stuck under the skin, and my arm was scratched from my elbow all the way down to my wrist. As I sat there, I gritted my teeth and started working on the largest of the slivers. It was almost out when I heard a splashing sound. I spun around and looked up at the tub and the pipe.

"Oh, no!" I said. Soapy water was flowing out of the end of the large pipe into the milk tub. I jumped up and looked into the tub. It was more than half full of milk. I ran to the stool and moved it into position as fast as I could. Then I climbed on top of it and pulled the valve closed. As the flow of soapy water slowed to a drip, I stared down at the milk in the tub. You really couldn't tell by looking at it that anything was wrong, and I stood there for a few moments, trying to figure out what I was going to tell Clyde.

I finally got enough courage to make my way out into the barnyard. The cows were standing around, chewing their cud, drinking from the water trough, and making little piles here and there. I made my way slowly into where the milking stalls were and saw Clyde working on the pipes, using a long-handled, soapy brush and a water hose.

"Thanks!" he called with a smile. I tried to smile back, but I don't think I did very well. I was having trouble breathing, and I probably looked half sick. He turned off the hose and asked, "Is something wrong?"

"Umm. Well, yeah. I . . . uhh . . . well . . . I tripped on the way into the milk room. And . . . uhh . . . I hurt my arm. And . . . I was looking at it . . . for . . . a while."

Clyde suddenly realized what I might be trying to say. His eyes got huge. "Didn't ya close the valve!" he yelled frantically as he went running past me to check it for himself. I caught up with him as he was leaning over the tub staring at the milk.

"I closed it!" I said. Then very quietly I added, "But . . . some water ran in before I did."

"How *much* water?" he asked quietly without looking away from the milk.

"Oh, uhh . . ."

He spun around and asked very quietly, "How much *water?*"

"It was only going for a couple of seconds!" I said as fast as I could.

"What? Five seconds, two seconds, what?" His eyes were intense.

"Umm, less than five seconds! I got up when I heard the

52

splashing and pulled the stool over and jumped up and closed it. Maybe four, three seconds. Three . . . or four."

He spun back around and stared into the tub. You couldn't tell by looking at it what had happened.

"Bein' from Utah an' all," Clyde said quietly, "I don't reckon you've ever felt the point of a cowboy boot on your backside." I got the distinct impression that he'd be pleased to give me the experience. He turned toward me, and I backed away from him. I tripped as I backed through the door, which probably helped my story about tripping on the way *into* the room sound more believable. I scrambled to my feet and took off running. I dove through the fence and ran up the slope to the front of the barn. I was scared to death, and all I could think about was finding a place to hide.

Dashing headlong into the barn, I ran for the ladder leading to the loft and started climbing. I hadn't heard anything from Clyde since my hasty exit from the milk tub room, but I wasn't taking any chances. When I reached the top of the ladder I tried to launch myself sideways onto the loft in an effort to get out of sight as quickly as possible. Either I was shaking too much out of fear for my life or that ladder rung was just too slippery, but for some reason, I made it only about halfway onto the loft, and as I stumbled backward, my foot knocked the block and tackle hook right out of its hoop.

Whoever had used the hook last hadn't bothered to tie off the end of the rope, and so, just like Clyde's dad had warned us, the heavy metal hook plummeted down as fast as gravity would take it. It made a huge crashing sound when it hit the floor; then there was a moment of silence, followed by a heavy thud and what sounded like several large wooden planks bouncing around.

I was still hanging halfway off the edge of the loft when the noise stopped. Carefully pushing myself the rest of the way up, I turned around and leaned over the edge to inspect the damage. The hook and pulleys were nowhere in sight. All I could see was a single rope running past me, down into a square black hole in the floor-boards, almost directly below my perch. If I had been scared before, I was petrified now. I couldn't believe all the damage that I had caused—first to the milk and now to the barn floor!

After staring at the hole for a minute or two, I realized that my heart had slowed down a little, and I wondered where Clyde was. Since he was nowhere in sight, I hoped he had decided to give me a break—at least for the moment. I decided I'd better try to clean up the mess in the barn before going back to face Clyde about the milk. Looking above me into the rafters, I saw that the rope was caught in a pulley. A knot in the end of the rope was wedged into the pulley, and that was all that was keeping the rope from slipping completely through and following the rest of the block and tackle down into the blackness.

The first thing I thought I'd better do was to try to get that block and tackle back up out of the hole it had made in the floor. Clyde's dad showed us how the pulleys made it a lot easier to lift the hook just by pulling on the one rope at the top. It looked like I could probably reach the knot stuck in the pulley in the rafters at the top of the barn if I climbed up on the bales of hay stacked in the loft. By jamming my toes in between the bales and grabbing the twine that was wrapped around each of them, I was able to climb about halfway up the stack. Then the stack started to tip in my direction, straight toward the edge of the loft!

I knew I was going to be in serious trouble if I didn't quickly find something to hold onto. The only thing close was the rope hang-ing from the pulley, so as the bales of hay fell out from under me, I lunged for the rope and grabbed hold of it with both hands and wrapped my legs around it. Unfortunately, the stacks were packed so tightly that when I pulled down the first stack, it took at least two other stacks with it. I just hung on for all I was worth as the bales of hay came falling down, crashing into me, the rope, and each other and the rope swung wildly around. Hanging on

54

desperately, I just hoped the knot on the end of it was big enough to keep the rope from pulling the rest of the way through the pulley.

When the hay finally stopped falling and my swinging slowed, I carefully slid down the rope to where I could reach the edge of the loft with my feet. Feeling pretty safe with my feet on something solid, but still holding onto the rope for extra security, I leaned over the edge to inspect the damage. There was hay everywhere! Many of the bales had broken open, and the hole in the floor was now completely buried under the mess.

With a disgusted groan, I closed my eyes and yanked on the rope out of frustration. As soon as I did it, I knew it was a mistake and my relatively bad day was about to get worse. That little heave was all it took to pull the knot the rest of the way through the pulley, and when the rope went slack, I lost my balance and found myself out in thin air, falling toward the pile of hay below me.

I think I pretty much did a flip in the air and landed on my back, but the hay didn't stop my fall. I just kept falling, through the hole the hook had made in the floor and on down into the blackness. Then I landed on something *really* hard, and loose hay settled in around and on top of me.

I had fallen a long way, and when I landed it knocked the wind out of me. My back hurt, and for a few scary moments I couldn't even breathe. When I finally quit gasping for air, I couldn't see anything, either. Some more hay must have fallen down and covered the hole I had fallen through, and it was totally dark.

I found the remains of the block and tackle assembly and the broken floorboards buried under the pile of hay I had fallen on, and I was glad all that hay had been under me when I landed.

After groping around some more, I realized I was in the bottom of a narrow shaft. It smelled damp in there, and the only thing I could hear was my breathing and my heart beating. I searched around, hoping there might be a way to climb out of the shaft, but except for a low opening to some kind of tunnel on one side of the shaft, the walls were solid. The place was pretty spooky, and I guess I began to panic a little. I called out to Clyde a couple of times, but there was no answer.

When I realized no one was hearing me and that there was no way to climb out of the shaft, I decided to explore the tunnel. The walls and sides of the narrow opening were lined with rough, wooden planks, and the entrance was only about a foot and a half wide. The ceiling was so low that I had to stoop to keep from hitting my head. I inched my way into the opening, feeling ahead of me with my foot to keep from tripping over anything. Tripping had been sort of a problem for me ever since breakfast.

I kept running into spiderwebs with my face, and I used my hand to try to clear the way as I moved slowly along the passageway. After walking for what seemed like several minutes, I stopped for a moment to rest. In the pitch-black darkness, it was hard to tell how far I had gone. All I could hear was the sound of my heart, which was getting louder and louder. It was beating faster, too.

I started to think I should go back, so I turned my head over my shoulder to see where I'd come from, but everything was black. After thinking about what to do for a moment or two, I decided to keep going and continued forward the same way for several more minutes. Suddenly I kicked something with my foot. I reached forward with my hands and felt a wooden wall. It was a dead end!

"Oh, great," I said out loud. I couldn't understand the point of a tunnel that went nowhere. I felt around the wall I had run into but found no opening, just a couple of extra boards that formed a big "Z." There was no opening in the ceiling either. Discouraged and getting a little angry, I turned around and started back the way I had come. I was less cautious now because I knew there was nothing to trip over. But I kept asking myself what the point of all this could be. Then I stopped short.

"That 'Z' is just like the braces on the gate going into our backyard at home," I whispered to myself. "Maybe it's a door!" Excited by the thought, I turned around again and headed back toward the wooden wall. My knee found it sooner than expected. "This is *not* fun!" I grumbled as I rubbed my knee in the darkness.

I pushed against the "Z", but the wall seemed pretty solid. I pushed harder and then started banging on it. Nothing budged. I ran my hands very carefully around all the edges where it met the walls on the sides. Then about waist high on the left side I found a slot cut into the wood, just big enough for me to fit my fingers in. I tried pulling the board toward me. It felt like it moved a little, but then snapped back. I got both hands in the finger groove and tried again. This time it *definitely* moved. It felt like it was free at the bottom but sticking at the top.

I can't even guess how many times I pulled on that thing, only to have it snap back into place. Sometimes it seemed like it was moving more than before and sometimes not. After working at it for several minutes, I stopped to rest for a moment. Then, practically biting through my lower lip, I gave the board the biggest yank I could possibly manage. Whatever was holding the door closed at the top gave way, and the whole thing swung toward me and hit my foot. I lost my grip, and the board snapped back into place. I pulled at it again, and this time I was able to keep hold of it as it swung toward me.

It *was* a door! I opened it until it lay flat against the wall on the right side of the tunnel. Everything was still pitch black, but putting one foot carefully forward and holding both hands out to my sides, I continued forward the same way I'd moved down the tunnel. When I heard the door bang closed behind me, I suddenly had this fear that I wouldn't be able to get it open again. I spun around as fast as I dared in the dark and pushed on the door. It didn't move, and I started to panic. But when I braced my feet and leaned on it as hard as I could, the door flew open, and I went tumbling back through the opening into the tunnel.

Feeling safe about being able to get back the way I came,

I turned around and went forward through the doorway again. I noticed that the floor was different, so I reached down to touch it. It felt like a sidewalk, and the walls weren't wooden anymore, either. Instead, they felt smooth, like cardboard. I moved my hands up and down and decided that I was standing between a couple of shelves loaded with cardboard boxes.

As I moved forward carefully and reached the end of the shelves, I noticed a sliver of light off to the right and slightly above me. My eyes almost didn't know how to react. I didn't know how long I'd been down in this tunnel, but I had really gotten used to the blackness. I couldn't tell how far away the light was, but it looked sort of like a long, fluorescent lightbulb running side to side. I moved slowly toward it with my hands out in front of me. I guess I wasn't being as careful as before because all of the sudden I ran into something with my shin.

"Ouch," I grunted. I'd hit it really hard, and I reached down to rub my aching leg. Then I tried to feel what I'd run into. It was a slab of wood just high enough off the floor for me to get my foot under it while it whacked my shin just above the ankle. It took only a second for me to realize I'd found a set of stairs and that I'd just donated blood to the bottom step. Looking up, I could now see that what I had thought was a fluorescent lightbulb was actually a sliver of light shining through the crack under a door at the top of the stairs.

I found a handrail and made my way up the creaking steps. There *was* a door at the top of the stairs, only *this* time it had a doorknob to go with it. I turned it and pushed, but the door didn't budge. I made quite a bit of noise pushing and pulling on the knob a few times, but the door was obviously locked!

I was devastated. Just when it looked as though I had found a way out, I'd run into another roadblock. Then it came to me. *If there's a doorknob, then maybe there's a light.* I stood up and began feeling around on the wall next to the door. The switches on the farm were not the normal flip-up-and-down kind. I think electricity was added after the house was built, so there were metal tubes running all over the walls and ceiling between the lights and plugs and switches. The switches were on little boxes mounted on the wall, and they had knobs that you had to spin. Spin it once and the light comes on, spin it again and the light goes off. The switch would always make a loud click when it was turned.

I found some tubing on the wall and followed it to a switch box. I spun the knob and immediately covered my eyes because the flash of light was so bright. After a moment of squinting and blinking I realized it must not *really* be very bright. There was just a single lightbulb hanging from the ceiling. I looked around the room. I was in Aunt Ella's cellar! And these stairs were directly under the stairs leading to the loft. The door where I was standing was right next to the kitchen. Aunt Ella was always either in the kitchen or in the nearby sitting room.

I started banging on the door. "Aunt Ella!" I called. "Anybody! Open the door! I'm in the cellar!" No one answered. I couldn't hear a thing, so I tried the door again. I couldn't imagine where she was, or everybody else for that matter. The only time I'd seen Aunt Ella leave the house during the past week was Saturday morning when she took Mom and Granny into town to do some grocery shopping and when we all went to church on Sunday.

Then it hit me. "No!" I almost cried as I realized that this was Saturday morning! Aunt Ella, Mom, and Granny were probably at the store with Daniel and Chelsea. Dad was at the library, and everyone else was probably playing either in the loft or outside. I was obviously going to be here for a while. I sat down on the top step and rubbed my sore shin.

After thinking about it for a minute, I remembered that when Aunt Ella had sent me to the cellar to "fetch" something, I had had to unlock the door. But it was one of those locks that you can see right through, as long as the key isn't in it. I looked into the lock, but it was black! That meant the key *had* to be in the lock, just like it had been the day I used it.

I remembered seeing a TV show once where a guy was stuck in a room with a lock just like this. He had slid a piece of newspaper under the door, right underneath the lock. Then he pushed something into the lock that forced the key out of the lock and made it fall onto the paper. He was then able to get the key by pulling the paper into the room where he was trapped. *Yes!* I thought. *It'll be cool to tell everyone how I got myself out of here!*

I started looking around for some paper. A small notepad hung on the wall near the top of the stairs, but the paper wasn't big enough. I would only have one chance to get the key to land on the paper, so it had better be a *big* piece. At the bottom of the stairs was a large brown paper bag with some napkins and paper towels and stuff like that in it. *I'm glad she chooses paper and not plastic at the grocery store,* I thought as I tore the bag apart and laid it open. I took it back up the stairs as fast as I could and slid it carefully under the door, hoping it was big enough to catch the key.

Now I needed something to push the key out of the keyhole. There was a pencil on a string next to the notepad. I yanked on it, and the string broke, but when I tried to push it into the hole, it was a little bit too fat. I decided I'd better look for something smaller. After searching for probably five minutes, I couldn't find anything but bottles, cans, and boxes. I opened a few of the boxes, but I couldn't find anything that looked like it would work. In my frustration I went back to the door and banged on it a few more times. Still no answer.

I tried the pencil again. This time I put the sharpened end in first and it made it almost up to the painted part before it got too tight to go in any farther. I figured it didn't have to go much farther, so after checking the position of the paper on the floor to make sure it was in the right place, I jammed the pencil with my hand as hard as I could. I think it did go in a little more, but it also broke off, leaving the tip of the pencil stuck inside the lock. And, of course, I never heard the key fall out the other side. I had just blown my chance to tell Dad that I'd finally learned something useful from TV.

I slumped down and sat on the top step for a while, rubbing the palm of the hand I'd used to jam the pencil into the lock. I started thinking about how I'd ended up here and went down to look at the door I'd come through. It didn't look anything like a door. It just looked like a wall made of wooden planks. But there was something painted on it. It was kind of hard to see because it was so faded and because the light was so bad. As I looked more closely, I could see that it was a temple that I'd seen a picture of before. It was white and had lots of windows. Below the painting was the word *Nauvoo* and an inscription that said "1 Nephi 2:2."

I stared at it for a moment before pushing the door open again. It still seemed to get stuck when it closed, but it was getting a little easier to open each time. I walked around the storage room and found that there were two other paintings on the walls. One was of a building with the word *Kirtland* painted below it. The other was of a group of people working in a large meadow or field or something. The word *Independence* was painted under that one. I pushed as hard as I could on each of these, but nothing moved. I had the feeling that these really were just walls and not more secret doors.

As I walked around the room, I noticed labels painted on the edges of several of the storage shelves. They were scripture references—such as "3 Nephi 14:16" and "2 Nephi 22:3." I thought about Aunt Ella telling me to search the scriptures. I laughed softly to myself as I whispered, "She probably arranged this whole ordeal just for my benefit! Too bad I don't have a Book of Mormon with me." There was one scripture reference that I recognized. It was Alma 17:2—the one about the sons of Mosiah searching the scriptures.

There was a small box on the shelf above this reference. I pulled down the box and found it contained a set of scriptures and some other books. There was a Bible and a triple combination, which included the Book of Mormon, the Doctrine and Covenants, and the Pearl of Great Price. I took the triple combination out of the box. The shelves closest to me were loaded with bottled fruit and were labeled 3 Nephi 14:16. I looked it up and read these words:

Ye shall know them by their fruits. Do men gather grapes of thorns, or figs of thistles?

"Huh?" I said aloud. I think hearing my own voice was helping me forget that I was alone. I read the scripture again then looked more closely at the bottles on the shelf. They contained what looked like small, dark cherries. One shelf down was the reference 1 Nephi 15:36. I looked it up.

Wherefore, the wicked are rejected from the righteous, and also from that tree of life, whose fruit is most precious and most desirable above all other fruits; yea, and it is the greatest of all the gifts of God. And thus I spake unto my brethren. Amen.

The bottles on that shelf had pears in them. *These are scriptures about fruit!* I realized. I couldn't believe that someone would use scriptural references to label shelves in a storage room. I read the first scripture again and the word *grapes* jumped out at me. I decided those must be bottles of grapes, not cherries. I didn't get the second one, though. Was Aunt Ella trying to say that pears are the "most desirable" fruit?

I moved to another shelf, loaded with smaller bottles full of what looked to be strawberry jam. The reference here was Moroni 8:25, which reads:

And the first fruits of repentance is baptism; and baptism cometh by faith unto the fulfilling the commandments; and the fulfilling the commandments bringeth remission of sins.

"First fruits," I said aloud. All I could guess was that strawberry jam was the first fruit that she bottled every year. I moved to another row, labeled 2 Nephi 26:25, and looked it up.

Behold, doth he cry unto any, saying: Depart from me? Behold,
I say unto you, Nay; but he saith: Come unto me all ye ends of
the earth, buy milk and honey, without money and without price.

The shelf above this reference held two bags of powdered milk
and several cans of honey. I looked up some others, just shaking my
head with each one. One of the references was Jacob 1:8, which
reads:

Wherefore, we would to God that we could persuade all men not
to rebel against God, to provoke him to anger, but that all men
would believe in Christ, and view his death, and suffer his cross
and bear the shame of the world; wherefore, I, Jacob, take it
upon me to fulfill the commandment of my brother Nephi.

That shelf held three large boxes, each labeled "Easter." I read
the scripture again a couple of times and thought about Jacob trying
to get all men to believe in Jesus Christ and that he suffered for our
sins. The shelf above the Easter shelf had a whole bunch of boxes
labeled "Christmas." The reference there was Alma 7:10, where it
reads:

And behold, he shall be born of Mary, at Jerusalem which is the
land of our forefathers, she being a virgin, a precious and chosen
vessel, who shall be overshadowed and conceive by the power of
the Holy Ghost, and bring forth a son, yea, even the Son of
God.

I just stared at these words for a while. I thought that maybe this
wasn't such a bad idea after all. I'd looked up every reference I could
find on the shelves. Then I looked again at the painting of the
Nauvoo Temple and turned to 1 Nephi 2:2:

And it came to pass that the Lord commanded my father, even
in a dream, that he should take his family and depart into the
wilderness.

At first I figured this scripture must mean that the door was a
way to get to the forest or outside. If you wanted to get from the house
to the barn without going outside because of snow or something,

then you could go this way. Then I thought maybe it was an escape route, like Lehi escaping from Jerusalem. I thought about the tunnel for quite a while before going back up the stairs to see if anyone might be where they could hear me now.

"Help!" I called. "I'm locked in the cellar!"

"Just a minute," came a man's voice that I didn't recognize. I heard a screen door slam. Then I heard the key being rattled in the lock. "The lock seems to be jammed," he grunted.

"I think there might be a piece of a pencil stuck in there," I confessed.

"Give me a moment," he called through the door. I could hear him working the key back and forth in the lock. After a minute or so the door swung open.

"There you go," the man smiled.

"Thanks," I said. "I've been stuck in there ever since breakfast."

"Happy to help," he said as he thrust his hand out for me to shake. "My name's Dr. Anthony."

CHAPTER 5

The Great Salt Lake Valley

"I knocked on the screen door a couple of times," Dr. Anthony said, "but no one answered. Then I heard you calling, so I thought I'd better come in and see if I could help. You say you've been down there since breakfast? Wow, it's past ten o'clock now. That must have been quite an experience."

I was too stunned to say anything. I just stood on the top step staring at him with my mouth open and my hand on the doorknob. In my other hand I still held the triple combination I'd been using in the cellar. The guy was tall and skinny. He wore glasses with wire frames and his dark, wavy hair hung down past his ears. His clothes looked like he'd slept in them several days in a row.

"How did you get stuck in the cellar?" he asked, but before I could answer he said, "You don't live here."

"I'm visiting my Aunt Ella," I finally managed to get out. I ignored his question about the cellar. "What are you doing here?" I asked suspiciously, "and why are you inside her house?"

"I came to visit your Aunt Ella," he smiled. "I believe I already mentioned that I came inside only after I heard you calling for help. Do you know where your aunt is?"

"I expect her at any moment," I said flatly. "But I think you should probably leave until she returns."

"Oh," he tried to sound reassuring, "I've been here several times before. I'm sure your aunt won't mind a bit if I wait around for a few minutes. I need to talk to her about . . ." He stopped short and grabbed the book from my hand. "Is that my book?" he gasped. "Where's the pouch?" He opened it with excitement but quickly realized that this was not the book he was looking for. I must admit, though, the cover of this book did look quite similar to the one on the mantel.

Just then the screen door swung open and Aunt Ella stood there staring at Anthony. "*Your* book!" she exclaimed. "What makes you think that anything in this house belongs to you?"

"Good morning, Mrs. Bellon," Dr. Anthony smiled as he turned to her. "So nice to see you again." He took a couple of steps toward her. "You know what I mean, of course. I was referring to the book that I've come so far to see. That original copy of the Book of Mormon that we've spoken about so many times. I was quite surprised when I thought the boy had it in his hand," he laughed. Then he winked at her as he pointed a finger into the air. "But now that I think about it, I'm sure it's still on the mantel where you always keep it, isn't it?"

Without waiting for a response, he spun on his heel and started through the kitchen toward the sitting room. "I just had to see it again," he exclaimed. "I can't wait a moment longer."

"Mr. Anthony," Aunt Ella called as she followed him through the kitchen. "I would appreciate it if you would not touch the book, please."

I followed, too, and saw Anthony with his hands on the mantel on either side of the book. I don't think he was touching it, but I couldn't be sure. Aunt Ella was staring at him with her head tilted slightly to one side. I couldn't see her face from where I was standing, but I sure got the feeling she was glaring at him.

"It's so refreshing just to look at it again," Anthony sighed.

This guy was weird. Aunt Ella had mentioned that he was persistent, but she'd never said anything about being so passionate. I, personally, would have used a few other words like "nuts," "whacky," and maybe even a little "slimy." His silky smooth way of talking gave me the heebie jeebies.

"Mrs. Bellon," he said solemnly as he turned to face her, "may I borrow the book for just a day or two? I'd really like to have some time to study it."

"Mr. Anthony," Aunt Ella copied his mood as she spoke, "would you be so kind as to leave. Now is not a good time. I will appreciate it also if, in the future, you will please telephone before coming to visit me."

Then I got scared. He didn't say anything for a moment, but his eyes turned dark and cold. When he turned to face Aunt Ella, he left one hand next to the book on the mantel. I could see his grip tighten and the knuckles on that hand turn white. He also clenched his jaw as he stood glaring at her. Then, almost instantly, he relaxed again.

"Please pardon my insensitivity," he said without feeling. "I shall certainly respect your wishes from this time forward."

Aunt Ella didn't move as Anthony removed his hand from the mantel and walked past her toward me. I backed out of the doorway into the kitchen, where Mom was standing with a large brown paper bag in her arms and Granny was setting another bag on the counter. He nodded in my direction as he hurried past. "Young man," he said. Then, looking at Mom, he said, "Ma'am." He never slowed down but went straight through the screen door and let it slam behind him. I heard a car door open and the engine start at the same time the car door slammed shut. If the driveway had been paved, I'm sure his tires would have squealed. Once he hit the road we could hear gravel spraying as he sped away.

"Maybe we shouldn't leave the book on the mantel anymore," I said as Aunt Ella walked through the kitchen.

"Who was *that?*" Mom asked. She sounded like she was as scared as I was.

"A man who wants something of mine that I am not interested in giving to him," Aunt Ella answered. Then she turned to me and asked, "Are you all right, Brandon?"

"I'm fine," I said, feeling rather overwhelmed by the whole morning. Then I added, "You never told me the guy's a fruitcake!"

"Well, he certainly has never been that bad before," she was shaking her head. "I can see now why I have felt so strongly about getting this taken care of." She turned and looked into the sitting room. "I think the book will be fine where it is for now."

From outside we could hear Jeff calling, "Aunt Ella! Mom! Come quick!" He came charging through the screen door as he yelled, "Something's happened to Brandon!" When Jeff saw me, he stopped dead in his tracks, screwed up his face, and asked, "How did you get in here?"

"What exactly do you *mean?*" I asked with a sly look. I wanted to milk this story for all I could get.

"We thought you fell into a hole in the barn and were stuck down there!" Jeff panted. "Clyde said he saw you run into the barn a couple of hours ago, and I've been looking for you. When I went into the barn, some of the stacks of hay had been knocked over and some had fallen into a hole in the floor of the barn. I got Clyde to come look at the mess, and since no one had seen you for a while, we figured you'd fallen down the hole. Right now Clyde's trying to get the bales that fell down the hole back out."

I just stood there smiling during Jeff's explanation.

"Do you know anything about this, Brandon?" Mom asked.

"Yes!" I said emphatically. "The block and tackle in the barn came loose from its hook and broke right through the floor. I was climbing up a stack of hay in the loft to try to get the block and tackle back out when the stacks of hay fell over and down into the hole. I was checking it out when I lost my balance and fell into the hole myself. A bunch of hay fell in after me, so I couldn't get out." I intentionally left out the part about yanking the rope out of the pulley. Turning to Aunt Ella, I asked, "Did you know that there's a tunnel leading from the barn to the cellar?"

Aunt Ella smiled as she shook her head back and forth. "As a matter of fact I did not know that," she said, "but it is no surprise to me."

"What do you mean?" I asked.

"You two go fetch Clyde so he knows that Brandon is all right," she said to Jeff and me. "Then you can show us the tunnel, and I will tell you about the man who built this house."

As Jeff and I got closer to the barn, my heart started racing again. I wasn't looking forward to facing Clyde about the soapy water in the milk. The mess in the barn looked worse than ever. By the time we got into the barn, Clyde had already pulled a couple of bales out of the shaft. He heard us come in and poked his head up through the hole in the floor.

"There ya are!" he said to me. I couldn't tell if he was still mad or what.

"Sorry about the milk," I said quietly. "What's gonna happen to it?"

"The truck done picked it up already," he said as he climbed out of the shaft. "I jus' told 'em to take five gallons off the total. They said it's fairly common an' so long as there ain't too much, it don't hurt nothin'. I think they said impurities are allowed up to a half a percent, 'r somethin' like that. An' that's the total for ever'thin' they pick up in a day. It ain't no problem. So, did ya fall down this here hole? I'm having a heck of a time getting them bales back outta there."

I was really relieved about the milk not being a problem, but it made me wonder how much of the milk we bought had soapy water in it. Or something even worse. I explained to Clyde about the tunnel leading to the cellar. He suggested we get the hay all stacked up again before I showed them what I'd found. I was sent to the blue shed for some rope. My back was hurting a little from the double fall I'd taken, so Jeff got the job of squeezing down the shaft and tying the rope around the bales that were still down there. We pulled up several bales and then a lot of loose hay from the bales that had come apart. Clyde suggested we leave the block and tackle where it was for his dad to take care of on Monday.

After all the hay was stacked up again we took a look at the opening to the shaft. It was actually a trapdoor. It was hinged and the door opened away from the front wall of the barn. It looked just like the rest of floor, though, so I don't think anybody would have ever noticed it if the block and tackle hadn't landed hard enough to break right through it. We put some wooden planks over the opening so nothing would fall into it while we were gone; then we headed for the house. Aunt Ella had some lemonade ready for us, but before we drank any, we all went down to the cellar so I could show everybody the door to the tunnel.

"There are flashlights in the box right there," Aunt Ella said, pointing to a box on one of the top shelves. The scripture reference on the shelf was Ether 3:4. Mom and Aunt Ella said they had "absolutely no interest" in going into the tunnel, but Clyde, Jeff, and I each took a flashlight and went in. I went first and shined my light to the end where I'd fallen down. It was far enough away that I could barely see it. But before, in the dark, it had felt like it was a lot farther. We got to the end, and I could see that there was more hay to be picked up. The tunnel was so narrow that we had to go single file all the way to the ladder Clyde had put down into the shaft that led up to the barn. We shined our lights up the shaft for a minute and then turned around and went back to the cellar.

While Mom and Granny put the groceries away, Aunt Ella was busy preparing lunch. She invited us to sit at the table with our lemonade while she told us what she knew about the farm.

"My father built this house," she began. "It was built in the early 1900s, before I was even born. Dad grew up in Salt Lake City during the time the Salt Lake Temple was being built. He used to tell us stories about the trouble some members of the Church had. Life was much better for them after leaving Nauvoo, but some members of the Church still feared persecution. Most of the Church leaders had hiding places on their own property."

Aunt Ella was pouring lemonade for everyone around the table the whole time she talked. "But they still had to run the Church," she continued, "they had to meet together and make decisions and carry on the necessary business. The rumors were—and apparently Dad believed every word of it—that they set up a system of tunnels between some of the buildings in downtown Salt Lake City."

"It's pretty well known," interjected Mom, "that there are tunnels now that go between the buildings on Temple Square."

"Really!" we all asked at the same time.

"Sure," she said. "When your dad was a missionary, he got to go from the mission home to the temple through one of the tunnels. But I have no idea how long they've been there."

"Well, according to your grandfather," Aunt Ella said to Mom, "they have been there since before the Salt Lake Temple was ever finished. The temple was completed in 1893. They at least had tunnels at that time. The ones they have now are most likely new."

"Wow," I breathed. "When was he born?"

"In 1880," replied Aunt Ella slowly as she tried to remember for sure. "He and my mother moved to this farm here in 1908, right after they were married. Of course there was no farm here then. It was just a valley of trees. He cleared all this land and built the house himself."

"Why did they come to Iowa?" Jeff asked.

"Well, my grandmother—that would be my dad's mother—was about eleven years old when the Saints were forced to leave Nauvoo and go west to Salt Lake. Dad said she used to love to tell stories about life in Nauvoo and the trek to the Great Basin. Her father never made it though. He died in 1846 as they were traveling, and he was buried along the trail here in Iowa. I am sure that is the reason my dad decided to come back and settle in this area. His grandpa Eli was his hero and his idol, even though he never met him. Elias Franzen was his full name."

"Can we go see his grave?" I asked. I'd completely forgotten about my lemonade by this time.

"We don't even know where it is," Aunt Ella smiled. "We just know that it was somewhere between Nauvoo and Winter Quarters."

"What's Winter Quarters?" Jeff asked.

"Winter Quarters is where the Saints stopped for the winter of 1846 and '47," Aunt Ella explained. "It does not exist anymore, but there is a museum in Omaha, Nebraska, that tells about it."

"Didn't we come through Omaha on the way here?" Jeff asked Mom.

Mom got a fake shocked look on her face. "How did you know that!? I thought you were too busy watching movies to notice anything outside the van," she smiled.

"Road signs are *slightly* more interesting than Tweety reruns," he smirked.

"But you're right," Mom continued, ignoring Jeff's "Tweety" remark. "Omaha is the last city we went through before hitting Iowa."

"But you didn't know about the tunnel?" I asked Aunt Ella, as I remembered my lemonade and took a sip.

"No. At least not for sure," she replied. "Whenever Dad would tell stories about Salt Lake and persecution and hiding out, he would always smile and add something like 'folks weren't too friendly 'round here neither, at first.' Then he would wink and say, 'That's why I took some precautions m'self.'" Aunt Ella smiled, "I used to wonder about hiding places or underground tunnels, but I had long since forgotten about the idea."

"Well," said Jeff as he scrunched up his face and made a fake laugh, "leave it to Brandon to fall right into it for you."

Shauna and Meg had been in our bedroom upstairs and came

wandering into the kitchen. We told them the whole story and invited them to look at the tunnel with us.

"Does it stink?" asked Meg.

Jeff and I didn't think so, but with Meg you can never be quite sure. Aunt Ella found her a plastic bag that she could carry just in case, and we gave them the tour. Meg stood at the Nauvoo door and watched us go down the tunnel. Shauna just kept saying, "This is so *cool!* This is *so* cool!" Every time she repeated it, she would emphasize a different word in the sentence.

Dad came back from the library at about five o'clock, just like the previous Saturday. We told him about the tunnel and showed him the hole in the barn floor where I'd fallen through.

"Why doesn't this open up into the lower level of the barn?" Dad wondered. Jeff and I just stared at each other.

"*I'm* clueless," I said eventually. Then, quickly, before he could say anything rude, I glared and said, "Be nice, Jeff!" His mouth was already open. He closed it and smiled.

Dad went back and forth between the milk room in the lower level of the barn and the opening of the shaft several times. Then he went into where the milking stalls were located. Jeff and I just followed him everywhere he went.

"What are you doing?" I finally asked.

"I'm trying to figure out where everything is," he said as he was looking up and down the wall that separated the milking stalls from the milk room. It turned out that the back of the milk room didn't go all the way to the front of the barn like the rest of the lower level. There was a space about four feet by twelve feet missing. But the shaft only took up about two of the twelve feet.

"Brandon, fetch me a flashlight," Dad said as he stared down the shaft.

"What?" I said, my eyes popping open. "Excuse me, but did you say the word *fetch* to me just now?"

Dad turned to me and smiled. "When in Rome!" he said.

"Huh?" I had no clue what he meant by that.

"When in Rome, do as the Romans do," Jeff explained helpfully.

I still didn't get it. "What do Romans have to do with flashlights?" I asked.

Jeff was exasperated. "Brandon," he said, "we're in Iowa, so Dad is talking like the people who live in Iowa!"

I just stared at Jeff and then Dad and back at Jeff.

"Just get me a flashlight, please," Dad smiled.

I took my time because I was still trying to figure out the "Rome" thing. When I got back, Dad was standing on the ladder partway down the shaft with his head twisted around looking over his shoulder.

"I think something is painted on this wall," he called up. "Is Brandon back with the Roman flashlight yet?"

"How rude!" I said, pretending to be offended. Jeff did his weird scrunched up face and fake laugh thing again as I handed the flashlight down to Dad.

He shined the light on the wall opposite the ladder for a moment before calling up, "Someone's painted a picture of the Salt Lake Temple on this wall."

Jeff's scrunched-up face returned to its normal bewildered look. I got excited as I realized what this probably meant.

"Push on it!" I yelled. "I bet it's a door."

I heard Dad grunt a couple of times, and then he disappeared. I climbed down the ladder into the shaft, and Jeff followed. We found Dad in a room that was about three and a half feet by ten feet. Shining the flashlight around, we could see that there were shelves on the narrow wall opposite the door. On the shelves were some very dusty bottles of fruit and an old oil lantern. There were also two or three moldy looking blankets with lots of holes in them. Spiderwebs were everywhere.

"It looks like the guy had a hideout set up in here," Dad said after a moment.

"Really?" asked Jeff from behind me. This room wasn't much wider than the tunnel below, so he couldn't see past me very well. He hadn't seen the shelves on the opposite wall, so he started straining to get a peek over my shoulder.

"Sure," Dad explained. "There's a lantern here and some matches. He's got bottled fruit and blankets, too. He was set up pretty well."

"This is really cool," Jeff said.

"Can we use this as our hideout?" I asked.

"It's okay with me," Dad said, "but you'll need to ask Aunt Ella first."

Jeff and I went running as fast as we could to the house. As we burst into the kitchen I blurted out, "You've gotta come see this! We found a secret hideout under the barn that you get to by going halfway down the ladder." I went up to Aunt Ella and began pleading, "Can we use it? Please! Can we make it into a hideout for us?"

"Wait a minute. What did you find?" she asked.

"You know the shaft that I fell down?" I said. "There's a secret door in one of the walls. It opens into a secret room behind the room where the milk tub is. It's got old bottles of fruit and blankets and stuff. We're asking if we can have it."

"Will a rocking chair fit in the room?" Aunt Ella asked.

"Huh?" Jeff and I both responded.

"If a rocking chair will fit in there, then I may just want to use it myself," she explained.

"Aunt Ella," I said slowly as I shook my head back and forth, "you're too *old!*" I suddenly realized what I had said. "I mean—you'd have to climb down the ladder and . . . and it's dirty down there and . . . and . . . oh, I'm sure a rocking chair wouldn't fit!"

I realized that everyone was just smiling at me. Everyone, that is, except for Jeff. He just looked at me and said, "Hello-o-o-o, Brandon-n-n-n!"

"I think Aunt Ella's just kidding," Mom suggested.

"Oh," was all I could manage after a moment. I looked over at Jeff, who pasted a fake smile on his face as he blinked about twelve times.

"If you boys would like to use the room," Aunt Ella smiled, "then go right ahead."

Well, I let out a cheer and ran to tell Dad the good news.

"But first bring everything to me that is already in there!" Aunt Ella called after me.

With Dad's help, Jeff and I got the room cleaned out and all fixed up that afternoon. Aunt Ella threw away pretty much everything we pulled out of there, except for the lantern. She decided it was an antique worthy of being displayed on a bookcase in the sitting room. Of course she cleaned it up first. She said she didn't dare even open any of the bottles of fruit. And the blankets were full of holes, dirt, and who knows what kind of animal life.

After we swept the place out, we filled our new hideout with stuff that Aunt Ella found for us. We put an old piece of carpet on the wood floor and furnished it with pillows and blankets. She had some old games and books that we loaded onto the shelves. Because of the size and shape of the room, any game that required more than two people at a time was pretty much worthless. It worked well for checkers and chess, though. Dad helped us hang a couple of flashlights from the ceiling, and we were set.

Before we got a chance to use our new hideout, Dad had us help him fix the trapdoor in the barn. But a hideout isn't really a hideout if it's not hidden, so we didn't mind helping him. The hinges for the trapdoor were pretty well trashed, so we went to the hardware store in town and got some new ones. Then we used some boards we found in the blue shed to make a door to replace the one ruined by the block and tackle crashing through it. Dad did a great job. Except for a slightly different color in the wood, you couldn't even tell there was a trapdoor, just like it was before.

The next Saturday Aunt Ella woke me up as usual for our

meeting in the sitting room. This whole vacation was beginning to fly by. The farm was actually turning out to be a pretty fun place, and I never felt like complaining anymore. Aunt Ella was really nice, and Clyde was fun to work with. He even seemed to have forgotten my mistake with the milk valve. Jeff and I were also having a great time with our new hideout under the barn. It was usually too dark after dinner to do much outside, so we got in the habit of playing chess every evening in our secret room.

"Today," Aunt Ella began, bringing me back from my daydream, "I would like to talk more about Joseph Smith. He had quite a time keeping the gold plates safe while they were being translated, and then he had just as much trouble keeping the manuscript safe once the translation was complete."

Aunt Ella told me that Joseph Smith had kept the gold plates hidden in a hollow log and then later under some stones in front of the fireplace. She also told me that when Joseph and his wife, Emma, moved from New York to Pennsylvania, they hid the plates in the bottom of a barrel of beans. Men were constantly trying to get the plates away from Joseph.

"As long as Joseph did his best to keep the plates safe, the Lord helped him succeed. You can read the details in the *History of the Church*," she said, pointing to the bookcase.

"Which book is it?" I asked, genuinely interested.

"See that set of eight blue books at the far left on the top shelf?" she asked.

My interest fell just a little bit—like a rock. "*Eight* books?" I asked.

"For the complete history," she replied. "There are actually seven volumes, plus an index. But you will find what we have been talking about in the first volume."

I was relieved to hear *that*. Then she told me about Martin Harris. When he heard about Joseph Smith and the work he was doing, Martin became interested in helping Joseph Smith with the translation. He had quite a bit of money and offered to help pay some of Joseph's expenses. Aunt Ella told me a cool story about how Martin Harris took a copy of part of Joseph's translation to some really smart guy in New York City, who said the translation was correct and even gave Martin a certificate saying so. But when Charles Anthon asked Martin where Joseph Smith had gotten the plates and Martin said it was from an angel, the professor told Martin Harris there wasn't any such thing as angels and to bring the plates to him, so Anthon could translate them. When Martin Harris said he couldn't do that, Professor Anthon took back the certificate and tore it up and wouldn't admit afterward that he had ever said Joseph Smith's translation was good.

That didn't matter to Martin, though. He was now convinced the Book of Mormon was true, and he helped Joseph as much as he could after getting back from New York.

Martin's wife was not happy about how much time he was spending helping Joseph. Martin thought that if he could just show his wife the manuscript he and Joseph were working on, she would see the value in it and let him continue to help Joseph. He was really worried also about how his wife would react once she found out that he was planning to pay for the book to be published.

Well, when Martin asked Joseph if he could show the manuscript to Mrs. Harris, Joseph prayed and was told "no." Martin kept pushing and pushing, and so Joseph kept praying about it. Finally, after praying for a third time, Joseph came back with a list of people whom Martin would be allowed to show the manuscript to. By then they had 116 handwritten pages, and Joseph Smith warned Martin to be very careful with the book. Martin took the pages home and showed them to his wife. He also showed them to everyone on the list and even some people who weren't on the list. When it came time to return the manuscript to Joseph Smith, it was gone. They never found it.

Aunt Ella explained to me how the Lord will sometimes give

you what you want if you bug him enough, but when we do that, it doesn't always turn out the way we want. That made me think about all the fasting and praying we had been doing for Dad to finish his research early. But that was something that was good for everyone, I thought, so it wasn't the same thing.

She also told me how the members of the Church had to keep moving around to escape from their enemies. They were in Kirtland, Ohio, for a while and some were in Independence, Missouri. Then they moved to Nauvoo, Illinois, but even that didn't work. Finally, they had to abandon everything again and go all the way to the Rocky Mountains, where they built Salt Lake City. I couldn't help wondering about all those paintings in the cellar and on the door to our hideout. Here are my notes from that morning:

Saturday, April 25. Third discussion with Aunt Ella:

JS—H. 1:61: Martin Harris gives money to Joseph Smith to help him move.

JS—H. 1:62: Joseph Smith copies some of the characters off the gold plates.

JS—H. 1:63: Martin Harris takes the writings copied by Joseph Smith to New York City.

JS—H. 1:64: Martin Harris shows the characters to Professor Charles Anthon. Professor Anthon says the characters are true and that Joseph Smith's translation is the most correct he's ever seen and gives Martin a certificate saying so.

JS—H. 1:65: Professor Anthon tears up the certificate when Martin tells him that Joseph got the plates from an angel.

That night as I was lying in bed, I tried looking up "Martin Harris" in the index of my triple combination. But I had to look under "Harris, Martin" before I found anything. There were a whole bunch of scriptures in the Doctrine and Covenants about him, and I read them all. That might be the reason I had the dream I did that night. It was the scariest dream I've ever had.

I dreamed that I was with Joseph Smith and Martin Harris and that we were running and hiding. First we had the gold plates and then after a while it changed to be the 116 pages. The whole time we were being chased by the professor from New York City. At least Martin and Joseph kept calling him Professor Anthon, but in my dream he looked exactly like Dr. Anthony. We kept thinking we were safe, but then he would show up again. We went from Kirtland to Independence to Nauvoo and then to Salt Lake City. We were safe there for quite a while, but then all of a sudden Professor Anthon showed up and yelled, "Give me my book!"

I looked down at the 116 pages that I was holding, but they turned into the old copy of the Book of Mormon that was on Aunt Ella's mantel. I was so scared that I woke myself up. I couldn't go back to sleep, so I took my scriptures with me down to the sitting room. For a few minutes I stood at the mantel and just stared at that copy of the Book of Mormon.

The butterfly clock read 4:35. I went to the sofa and started looking up some scriptures. By the time Aunt Ella slipped quietly out of her room and came into the sitting room twenty-five minutes later, I was ready. I told her about my dream. "I think we should keep the Book of Mormon in a safer place," I said.

She was sitting next to me on the sofa. "Because of your dream?" she asked.

"Yes!" I said emphatically, "because Heavenly Father often warns people through dreams."

"Oh, really?" she smiled. "Why do you say that?"

"Because," I said, opening my copy of the Book of Mormon, "I found some examples. Lehi had lots of dreams that told him what he should do. The story about the tree of life came to him in a dream. In First Nephi, chapter eight, verse two, it says, 'And it came to pass that while my father tarried in the wilderness he spake unto us, saying: Behold, I have dreamed a dream; or, in other words, I have seen a vision.'" I looked up from the book and said, "And his tree of life vision told about his family and what was going to happen to them."

Aunt Ella smiled at me. "Did you find any other examples?" she asked.

"Uh-huh," I said, barely taking time to breathe. "In First Nephi, chapter two, verse two, it says, 'And it came to pass that the Lord commanded my father, even in a dream, that he should take his family and depart into the wilderness.' And in First Nephi, chapter three, verse two, it says, 'And it came to pass that he spake unto me, saying: Behold I have dreamed a dream, in the which the Lord hath commanded me that thou and thy brethren shall return to Jerusalem.' Those are examples of Lehi being told exactly what he was supposed to do," I said.

"Sounds to me like Lehi was the only one who had dreams," said Aunt Ella, with a twinkle in her eye. But I was ready for that argument.

"Oh-h-h, no," I corrected her. "Look what it says right here in Ether, chapter 9, verse 3: 'And the Lord warned Omer in a dream that he should depart out of the land; wherefore Omer departed out of the land with his family, and traveled many days.' There's more, but it's not important."

"So what *is* important?" asked Aunt Ella very seriously.

"What's *important*," I said emphatically, "is that each time one of these guys was warned in a dream or told to do something in a dream, they did it. Lehi sent Nephi and his brothers back to Jerusalem. He also told his sons about the tree of life and tried to get them to learn from it. And right here in Ether it says that Omer was warned, and so he took his family and left."

"And your point is?" Aunt Ella smiled.

"My *point* is," I said, trying to make myself be perfectly calm, "I think that my dream might be a warning. It's a warning that we need to keep that copy of the Book of Mormon safe from Dr. Anthony."

Neither of us said anything for a moment. Finally Aunt Ella smiled and said, "Perhaps we should pray about it. Will you offer the prayer?"

"Okay," I said and then I prayed. I mean, I *really* prayed. I was sincere about wanting to keep this book safe. And all of *us* safe as well. That Anthony guy worried me. When I was done with my prayer Aunt Ella just sat with her head bowed and her arms folded for a few more moments. All I can figure is that she was saying her own prayer. Finally she looked up.

"I think the book will be all right on the mantel for now," she smiled. "What do you think?"

I could tell there was no use arguing, so I offered a reluctant "Okay," and she went into the kitchen. I wanted to remember what I'd found, so I added the following notes to my notebook:

Sunday, April 26. My research about dreams.

1 Nephi 2:2: Lehi is commanded to take his family into the wilderness.

1 Nephi 3:2: Lehi has a dream telling him to send his sons back to Jerusalem.

1 Nephi 8:2: Lehi tells his family he's seen the tree of life in a dream.

Ether 9:3: Omer warned in a dream to depart out of the land.

The more I thought about it, the more I felt like I was pushing my luck, the same way Martin Harris had when he asked for the 116 pages just one too many times. But it was still Aunt Ella's book, so I would just have to go along with what she wanted. I just couldn't get Dr. Anthony out of my mind.

CHAPTER 6

My 116 Pages Get Lost

For the first few days after Aunt Ella and I talked about my dream, it was hard to think about anything other than Dr. Anthony. Eventually, though, I started to relax a little. We were still busy most of every day doing homework. Mom had us working so hard that I was starting to think that Dad wouldn't be the only one who got all his work done in a month. I already had most of my assignments completed and sent off to my teacher. And Mom was checking everything for me pretty carefully before it got sent, so I was hopeful that I wouldn't have to redo anything—Mom was already giving me plenty to do over again.

Once Mom had dished out all the torture she could manage each day, we were able to spend the rest of the afternoon and evening doing pretty much whatever we wanted. Jeff and I had brought a soccer ball with us, and we practiced almost every afternoon for the first two or three weeks we were at the farm, which was a constant reminder about my soccer tournament. But it was starting to get too hot to be outside in the afternoons. I couldn't believe it was May already.

Aunt Ella woke me on Saturday at the usual time. I said the prayer and "fetched" the book from the mantel. This time she placed it in her lap without removing it from the pouch.

"What are we going to talk about today?" I asked as I tried to hide a small yawn. I wasn't bored, just still a little bit sleepy.

"What *is* today?" she asked, "or better yet, what is tomorrow?"

I had to think for a moment. "Fast Sunday?" I asked, not sure if that's what she was talking about.

"Correct," she smiled. "How did your fasting go last month? And have you decided what you will be fasting for this time?"

"Well, . . ." I responded slowly, "last month I was fasting for something that I still won't know about for a while, but so far things seem to be going pretty good."

She nodded her head up and down a little as she said, "It pleases me that you are able to work on spiritual things that do not necessarily happen overnight. Do you remember Alma 17, verse 2?"

She was kidding, right? I practically had it memorized by this time! I grinned and said, "That's the one about the sons of Mosiah searching the scriptures and fasting and praying."

"And what did they get from doing all that?" she asked.

"Umm, sound understanding, right?"

"Correct again," she answered. "And how much time do you think they spent searching the scriptures and fasting and praying before they achieved sound understanding?"

"I don't know," I said honestly. I'd never really thought about it before. "Probably months," I said. "Or maybe years. I think understanding the scriptures or spiritual things probably happens just a little at a time."

"That is very true," she said seriously, "and it is probably the first and most important thing we all need to learn." She nodded her head slightly as if she all of a sudden approved of me. I decided I kind of liked feeling approved of. "So," she continued, "will you be fasting for the same thing this time?"

"Well, partly, I guess," I answered. "I mean, what I fasted about last month is still important to me, and it hasn't happened yet, but . . ." I paused for a moment.

"But what?" she asked, without being pushy.

"But . . . I've been wondering about something else lately that I think is probably a lot more important right now," I finally replied. She stared at me, and I felt a little uncomfortable. I couldn't tell if

84

she knew what I was thinking or not. I mean, about Dr. Anthony and how scared I was of him.

"Good for you," she broke the silence at last. "It is wonderful that you have spent time thinking about your fast in advance of beginning your fast. I feel certain you will pray about it thoroughly before you begin, will you not?"

"Yeah," I smiled.

She smiled back.

Then she began with new energy. "Well, today, I would like to tell you more about this book." She handed me the copy of the Book of Mormon that she'd held so carefully on her lap each of the last three Saturday mornings. "Look it over and ask me anything you would like to know," she said.

She handed it to me, and I had this funny feeling—like I was holding something that wasn't just fragile but very precious.

"Okay," I said softly, trying my best to control the smile that I could feel tugging at the corners of my mouth. I couldn't believe she was actually going to let me look inside it after all this time. I started by carefully removing the book from the pouch. The book opened easily, and I quickly found what looked like very old hand-writing inside the front cover. It read:

My dearest Hannah,

This book is very important to me. But now that we must leave Nauvoo, I reckon you shall be needing it more than I. Please accept it with my love.

D.

"Who's Hannah?" I asked. "And who is the person who signed it just 'D' period?"

"I have told you a little about Hannah already," she answered, "but I just never told you her name. Hannah is my grandmother. She is the one who left Nauvoo with the Saints when she was about eleven years old. This book was given to her at that time by her father."

"Did his name start with a 'D'?" I asked.

"No, his name was Elias Franzen. Inside the leather pouch you will find the small letters 'E. F.' burned into the flap. So I imagine that 'D' is short for 'Dad.' Or perhaps 'Daddy.' That is what she always called him. He is the one who died and was buried along the trail somewhere in Iowa."

"Oh, yeah," I said, remembering the story she told us before. It seemed weird to be holding a book that had been held by someone who was now dead.

"What did he mean by 'you'll need it more than me'?" I asked.

"I am not sure." She paused for a moment before adding, "Maybe he knew that he would not make it very far on the trek."

"That's really sad," I said quietly. As I turned through the pages in the book, I found some marks made by hand with dark blue ink. Nothing was written in the printed area, but there would be a line running up and down the margin next to the words. I also noticed that the paragraphs in the book were printed just like a normal book.

"This looks like a novel. Why aren't there any chapters or verses?" I asked.

"This is from the very first printing," Aunt Ella replied. "When translated from the gold plates, the Book of Mormon was divided only by the book names like First Nephi and Second Nephi. The chapters and verses were not marked until about fifty years later."

"Wow," I said, "so how could you find a scripture that you were looking for?"

"You would have to know the book very well," she smiled. "I suppose they would just have to remember approximately where the reference was on the page or perhaps the page number."

"Oh, I know!" I beamed. "You can just use the index!" Shauna had taught me that trick, and I'd used it several times now to find things I was looking for in the scriptures. Before I could finish turning to the back of the book to find the index, Aunt Ella began to laugh.

"There was no index, either!" she giggled. I couldn't believe she was laughing at me. But not just laughing—giggling! This 80-something-year-old lady was giggling. At me! I tried not to act too annoyed by her reaction. I guess it just really surprised me. She still had a huge smile on her face as I tried to get the conversation moving again.

"It would be really hard to find something in the book of Alma," I said, "'cause it's huge!"

"That is true," she was still smiling. "So how about seeing just how difficult it really is. See if you can find what we know as Alma, chapter 17, verse 2."

"Okay," I said as I started carefully turning the pages. It took a couple of minutes, but I finally found it. She giggled a couple more times while I was turning through the pages, but I just tried to ignore her. Next to the reference was one of those vertical lines written in the margin. "Is this how they marked important scriptures?" I asked.

"I imagine so," she answered. "They obviously did not have anything like a fluorescent highlighter or even a red pencil that they could use to underline sections without covering the text. Actually it was uncommon then to write in a book of scripture at all, other than inside the front cover. I was quite surprised to find these markings when my grandmother gave me the book. She said the marks were there when she received the book from her father, so I would think that he probably put them there."

I turned a few more pages, and the book fell open at Third Nephi because there was a scrap of paper between the pages. The paper was very worn and looked as though it had been torn along a couple of edges. The handwriting on it was similar to that in the front of the book. "What's this?" I asked, as I pulled the scrap from between the pages.

"Grandmother used that as a bookmark. She told me that this is her father's handwriting and that it was in the book when he gave it to her. I think she kept it just to remember her father by."

The ink on the paper was faded, and there were only four short lines that I could read:

Valley of Lemuel

Lamanites, A.D. *30*

Mount Zerin

Mormon and Lamanite king

There was one more line written below this, but that part was torn and faded, and I couldn't make it out. I started to read in the Book of Mormon where the bookmark had been. It was the part that talked about Jesus Christ appearing to the people in America. I read a few paragraphs until I came to a part that I later found to be 3 Nephi 17:3. It says: "Therefore, go ye unto your homes, and ponder upon the things which I have said, and ask of the Father, in my name, that ye may understand, and prepare your minds for the morrow, and I come unto you again."

I was really surprised by this scripture, so I read it a couple more times. "I've never noticed this before," I finally said to Aunt Ella. "They tell us all the time that you're not just supposed to believe what the prophet or apostles tell you in general conference but you're supposed to pray about it and get your own testimony. Well, here it says that even if you're standing right there in front of Jesus Christ himself and he's talking to you face to face, you're still supposed to pray for understanding."

Aunt Ella just smiled knowingly and let me continue.

"In fact, he's the one who told the people to go home and ponder his words and pray for understanding and to get prepared for the next day because he was coming back to teach them some more. It doesn't matter who's talking to you. You're supposed to search the scriptures, think about what you've heard or read, and then pray about it."

I spent a few more minutes looking through the book and reading some of the paragraphs that had lines next to them in the margin. Aunt Ella just sat quietly while I was doing so, then she told me more about her great-grandfather Elias Franzen. He and his family came from Kirtland, Ohio, at the time Joseph Smith got the land for Nauvoo, and they were among the first to arrive there, when it was still mostly a swamp. He helped dig huge ditches to drain the land and get it ready for the Saints to build houses on. It was a lot of work because there was so much rock in the area. He also helped dig wells and did all sorts of other stuff that was needed when Nauvoo was first being built. We talked about him for a long time. He seemed like a pretty cool guy.

"Do I get to keep the book now?" I asked hopefully, when our discussion looked like it was done for the day. After all, she had let me hold it and look through it, and she'd never done that before.

"You tell me," she replied.

"Yes!" I beamed. "We've had *four* meetings now, and I think I understand what I need to do to take care of the book."

"We agreed on four *weeks* after the first meeting," Aunt Ella smiled, "and it has only been three."

"Okay," I said, heaving as deep a sigh as possible. I stared at her for a few seconds with the most pitiful look on my face that I could manage.

She just smiled and bowed her head as she said, "I think we need a prayer. Will you offer it, please?" When I said the prayer I was sure to mention something about being grateful for the opportunity to develop patience. I noticed her shaking her head just a little bit as she stood and went into the kitchen.

Forty minutes later we were all at the big, round table, finishing up another one of Aunt Ella's fabulous breakfasts.

"I don't think I'll be going to the library today," Dad said after he swallowed his last bite of pancakes and wiped his mouth with a napkin. I had been reading the milk carton, trying to find something about the allowable percentage of impurities, but I almost dropped it when I heard what Dad said. Good thing it still had the lid on. Shauna and Jeff looked equally shocked. We all sat there frozen for a moment. Jeff's fork was stopped in midair, about three inches from his mouth.

"What do you mean?" Jeff asked in astonishment.

"Why not?" Shauna and I both added.

"Guys," Mom said, "what's your problem? If Dad doesn't want to go to the library today, he doesn't have to! You're going to make him *feel* bad."

Shauna was sitting next to Dad. She leaned her head on his shoulder and started rubbing his arm. With a sad face she said, "Don't feel bad, Daddy! We just want you to be sure to get all your work done so you won't have to worry about it anymore!"

"Thank you for your concern," Dad replied, but I'm not sure he bought it. "My research is going very well," he continued. "It's going so well, in fact, that I'm sure I'll be done much sooner than expected. That's why I'm not planning to go to the library today. I thought maybe we could do something fun together for a change."

"Like *what?*" I asked. I honestly couldn't think of anything we could do. Usually when Dad suggested we do something fun, we would go for a bike ride or swimming or something like that. But we couldn't do any of those things here. At least not as far as I knew.

"Well," Dad said, "yesterday I was talking to the man who works Aunt Ella's farm . . ."

"You mean Clyde's dad?" I interjected.

"Clyde's dad. Yes," Dad answered me. "And Clyde's dad has his very own name, you know. It's Mr. Hansen. And Mr. Hansen— Clyde's dad—told me that he would be needing to sell some of the pigs soon, and so he's planning to go to the auction in town today to see how much pigs are going for. And he's invited all of us to go with him."

"What's an auction?" asked Meg.

"That's where people bring stuff they want to sell and other people bid how much they're willing to pay for it," Shauna explained.

"Huh?" replied Meg.

"Tell you what," Dad jumped in, "let's all go to the auction and we'll show you how it works."

The auction didn't start until nine o'clock, so we didn't have to leave for another hour or so. Mom, Granny, and Aunt Ella took Chelsea and Daniel and went grocery shopping right after breakfast. Mr. Hansen showed up at the screen door about 7:45. "I reckon we better be movin' if I'm gonna git a chance to look them livestock over 'fore the biddin' starts," he said.

"Shall we all ride in the van?" Dad suggested.

"Suits me jus' fine. Is ever'body comin' with us?"

"Just me and the four oldest kids," Dad replied.

The town we went to was only about twenty minutes away. It was obvious where the auction was being held by the number of pickup trucks parked all around the building. The building was round and made of wood and had double doors in the front. It was two or three stories high, I think, but it was hard to tell because the only windows were at the very top. It sort of reminded me of Aunt Ella's grain silo, but it was a lot fatter. Behind the building was a yard with a bunch of holding pens full of animals. Each pen had a number on it. There were cows, bulls, calves, horses, and pigs of every size.

There wasn't any parking anywhere close to the front of the building, so we parked in back next to one of the holding pens.

"This is better anyhow," Mr. Hansen said, "seein's how we wanna check 'em out first."

We pretty much just followed him around as he went to each pen that had pigs in it. If the owner of the animals was around, he'd ask how much the big ones weighed and how old the little piglets were. Sometimes he'd ask what they'd been raised on. Judging from the answers he got, I think that meant what food they'd been eating. In one pen were about eight little, tiny pigs, but no one was there to answer questions about them.

"Them piglets can't possibly be weaned," he exclaimed. "I can't believe some fool thinks he can sell 'em off when they's still that young."

After a good half hour of looking over the pigs and watching Meg gag, we went inside. The inside of the building was just one big room with a round dirt floor in the center. There was a five-foot-high wall that went all the way around the dirt floor. At the top of the wall was a short railing with a wooden walkway that looked down over the arena. The rest of the space was filled with bleachers that started above the walkway and went up from there on all sides.

There were two sets of stairs leading up to the walkway; one went to the front of the building and the other led to the back. There was a large gate that opened to the yard behind the building, and above the gate was a small platform with a wooden stool and a microphone stand on it.

The bleachers were probably two-thirds full by the time we came up the back stairs onto the walkway. The railing hit me about knee high. I was a little nervous standing next to it because it was a long way down to the dirt floor on the other side. There weren't any stairs to get up the bleachers, so we had to climb over people and say "excuse me" a lot.

We found places to sit almost at the top and waited for the auction to begin. As we sat there I looked at the people on the bleachers around us. As far as I could tell, we were the only ones there not wearing hats or boots. Almost everybody had a cowboy hat on, but there were a few baseball caps around, too. A man in a white cowboy hat and very pointed cowboy boots climbed up onto the platform and stood next to the stool instead of sitting on it. He had skinny legs and a big belly that hung way over his belt.

"We got ourselves a downright good-lookin' crowd here today," he drawled into the microphone. "Hope ya brought yer billfolds with ya, 'cause we got some fine animals to git rid of this mornin'. Hope ya had a chance to look over what we got available t'day. We'll be startin' this mornin', as usual, with the calves. Then we'll move to cows, bulls, pigs, and horses in that order. Ever'thin' else we'll bring in at the end, 'cause we got only one er two of each critter after that."

No one seemed to be paying very much attention to him. Then all of a sudden he yelled, "Let's begin-n-n!" into the microphone, and immediately a man came from the yard through the gate pulling a calf. "Okay," the man in the white hat said while he looked at a clipboard. He announced the name of the person selling the calf and the age and weight of the animal very clearly and distinctly. And then he let out a yell into the microphone that almost scared me out of my seat.

For the next sixty seconds I couldn't understand a word he said. His mouth was moving ninety miles an hour, and he'd mumble along real low and then all of a sudden somebody would yell out a word that I couldn't understand, and he'd yell something back as he pointed to them. Then he'd jabber along some more until someone else called something out. The guy never even took a single breath. The man with the calf kept leading it around in circles while all this was going on.

I realized after a minute that there were a couple of other guys helping the one at the microphone. They were standing at the bottom of the bleachers on the walkway, right along the wall, and when someone would raise a hand or call out something, they'd point at him and call out something to the guy in the white hat. That's when his voice would change from low and fast to high and fast for a couple of words. But then he'd go right back to the low jabbering again.

Then before I knew it, the man on the platform took a big wooden hammer and banged it down on the railing next to him and yelled, "Sold!" right into the microphone. "You can pay Mr. Milburn right back there," he said as he pointed toward the yard. A man in the bleachers stood up and followed the calf being led away. At the same time another calf was being brought in. Then the whole thing started all over again.

"What happened?" Meg asked.

"That man just bought that calf," Dad told her.

"He did?" Meg asked with her nose wrinkled up on one side.

I just sat in amazement as Dad tried to explain what had happened and how the whole thing worked. The guy never spent more than a minute or two with each animal, and I'm absolutely sure that I didn't understand more than two words the whole time the bidding was going on. After about forty-five minutes, they finally got to the pigs. Clyde's dad looked completely bored while the calves, cows, and bulls were auctioned off. I was expecting him to act at least a little more interested about the pigs, since that's what we came for. But his expression didn't change a bit.

Once they got going, I noticed that he would sort of shake his head after each pig or group of piglets was sold. Finally he leaned over to Dad and said, "They ain't gittin' nothin' for 'em this year."

I was starting to get bored with the auction, so I began looking around the room. All of a sudden I saw someone who caught my attention. It was Dr. Anthony! I was sure of it. He had a big cowboy hat on that he used to hide his face the second he saw that I had noticed him. He was standing right at the top of the stairs leading to the yard in the back. He glanced back over toward where we were sitting and then started quickly down the stairs.

"Dad," I whispered as loud as I dared, "that's that Anthony guy we told you about."

"What?" he asked, looking in the direction I was pointing.

"The guy who came to Aunt Ella's house looking for the Book of Mormon that she's giving to me," I explained. "That's him going down the stairs!"

"Put yer hand down!" Mr. Hansen hissed at me. "You just bid on them piglets! We ain't here t' buy nothin', and you sure as you-know-what don't want to make yer father pay fer them six piglets and haul 'em back to Utah with ya!"

I stared at Mr. Hansen and then at the man with the microphone. I could feel my face getting hot all of a sudden. "Sorry," I whispered. "Sorry, Dad. I'll pay for them!"

"Settle down," Mr. Hansen cut in. "Yer off the hook. Some feller over there made a bid. But now keep yer hands down!"

When I looked back toward the stairs, Anthony was gone. Dad turned to Mr. Hansen and said, "I'm going outside."

"We can all go," Mr. Hansen replied. "I ain't got no interest in any more o' this. But wait till they's done with this group o' piglets."

We waited a few seconds until the hammer banged down and the man yelled, "Sold!" It took us a minute or so to work our way through the crowd and down the bleachers. I glanced up at the man on the platform, and he didn't look too pleased that six people were disturbing his fine mumbling performance. The people who had to move to let us through didn't seemed too happy either. I think Shauna and Meg were the only girls in the whole place, and I heard someone say, "I reckon them fillies have had enough."

When we got out into the yard, Dr. Anthony was nowhere to be seen. Dad looked around a little as he walked slowly toward the car.

"Well, I guess he's gone," Dad sighed. "I was hoping to get a better look at him."

"Who?" Meg asked.

"It's not important," Dad smiled. He pulled Meg to his side and headed to the car. "Who wants ice cream?" he asked.

"I do," Meg said with an excited giggle. We all agreed, and Mr. Hansen said there was an ice cream shop just down the street.

We all climbed into the van, and Dad started the engine. He asked, "Everyone got seat belts?" Then, without warning, he yelled, "Hey!" as he threw his door open and jumped out. He sounded mad. I was sitting on the very back bench on the right side of the van. At the same time Dad yelled, the side of the van that I was on felt like it fell into a six-inch hole. Then the whole van rocked back and forth a couple of times.

Dad ran around the front of the van and down the side past where I was sitting. I turned to see where he was going and caught a glimpse of Dr. Anthony several cars away. He was running as fast as he could and didn't bother to slow down when his hat came flying off. He jumped into a small, dark blue car and sped away before Dad could catch up with him. By this time Mr. Hansen had climbed out to see what was happening, and so the rest of us followed.

"What in tarnation is goin' on!" he called to Dad as he walked quickly back to the car. "Looks like that guy jus' slashed yer tire. Who was that?"

"Someone who's been harassing Ella," Dad answered, "but I don't think he's ever gone this far before." He looked down at the tire. "Let's get this changed and get back to the farm and make sure she's all right."

"Do ya think that's where he's goin'?" asked Mr. Hansen.

"Why else would he slash the tire?" Dad asked grimly. "I'm afraid he's just trying to slow us down so he can get back to the farm before we do."

I've never seen Dad move so fast. He pulled the jack out and gave it to Clyde's dad. Then while Mr. Hansen began jacking up the van, Dad unloaded the spare tire. Between the two of them they had the tire changed and the jack down again in just a couple of minutes. Dad yelled for everyone to get in quick as he just tossed the jack, the ruined tire, and the hubcap into the back of the van. The tires squealed as Dad took off down the road.

"Are we still going to get ice cream?" Meg asked.

"I don't think so," Shauna answered. "We need to go check on Aunt Ella first, but I'm sure we'll get some ice cream later."

"*Ohh!*" Meg pouted.

I don't think Dad was too concerned about speed limits or any other traffic laws. No one had to remind me to put my seatbelt on this time. Dad took the first corner so fast that my head bounced off the window. Somehow I managed to buckle the seatbelt with one hand while I was rubbing the side of my head with the other. I'd never seen him drive like this before. He was usually very careful and cautious. Mom, on the other hand, was *always* in a hurry when she was driving, so I knew what it was like to be tossed around in the car.

When the farm came into view, we could see the blue car parked out front. Aunt Ella's car was there, too, so they were already back from the grocery store. As we got closer to the house we saw Anthony charge out through the screen door and jump into his car. He was carrying what looked like a small bag or satchel in his hand.

"He's got somethin'," Mr. Hansen shouted.

"Let's check inside the house before we worry about that," Dad said quickly. He sounded intense.

Aunt Ella's driveway formed a small semicircle that connected to the gravel road at both ends. Instead of pulling into the driveway behind Anthony's car, Dad pulled the van sideways so it blocked the entire road leading back to the main highway. Anthony pulled his car onto the road and headed straight for the van, but he skidded to a stop about fifteen feet away, with his car pointed straight at Dad's car door.

"Go inside and make sure everyone's okay," Dad called back as he jumped out of the van and ran toward Anthony's car. The rest of us jumped out of the van, too. It must have looked to Anthony as though he was about to get mobbed. He had a look of shock and fear on his face, and I think I even heard him scream from inside his car. It sounded like a girl! He put his car in reverse and sprayed gravel as he backed down the road and into the driveway again. Dad stopped charging and turned to protect himself from the flying rocks.

We ran inside yelling, "Aunt Ella! Mom! Granny! Is everyone okay?"

"Everyone is fine," Aunt Ella said calmly, "but Mr. Anthony took the book."

"What?!" I yelled. "No!" I spun on my heel and went crashing back out the screen door.

As the screen door slammed behind me, I heard Meg ask, "What book?"

Anthony had gunned his car in the other direction on the gravel road, and Dad was standing a few feet from the van, helplessly watching the blue car race past the pig shed and then disappear around a curve in the road.

"Is anyone hurt?" Dad called over to me.

Mr. Hansen had followed me out of the house. "No," he hollered, "ever'body's jus' fine."

"But, Dad!" I cried, "he's got the book! He *stole* my book!"

CHAPTER 7

Seek and Ye Shall Find

Aunt Ella, Mom, and Granny appeared at the screen door.

"What's going on?" asked Meg from behind them.

"Call the sheriff," Mr. Hansen told Aunt Ella, "and tell 'im to git to the north end of this here access road. If 'e can git there within 'bout five minutes, we'll have the varmint trapped!"

Aunt Ella scurried back inside to call the sheriff.

"Ya feelin' up to runnin' this guy down?" Mr. Hansen asked Dad, as he ran toward the van.

Dad didn't answer but just turned and jumped into the driver's seat.

"Wait for me!" I yelled.

"Me, too!" Jeff called from right behind me. Every door on the van was open, so we were able to jump in without even slowing down.

"This road ain't got no turnout fer 'bout five miles," Mr. Hansen said, as Dad straightened out the van and made a spray of gravel of his own. After the way Dad had been driving on the way here, I immediately fastened my seatbelt again, and Jeff took care of his, too, without any prompting. The road wasn't very wide, and Dad seemed to be using every inch of it that he possibly could as the van swayed back and forth with each curve.

Mr. Hansen was holding onto the dashboard with both hands. He kept glancing over at Dad, and he acted more and more annoyed each time a strong curve knocked him against the car door.

"If Ella can git the sheriff in time, then we ain't got no problem cornerin' this guy," Mr. Hansen said, as he stared at what was coming next in the road. I think that was his subtle way of trying to suggest that Dad ought to slow down.

"But if the sheriff isn't there in time," Dad countered, "then we might lose him altogether."

"I see yer point," Mr. Hansen replied grimly.

After at least five minutes of swerving and swaying in silence, we began to hear a police siren.

"Maybe they caught him!" I said hopefully. For the next twenty or thirty seconds, the siren seemed to be coming closer. Then, all of a sudden, as we came around another curve in the road I saw Anthony's dark blue car heading straight for us with a police car not far behind. I thought for sure we were going to hit head-on.

Dad hit the brakes, and my chin hit my chest. I felt the safety belt pull tight across my shoulder. When I looked up again our van was sliding sideways in the gravel, blocking the entire road. Anthony's car swerved to miss us and went off the road and into a ditch on the right side. The police car started sliding sideways just as our van had and ended up side-by-side with us, only facing the opposite direction. I looked out the side window of the van and read the word "Sheriff" painted across both doors of the car next to us. It was only about three feet away.

The sheriff got out of his car, but instead of running to the ditch to catch his criminal as I expected he would, he walked slowly around the back of his car, acting only mildly concerned as he was asking if we were all right. Judging from the size of this man, I don't believe he could have run anywhere anyway. It looked like it took every ounce of strength he had just to maneuver the large stomach that was hanging proudly over his belt. Dad and Mr. Hansen already had their doors open and yelled, "We're fine!" almost at the same time. Then Dad added, "Catch that guy," and Mr. Hansen asked, "Where'd 'e go?"

I got out of the van and could see nothing but the back bumper of the blue car showing above the side of the road. Jeff and I got to the edge of the ditch about the same time. The front of the car was either smashed in really good or it was about a foot deep in mud. The driver's side door was open, and Anthony was nowhere to be seen.

"Shh-h-h!" the sheriff hissed, and we all listened. I watched the sheriff carefully scanning the cornfields in front of us, watching for the slightest movement and listening for any sound. The corn was only about two feet high, so if Anthony was out there, he had to be lying down, and if he was moving, then we should have been able to see the short cornstalks moving too.

There was a gentle breeze that moved over the field. "Well, 'e can't be too far off," the sheriff said as he climbed down into the ditch and went over to inspect the car. "Wha' did ya say this guy stole from ya?" he called up. He was standing next to the car, ankle deep in mud, leaning over with his head in the backseat.

"A book," I answered. "A really valuable, *old* book. It's in a brown leather pouch."

All we could see of the sheriff was his large backside from the waist down. We could hear him moving things around in the car, but he didn't say anything.

"He apparently claims to be a historian or professor of history or something, and he's been interested in this book of Ella's for some time now," Dad explained as he and Mr. Hansen followed the sheriff into the ditch. The sheriff didn't respond for a moment.

"I ain't never seen s' much junk," the sheriff muttered as he rummaged through stuff on the floor of the backseat. "Looks like he's been sleepin' and eatin' in here for a while. He sure must like Twinkies." He climbed partway into the backseat and asked, "Don't see what yer missin' in here anywhere, do ya?"

Just then I heard a sound behind me.

"There he goes!" Dad yelled. I turned around and saw Anthony running across the road and into the trees on the other side. He had apparently made his way partway down the ditch and hidden behind some tall weeds before we got to the edge of the ditch looking for him. He was carrying the same satchel we saw when he first came running out of Aunt Ella's house. Dad and Mr. Hansen scrambled up out of the ditch and took off after him while the sheriff slowly shut the car door and brushed off the knees of his pants. I couldn't believe he wasn't doing anything!

"Aren't you going to pull your gun and at least yell 'Stop or I'll shoot'?" I complained. "I mean, that's what you have a gun for, right?"

"Listen, son," the sheriff wheezed as he slowly climbed out of the ditch, "he ain't gonna stop, and I ain't gonna shoot, so what's the point in hollerin' 'bout it? That boy's already into them trees. He's younger an' faster than me, and he's got a head start. Not t' mention the fact he prob'ly weighs only 'bout half o' what I do. I ain't gonna be able t' catch 'im. But on the other hand, he ain't gonna be able t' git outta them hills without us findin' 'im first. So jus' settle down a minute."

I let out an exasperated sigh and looked over at Jeff. I imagine I looked just as surprised and disgusted as he did. The sheriff moved to his car door, which was still open, and allowed himself to fall backward into the seat with a grunt, leaving his legs and muddy shoes stretched out onto the gravel road. He picked up the microphone to his two-way radio and started talking. Some lady named "Mabel" was on the other end. "Git ahold of ever' deputy an' git 'em out here as soon as possible," the sheriff instructed. "Have 'em start on t'other side an' work their way over th' hill. All 'cept Hank, that is. Tell 'im t' bring the dogs an' meet me here. Sheriff out."

"Wow," I said, looking at Jeff.

"Sounds fun!" Jeff laughed.

The sheriff heaved himself to his feet and stood next to his car, still holding the microphone. There was a large bullhorn mounted on the top of the car, which he spun around and pointed up the hillside toward where Anthony, Dad, and Mr. Hansen had disappeared.

"C'mon back now, boys," he drawled into the microphone. His message came blaring out of the bullhorn. "The dogs'll be here in a few minutes. He ain't gittin' away." He paused for a moment and then added, "An' you, sir, the boy who done stole the book. If'n I was you, I'd hightail it back down here 'fore them dogs show up. Ya see, they ain't trained too well. They know how t' catch people, but they ain't too good at knowin' just how t' treat 'em while they's waitin' fer us to catch up and slap the handcuffs in place." He paused another moment and added, "Big dogs, they is, too. Lots o' teeth."

Dad and Mr. Hansen emerged from the trees a couple of minutes later and made their way down to the road. "That's a pretty convincing story you tell," Dad smiled.

"Prob'ly 'cause it's mostly *true*," the sheriff said. He wasn't smiling. "Anybody here know what this feller's name is?"

"Charles Anthon," I said with authority.

"I thought you said it was 'Anthony,'" Dad questioned.

"Oh, yeah," I said quietly. "Yeah, it's Anthony."

"Is his first name 'Charles'?" Dad asked.

"Uhh, I don't know for sure. Maybe not," I smiled weakly. "I guess I was thinking about someone else."

"Ain't no matter," the sheriff responded. Then he spoke into the microphone again. "Mr. Anthony, sir, it ain't possible fer ya t' git outta them hills without us findin' ya first. You'll save us all a heap o' trouble if'n you jus' c'mon down right now. Judge Myrup's gonna look real close at what goes on here, so the sooner ya c'mon down, the easier it'll go on ya." He paused and then added, "You can try to run from th' dogs, but that's just like stompin' in the mud—it won't do ya no good."

The sheriff fell back into the driver's seat of his car. He pulled out a clipboard with some papers on it and started writing stuff down. He obviously wasn't too concerned about either Dr. Anthony or my book.

"What did he mean about the judge looking close at what happens?" I asked Dad as we both stood scanning the hillside for any sign of Anthony.

"I think he means that if Mr. Anthony turns himself in voluntarily, before the dogs have to chase him all over the hill, then he might get a lighter sentence."

"A lighter sentence?" I wondered out loud. "So he'll get out of jail sooner and be able to come try to steal my book again?"

"Well, I suppose so," Dad answered, "but sentences are supposed to help people change their desire to commit crimes."

"Haven't you heard, Dad?" I said with half a smirk, "rehab doesn't work—especially for lunatics like this guy!"

Dad just smiled as he looked over the hillside.

"So the more work it takes to catch this guy, the longer he could stay in jail?" I asked.

"Something like that," Dad responded as his head bobbed slowly up and down.

"Go-o-o, Anthony!" I yelled. "You can make it! Don't worry about the dogs, they can't possibly be as bad as he says! Go! Go! Go!"

As I yelled those last three words, I was jumping and throwing my arms into the air with each word. I had a huge grin on my face as I stared at the trees now. I suddenly had the feeling that someone was looking at me, so I looked over to one side and then the other. I was wrong, though; *everyone* was looking at me.

Dad was still facing the hillside, but his head was turned in my direction and his mouth was hanging half open. Behind Dad I could see the sheriff still sitting halfway in the car with his legs hanging out. His head was slightly cocked to one side. He was still holding the clipboard, and his pen was still on the paper, but it wasn't moving. It was as if he'd quit writing right in the middle of a word. My smile faded a little as I turned to look the other way. Mr. Hansen and Jeff were both staring at me, too. Mr. Hansen's hand was on his forehead shading his eyes from the sun.

Everyone had a blank look on their face. Everyone, that is, except for Jeff. His mouth was hanging completely open, and he had a look on his face that was an amazing combination of shock, pain, and just downright confusion.

"*What* are you *talking* about?" Jeff finally spit out. My expression didn't change as I slowly looked around at each person and realized that they were all very interested in my answer to Jeff's question. As my brain stumbled and fumbled for a moment, I quickly realized that what had made perfect sense when I was yelling at the hillside now made no sense at all. I was about to try to explain myself when I heard a siren in the distance. The noise turned everyone's attention away from me and provided some hope of being able to get out of this situation without having to confess what I had been thinking.

Within a moment we heard a couple more sirens. One of the sirens sounded like it was getting pretty close.

"That would be Hank," the sheriff said to no one in particular as he struggled to free himself from the car seat. He closed the car door and put his clipboard on the hood. As a pickup truck with a flashing red and blue light bar came around the bend, the siren wound down and the truck came to a stop. A tall, skinny deputy stepped out.

"What's the story, Sheriff?" he asked as he ambled over to where his boss was standing. The sheriff began to explain the situation while Jeff and I went over to check out the truck. It was the same color as the sheriff's car and also had the word "Sheriff" painted along each side. The bed of the truck had a shell on it, and we could hear some scratching and rustling coming from inside.

"Well, let's get to it," the deputy said as he walked back to his truck. He opened the door to the cab and pulled two leashes from inside before moving around to the back and opening up the door to the back of the shell. He reached in to hook up the leashes and then out jumped two of the biggest German shepherds I'd ever seen. They immediately started sniffing around and straining against the leashes. I didn't think the scrawny deputy would be able to hold on.

"Settle down, boys," the deputy said, pulling the two dogs in the direction of the car in the ditch. "Take a minute in here and then let's go find this guy," he said as he opened the car door.

The dogs immediately jumped into the car. One was in the front and the other in the back. They were sniffing about wildly and leaving muddy footprints everywhere. After a few seconds, Hank said, "Let's do it, boys!" The dogs jumped out of the car and started sniffing around and pulling Hank down the ditch. One of them began barking and started to run. Hank was getting stretched between the two leashes until the second dog quit sniffing and romped after the first one. They both slowed when they got to the place where Anthony had crossed the road, then, after sniffing in circles for a moment, they scampered out of the ditch and dragged Hank across the road and toward the wooded hillside.

"Looks like they've marked 'im!" the sheriff called over to Hank.

"Hold on, fellers," Hank said to the dogs as he struggled to slow them down. Somehow he managed to get a hold on one of the collars and unhook the leash. The dog took off up the hillside on a dead run. I thought the second dog was going to go nuts until he got free. Then Hank unhooked his leash, and the dog also bounded into the trees. "Go get 'im, boys!" the deputy yelled, and he started jogging after them. I don't know why he bothered to say anything because they were already long gone!

While Jeff and I stared in the direction of the barking dogs, the sheriff started asking Dad and Mr. Hansen some questions. They gave him the whole story about how we had seen Anthony at the auction when he slashed the tire, about rushing home, and finally about chasing him to where we had run him into the ditch. I noticed that Dad conveniently left out the fact that he broke every speed limit from the auction all the way back to Aunt Ella's. The sheriff didn't write too fast and didn't remember very well either, so Dad had to keep repeating most of what he said. He asked me a couple of questions about the book and where Aunt Ella usually kept it, but I was pretty well entranced by those barking dogs. The barking kept getting more faint as they moved up the hillside.

After about ten minutes we heard Hank's voice on the speaker in the sheriff's car. "We got 'im, Sheriff," came the crackly voice. "He's got a small satchel with 'im. Was there anythin' else that we should be looking fer?"

"Naw, that's it," responded the sheriff.

"Good 'nough," said Hank. "It's all downhill from here, so we should be back down in jus' a couple o' minutes."

"Ya got somebody there with ya to help with the escort?" the sheriff wheezed.

"Sure 'nough, Sheriff. Dave an' Jimmy jus' followed the sound of the dogs, and we all got to the perpetrator 'bout the same time. Dave's comin' down with me, an' Jimmy's headin' on back to pick up their vehicle."

"Sheriff, out," was all the sheriff replied, and then he put the microphone back on the dashboard.

"I wonder if my book's okay!" I said to no one in particular, but secretly I was hoping the sheriff would get the hint that I was more than a little worried about my stolen property. I thought he ought to call Hank back and ask him about it. I really wanted to know, but I didn't feel brave enough to just come right out and ask him. I was trying to avoid calling too much attention to myself since everyone had so kindly chosen to forget about my little yelling incident without making me explain it.

After a few minutes of anxious waiting, watching the sheriff scribble notes, I saw a deputy I hadn't seen before escorting

Anthony out of the trees. The prisoner had his hands behind him and was wearing a pair of handcuffs. Hank followed close behind them, pulling back on the leashes as the dogs kept nipping at Anthony's heels.

"Ouch!" Anthony growled. "How many times do I have to tell you to keep those dogs away from me?"

"They's jus' doin' their job!" Hank smiled. "Now don't you go an' git 'em all riled up agin! If'n you was to move a tad faster, I 'magine they'd leave ya be. But ya know how dogs git when it's past their supper time."

"No, I *don't* know how dogs 'git.'" Anthony emphasized the word *git*, mimicking the way Hank pronounced it. The men and dogs were almost to the road now.

"Well, I'll tell ya, then," Hank smiled again as he looked over at the other deputy. "When they git the itch t' chew on somethin', jus' ain't much I can do t' prevent it."

Anthony stumbled onto the gravel road and immediately began complaining to the sheriff. "I intend to file a formal complaint about the treatment I've received from these dogs!" he yelled.

The sheriff just opened the back door of his car and looked at Anthony. "That'll go nicely with th' report I'll be makin' 'bout you evadin' arrest and costin' the taxpayers plenty fer makin' us drag these animals out here to fetch ya," the sheriff answered.

Anthony jumped toward the car. "They're still biting me!" he yelled.

"They's jus' encouragin' ya to git in th' car," Hank answered. "I ain't allowed to put 'em back in th' truck 'til you's in custody in that there vehicle."

"Sheriff!" Anthony started to complain again, but the sheriff interrupted him.

"Jus' shut up and git in the car, son!" the sheriff said, sounding like he couldn't believe how dumb this guy was. "The deputy's already told ya that the dogs git put away jus' as soon as you's in the back o' the car." Then the sheriff turned to the deputy and said, "Obviously English ain't his native language, Hank. Ya better find out what it is an' then read 'im his rights again."

Jeff and I started to laugh, but Anthony's vicious glare was enough to make us sober up really fast. He then gave the sheriff a look of disgust and climbed into the car with a defiant kick in the direction of the dogs. I thought those dogs were going to pull Hank right into the backseat with them as they both lunged at Anthony, but Hank somehow managed to hang on.

"Shut the door!" yelled Anthony, suddenly realizing how dumb that move was.

"Happy to," answered the sheriff as he gently snapped it closed.

The second deputy handed Anthony's satchel to the sheriff. I'd almost forgotten about it. Jeff and I both hurried over to watch the sheriff open it. "This yer pouch?" he asked as he pulled Aunt Ella's Book of Mormon from the bag.

"That's it!" I gasped as I reached for it.

"Make sure there ain't no damage," the sheriff said as he handed it to me. Carefully, I opened the pouch, pulled out the book, and looked it over. Everything seemed fine. I opened the book and found Hannah's bookmark with her dad's handwriting still in place.

I looked over at Anthony because he was yelling something in the back of the sheriff's car. But all the windows and doors were closed, so I couldn't tell what he was saying.

"Let's move over this way a bit," the sheriff suggested as he walked slowly down the road, away from the car. "So's we don't have t' listen to all that racket."

"Do you need to keep the book as evidence?" Dad asked.

"Naw," replied the sheriff. "We got several witnesses. Go ahead an' take it home. We can have ya bring it to th' station later if need be. Jus' be sure t' keep it in a safe place."

"Aunt Ella has been keeping it on the mantel," I replied. "I tried to get her to move it before, but she wouldn't."

"She jus' might be willin' to turn an ear in yer direction now," he said. Then he pointed to the deputies and said, "These boys'll be followin' ya back to the house now to get some more statements from them folks what's there. Ya might wanna mention it to 'er when ya git there."

I nodded in agreement.

"This yers, too?" the deputy asked, holding out a single piece of paper inside a clear plastic cover. I stared closely at the paper as the deputy held it out to me. It was handwriting on yellowing paper that was obviously very old.

"I've *never* seen this paper before," I said, "but I think I know who wrote it."

I quickly opened up the old Book of Mormon again, pulled out the bookmark, and held it next to the paper in the deputy's hand.

"You're right!" Dad exclaimed. "That handwriting *is* the same." Then he pointed to the bottom of the paper and added, "And just take a look at who signed it."

I looked where Dad was pointing and read the words *Elias Franzen.*

"May I read this?" Dad asked the deputy as he carefully took the paper from his hands.

"He'p yerself," he said.

"I think this is a letter to Joseph Smith from your triple-great-grandfather," he said with excitement.

"Cool!" Jeff and I both said at once. With one of us looking over the sheet from either side of Dad, he read the letter out loud as we followed along. Here's what it said:

This, the thirtieth day of July, in the Year of our Lord 1838
Dear Brother Joseph,

By the good grace of God, may this brief find you filled with His peace and good blessings. Owing to the responsibilities on both your shoulders and mine, it is already some long time since I have had the good pleasure of your kind company and that of your dear wife.

I feel certain you will recollect that this last meeting was the time when you gave me charge over certain items in the Kingdom that are of some great import. Likely you will also recollect the great treasure entrusted to me and the charge over the same which was so generously granted me at your hand.

This brief then, is intended as an assurance to your mind that I have been diligent in the charges given and that I will expound in detail at such time that God sees fit that we may enjoy one another's company once again. Regarding the great treasure and map received at your hand, the details of which being written down by your scribe at the time, I wish for you to be assured that I keep the writing as near to me as my precious Book of Mormon at all times, that it may always be at hand. My greatest gratitude is extended toward you for that with which I have been entrusted.

May God be with you until the time of our reunion. Your fellow servant in Christ,

Elias Franzen

"That is *really* cool!" Jeff breathed.

"Yeah!" I agreed.

"But ya said ya ain't never seen this b'fore?" the sheriff asked.

"No," we all answered.

"He must have already had it," Dad suggested, as he handed the plastic-covered letter back to the deputy. The deputy returned it to Anthony's bag, zipped it closed, and gave it to the sheriff.

Just then there was a loud crash behind me, and I spun around to see little pieces of glass flying from the back door window of the sheriff's car. Anthony's feet were sticking out where the window used to be. The sheriff and his deputies just stared at the car and then at each other as if they'd never seen anything so dumb.

The sheriff lumbered toward the car as Anthony pulled his muddy shoes back inside and struggled to get himself back into a sitting position.

"What'sa problem in there, son?" the sheriff asked.

"That paper's mine!" Anthony yelled through the window opening. "You have no business letting those people read it! Give it to me, now!"

"It's already been returned to yer bag," the sheriff said, shaking his head. "You done busted m' window on account o' that?"

"It's none of their business what's in that letter!" Anthony screamed again.

"We's jus' makin' sure we understand what they claim was stolen and what weren't," the sheriff explained. "Did ya steal that there book like they say, or are ya suggestin' it's yers also?"

Mr. Anthony started to say something but stopped abruptly. He just closed his mouth, glared at the sheriff for a moment, and then stared straight ahead without saying anything else. The sheriff told Hank to add the broken window to his report; then he climbed in the car and drove away with Mr. Anthony.

The deputies followed us to Aunt Ella's house. They spread out some papers on the kitchen table and asked everybody there what they'd seen when Anthony came to the house. According to Mom, Granny, and Aunt Ella, he had just barged in, grabbed the book, and run out again before anyone really even had a chance to figure out what he was up to.

Another deputy showed up as Hank was writing down what everybody had said about Anthony's little visit. Aunt Ella made sandwiches and lemonade for each of them. Hank did all the work, while the other two just kept eating and saying, "Thank ya kindly, ma'am," and "Sure do 'preciate yer hospitality!" After finishing all the paperwork, Hank told us that Anthony would be appearing before Judge Myrup, probably on Monday morning, and so someone would come by afterward to tell us what had happened. The deputies all left pretty quickly once the sandwiches were gone. By that time it was about noon, and the rest of us were pretty hungry.

We helped Aunt Ella make more sandwiches and lemonade. Then we sat around the kitchen table talking about the day's events. I was certainly feeling a lot safer, now that Dr. Anthony was in jail. Aunt Ella reminded us all that dinner was at five o'clock and that we would begin our fast right after. "Allow me to invite you children once again," she smiled, "to spend some time preparing for your fast and deciding what you will be fasting about."

"Okay," we all said as we left the kitchen. Jeff, Shauna, and I all smiled at each other knowingly. There was no doubt in any of our minds what we were fasting for. The fact that Dad had stayed home from the library today said a couple things to me. First, that meant that he felt good about his progress. In fact he'd said and done a lot of things in the last week that led me to believe that he was going to be finished with his research very soon and that I might really be home in time for my soccer tournament! Second, it was impressive to me that he would choose to stay home on the same day that Dr. Anthony finally went ballistic.

I thought about the second thing for a long time. Dad had been home when we needed him. I had been worried about our family's safety and was thinking about making that the focus of my fast this week, but apparently that wasn't necessary. I mean, Anthony landed himself in jail just hours before we were going to begin our fast, and I had the feeling that our family would be long gone before he ever even had a chance to think about getting out. I decided there was no point in changing what I would be fasting about. Everything seemed to be going just fine. I thought about praying about it, but I already felt so good that I didn't bother.

Two days later, we were just finishing up our morning home-work when we heard police sirens wailing in the distance. Mom was helping Aunt Ella make lunch, and the rest of us were clearing our books from the kitchen table. As the sirens got closer we all went outside to see what was going on. Two sheriff's cars were barreling along the graveled road, coming from the direction of the main highway. They pulled off the road and came sliding to a stop in the dirt driveway in front of Aunt Ella's house. We could also hear another siren coming from the other direction. Hank jumped out of the first car and ran through the dust cloud his car had just made. He looked really anxious.

"Have ya seen Mr. Anthony?" he asked.

"W-What do you mean?" Aunt Ella stammered. We were all wondering the same thing.

"He's done escaped!" Hank exclaimed.

CHAPTER 8

The Liahona

"We got here as fast as we could!" Hank panted. His eyes darted around wildly.

Another deputy we'd seen on Saturday got out of the second car and started looking up and down the road and around the sides of the house.

"So I reckon this means ya ain't seen 'im?" Hank said, trying to get a firm answer.

"No, we have not," Aunt Ella replied soberly.

"How did he get out?" I asked, imagining Anthony sawing through the bars of his jail cell with a hacksaw blade smuggled in by some evil girlfriend. She'd probably hidden it in a cake and gotten away with it by offering to bake another one for the guards.

"We was takin' 'im t' th' courthouse to see Judge Myrup, an' he jus' ran off after we got 'im outta the car," Hank explained. "Handcuffs an' all!" He was shaking his head back and forth like he just couldn't understand how it had happened. I was feeling the same way. "He ran into a mess o' bushes next to th' courthouse an' jus' disappeared. I ain't got no idea how 'e done it. We searched fer quite a while an' then figured we'd best hightail it out this way jus' t' make sure you was all safe an' sound."

The siren from the other direction got closer, and another car pulled up. I knew it was the sheriff's car because the back window was missing on the driver's side. The sheriff turned off the siren as he got out, but he left the red and blue lights flashing.

"Mornin', folks," he said as he walked slowly over toward us. "Ya got these folks apprised of th' situation, Hank?" he asked.

"Sure 'nough, Sheriff," Hank replied, "but I still can't figure out how the whole thin' happened. It don't make no sense."

"We'll git 'im," the sheriff tried to reassure us. "Now, don't ya be worryin' 'bout that. In the meantime we'll be leaving a deputy at th' farm here twunny-four hours a day. If'n ya need to be off somewhere's, jus' let us know an' we'll also send a escort with ya."

I couldn't believe it! How does a guy in handcuffs get away from a bunch of deputies right in front of the courthouse? It didn't "make no sense" to me either.

"By th' way," the sheriff said to Aunt Ella as he was leaving the house, "I wouldn't leave that book on the mantel no more, if'n I was you." He nodded his head slightly with a solemn look and then let the screen door slam behind him.

I felt pretty tense for the next couple of days. I don't know how many times I thought about how I was going to fast for our safety last Sunday but then hadn't done it. I was so uptight that I had trouble eating very much. Everyone else in the house seemed to be feeling pretty much the same way. I kept thinking, *If Dad would just hurry and get done then we could just go home.* I was sure we'd never see Anthony again once we left Iowa.

The deputies took turns watching the farmhouse. There were four of them switching off on six-hour shifts. Most of the time they'd just sit in the car and read or listen to the radio or sleep, but they always came in when it was time to eat. We all took turns taking cookies and stuff out to them every couple of hours. Unlike the rest of us, the deputies' appetites didn't seem to be affected at all. One time, after I had taken some cookies out to Hank, I stayed in the car for a minute and listened to the radio program that was on. Two guys were having some big discussion about "winter wheat prices" and other stuff I'd never heard of. Iowa felt like a whole different country. Maybe that's why it seemed like going home would make this nightmare go away.

The sheriff came by every day that week, and the story was

always the same. Nobody had seen or heard anything about Anthony. Toward the end of the week, I think we were all starting to relax just a little. The sheriff started saying things like, "He prob'ly ain't even in Iowa no more," and "Won't be needin' t' keep m' deputies here much longer." Dad was still working long hours at the library, but he seemed happier and happier each day he got home. I had the feeling that he was getting really close to being done.

Five A.M. Saturday came as usual. I wasn't really thinking too much about the old Book of Mormon as I followed Aunt Ella down the stairs. They didn't creak at all because I'd learned where to step to keep them quiet, even while carrying my scriptures and holding the quilt around my shoulders. We took our usual places in the sitting room. I was waiting for her to start, but she didn't say anything for a few moments. I looked at her and was surprised by her appearance. She looked excited and content all at the same time, and her face was absolutely shining. I'd never seen her look like that before, and I wondered what she was thinking.

"Do you know what today is?" she asked with sparkling eyes.

"Saturday," I said slowly. "It's not fast Sunday," I continued, remembering my fasting disaster from last weekend.

"How long has it been, now?" she asked with more excitement. With all the events of the previous few days, I was completely clueless about what she was getting at.

"How many weeks?" she said, trying to lead me to the correct answer.

"Oh!" I gasped. Then I could hardly talk! "It's been four! I get the . . . ! Has it been . . . ? Yes! Hasn't it . . . ?" Then a big smile crept slowly across my face. "Today's the day, isn't it?"

"Yes, Brandon," she responded with a small laugh. "Today is the day. You have been coming here faithfully for four long weeks now."

"Did you say 'faithfully'?" I asked. "Does that mean I pass the test?!" She just laughed at my question, and before she could answer

I said, "Well, it was supposed to be a test, wasn't it? That's what we talked about. Joseph Smith had to prove himself faithful and worthy to take care of the plates." My own words hit me like a board across the top of my head.

"Oh," I said with much less excitement. "That means that now I've got to keep the book safe by myself." I looked over at the mantel where the book had been ever since we got it back from Dr. Anthony last Saturday. The butterfly clock was spinning slowly back and forth. I thought about Anthony again as I stared at the book.

Aunt Ella broke the silence. "People will help you keep it safe. Remember how many people helped Joseph Smith? You will be just fine," she reassured me. "Look at all you have been through these past few weeks! I am not worried about you one bit."

She was smiling at me warmly, and I had the feeling she wasn't just talking about the book. All of a sudden I wasn't worried either. I felt confident that everything would be okay.

"Should I fetch the book?" I asked.

"Please."

She placed the book on her lap for what I assumed would be the last time.

"Tell me what you know about the Liahona," she began.

Her question caught me by surprise. I wasn't really expecting a discussion today. I thought there might be a little ceremony— maybe a graduation certificate or something—then she'd give me the book.

"Well, . . ." I said, trying to remember what I knew about the Liahona. "It was a gold ball that Lehi and Nephi used to find out which way to go in the wilderness."

"Do you remember where it came from?"

"I think Lehi found it inside his tent one morning. Or was it Nephi?" I had to think about it a minute. "No, wait, it was Lehi."

"That is correct. However, both Lehi and Nephi used it, but

Lehi found it *outside* his tent, on the ground," she added. "Do you remember how it worked?"

"I guess it worked great," I laughed.

Aunt Ella didn't appear to be amused.

"I meant," she said, "do you remember how it functioned?"

"Well, there were two pointers inside the ball, and one showed them the direction they should go."

"Right again," she smiled. "Was that all?"

"No-o-o. It also had writing on it that changed once in a while."

"Good," she said, as if I'd passed the quiz. "Now, you said that the Liahona 'worked great.' Was that always the case?"

I remembered something about that. "Didn't it work only when they were being righteous?" I ventured.

"What do you mean, 'being righteous,'?" she probed.

"Well, when they had faith and stuff and were being humble and not complaining, then it would work. But when they murmured it wouldn't work."

"Very good," she said. "We should look up some scripture references just to remind ourselves of the details about the Liahona."

"Okay," I said, pulling my scriptures from under the quilt. She just continued to look at me. Finally I asked, "What should I read?"

"You tell me," she responded.

I paused for a moment as I started to unzip the scripture cover of my triple combination. "Can I look in the index?" I asked.

"Good idea," she said with a nod.

We read every reference I could find about the Liahona, and I learned several things that I hadn't known before. First of all, it was made of brass, not gold. And it said that the writing on the ball gave them understanding about the Lord's ways. I had always sort of thought it said things like "turn right at the second big rock" or something like that.

Also, Alma told his son Helaman that *Liahona* means *compass*. I didn't remember ever hearing that before, but it made sense.

119

I thought maybe that's what the second pointer inside the ball was for, like a real compass. The last thing we read was something else that Alma told Helaman, and I think it was the thing that hit me the hardest. He said that the Liahona is a symbol of Christ, that Christ points in a straight line exactly the way we should go and that following Christ is as easy as looking at the spindles in the Liahona and following the direction they are pointing.

This is what I wrote in my notebook:

Saturday, May 9, Notes from 5th discussion with Aunt Ella

1 Nephi 16:10: Lehi finds the Liahona outside his tent.

1 Nephi 16:26–27, 29: Writing on Liahona gives understanding of the ways of the Lord.

1 Nephi 16:28: Liahona worked according to faith and diligence and heed.

1 Nephi 18:12–14: Liahona quit working when Nephi was bound.

1 Nephi 18:20–21: Liahona worked again when Nephi was untied.

Alma 37:38: Liahona means compass.

Alma 37:43–45: Liahona is a shadow or symbol of Christ; Christ is as easy to follow as a compass.

"Good work," Aunt Ella said with a satisfied nod when we had finished looking up scriptures and I closed my notebook. Then she got a very intense look on her face. "This," she said, picking up the Book of Mormon from her lap, "is *your* Liahona, Brandon."

I wasn't exactly sure what she meant by that. She went on before I had a chance to give my typical intelligent "huh?" response.

"This book will show you exactly which way to go. It contains the words of Jesus Christ. It teaches you how he interacts with his people. It contains examples of what happens to those who are faithful and diligent and what happens to those who choose not to follow the compass. This is everything you need. If you study it often and follow the principles in this book then *you* will *belong* to Christ."

As she said the word *Christ*, she held the book out for me to take. I didn't reach for it immediately. I felt like I'd just received a promise or a prophecy or something. It reminded me of how I've felt when Dad has given me a priesthood blessing. I reached out and took the book from her hands. I didn't know whether to thank her and promise that I'd protect the book or to make a commitment out loud right then and there that I would treat it like Nephi treated the Liahona for my whole life. But I just couldn't say anything. I felt completely overwhelmed.

I noticed that her eyes were slightly moist as I looked back and forth between them. They were absolutely shining. I could tell that she wasn't expecting me to say anything. The look on her face was a combination of happiness and love. After about ten seconds of silence, she patted my hand and whispered, "Thank you." She spoke so softly that I could barely make out the words. Then she stood and went to the kitchen.

I stayed on the sofa for another couple of minutes. I was really hot, so I pushed the quilt off my shoulders and then sat there just staring at the book for another moment or two. I think I realized for the first time that I was only just beginning to understand the treasure I held in my hands. Then I took the book up to the loft and tucked it carefully into my backpack.

Later that morning Mom announced that she and Granny and Aunt Ella would be going to Waterloo to do some shopping and then pay a visit to some old lady relative of ours who lived there. "We probably won't be home until well after dark," Mom said. "You know how much Granny loves to shop," she smiled. Aunt Ella added, "And there is no telling how long we will be at Cousin Bertha's. She doesn't get many visitors, and she will probably talk our legs off."

Mom turned to Shauna and asked, "If we take Chelsea and Daniel with us, do you think the four of you will be all right by yourselves? Dad should be home about dinnertime."

"Sure," Shauna answered. "We'll have a great time, won't we guys?"

"Yeah," Jeff and I responded in unison. "We can play hide-and-go-seek with Meg out by the hog house," I suggested.

"You be nice," Mom said with her lips scrunched together.

"Just kidding!" I smiled.

Just then we heard a car pull up outside, and a moment later the sheriff knocked on the screen door. He and the deputy who'd been watching the house since 6:00 A.M. came into the kitchen.

"Mornin', Miss Bellon," said the sheriff as he lowered himself onto a chair. "Jus' come by t' tell ya that I think it's all right for us to back way off on this guardin' the house thin' now. I doubt that boy's even still in th' state. Ever' law enforcement official in Iowa has been on the lookout fer 'im all week. He jus' ain't 'round no more."

I could tell what was coming, and I think Aunt Ella could, too. But she was taking it a lot better than I was.

"What we're gonna do fer the next couple o' days is go ahead an' leave a car parked out front but with no deputy in it. We'll still come by a couple o' times ever' day and check on ya, but I think this is the correct course of action fer now."

I started to protest, but Aunt Ella calmly held up her hand in my direction, so I just shut my mouth. My lips were pushed up so far that they almost touched my nose.

"I want to thank you, Sheriff," Aunt Ella said sincerely, "for all that your department and you personally have done for us. I feel certain that you are making the best decision under the circumstances."

I wanted to jump up and down and make it clear that I certainly didn't feel that he was making the best decision under the circumstances. I was also starting to wonder if it was such a good idea for all the adults to be gone for the rest of the day. After the deputy and sheriff both left in the sheriff's car I told Mom what I was thinking.

"If you really want us to stay here," Mom said, "then we will."

"We'll be all right!" Shauna said as she jabbed me in the ribs with her elbow. "Won't we?" she asked with a look on her face that just dared me to disagree.

"I guess so," I responded without much conviction.

"We'll have a prayer, with you before we leave," Mom said. "I'm sure you'll be fine."

Well, we had a prayer, and they left and after a while I forgot about being worried. I started to believe that I was just getting paranoid. Shauna, Meg, Jeff, and I had a great time all afternoon. We played all sorts of games in the house that we couldn't have if everyone else had been there. We played sardines for a while and then it sort of evolved into a game of tag. After knocking over a couple of things, which *thankfully* didn't break, we came to our senses and went outside for the rest of that game.

About dinnertime we heard Aunt Ella's phone ringing. We all followed Jeff as he ran inside to answer it. "Oh, hi, Dad," Jeff said into the phone. "No, they're all in Waterloo. Shauna is baby-sitting me, Meg, and Bran." He listened for a moment and said, "Yeah, just a minute." He held the phone toward Shauna and said, "He wants to talk to you."

"Hi, Dad," Shauna smiled into the phone. I didn't hear what she said next because Jeff was telling me that Dad was wanting to stay at the library a little later tonight.

"No problem," Shauna said. "You take as much time as you need, and we'll see you when you get home. We'll be fine." She listened for a few seconds and then replied, "Yeah, I'm sure. Just do what you need to do." Then she said, "Bye!" and hung up.

"Guess *what*, guys!" she practically yelled.

"I know," giggled Meg. "Dad's not coming home for a long time, so we get to play some more!"

"Right!" said Shauna, "but there's more. He asked me to make dinner because he said he needs to finish the thing he's working on and—get this—he said if all goes well, then he'll have some very, *very* good news for us when he gets home."

"Like what?" Meg asked, jumping up and down like she just couldn't stand the suspense.

"I'll bet," Shauna said with a sly look, "that he's all done with his research, and you know what that means, don't you?"

"We get to go home!" I yelled as I jumped into the air with my head back and my fists straight up. "My soccer tournament starts next Saturday, and I'll *be* there!" I yelled as I jumped again.

"And I'll be home in time for *junior prom!*" Shauna yelled. "Oh," she whispered, "I can hardly *believe* it!"

We all sat around the kitchen talking about how great it was going to be to get home again at last. We pulled out some of Aunt Ella's homemade bread and had sandwiches and lemonade for dinner. It's amazing how fast you can get used to something. Before we came to Iowa I can't imagine the four us ever having sandwiches and lemonade for dinner on a Saturday night when we were left by ourselves. We probably would have scraped some money together and ordered a pizza to be delivered. And I'm sure we would have gotten a 2-liter bottle of root beer to go with it. I think I had had more lemonade in the month we'd been at the farm than in the whole rest of my life combined.

By then it was getting dark, and there were no signs of the grown-ups getting home. Shauna suggested that as long as the little guys weren't around to make us switch in the middle, that we watch a video in the sitting room. While she was sorting through the stack of movies, I ran up the stairs to the loft to "fetch" the pillow off my bed. I, personally, don't believe it's possible to watch a movie without a pillow to lie on. The light by the stairs was bright enough that I didn't bother turning on the bedroom light when I went in. I just grabbed my pillow and spun around to head right back down the stairs, when something outside the window caught my attention.

I went over to the window and looked across the road at the grove of dark trees on the other side. There was someone out there with a flashlight!

CHAPTER 9

A Thief in the Night

I almost tripped twice as I lunged down the stairs two at a time. "Shauna!" I yelled, "there's somebody across the road with a flashlight!" I burst into the sitting room. "It's him! It's Dr. Anthony! I know it's him!"

"Did you see him?" she asked, all wide-eyed.

"No, but I *know* it's him," I panted. "And even if it isn't, there shouldn't be anybody out there with a flashlight anyway!"

"You're right," she said as she glanced quickly around the room. "Quick, turn out the lights. I'll call the police, and you guys go lock the front and back doors."

Turning out the lights as he bolted out of the room, Jeff followed right behind Shauna. He called back to me, "I'll get the back door; you lock the front one!"

I ran through the kitchen where Shauna was reaching for the phone and threw myself into the front door, slamming it shut and then quickly locking it and putting the chain in place. As soon as I did so, I shuddered. I wanted to peek through the window to see if I could still see a light across the road, but I didn't dare. Instead, I ran through the darkened house back into the kitchen.

"Does 911 work here?" Shauna asked. "Nothing's happening." She hung up the phone and then put the receiver back up to her ear. Her eyes got huge as she whispered, "There's no dial tone!" She hit the button two or three times. "Oh, no!" she said breathlessly. "The phone's dead!" She dropped the receiver and left it swinging on its cord from the wall.

Meg was standing in the doorway between the sitting room and

126

the kitchen. Jeff had returned to the kitchen after locking the back door. We all just stood there in the dark, not knowing what to say.

"Do you think he cut the phone line?" I finally asked.

"I think the phone pole is over by the barn," Jeff replied. "We can probably see it from the sitting room." We all followed Jeff into the sitting room and carefully pulled back the curtains in a couple of places trying to get a look at the phone pole.

Suddenly there was a crash of breaking glass coming from the front door. We all jumped, and Meg screamed. I think I actually jumped twice—once when I heard the glass breaking and again when Meg screamed!

"What was that?" Jeff asked what we all wanted to know but were way too afraid to find out. Shauna tiptoed over to the kitchen doorway and leaned her head around to where she could see the front door. Just then a flashlight beam swept briefly through the darkened house.

"Somebody's coming in!" she hissed. We could hear the door-knob and chain rattling, and she scampered back toward us. "Somebody's reaching in through the broken glass and trying to unlock the door!" she whispered frantically.

"What are we going to do?" I mouthed.

"Let's get out of here," Jeff responded. But as soon as we started to move, we all realized that we had to go through the kitchen to get to either the front or the back doors. We were trapped! We stood paralyzed in silence until we heard the chain on the front door quit rattling.

"Open a window," Shauna hissed, and Jeff immediately turned back to where we'd just been peeking out and started searching for the latch.

"I don't know how they work," Jeff grunted tensely. His hands were shaking, and he moved quickly to the next window. Just then we heard the front door swing open and heavy footsteps on the hardwood floor of the entryway. Meg screamed again. That was all the intruder needed to come straight to where we were huddled.

Pointing his flashlight at us, a man shouted, "Don't move an inch!" He swept the room with the beam of his flashlight, looking for the light switch. He found it and flipped it on. It was Dr. Anthony. He was dirty and grimy and breathing so hard I'd have thought he'd just run a marathon. He was also holding a gun, pointing it at the ceiling above our heads.

"You're all here!" he smiled a sickening smile. "Good. I've been watching the house all day, so I know that you're the only ones at home." He was still breathless. "Now, I don't want to hurt anybody, so just don't try anything stupid. All I want is my book."

He looked over at the mantel where Aunt Ella had always kept it.

"What!" he yelled. "Where *is* it?" He stumbled over to the mantel and frantically started pushing things around, searching for the book. He suddenly stopped short, and we could see him get tense. He just stood there with his back turned halfway to us. None of us dared move or even breathe. After what seemed like an eternity, his shoulders slowly began to sag until he seemed to go completely limp.

"No!" he whispered. "No, no, no!" Then he turned to us and said, "She's hidden it, hasn't she?" But he wasn't expecting us to respond. "She's hidden it from me." He seemed totally defeated as he walked across the room and slumped onto the couch. None of us made a sound. We just waited to see what he would do next. The gun was still in his hand, but he seemed unaware of anything in the room. He just stared into space. After about a minute of staring and shaking his head slowly back and forth, he let out a determined sigh.

"Okay," he said, looking up at us. "You know what I really want, don't you?" He looked back and forth between me and Jeff. "You read my letter when you were out there on the road, so you know

now that this Elias Franzen guy had a treasure that he was hiding for Joseph Smith. And you also know that he was keeping a map of where it was hidden with that Book of Mormon of his."

I looked over at Shauna. Her eyes were huge. Meg was huddled next to her.

"You can even keep the book if you want," Anthony continued. "All I really want is the treasure map. Where is it?"

Shauna, Jeff, and Meg all looked at me as if I might know something about it. I couldn't say a word. I just shrugged my shoulders and slowly turned the palms of my hands upward. My mouth was dry and partially open as I looked at each person and my stare stopped on Dr. Anthony.

"Well, I don't believe she'd take it out of the house," he said after staring back at me for a moment. "She's had it here for years. So it's got to be here somewhere." He looked us over and said, "I don't suppose any of you know where it is." None of us flinched. "And I don't suppose you'd tell me, even if you did." We still didn't move.

"When is someone else going to be home, young lady?" he asked Shauna.

Shauna gulped so loud that I could hear it. "They didn't say for sure," she replied weakly. "They just said they'd be late."

"Good enough," he said more to himself than us. "It's a small house. I'll just have to find it myself." Then he looked over at us again. "I guess I'd better lock you kids up somewhere. Can't have you in the way, and I can't let you run away for help either." Then he smiled at us as he said, "I was smart enough to cut the phone line, so don't think you're dealing with some amateur here. I saw you trying to call somebody before I came inside. It was easy enough to do. That phone pole across the road out there is right next to a huge tree that was quite easy to climb. I definitely know what I'm doing, so you just watch yourselves, and no one will get hurt."

He seemed to be feeling better now and stood up quickly from the couch. "Enough small talk," he said. "Let's find a place to lock you guys up for a while."

"Please, not in the cellar," I said quickly.

Shauna, Jeff, and Meg all swung their heads around to glare at me at the same time.

Anthony's eyes narrowed. "Now, why would you say that?" he asked. Everyone's stare now returned to him. "Is that where the book is hidden? Are you trying to get hold of it before I do?" He watched me for a moment, and I could feel myself getting faint. "Or are you just saying that because that's the place you really want to be? As I recall you spent a rather frightful morning down there by yourself not too long ago." He paused another moment.

"No matter," he said finally. "If the book is down there, I'll find it eventually. It won't be getting away from me."

He backed into the kitchen and motioned with the gun for us to follow. Because he'd helped me get out of the cellar the first time I'd met him, he knew right where it was. None of us had any interest in challenging him in any way, so we moved quickly down the steps, and he locked the door behind us. He banged on the locked door and called, "I'll be back in a few minutes to check on you, so don't try anything."

Meg was crying. "I don't like it down here," she whimpered as she looked up at us with big puppy-dog eyes. "Is that man going to hurt us?" she asked.

"I don't think so, Meg," Shauna reassured her. "As long as we do what he says."

"Guys, this is perfect," I whispered.

"Huh?" Jeff said.

"I thought you'd been acting really strange ever since this thing with Dr. Anthony began," Shauna said, "but now I'm absolutely sure you've *lost* it. Bran, that guy's a lunatic."

"I know," I said, "but—"

"And he's dangerous," she interrupted.

"I *know!*" I was trying to speak softly, but it was frustrating, trying to explain what I was thinking.

"We need to be *really* careful!" she said. "I just hope he finds that book and leaves us alone."

"*Wha-a-at?*" I said. "*You're* the one who's crazy. That book's *valuable!*" I drew a deep breath and tried to calm myself. "But it's okay because we can get out of here."

"Bran," Shauna said seriously, "do you know anything about a treasure map?"

"No!" I said honestly. "I have no clue what he's talking about. The only thing I ever saw with the book was a bookmark. And it was no treasure map. It just had some Book of Mormon words on it."

"Okay," Shauna sighed. "I know you think the book is valuable, but nothing is more valuable right now than our safety."

"Fine," I replied. "That's why I wanted him to put us in the cellar. So if you want to be safe, let's go through the tunnel and get out of here! We can get to the main highway and get somebody to call the sheriff for us before Anthony gets away."

"Oh, yeah! The tunnel!" Shauna cried.

"Sh-h-h-h!" I hissed at her. "He might be able to hear us!"

We all stopped to listen. We could hear what sounded like books hitting the floor one at a time right above us.

"He must be going through the bookcases in the sitting room," Shauna whispered. "Do you think Meg can make it to the highway? What if he comes to check on us before we get very far?" she asked.

"She could hide in the woods," I said. "We don't all have to go all the way to the highway. Once we get out, you and Meg can hide in the trees across the street while Jeff and I go to get help."

"I suppose that might work," Shauna replied thoughtfully. "Then if he finds the book and leaves we'll be able to see which way he goes. But Meg might get cold while we're waiting."

"No problem!" I said. "We've got blankets in the hideout. And there are flashlights there, too."

"But what if he comes down before we're out of the tunnel?" Shauna asked.

"He'll never be able to find the door," Jeff said. "Look at it! It doesn't look anything like a door. He'll just think we're hiding in here somewhere. And we can get out so fast that even if he does find the tunnel we'll already be long gone."

"Okay," Shauna said with determination, "let's go!"

After listening to make sure Anthony was still in the sitting room above us, we pushed the door open and went into the tunnel. Then I pushed the door closed behind us, and we were plunged into absolute darkness. Jeff and I assured the girls that we'd be fine, because we'd done it a hundred times already. But Meg began to cry again.

She was holding on tightly to Shauna. "I'm scared," she whimpered. "It's too dark in here."

"Just stay here, and I'll go get the flashlights," Jeff said. I could hear him move ahead down the tunnel.

"You're okay, Meg," Shauna said. "You hold on to Brandon, and I'll open the door a little so we have some light until Jeff gets back."

Meg didn't say anything until I turned around and found her shoulders. She instantly threw her arms around my waist, and I pulled her in close.

"Okay," Meg finally said, sounding like she was being as brave as she possibly could. Shauna made her way back to the door leading into the cellar and carefully opened it. The light immediately seeped into the passageway.

"Is that better?" she called back softly.

"Uh-huh," Meg responded but too quietly for Shauna to hear.

"She says she's okay now," I said to Shauna. "Can you still hear Anthony upstairs?"

"Yeah, I can hear him."

We all stood in silence for a minute or so. Jeff made it back pretty quickly with two flashlights, and Shauna pushed the door shut. He kept one, and we gave Meg her very own, hoping it would help her feel a little safer. Her spirits were obviously brightened as we moved down the tunnel together. I could see her light bouncing all over the place past me. We got to the ladder and started climbing. I held Meg's flashlight, pointing it down the ladder, while Shauna stayed close behind her to make sure she didn't slip or fall.

"Let's go all the way up into the barn, and then I'll come back for the blankets," Shauna said as she climbed past the hideout.

Jeff got to the top, and I could hear him straining, trying to push the trapdoor up. He grunted two or three times and then called down, "It's stuck! I can barely even budge it!"

"Have you guys been using that door?" Shauna called up from the darkness.

"Yeah, we use it all the time," I said.

"The only other time we've had any trouble," Jeff offered, "was when they delivered the new bales of hay and the guys piled a bunch right on top of the door. We had to go around the other way and move it all."

"Oh, no!" I said. "I saw Mr. Hansen in the barn yesterday, and I think he was moving some hay around. He said there was more coming in next week!"

"Oh!" Meg cried. "I want to get *out* of here!"

"Can you move it at all?" Shauna called up.

"A little bit," Jeff responded. "Bran, let's try something different. Here, hold my flashlight."

I put Meg's flashlight in my back pants pocket pointing straight up at Jeff; then I handed his down to Shauna. I watched as Jeff turned around backward on the ladder and put his back against the door. His feet were on the second step from the top, and his hands were on the opposite wall. Then he pushed as hard as he could. The trapdoor opened only about eight inches before he let it fall slowly back down.

"That's the best I can do," he panted.

"I think I can fit through there," I said. "Then I can move the hay out of the way for the rest of you."

I climbed up next to Jeff, and he pushed the door open again. I was able to push it open a little more. It was a tight squeeze, but I made it through with only a small scrape on my arm for the trouble. I was now sitting on the floor of the barn. I took the flashlight from my pocket and shined it at the trapdoor. There was hay on top of the door, all right. Luckily, the bales had only been stacked about halfway over the door; otherwise, I'm sure we'd have never been able to move it. I let the light drift up the stack of bales. I almost fell over backward trying to see the top of it. It reached all the way to the ceiling of the barn!

"Oh, no!" I said out loud to myself.

Just then the stack began to shake a little and I heard Jeff's muffled voice ask, "What's going on, Bran?"

I looked down at the trapdoor. He had opened it about an inch, and I could see Shauna's light faintly outlining the opening around the door.

"It's stacked all the way to the roof!" I exclaimed. "It'll take me forever to move it all!"

I heard Jeff heave a big sigh and then say something to Shauna. I didn't hear her response, and then he let the door close again. It reopened a moment later.

"Shauna wants to know if you can find something to wedge in the door to prop it open," Jeff said through the small opening.

"Just a sec," I said as I began to shine the light around the barn. All I could see were bales of hay everywhere. I moved toward the back of the barn, where some hay had been broken out of a bale and spread around. There was a pitchfork stuck in the pile. It had a long wooden handle and four sharp spikes about six inches apart.

I picked it up and noticed that the handle was quite worn and had deep creases in it.

"Doesn't Aunt Ella own *anything* that's new?" I muttered as I made my way back to the trapdoor. It was closed again, so I used the handle to knock on it a couple of times.

"That's loud!" Jeff hissed through the crack after the door opened again slightly. "You scared me!"

"Sorry," I whispered, "but I found a pitchfork that we could maybe use to prop the door open."

"Okay," Jeff panted, "I'll push the door as far as I can. You get ready to wedge the handle in and hold it open."

I got the pitchfork in position and waited. About ten seconds later the door popped up, and I quickly slid the pitchfork handle across the opening as close to the hinges as I could get it.

"Get it all the way across both sides," I heard Shauna call up. Jeff was grunting as I positioned it and pushed it as far back as possible.

"I'm putting it down now," Jeff gasped as he lowered the door. It stayed open but only about six inches.

"If you can lift it up again, then I'll try to kick it farther back," I said.

"Okay," Jeff breathed, "but give me a minute. This is hard." I could hear Meg asking Shauna some questions while I waited for Jeff to catch his breath.

"On three," Jeff said as he positioned himself again. "One . . . two . . . *three!*" he called as he hit the door with his back as hard as he could. I kicked the handle of the pitchfork right at the same time, and we gained another couple of inches. After two more attempts it looked like the door was staying open at least ten or twelve inches.

"I think I can fit through there now," Jeff said. "Should I go ahead?" he asked Shauna, "or should we try to get it farther open first?"

"Go ahead," Shauna replied. "I'm sure I can fit through."

Jeff was able to get out pretty easily, but he lost his balance as he started to stand and ended up falling against the open edge of the trapdoor. The extra weight was enough to snap the old pitchfork handle in two places, and the broken ends went sailing through the air. There was a loud crack, and Meg screamed. The end of the pitchfork with the spikes barely missed my shoulder before it landed somewhere behind me. It's a good thing, too, because there was no way I could have moved out of the way in time. The trapdoor was now only open a crack, with the middle section of the broken handle still wedged on one side.

"Sorry, Shauna!" Jeff called desperately through the small opening. "Are you guys okay?"

"We're fine," came the reply, "but I think I have another idea."

"What?" Jeff and I asked at the same time.

"How about if Meg and I just stay in the hideout while you two go get help," she said. "I don't think it's safe for us to try to get out this way."

We argued back and forth for a moment before finally agreeing to her plan. The more I thought about it, the better it sounded. They would have blankets and light in the hideout, and there was probably less danger of being caught by Anthony if they stayed there than if they hid across the street, where he might see them.

Jeff and I slowly pushed open one of the huge barn doors just far enough for us to creep out. There was quite a bit more light outside the barn than inside, which was good because we were afraid to use the flashlight where we could be seen from the house. The sky was clear, and stars were beginning to show. The light outside the front door of Aunt Ella's house lit up the dirt driveway and almost reached across the gravel road. We had to go past the house to get to the main highway.

Carefully, we crossed the road and entered the trees, figuring we'd be a lot safer there. We didn't want to take a chance in case Dr. Anthony happened to look out and see us. We stayed just about ten feet from the road as we began making our way through the trees. When we were directly across from the farmhouse, Jeff said, "Hey, there's the phone pole." We both stopped and looked up at the pole. I could see the tree Anthony had told us about; the one he climbed to reach the phone line.

"I bet I could get up there and fix it," Jeff said after looking over the tree.

"What good would that do?" I asked. "Besides you can't do it without a light, and he might see it."

We looked over at the house. Just then the light went on in Aunt Ella's bedroom.

"He must be done searching the sitting room," Jeff said. "Where's the book? You did say she gave it to you this morning, didn't you?"

"I put it in my backpack," I responded. "I think it's on the desk in our bedroom."

We stood silently watching the house for a minute. Through the curtains we could see Anthony's shadow moving around in Aunt Ella's bedroom.

"I'll bet I could get it," I said flatly.

"*What?*" Jeff said. "You really are crazy!"

"No, listen!" I said excitedly. "He's in Aunt Ella's bedroom. I could sneak in the back door and go up the stairs without ever going past either of the doors to her room."

"The stairs squeak," Jeff reminded me.

"But I know where to step so they *won't* squeak," I said without looking away from the shadow in the window.

"Don't do it, Bran," Jeff said, but the way he said it told me that he already knew I'd made up my mind.

"I can't let him find that book," I said. "I'm going to get it."

As I took a couple of steps toward the road, Jeff asked, "So what am I supposed to do if you get caught?"

"I won't."

"But if you do?" he asked again, "what am I supposed to do? The first thing he'll do is take you back to the cellar and find out that we're all gone. Then he'll go nuts. There's no telling what he'll decide to do then. Don't do it, Bran. We're all safe now. We just have to get to the highway and let the sheriff take care of it. Don't, Brandon."

"If I get caught," I said, "then you run like crazy to the main highway. You're fast. He won't find Shauna and Meg. Just run."

With that I headed toward the house. About halfway across the road I heard Jeff hiss something about staying away from the light, so I turned and headed back toward the barn. I wasn't too worried because I could see where Anthony was. Still I stayed close to the barn and then circled around the back of the house where there was no light. I started getting a little nervous now just because I couldn't watch his shadow anymore.

As I slowly crept up to the back door I began to wonder if he might choose now to go back to the cellar and check on us. It didn't look like he'd bothered to do it so far, so why would he choose now? I got to the back door and tried to turn the knob. Instantly, I remembered that Jeff had locked it when all this had started. My only way into the house was through the front door.

Aunt Ella's room was located in the front corner of the house with one door leading directly into the sitting room and the other door leading into the small hallway that accessed the bathroom, the cellar, and the kitchen. If I went in the front door, then I'd have to go past that hallway. And if the door to Aunt Ella's room was open and Anthony was in the right place, he'd be able to see the front door opening.

"He's not going to see me," I whispered to myself with my hand still holding the doorknob on the back door. Slowly I made my way around the side of the house and to the front door. I went around the side where the kitchen was, not the side with the sitting room and Aunt Ella's bedroom. The small porch was lit by a single bulb above the door. As I reached for the doorknob I was sure that I could hear Jeff gasp from clear across the road.

After breaking the glass and getting into the house, Anthony had closed the door but not locked it. When I turned the knob, I felt the door latch release, and I slowly pushed the door inward. There was glass on the floor. As I tried to decide where I would have to step, I realized that I could get into the house only about six inches before I'd be in full view of Aunt Ella's bedroom door. I could hear the sound of things being tossed around in there.

Before I dared step into the house, I carefully leaned forward and looked down the hallway. The bedroom door was open, but I couldn't see Anthony. I stepped in, staying close to the door, and gently pushed it closed behind me. It took only three more steps to make it quietly past the glass on the floor. Once completely out of view of the bedroom door, I paused in the kitchen for a moment to try to relax. My heart was pounding in my ears, and my throat was dry.

After the pounding quieted slightly and I reassured myself that Anthony was far too involved in his hunting to be worried about me, I moved out of the kitchen into the sitting room. I could see that this door to the bedroom was open too, as was the door up to the loft. I gently placed my foot on the far left of the first step. This one had a loud squeak everywhere but the one side.

I worked my way slowly up the staircase, gaining confidence with each step I took. I was suddenly grateful for all those 5:00 A.M. Saturday morning sessions, which had taught me how to negotiate the staircase without making any noise. It was quite dark up in the loft, but the night-light was still on. I made my way into the bedroom and over to the desk, where I'd left my backpack. I strained my eyes before each step, trying to be as careful and quiet as possible.

When I reached the desk I released a huge breath. I think I'd been holding it all the way across the floor. Slowly I unzipped the backpack, cringing at the noise it made. I reached in and breathed a sigh of relief as I removed the book. I'd half expected it to be gone. After taking a couple more deep breaths to try to calm the pounding that was still in my ears, I started back toward the stairs. As I turned, my foot caught the leg of the chair that was only partway under the desk. The chair slid a good six inches across the wood floor, making a scraping noise so loud that it was almost deafening compared to the silence around me. I froze in absolute panic.

Quickly I determined that I was approximately above the front door or perhaps the small hallway leading to Aunt Ella's bedroom. Only a miracle would have kept Anthony from hearing all that noise. The book in my hands began to shake as I listened intensely for the slightest sound from downstairs. I knew he had to have heard me. He had to be coming.

Thirty seconds went by, and I began to hope that I just might be the luckiest dog in the world, when suddenly a sound that I'd heard a hundred times before made my heart stop. It was the creak of the bottom stair. Anthony was coming up the staircase.

CHAPTER 10

The Answer to My Prayer

I was trapped, and I knew it. There was only one staircase. There wasn't even a decent place to hide. But I didn't want to hide—I wanted to *escape!* In sheer panic I scanned the room until the window caught my eye. Holding my breath, I turned quickly and reached for the latch that was closest to me. From the look of the thick coating on the latches, I could only imagine how many dozens of times these windows had been painted. I was certain that opening the latches would be impossible, but I had to try.

I glanced quickly toward the stairs and listened. I saw and heard nothing. Returning my attention to the window, I was shocked to find that two or three silent grunts on the first latch was enough to open it. The other latch was not nearly so kind. I pushed on it as hard as I could with the palm of my hand, but it didn't even begin to budge.

Setting the book on the windowsill as quietly as possible, I placed one thumb on top of the other and planted my feet. I pushed until I could feel my eyes started to bulge out, so I forced myself to take a huge breath. Pushing it for all I was worth, the latch finally gave way, but so did my feet. I have no clue which sound was the loudest—my knees hitting the floor, my head hitting the window, or my elbow hitting the book and knocking it from the sill.

"Hey!" I heard Anthony yell from somewhere down the staircase. "Who's up there?" Anthony apparently hadn't moved any farther up the stairs since the bottom step had been good enough to give me its creaky warning. He must have just been waiting, listening for more signs of life. But now he was charging up the steps, and

I had about one-thousandth of a second to figure out how to handle more adrenaline than I'd ever experienced in my life. What I decided was to jump from my knees, grab the book with one hand while pushing the window open with the other, and simultaneously launch myself through the open window. As nearly as I could tell, I accomplished all this without my feet even ever touching the floor, the windowsill, or anything else.

It wasn't until I was airborne that I first considered how long I might have to flap my wings before finding an acceptable place to land. But it was far too late to abort the mission now. I looked down just in time to see something flat and dark coming toward me *very* fast. There wasn't even time to figure out what it was before I belly-flopped onto the small roof that covered the concrete slab leading to Aunt Ella's front door.

As I raised myself to my elbows, I looked back up at the window and saw Anthony lunging toward me, his hand reaching frantically for my ankle. My only thought was to jerk my leg out of his reach, so that's what I did. It was then that I remembered how small this little roof was. I imagine I looked something like an old windmill or a sideways helicopter as I fell off the edge of the roof and landed right in a huge rhubarb bush. There would definitely be some of Aunt Ella's homemade rhubarb pie tomorrow, if I was lucky enough to be around to enjoy it.

"Get back here, you little thief!" Anthony yelled after me as he scrambled through the window onto the roof. I was already on my feet and halfway down the dirt driveway. I whacked the hood of the sheriff's car with the bottom of my fist as I ran past.

"Correct course o' action under th' circumstances," I grumbled, doing my best to imitate the sheriff and sound disgusted all at the same time. Sprinting all the way to the main highway now seemed like the "correct course of action" for me under the circumstances. When I got to the gravel road I glanced back over my shoulder in time to see Anthony timidly adjusting himself into a sitting position on the edge of the little roof. I slowed down a little and watched him as he let himself fall to the ground.

"Ouch," he grunted, falling to one side. He got to his feet and started limping in my direction, alternately mumbling under his breath and threatening to "catch me no matter what" and "make me regret it."

That gave me another shot of adrenaline, and I started running a lot faster. I stayed along the edge of the road, where there wasn't so much gravel because it was a lot easier to run there. Anthony started jogging a little, but he was not getting any closer. After a couple of minutes I quit worrying, remembering that I had finished first in my class the last time we did the two-mile run at school. I wasn't the fastest sprinter, but I had good endurance for long-distance running. And luckily, my little flying-out-the-window-and-falling-off-the-roof trick gave me a bit of a head start.

I kept looking back as I ran just to make sure Anthony could still see me and that he was still after me. I was hoping that with Anthony gone, Jeff would be able to get Shauna and Meg out of the hideout and they'd all be safe until I got someone to call the sheriff.

I had been running for about ten minutes when I turned to check on Anthony again. He was nowhere to be seen! And I got scared. *Where could he have gone?* I wondered silently. Had he gone back or hidden in the trees or what? I could feel the fear rising in my throat again, so I decided to just run for all I was worth and get help as fast as I could.

Another couple of minutes went by, and I heard a siren. It was coming from the highway. Even when I realized it was coming in my direction, it still didn't help me settle down. When the headlights hit me, I started jumping up and down and waving my hands in the air.

"Hey there, Brandon," Hank said as I jumped into the passenger seat. "Are you all right?"

"I'm fine!" I gasped, "but Dr. Anthony was chasing me down

this road until a couple of minutes ago." I took a deep breath. "Now I don't know where he is!"

The car started forward again. "Where's ever'body else?" Hank asked.

"Jeff was hiding in the trees and Shauna and Meg were hiding in the . . . uh . . . the barn," I gasped. "Everyone else is still gone. But how come you're here?" I asked. "How did you know we were in trouble?"

"Yer brother called the dispatcher," Hank replied. "Said Anthony done trashed the house and was chasin' you toward the highway."

"Jeff?" I asked. "Whose phone did he use? Aunt Ella's phone is dead. Shauna tried it, and Anthony told us he had cut the line."

"I don' know nothin' more," Hank said, shaking his head back and forth as we pulled up in front of the house. Jeff, Shauna, and Meg came out the front door to meet us. Hank turned the siren off but left the emergency lights flashing.

"Oh, Brandon," Shauna breathed as I got out of the car, "are you okay?"

"I'm fine," I answered, "and so's the book." I smiled and held it up for everyone to see. "But how did you guys get the phone to work?"

"*I* fixed the wires!" Jeff smiled with pride. "Once I saw Anthony take off after you up the road, I figured it was safe to climb the tree and turn on the flashlight. He cut the line right where there was a big loop, so both ends were just hanging right there next to each other. I had to bite the plastic off the wires before I could twist them back together, but I came into the house, and the phone worked!"

"*All right, Jeff!*" I yelled.

"After I called 911, I went and got Shauna and Meg." He shrugged his shoulders like the whole thing was no big deal. Hank was back at his car using the two-way radio.

"Ever'body's safe 'n' sound at the house here with me," he said.

"Looks like the suspect's prob'ly back in them hills somewhere between the house and the highway. One o' th' victims here says the suspect chased 'im 'bout halfway to th' highway, but then 'e don't know where 'e went." He looked down the gravel road, but it was too dark to see much. "Deputy Mills, out," Hank said into the microphone and then put it back on the hook inside the car. "Let's go on inside an' see what the feller's done this time," Hank said to us.

We went inside to find piles of books in the middle of the sitting room and all over Aunt Ella's bed. Some had spilled from her bed onto the floor.

"Whew!" Hank whistled. "What a mess. Well, let's don't touch nothin' till the sheriff gets here."

The sheriff was at the farm within a couple of minutes, and we could hear other sirens in the distance. The dogs came again, and one of the other deputies chased them down the gravel road in the direction Anthony had chased me. When I took Hank upstairs to show him the window I'd used to do my Michael Jordan imitation, we found Anthony's gun on the floor by the desk. I'd completely forgotten about it. When Hank discovered that none of us remembered Anthony wearing gloves, he smiled at the thought of getting some nice fingerprints from the weapon.

Aunt Ella's house was like a circus for the next couple of hours. There was a police photographer walking around the rooms taking pictures of all the messes he could find. He even took a picture of my piles of dirty clothes before I had a chance to tell him that Anthony had nothing to do with that. Shauna, Meg, Jeff, and I were answering all sorts of questions as the deputies filled out their reports. Dad got home, and we explained everything that had happened since he had called. Aunt Ella and Mom and Granny got home just as we finished telling Dad all about it, and so we explained it all over again.

When the photographer left, we started cleaning up the place.

Dad covered the broken window in the front door with a piece of wood he found in the big blue shed. Jeff took one of the deputies out to show him how he'd fixed the telephone wire. The deputy wrapped some black tape around the cut wires that Jeff had twisted back together and then said that it would probably be just fine until the phone company could come out on Monday to redo it. The rest of us started picking up all the books that had been thrown everywhere. My book, of course, went carefully into my backpack up in the bedroom.

We were all starving, so Granny and Aunt Ella put together a great dinner while the rest of us finished cleaning up. There were still a couple of sheriff's cars in the driveway, with others coming and going when we sat down to eat. We could hear the noises of the police radio outside as Mom said the blessing on the food. Her prayer was more about being thankful that we were all safe than about food, though. It was then that I realized that we hadn't heard anything about Anthony yet.

"Did they catch Dr. Anthony?" I asked, once the food started being passed around the table.

"I don't know," Dad answered. "I didn't hear them say anything about it."

"The truck for the dogs is still in the driveway," Jeff added, "so I don't think they've found him."

I didn't think anybody had really forgotten about Anthony, but I was just glad that my book was okay. I guess with all the adults around and the police outside I was feeling pretty safe. But once Jeff told us that the dogs were still out searching, nobody at the table said too much.

About the time we were finishing our meal, the sheriff knocked at the front door.

"May I offer you and your men something to eat, Sheriff?" Aunt Ella asked after he had followed me back into the kitchen.

"No, thank ya kindly, ma'am," he answered soberly. "I's here 'cause you should know that we ain't been able to apprehend the suspect as of yet. We're bringin' the dogs back in 'cause they jus' cain't seem to pick up on any trail."

"I see," Aunt Ella responded. "So you are discontinuing the search for now?"

"We got a bulletin out right now for the county and the state," the sheriff continued. "We feel certain that he jus' ain't in them hills no more. He musta had a vehicle stashed somewhere or somethin'. But anyhow, we'll be leavin' a deputy here again. Apparently that was enough to keep the suspect away from the house all week. I do apologize that we ain't got 'im in custody yet."

"There is absolutely no need to apologize, Sheriff," Aunt Ella smiled. "We have full confidence in you and your deputies. Thank you for the information."

The sheriff just sort of mumbled as he nodded his head and left. I think he was feeling pretty bad about the whole situation. Especially since Anthony broke into the house on the very same day the deputies quit guarding outside. I felt kind of sorry for him as he slowly walked out and I closed the door behind him. I returned to the kitchen table and slumped quietly into my chair.

"I'm glad we're at least going to have a guard outside again," Mom smiled. "We can all feel safe tonight. But now, I think we should change the subject to something a little happier."

"Oh!" Dad exclaimed with his face lighting up. "I *almost* forgot the good news!"

"What?" I asked, thinking I knew exactly what he was about to say. I pictured myself scoring a goal the following Saturday in my team's first game of the tournament, with more than a thousand miles between me and Dr. Anthony.

"That's right!" Shauna smiled. "You said you would have some *very* exciting news when you got home."

"Tell us! Tell us! Tell us!" Meg cried.

"Everybody be quiet!" Jeff yelled. "He'll tell us if we'll just listen!"

"Not quite," Dad smiled mischievously. "I'll tell you as soon as you all have your PJs on."

"Oh!" Meg pouted.

"Let's go!" I called over my shoulder as I jumped from my chair and headed for the stairs. Jeff and Shauna were right behind me, but Meg still had her lips pushed together and sticking out from her face about an inch and a half.

We all ran around like mad upstairs, and in a few minutes had our pajamas on and had raced back down to the kitchen to hear Dad's big announcement.

"We're ready!" I smiled. I was perched on the front edge of my chair, waiting for the news. My knees were bouncing up and down with excitement.

"Well," Dad smiled. "You all know how much time I've been spending on my research and how hard I've been working. We've been telling you all along that I had two months' worth of work to do, but I was secretly hoping that it wouldn't take that long."

"Us, too!" I interjected.

"Oh," Dad looked over at me. "Then what I have to say should make you very happy."

"We're listening," Shauna giggled.

"I wanna know!" Meg whined excitedly.

"I'm done!" Dad said.

As soon as the words were out of his mouth, I jumped straight up into the air. "Yes!" I called with my arms extended and my head thrown backward.

"Good job, Daddy!" Shauna closed her eyes and smiled as she began swaying slightly from side to side. I knew what she was thinking.

"It gets better," Dad said without warning.

My dance stopped abruptly with one of my feet still in the air.

Shauna quit smiling and opened her eyes as she still leaned slightly to one side.

"What is it?" Jeff asked.

"We," Dad smiled and looked around at every one of us, "have a condo in Branson, Missouri, starting Thursday. I don't have to be back to the office for another month, and Mom tells me that you all have your homework done for the rest of the year, so now it's time to play! Our family vacation has only just begun!"

I was stunned by the announcement. I looked over at Shauna, and I could tell she was in shock, too.

"What's a condo?" Meg asked.

"It's like a big hotel room," Mom answered, "only it has a kitchen and separate bedrooms. There's a swimming pool and tennis courts. And the best part is that we'll be just a few miles from an amusement park."

"What's a 'muse-ment park?" Meg asked, tilting her head.

"It's like Disneyland or—" Dad began, but Meg didn't let him get any more out of his mouth before she breathed a huge gasp.

"We're going to Disneyland?!" Meg yelled.

"No," Mom said quickly. "Dad said it's *like* Disneyland. This place is called Silver Dollar City. It has rides and lots of other fun stuff. Granny used to take me there every summer when I was a kid. My favorite part was eating funnel cakes. They make them by pouring cake batter through a funnel into hot oil so it's deep fried. They are *so* good. I know you guys will have a great time."

"We're going to be there for a week?" I asked.

"Oh," Dad grinned, "it doesn't stop there. We'll be in Branson for a week, yes. But we're going to be visiting some Church history sites both before and after we get there. We'll take a couple of days driving down, stay there for a week; then we'll take a few more days and drive to Nauvoo and see where the temple used to be, and we'll see some other things also. I promise, you guys are going to have a great time!"

149

"So when do you think we'll be getting home?" Shauna asked weakly.

"I don't know for sure," Dad was still smiling. "Probably about two or two and a half weeks. And we're just going to be playing the whole time. Doesn't that sound like a fantastic end to our vacation?"

Shauna, Jeff, and I each did our best to act excited, but I don't think we really did that well. Luckily, Meg was jumping up and down and singing something like, "We're going to a place like Disneyland! We're going to a place like Disneyland!"

Chelsea started saying, "Disneyland? Disneyland?" Her eyes were sparkling as she looked from person to person. Mom and Dad tried to explain the difference to her while Meg was still dancing around the kitchen. All the commotion caused by Meg and Chelsea was enough to keep our disappointment pretty well disguised as we all helped clean up the dinner dishes.

"I don't get it!" I said to Shauna and Jeff later when we were all upstairs again. "It didn't work! We didn't get what we prayed for!"

"I think we probably did," Shauna said with disgust.

"What are you talking about?" I asked.

"What was your goal, Bran?"

"To go home a month *early!*" I practically yelled.

"No it wasn't!" Shauna responded. "At least that's not what you prayed for. I heard you. It's not what I prayed for, either."

"What are you talking about?" I asked in astonishment. "Of course that's what I prayed for."

"What we prayed for," she stated sadly, "was to help Dad *get done* a month early. We never actually mentioned the part about going home. Probably because it sounded better than praying to go home for a silly date or a soccer tournament. Think about what you said. We all did the same thing."

"No," I said under my breath. I was getting a sick feeling in my stomach as I realized she was right. I *had* just prayed for Dad to get done early, without actually asking for help to *go home* early. We all just stared at each other for a few moments as we realized how close we'd come.

"Well," Shauna tried to smile. "Maybe it'll be fun." She didn't sound convinced. And when neither Jeff nor I said anything in response, it was obvious that we weren't convinced either. Before climbing into bed I pulled out my notebook and added just a short note:

Saturday, May 9

My prayer was answered—Dad got done a month early.

CHAPTER 11

Independence

Sunday morning I woke up to the sound of rain beating down on the roof. I had learned over the previous month that when it rains in Iowa it *really* rains. In Utah a rainy day means the rain usually comes and goes several times during the day, sometimes even with sunny skies in between. But Iowa rain falls constantly for a day or two without even a hint of a break.

I'd seen several rainstorms since coming to Aunt Ella's farm, but this one turned out to be the worst one yet. Or at least the longest. It didn't stop for four days. Dad's research was done, so he was home. Our schoolwork was done, so we were free to do whatever we wanted. But obviously we had to do it inside because the farm had turned into one huge mud pie. It was fun to have Dad home, though, because he spent time playing board games with us and even started reading a book out loud to us. He read two or three chapters a day from *The Adventures of Tom Sawyer* by Mark Twain. I'd seen a couple different versions of this story on TV or videos, but it was really fun to get the real story straight from the original book.

The rest of the time Jeff and I played games in the hideout or watched videos with Shauna and Meg. That is, of course, whenever Danny and Chelsea were occupied with something else. A sheriff's car was still parked outside, and it was a gut-twisting reminder that Anthony was still on the loose and still dangerous. I was starting to feel trapped. I really wanted to get out of this place. Here I was— stuck in Iowa, stuck inside the farmhouse, and dependent on a guard outside the front door. I could hardly wait to go to Branson.

Of course I would have much preferred going home, but Branson would be acceptable under the circumstances.

Early Thursday morning we were in the van heading south. The rain had finally quit sometime during the night, and the sun was shining. I can't even begin to describe how good it felt to be going away. I really enjoyed the farm, and Aunt Ella was really cool; it was just that freak Anthony who was making me so uptight. Aunt Ella had made a fantastic breakfast, as always, and then gave us all huge hugs as we headed out the door.

"I'll see you in a few days," Aunt Ella smiled. "Have a wonderful trip!"

Dad's plan was to go south to Branson, Missouri, for a week, come back north and spend two days in Nauvoo, Illinois, and then return to Aunt Ella's farm for one day before heading home to Utah. Of course there were several other places he wanted to stop and see along the way. Dad called it a big circle, but I found the atlas and checked it out. His route didn't look like any circle I'd ever seen. It was more like a half moon or a deformed, rotting piece of fruit. It had obviously been a while since Dad had taken a geometry class.

Mom and Dad were in the front of the van talking about the different places we were going to visit on our way to Branson. At first Dad had said that we would be taking two days to get there, but after looking at the list of Church history sites he wanted to see, he had decided that one day would probably be enough. The plan was to make four stops on the way, but none of them would be very long.

The TV/VCR was playing some cartoons for Chelsea and Daniel, but the sun was glaring on the screen so badly, I don't know how they could tell what was going on. I decided that it was probably one of those tapes they've already seen a hundred and twenty times, so they didn't really even need to see the screen to know what was playing.

I climbed into the front bench and sat next to Granny. She was reading a Louis L'Amour novel with a picture of a cowboy sitting on a rock on the front cover. I knew better than to say anything to Dad before I'd strapped myself in, so after my seatbelt was fastened, I leaned forward, putting my hands on the cooler that Mom and Dad had on the floor between their seats.

"Dad?" I grunted because the seatbelt was cutting me in half. He glanced sideways at me and then returned his eyes to the road.

"Hi, Bran," he said. "What can I do for you?"

"Where are those papers you brought home about Independence and stuff?" I asked.

Dad had found some Church history information on the Internet at the library and printed out several pages. There were descriptions of Church history sites everywhere from New York to San Diego. He used a yellow highlighter to mark the ones we were planning to see.

"Here you go," he said, holding the papers out where I could reach them.

"Thanks," I said as I leaned back and started sorting through the pages. I flipped them over one at a time until I found some of Dad's yellow markings. I read the description below the words *Nauvoo, Illinois*, and then glanced at the other markings on the page. *Carthage, Illinois*, and *Council Bluffs, Iowa*, were also highlighted.

"Which ones are we going to see first?" I asked, remembering that we weren't going to be hitting Nauvoo until after we'd left Branson.

"They're all numbered," Dad replied. "Today we're seeing all the ones in Missouri. They should be numbered one through four."

Looking back at the page I'd just read, I found numbers in the left margin that I hadn't noticed before. There was a number 5 next to Nauvoo, a 6 by Carthage, and the number 7 by Council Bluffs, Iowa. I turned the page and found more highlighted words. The numbers 1, 2, 3, and 4 were in the left margin next to the headings

Gallatin, Missouri; Far West, Missouri; Liberty, Missouri; and Independence, Missouri. I started reading the description for Gallatin. I figured we'd be going there first, since it had the number 1 next to it. It mentioned a place called "Adam-ondi-Ahman," which wasn't very far from Gallatin and was supposedly the place where Adam had gathered all of his descendants and talked to them before he died. I'd never heard anything like that before.

"Adam lived in *Missouri?!*" I burst out, my head popping up.

Dad turned his head slightly, and it looked like there was a smile on the half of his face that I could see. "Well, it wasn't Missouri at the time!" he laughed. "But this is where Adam was living not long before his death."

"How do we know that?" I asked, not sure I believed it. "I thought all those old guys lived around Jerusalem before the Lord started telling them to build boats and sail to America."

"Old guys?" Dad laughed.

"Well," I stammered, "old prophets, you know . . . and all their people."

"I know what you mean," he chuckled. "And you're right; from the Bible we know that Abraham and Melchizedek lived in the area around Jerusalem or Israel, but that was at least a thousand years after Adam died, and it was also after Noah and the flood. We don't really know where Noah started from, but he probably landed not far from where Israel is today. In fact, some people think they've found the wreckage of the ark somewhere in Turkey, which is not too far north of Israel. But to answer your question about Adam-ondi-Ahman: it was revealed to Joseph Smith. It's in the Doctrine and Covenants. Why don't you see if you can find it? That'll be good preparation for you before we stop to see it."

After finally getting Jeff to stop watching Danny's video long enough to get my scriptures for me, I looked up "Adam-ondi-Ahman" in the index of my triple combination. I actually found three references. The first one was in section 78 and said something about the Lord establishing the foundations of Adam-ondi-Ahman, whatever that means. The second was in section 107, verses 53–57. There it said that Adam gathered all his righteous descendants together at Adam-ondi-Ahman three years before he died, and he gave them blessings. It also says that the Lord came to him and comforted him and told him that he would be prince over a multitude of nations forever. Then Adam prophesied about all of his descendants down to the last days.

"Well," I said to Dad after reading this scripture, "I found the place that says Adam gathered his righteous descendants together three years before he died, but it doesn't say that it was in Missouri. I still have one more to read, though."

The last reference was section 116, verse 1. It turns out that section 116 has only one verse, so verse 1 is all there is. The first thing it said is that some place named Spring Hill was really where Adam-ondi-Ahman used to be.

"Where's Spring Hill?" I asked.

"I think it doesn't really exist anymore," Dad replied, "but it was not too far from Gallatin. Just north of it, I think."

I read the rest of the verse.

"Hey, Dad," I exclaimed. "This doesn't say anything about Adam talking to his descendants before he died, but it *does* say that he's going to come here to visit his people later. So he's coming back?"

"Sure," Dad said. "That was prophesied by Daniel in the Old Testament when he was talking about the Millennium."

"Wow," I breathed. "So we're going to see not only the place where Adam *was* thousands of years ago, but this is the place he's coming back to during the Millennium? That's cool!"

"Adam was the leader of the first dispensation, and he's supposed to judge the people who lived in that dispensation," Dad continued. "I imagine that Joseph Smith will probably be meeting with us at the same time. He's the leader of our dispensation."

"Really?"

"Yep," Dad answered. "Each prophet who leads a dispensation will judge all the people of that time to see how well they obeyed and followed the prophets. Joseph Smith will want to know what we've done to build up the Church and spread the Book of Mormon."

"That'll be cool!" I said. This was starting to look like a pretty fun day after all. "So what are we going to see at the other places?" I asked.

"Well," Dad replied, "next we'll be driving just south of Gallatin to a place that was called Far West. The early members of the Church were going to build a temple there, and we'll see the cornerstones that they laid. The people were driven out of Missouri before they got any more of it completed."

"I thought we were going to see cornerstones from a temple that was in Nauvoo," I said.

"We'll see some there, too," Dad answered. "They actually completed the temple in Nauvoo, but it was destroyed, and so all that's left is the foundation. Nauvoo is where the Saints went after leaving Missouri. They were driven out of Illinois just a few years later. They were just finishing the temple at the same time that some groups of Saints were leaving to go west. But in Far West they never had time to do anything other than lay the cornerstones."

"Man!" I said. "That's not fair! I can't believe people kept kicking them out of wherever they went."

"Well," Dad sighed, "the members of the Church were very different from most people, and there were a lot of them. The Missourians realized that as soon as there were more Saints than everyone else, they would basically be able to take over the local government because they could vote anyone they wanted into office. Plus, some of the early members of the Church did some things that made people feel quite uncomfortable. For example, it was revealed to Joseph Smith that Independence was to be the gathering place for the Saints in the last days, so they came charging in and started building a city so fast that it's no wonder everyone else was worried that they were going to be overrun by these 'crazy religious zealots.'"

"Oh," I said. "I get it. So they should have been a lot more careful."

"Probably," Dad nodded, "but there were other things, too. The Lord gave some very specific instructions about how the gathering in Independence should be carried out, and the people didn't follow very well."

"So it was their own fault?" I asked.

"Pretty much," Dad sighed. "The situation got really bad by the time they left. Joseph Smith and several others were in jail for months at the same time the Saints were leaving for Nauvoo. Liberty Jail is another place we're going to stop today. We'll also see the visitors' center in Independence, which explains the whole story."

I leaned back again and read through the descriptions of Far West, Liberty, and Independence. I dropped the papers onto the bench next to me and tried to imagine what it must have been like to be driven from state to state just for trying to find a place where you could build a temple and worship Heavenly Father. Then I thought about Aunt Ella's and Granny's great-grandfather Elias Franzen. Aunt Ella had said that he was one of the first in Nauvoo and had helped to build the city, and then he died on the trail somewhere in Iowa. His daughter Hannah was only eleven years old when it happened. That was *my* age. I couldn't even imagine what it must have been like.

Then I started thinking about Dr. Anthony. This guy was no problem *at all* compared with whole mobs driving people from their homes. I don't know if it was because we weren't at the farm anymore or because I began to think about how easy *my* life was compared to what the early Saints had to deal with, but all of a sudden

I was starting to feel great. I didn't feel trapped anymore. It just seemed fitting that we were going to be visiting a place called "Independence" on the same day that I felt that I just got my independence back. I smiled to myself as I thought about it.

About eleven o'clock Dad pulled off the highway. We wound around for a couple of minutes and then found what Dad claimed was the road to Adam-ondi-Ahman, but it looked more like a goat path to me. The farther we went, the narrower it got. It was barely wide enough for our van. We had to go really slow and pull partway off the road whenever a car came from the other direction. The sides of the road were kind of steep in some places and really muddy. I figured it must have been raining for the last four days down here as well as in Iowa.

Just after Dad announced that he thought we were about a mile away, I saw this huge, red pickup truck coming straight at us down the road. And it was flying. Dad slowed way down, but the sides of the road were really steep, so he didn't want to get too far off to the side.

"Slow down, friend," I heard Dad mutter. "We're here, too!"

Mom looked up to see what Dad was talking about and let out a gasp and grabbed the armrest. The truck obviously had no intention of slowing down, and when he was about thirty feet from us he laid on the horn. And it was loud. Granny jumped and Meg screamed. Dad hit the gas and took us off the side of the road just in time to miss a head-on collision with this lunatic. As soon as the truck had passed, Dad turned the wheel hard to get us back up onto the road, but I could feel the back end of the van going farther down the side.

"We're going to get stuck!" Dad called out.

I looked out the back window and saw mud flying everywhere. The wheels were obviously spinning, but we kept slowing down. Finally we quit moving forward and started sliding even farther away from the road. Dad hit the brakes, and the van slid backward to a stop. By now the van had turned so we were facing the side of the road. The front was probably only about ten feet from the edge of the road, but the bank was steep enough and muddy enough that we couldn't get back up.

Dad heaved a sigh, looked over at Mom, and said, "We're stuck."

"At least no one's hurt," Mom forced a smile.

"That's my truck!" Jeff yelled without warning.

Everyone turned to stare at him.

"A bright-red Dodge Ram with an extended cab and a roll bar," Jeff went on. "That's the truck I'm going to have. Except mine is going to have four lights mounted across the top of the roll bar so I can go four-wheelin' at night."

"Jeff!" I yelled back at him. "That guy almost killed us, and *now* you want a *truck* like that?" Jeff has serious problems comprehending certain situations.

"I've *always* wanted a truck like that!" he said defensively.

"The guy's evil!" I stammered. "He tried to kill us!"

"Laban was evil," Jeff said with his chin sticking out, "and he tried to kill Nephi's family, but they *still* wanted his brass plates."

That comment didn't even deserve a response. And it's a good thing, too, because I didn't have one. Shauna was the only one who had anything to say.

"*What?*" she breathed, forcing a long slow blink.

"Well, it's true," Jeff said quietly.

I turned back around and stared out the front window, shaking my head. Our family obviously had bigger problems than just being stuck in the mud.

Dad got out and told everyone else to stay in the van so we wouldn't get muddy, and he hiked up to the road, slipping and sliding the whole way. Within a couple of minutes a car stopped. It turned out that they had a cellular phone, and so Dad was able to call a tow truck.

"The tow truck should be here within forty-five minutes," Dad announced as he climbed back in. "So I think it's time for lunch."

Mom broke out the homemade bread that Aunt Ella had packed for us and started making sandwiches. I got to pass everyone's plates back to them since I was still sitting on the front bench. We also had chips and oranges and apples and soda to go with it. It turned out to be pretty fun trying to balance everything when there wasn't a flat surface anywhere to put anything down on.

Several more cars passed by and most of them stopped to ask if we needed help. Dad kept his window rolled down and called up to them that we already had a tow truck coming but thanks for stopping. The tow truck showed up just as we were finishing our lunch.

"Perfect timing!" Dad said as he hopped out into the mud to go talk to the driver. The two of them stood at the edge of the road pointing and talking for about five minutes before Dad slid back down the hill to the van.

"What's going on?" Mom asked.

"Well," Dad sighed, "he says we're too far off the road, and he doesn't dare try to get us out. He's afraid we'll both end up stuck. He did say that he'd take me to one of the nearby farms so I could see if there's someone who'd be willing to use a tractor to pull us out."

"Okay," Mom said. "We'll just wait here till you get back, I guess. Have fun!"

"Be back as soon as I can," Dad said with obvious regret in his voice.

"We'll be fine," Mom reassured him. "We've got movies, games, and food! You know very well that's all I need to be happy."

I watched in dismay as Dad slopped back up the hill and climbed into the cab of the tow truck. There was no telling how long he'd be gone. I had seen Mr. Hansen driving Aunt Ella's tractor, and I'm convinced it never went more than about three miles an hour. I could just imagine how long it was going to take for Dad to first find someone willing to help and then for the silly tractor to travel who knows how many miles out to where we were.

Mom was right, though, about us having everything she needed to stay happy. As far as I was concerned, however, there was at least one problem with each thing. We had food all right, but we'd just eaten, so who wanted to eat? If we'd had some decent cookies, I probably could have eaten five or six, I guess, but we didn't have any. We had movies, too, but it was obvious whose videos were going to be playing as long as Danny and Chelsea were awake. So that left the games. We quickly determined that the only games available were a couple of decks of cards: Rook and hearts.

Jeff, Shauna, and I tried to play Rook for a while, but it didn't take long for us to figure out that it's almost impossible to play a card game without a flat surface. Besides that, I had to turn around and lean over the back of the bench. It didn't work too well, and so after a while we all pretty much gave up and just started doing our own thing. I pulled out my new, or rather, old, Book of Mormon and carefully looked through the pages that I'd discussed with Aunt Ella the first time she let me hold the book. I was still feeling just as reverent about it as I did then. I pulled the old bookmark out and read the four lines of writing again:

Valley of Lemuel
Lamanites, A.D. *30*
Mount Zerin
Mormon and Lamanite king

I thought about Anthony insisting that there was a treasure map with this Book of Mormon, but reading over these words again convinced me that this couldn't be what he meant. I tried to remember what Elias Franzen had said about a treasure in the letter that Anthony had, but I could hardly remember anything about it. Then the last line caught my eye because I realized I didn't remember anything in the Book of Mormon about Mormon and a Lamanite king. Meg came climbing up to the front of the van and sat in the driver's seat so that she could say something to Mom. After a minute she looked over at me and asked, "What's that, Bran?"

I put the bookmark back between the pages and closed the book. "It's my Liahona," I answered.

"What's a Liahona?" she asked with one side of her nose wrinkled up.

"It's something used by Heavenly Father to give direction," Mom answered.

"That's right," I said. "This is something that I got from Aunt Ella that gives me direction."

"I don't get it," Meg confessed.

"The real Liahona was a ball with two arrows in it that Heavenly Father gave to Lehi and his family to show them which way to go in the wilderness," I explained. "Aunt Ella just called this my Liahona because it's supposed to show me what to do but in sort of a different way."

"Oh," Meg said, but she acted like she still didn't understand. "Is it like a clock? A clock is a ball with two arrows."

I laughed, "Close enough." Then I told her the story of Hannah getting this book from her father. I figured she'd enjoy hearing about an eleven-year-old girl who lived so long ago. I noticed that Mom and Granny seemed to be listening, too.

Over an hour later we heard the faint sound of a tractor approaching. Gradually it got louder and louder until we finally saw it in front of us up on the road. It stopped right at the edge of the road, facing us. Dad and a man got out of the cab. The man looked pretty much like most of the Iowa farmers I'd seen while staying with Aunt Ella. He was dressed in a red plaid shirt and dark blue overalls. Dad and the farmer started acting just like Dad and the tow truck driver had acted earlier. They were talking and pointing back and forth at the van and the road. This went on for about half a minute before the man climbed back into the cab, handed Dad a chain, and then started turning the tractor around.

Dad slid down the hill and vanished under the front of the van. We could hear him clanking around with the chain for a minute or so before reappearing. I saw him heave a huge sigh before he trudged up the hill one more time. I'm sure he was getting tired of this muddy mess. He got up to the edge of the road just as the tractor was backing into position. The man took the end of the chain Dad had carried up the hill and hooked it onto the tractor. Once more Dad made his way to the van, this time holding the stretched-out chain all the way down.

"Hi," Dad sighed, opening the door and dropping himself into the driver's seat. "Looks like we might be in business. How did everything go here?"

"We had a great time," Mom responded. "Didn't we, guys?"

Dad started the car and shifted it into gear. Almost immediately the tractor started moving, and we felt the van lurch forward. The tractor was slow, but it had no trouble pulling us back onto the road. I watched the tractor go down the other side of the road as we moved up on top.

Once we were completely on the road, the tractor backed up slightly and the farmer hopped out. Dad met him at the edge of the road as they removed the chain from both vehicles and spoke with each other for another couple of minutes. At one point, Dad pulled his wallet from his back pocket, but the farmer immediately shook his head back and forth and held up his hand. He obviously had no intention of letting Dad pay him for his help.

"How come he wouldn't take the money?" I asked when Dad climbed back into the van.

"He said it was no trouble," Dad smiled, fastening his seatbelt, "and just considered it part of his Christian duty."

"Wow," I said, "that's really cool!"

"That's neat," Shauna agreed.

We were on the road now, but we were still facing sideways, and the road wasn't very wide. It took Dad seven or eight back-and-forths before we actually were facing the right way on the road. Two cars waited while we did our little stutter step. Dad was probably a little overcautious about avoiding the edge, but I had no trouble understanding why. We had finally been rescued more than two hours after Jeff's loony friend forced us off the road.

A couple of minutes later we were parked next to a historical marker and got out. Three other cars were also there. I'm not sure what I was expecting, but I was surprised by what I saw. It was nothing but a huge open meadow with several large clumps of trees off in the distance. I walked a little way from the van and stood there looking off in all directions for a while.

As I stood there I tried to imagine Adam and all his descendants gathered to receive blessings from him before he died. This was an amazingly peaceful place. I couldn't compare it to any place else I'd ever been. Then I started thinking about Adam coming again during the Millennium and meeting many of those same people and judging how they'd done in carrying on with his teachings. This was definitely a cool place. It was even worth the wait—though I wouldn't want to do it again.

We got back to the van, and a little while later we were at Far West looking at the cornerstones that had been laid for the temple there. This place was pretty neat, too. I think Jeff and Shauna agreed.

It was already well into the afternoon by the time we left Far West.

"It's getting late," Mom said to Dad, "and the little guys are tired. What would you think if we skipped the visitors' center in Independence? We could still hit Liberty Jail and then go straight to Branson from there."

"Sounds like a good idea," Dad agreed. "I'm getting tired, too. It would be nice to get settled in the condo before it gets too late."

A couple of hours later we arrived at the small visitors' center in Liberty, Missouri. We had just finished another sit-in-the-car meal using Aunt Ella's homemade bread. Then we all stumbled out of the van and went inside.

This place was very different from the others we'd seen earlier. It was interesting to see the jail where Joseph Smith had been held for so many months while the Saints were being driven from Missouri and to learn about all the revelations he received while he was here, but I didn't like the feeling. Where the other places felt peaceful and calm, the jail felt sad and depressing. I was more than ready to leave by the time we all piled back into our seats.

We finally arrived at the town of Branson about ten o'clock and spent a few minutes hauling all our junk into the condo. I was surprised to see how big it was. There were two bedrooms, two bathrooms, and a large open room, which included the kitchen, dining area, and family room. Mom and Dad got one of the bedrooms, while Granny and Shauna got the other. There was a sofa bed in the family room for two people and room for two sleeping bags on the floor next to it. Jeff and I would have to trade off each night with Meg and Chelsea for the sofa bed or sleeping bags.

Once all our stuff was in from the van, everyone was assigned different things to put away or take care of. It was my job to set up Danny's portable crib in Mom and Dad's room. I had just gotten started when Dad came in, sat on the bed, and picked up the phone.

"Who are you calling, Dad?" I asked.

"I just want to check in at home," he answered.

"You're going to tell Aunt Ella where we are?" I questioned.

"Not that home," Dad smiled. "You must have really liked it there, if you're calling it home now! I'm talking about our home in Utah. Aunt Ella already knows where we are, but I want to tell the lady who's house-sitting for us where we're going to be for the next few days."

"Oh," I said, returning to my work with Daniel's crib.

"Hello, Karen," Dad said into the phone. "It's Craig. I just wanted to call and see how everything was going. I hope 9:30 is not too late for you."

There was a long pause.

"I see," Dad finally said. "So the police are there now?" he asked, his voice tense. I stopped what I was doing and looked over at him.

"Thank you," Dad said after a moment. "I'll speak with you later."

There was another pause. I wanted to ask what was going on, but I didn't dare.

"Hello, officer," Dad said. "Can you tell me what's happened?"

A short pause.

"Yes, I'll do that," Dad said grimly. "One moment please."

Dad then placed the phone receiver on the nightstand without hanging it up. He stood quickly and walked to the bedroom doorway.

"Sarah," Dad called into the kitchen. "The police are at our home in Orem. I've got an officer on the phone right now. How about getting on the phone in the kitchen so we can both get the details at the same time."

CHAPTER 12

Hannah

"Go ahead, officer," Dad said into the phone. "We're both on the line now."

I didn't even pretend to be working on Danny's crib anymore. I wanted to know what was going on at home. The first few minutes of Dad's side of the conversation were simply long pauses broken up every once in a while by "Yes" or "I see" or something like that. Finally Dad said, "I think I probably know who's responsible for this. His name is Dr. Anthony."

What!? My mind raced with the possibilities of what Anthony might be doing at our home in Utah! How in the world did he even find out where we lived? Had he gotten into our van sometime and found our address written somewhere? Just when I was convinced that he was out of my life something like this happens! So much for our sightseeing representing my independence! Then I remembered that we never made it to Independence, Missouri, as we had planned. I knew that there was *no way* that had anything to do with it, but the idea gave me the creeps.

Dad described a few of the details about what Anthony had done in Iowa and gave the officer in Orem the Iowa sheriff's name and phone number so they could contact him for complete police reports. Then he asked to speak to the house-sitter again.

"The home-owner's insurance information is in the second drawer of the filing cabinet in my bedroom," Dad explained. He listened for a moment. "We'd really appreciate that, if it's not too much trouble," he continued. Another pause. "Yes, just use the same color. If we're lucky, maybe they can have it finished before we're home."

There were a few more typical conversation-ending comments before Dad finally got done. There hadn't been enough information on Dad's half of the conversation to get any clue about what was going on—only that it had something to do with Dr. Anthony. So I was pretty much going crazy by the time he finally hung up the phone.

"What happened?!" I breathed anxiously. I blurted it out before the phone receiver had even quit rocking back and forth on its base.

"Come into the sitting room, and we'll tell everyone at the same time," Dad said as he left the room, expecting me to follow. He probably wasn't expecting me to follow so closely that I accidentally stepped on his heel, though.

"Should we have everyone come and sit down for a minute?" Dad asked Mom.

Mom hesitated. "Let's put the little guys down first," she suggested as she forced a smile. Turning to me she continued with, "Is Daniel's crib ready?"

I grunted in frustration. "No . . . I . . . well . . ." I sighed. "No, I'll go finish it." Mom obviously didn't want "the little guys" to be around when they told us what had happened, so I ran back to get Danny's crib ready as fast as possible.

"Aren't you done with that yet?" Jeff called after me, but since I was already through the door he didn't get the pleasure of my smirk. I could have returned to the doorway to share it with him, but at this point I was more interested in getting my job done so we could find out what was going on.

It was probably half an hour before Danny was *finally* asleep in his crib and Meg and Chels were snuggled together, zonked out on the sofa bed. Of course we all had to get our pajamas on, and we'd had family prayer, and Dad read a chapter out loud from *Tom*

Sawyer with Danny on his lap and the girls in bed so they would all fall asleep while he was reading. I have no idea what he even read because I was going nuts just waiting for him to tell us about Dr. Anthony.

Jeff and Shauna had absolutely no clue what was going on, and when I tried to tell them what I knew, Dad cut me off and made it clear that "now was not the time." Twice while Dad was reading, I *carefully* interrupted him and mentioned that Danny, Meg, and Chelsea were all asleep, so could we start talking about "you-know-what" now?

"Brandon," he smiled the second time, in a way that made it clear that I was lucky he was still smiling, "please wait until I've finished the chapter, all right?"

"Sorry," I mumbled. Jeff and Shauna looked at me and then at each other with the identical expression, which clearly communicated, "What's *his* problem?" After Dad finished the chapter and put Danny in the portable crib, we gathered in the other bedroom, where Granny was stretched out reading her Louis L'Amour book.

"Someone broke into our home in Utah," Dad began, "and we think it was probably Dr. Anthony."

"How do you know?" Shauna asked.

"Well, nothing appears to be missing as far as the house-sitter can tell, but all the books in the house were thrown into big piles. Sound familiar?"

"Uh-oh," Jeff said as he twisted one side of his mouth. "Sounds like Dr. A., all right."

"The only other damage," Dad continued, "was some spray paint on the walls in each of the kids' bedrooms. The words 'Give me my book' were painted in each room."

"It *had* to be Anthony," I breathed. "But why did he paint just in the kids' rooms?" I asked.

"We don't know," Mom replied. "Maybe he was looking for your room, Brandon, but didn't know which one it was."

"Meg and Chelsea's room is *pink!*" I exploded. "Like he's going to think I have a *pink* bedroom?" I was totally disgusted.

"We don't *know*," Mom repeated. "The man obviously isn't all there. There's no way of knowing what he was thinking."

"Like I would have a *pink* bedroom," I muttered. Jeff laughed.

"It's okay, Bran," Shauna smiled.

"Anyway," Dad continued, "the police in Orem will be contacting Ella's sheriff so they can compare notes. Hopefully, they can get everything resolved before we get home."

"Yeah," I complained, "but we'll be going home to a huge mess."

"Actually," Mom said, "Karen offered to take care of everything. She's even going to try to have the rooms repainted before we're back."

"All right!" yelled Jeff. "Do we get to choose the color?"

"No," Dad shook his head. "I told her to just do them the same color they were before."

"Oh!" whined Jeff. Then he asked, "How about something exciting—like bright red?"

"What?" Shauna asked.

"Let me guess," I squinted at Jeff. "You want something to match a particular Dodge Ram, am I right?"

"Yeah!" he smiled.

"Maybe if you begged long enough," I continued, "they could even install a roll bar on your bed with four lights across the top."

"Oh, yes!" Jeff shouted. "That would be so *cool!*" Then, turning to Dad, "Let's do it, Dad! Can we? It'd be great!"

Dad just stared at him for a minute before answering, "Right! As if I want to remember some Missouri lunatic in a Dodge truck every time I walk into your room." Dad headed for the bedroom door as he added, "I don't *think* so!"

Shauna, Jeff, and I spent a few more minutes talking about Anthony and our house and what a freak he is before we went to bed. We couldn't figure out how he could have found out where we live. We decided he probably was pretty smart. I just hoped he wasn't smart enough to figure out where we were now.

The next morning Dad woke us at about nine o'clock and told us to shower and eat as soon as we could. Apparently Mom and Granny were off trying to find the best deals they could for some shows and Silver Dollar City and whatever else they could find. We were pretty excited about the thought of hitting an amusement park after an entire month on a dairy farm, so we were all ready to go in less than an hour.

We talked about doing some other things, too, like swimming and playing tennis at the condo. Mom and Granny were taking a long time, and it started to get boring after a while, so Dad let us take a walk down to the swimming pool just to check it out. All the way there and back we kept glancing toward the main entrance for Mom and Granny so we could take off as soon as they got back. The whole condo area was surrounded by huge, thick woods. It was like the hills around Aunt Ella's farm, but the trees were even bigger and closer together.

Watching other kids in the swimming pool got boring, too, after a while, especially since Danny kept saying he wanted to go swimming and we had to keep telling him that we were going someplace a lot more fun than swimming as soon as Mom got back. This was obviously way too far in the future for him to comprehend, and for some reason he just didn't buy it anymore after about the seventeenth time we told him that. In fact, I was starting to think we were going to miss half the day if they didn't get back pretty soon.

Finally we wandered back to the condo, where we sat around watching TV or playing games or doing anything we could think of, eventually resorting to just complaining to Dad. It was already past eleven-thirty, with no sign of Mom and Granny, so Dad said that we could go swimming until they returned. I should have guessed that as soon as we struck upon an alternate plan that everybody seemed happy with, Mom and Granny would suddenly show up.

It took another twenty minutes to get everyone in swimming suits and find towels and sandals and blow up eight different pool toys. But we finally got everything ready. Danny was standing in the kitchen in his swimming suit, sandals, and bright blue and green sunglasses with safety floats around his arms and an inflatable dinosaur tube around his waist, saying, "Let's go swimming now!" just when Mom and Granny opened the door. We should have tried this method of getting them home two hours earlier.

"Hi guys!" Mom bubbled. "We have the greatest tickets to all the neatest stuff. You're all going to love it." She looked around at everyone and said, "You're going swimming? You can't go swimming! We've got tickets to Shoji Tabuchi in an hour. He's a *fabulous* violinist! You're going to love it!"

I've intentionally avoided mentioning the following fact up to now, hoping that it wouldn't be necessary for this story, but the truth is, well, I play the cello. It's not that I'm ashamed of it or embarrassed by it or anything like that, it's just that most people—especially those my age—don't appreciate it too much. So I usually mention it only if the situation requires.

Mom played the violin when she was a kid, and she still pulls it out once in a while. So she decided that each of her children would play an instrument also. Either she loves it or didn't want us to miss out on the parent-child practicing wars. In any case, I play the cello. And because of it, I generally end up practicing every time I'd rather be doing something else.

My only consolation is that everyone else in my family is in the same boat. Shauna and Meg play the violin, and Jeff plays the viola. I'm sure Danny and Chelsea will eventually end up playing something, also. That is, unless the older kids happen to finally win the practicing wars and make Mom so miserable that she can't take it anymore and decides not to inflict the same abuse on them. I must say that I have always been extremely valiant in my efforts in their behalf.

The point of this confession is that since we all play stringed instruments, Mom thought we'd really enjoy hearing a violinist perform the entire afternoon on our first full day of *real* vacation. (For some reason, I never really considered doing homework on a dairy farm in Iowa for a month a *true* vacation.) It seems highly unnecessary to try to describe the scene that erupted after Mom's announcement. We got dressed again, though, ate a quick lunch, and went to the show. I wasn't too happy about it at the time, but I must admit: He was good!

Mom and Granny had bought tickets to several shows in Branson and said we would be there for four days. That meant we would be spending only two days in Silver Dollar City, which didn't make us kids all that happy. I complained a little, but it actually turned out that a couple of the shows we saw weren't too bad, especially the magic show. The guy was really good and pretty funny, too. The rest of the time we spent swimming or finding other things to do. The swimming was really nice because it was always so hot and muggy. One day we even took a ride out on the lake on this old army machine they called a "Duck" that could go on either land or water. It was pretty fun.

We were really excited when Tuesday arrived and we finally got to go to Silver Dollar City. It is an amusement park that was made to look like an Ozark Mountains village, filled with old-time saloons and cabins and stuff like that. There were also quite a few rides, and every one of them got you wet. That was great, though, since it was so hot. They also had some shows that were pretty good.

The best show we found at Silver Dollar City was the Nickelodeon Show. It was like a TV game show. They chose people out of the audience and had them come up on stage and answer questions. If you gave the wrong answer, you got hit in the face with a huge cream pie or they would dump green slimy stuff over your head or something cool like that. The audience even got to help by playing volleyball with twelve huge beach balls that everyone hit back and forth across a net that was set up through the middle of the seats. It was great!

Mom and Dad got tickets for every show they could, so we didn't get to go on too many rides the first day. They told us if we saw all the shows then we could decide if we wanted to see any of them again the next day. Shauna, Jeff, and I definitely all wanted to go to the Nickelodeon Show again.

Later in the afternoon, Dad found a ride called "Fire in the Hole," which supposedly didn't get anybody very wet, so he decided everyone should try it. It was like riding through a mine shaft in a mine car, with explosions and beams that acted like they were going to come crashing down. At the end, the mine car went through a river that made a pretty big splash. We all got quite a bit more wet than the man had told us we would, but everyone really liked it—at least everyone but Danny.

When we climbed out of our cars, I noticed that Danny had a big pout on his face. His hair was matted down on one side, and there was water dripping from the end of his nose. He was standing on the platform with his shirt drenched.

"Did you like the ride?" I asked him. Everyone else was laughing and smiling.

"No!" he insisted, his pout getting even bigger.

"Didn't you like getting wet?" Jeff asked.

"No!" he shouted again, acting even more insulted.

"What's the matter?" Shauna asked.

As deliberately as a three-year-old can, he shouted each word, *"It made me mad!"*

We all started laughing, which of course didn't make him feel any happier. Dad scooped him up as we headed outside, promising him that he wouldn't have to go on that ride again. Even after

Mom dried his hair and hugged him, Danny continued to pout for at least another forty-five minutes.

We got some drinks and started wandering back toward the entrance of the theme park. We found that one end of the park was basically an old homestead. There were several cabins, one of which had really been built over a hundred years ago. There were people dressed up like they lived there, doing chores and stuff. Each cabin only had one room inside with maybe a ladder going up to a loft. There were big stone fireplaces and just a few pieces of furniture. The old beds were filled with straw that poked out on the sides and underneath, and there were rugs covering most of the floor space. It was okay, but I guess I wasn't quite as interested as everyone else, so I ended up getting through the first couple of cabins ahead of the rest.

At the next cabin there was a lady sitting on the front porch doing some knitting. She was wearing a long dress, an apron, and a bonnet, which was tied tightly under her chin. She didn't bother to look up as I walked past her through the open door. The inside of this cabin looked pretty much like the others. In the corner was a large porcelain bowl on a small table where a young girl stood rinsing her hands. She turned and smiled at me as she wiped her hands on the front of the long apron she was wearing.

From behind me came the voice of the woman on the front porch. She said something about checking the fire in the smokehouse.

"Would you like to come with me?" the girl asked.

She looked like she was about my age, maybe a little younger. She was two or three inches shorter than I was. Her long dress had little brown and white squares all over it, and she was wearing a bonnet like the lady on the porch, except the strings weren't tied.

"It's just out in the back here," she explained when I didn't answer right away.

"Sure," I said, shrugging my shoulders.

She smiled again and went out the back of the cabin with me following. I paid careful attention not to step on her heels. There was a small clearing behind the cabin with paths that led to the other cabins I'd already been to. I noticed Shauna sticking her head out one of the windows of the first cabin. The ground sloped downward toward some tall trees that were so thick you could see only a few feet into them.

Right next to the edge of the trees was a small building that couldn't have been more than about six feet high. The inside probably wasn't even big enough for a normal sized bed. There was a small wooden door on one end, and smoke was seeping out of every crack around the roof.

The girl walked around to the back of the building where there was a metal plate about the size of an oven door. She used a stick to move the metal plate out of the way, exposing a small fire and a room full of smoke, most of which escaped through the opening where the plate had been. After stirring up the fire with the stick for a minute or so, she motioned for me to come for a closer look.

"Have you ever seen one of these?" she asked.

"Nope," I responded, not even sure what "one of these" was.

"This is a smokehouse," she continued, as if reading my mind. "If you look inside you can see meat hanging in there. We do this to preserve the meat and give it a nice flavor."

"That's pretty cool," I said. The smoke was starting to make my eyes water.

"This is hickory wood," she said as she picked up a couple of small logs from a nearby pile and placed them onto the fire. "We're making hickory-smoked beef jerky."

"Sounds great!" I said. Now my *mouth* was beginning to water as well as my eyes.

"It's really good," she agreed. I noticed she had a pretty smile.

I just watched her as she used the stick to push the metal plate back in place to keep the smoke inside the smokehouse. It wasn't until she was pretty much done that I realized I should have offered to help.

"I've got it, thanks," she smiled again. She really did have a nice smile.

She headed for a small barn next, and I followed without being asked. The barn was nothing like the huge thing on Aunt Ella's farm. This place had only small handmade tools and just a few animals. The girl asked me what I thought about Silver Dollar City and if I was enjoying Branson. We talked for a while about all sorts of stuff as she took care of some things in the barn.

"Brandon!" I heard my Dad call faintly from somewhere outside the barn.

I stuck my head out of the barn door and saw him standing in the path behind one of the cabins. "I'm over here, Dad," I said.

"Are you done?" he asked. "Let's go get some dinner."

"Coming," I called. Then I turned back to the girl. "Are you here every day?" I asked.

"Most days," she smiled again.

"Are you going to be here tomorrow? My mom got us passes for tomorrow, so we're coming back."

"I should be here tomorrow," she answered.

Now I smiled. "Good," I said. "I'll see you tomorrow, then. Bye."

I left the barn and started up the path around the side of the cabin leading to the front, where I could see the rest of my family gathering.

"Oh!" I said, spinning in my tracks. She was standing at the barn door. "You never told me your name!"

"You never asked," she smiled for a moment. "It's Hannah."

"My name's Brandon. See you tomorrow!" I called as I headed back up the path.

"Hey, *Hannah* was the name of my . . ." I whipped around as began to speak, but she was nowhere to be seen. I stood there for a moment looking all around. I couldn't imagine where she'd gone, so I shrugged and went to join my family for dinner.

CHAPTER 13

A Little Child Shall Lead Them

That night I had another dream. Well, actually, it was the same dream I'd had before about being with Joseph Smith and Martin Harris when Professor Anthon was chasing us. I hadn't thought much about Dr. Anthony for several days, not since we'd learned that he'd been at our home in Orem. But after having the dream again I couldn't get him off my mind. I lay in bed for a couple of hours before anyone else woke up. The image of Dr. Anthony dressed in old-fashioned clothes trying to grab my old Book of Mormon just wouldn't go away.

I got out of bed and took the book out my backpack and just held it for a while. It seemed so fragile I thought I'd better do something to protect it. I fumbled around in the dark kitchen until I found a large plastic bag. I put the book in the plastic bag, zipped it shut, and returned the book to my backpack. Then I climbed back into bed.

I felt a little better, but the dream still gave me a spooky feeling, so I tried to concentrate on something else: Hannah. She really had a pretty smile. I definitely planned to find her when we went back to the amusement park. It was obviously going to be my last chance to see her, since I was sure I'd never be coming to Branson again. Once everyone else was up and getting ready to leave, I found myself still thinking about Dr. Anthony on and off. I kept glancing nervously over at my backpack, where I was keeping my

Book of Mormon. Just as we were headed out the door, I grabbed my backpack almost without thinking and brought it with us.

When we arrived at Silver Dollar City for our second day, Dad organized us into groups depending on what we wanted to do. Agreeing to meet in twenty minutes at the saloon, Shauna, Jeff, and I took off to get more Nickelodeon tickets. I put the tickets into one of the pockets of my backpack. I had almost left the bag in the car, but for some reason I just didn't dare let it out of my sight. I knew Anthony wouldn't be able to find us here, but I just felt better knowing for sure that the book was still safe.

Since we still had a few minutes before we needed to meet the rest of the family, I suggested we take a longer route, which just happened to take us right past the homestead area of the park. The same woman was knitting on the front porch of the cabin where I'd met Hannah the day before. Just as before, she didn't bother to look up as I walked past her into the cabin. No one was inside, so I went to the back door and looked around. There was no sign of Hannah anywhere.

Returning to the front porch, I said, "Excuse me, ma'am. Is your daughter here today?"

"I don't have a daughter," she smiled, looking up at me.

"Oh!" I laughed. "I mean the girl who was here with you yesterday! I guess I just figured she was your daughter."

The woman's smile turned into a perplexed look. "There was no girl here yesterday," she said. "Some of the folks bring their children with them once in a while, but there haven't been any youngsters here all week, I reckon."

"B-b-but you sent her to check on the smokehouse when I was here," I stammered. "And I helped her with some chores in the barn—well, I watched her, anyway . . ."

"Can't help you, son," she replied, shaking her head slowly.

I was completely confused. This didn't make any sense at all. I wanted to shake her and tell her to snap out of it. I saw Jeff and

Shauna checking out a concession stand not too far away, and so I started to wander over where they were. Two or three times I stopped and almost went back to the lady on the porch again, but I didn't really know how to ask my question any differently than I already had. What had happened to Hannah?

"What's the matter?" Shauna asked when I finally got to where they were standing.

"I-I'm not sure," I hesitated. I shook my head and released the breath I'd been holding. "Do you guys remember the girl I was talking to at the homestead yesterday?"

"What girl?" Jeff asked.

"I don't remember you talking to anybody," Shauna replied, shaking her head. "Where were you talking to her?"

"We were behind the cabins," I answered. "I helped her with the fire in the smokehouse and then we did some chores in the barn for a few minutes. You mean neither of you saw her?"

"Was she cute?" Jeff grinned.

I was already way too frustrated to get overly annoyed at Jeff's silly question.

"Sorry, Bran," Shauna said, showing a lot more sympathy than Jeff was obviously capable of. "I guess we're no help. Were you trying to find her again?" she asked.

"Yeah," I sighed. "I just wanted to say, 'Hi.' I asked that lady over there, but she says there haven't been any kids around there all week."

"That's weird," Jeff said.

"We can try again later, Bran," Shauna suggested, "but I think we'd better go meet everyone else at the saloon."

We were the first group to arrive at the meeting place, so we bought a bag of sugar-coated popcorn and found a log fence to sit on while we enjoyed our second breakfast. Everyone else arrived within a few minutes, and we made plans for the rest of the day. Shauna, Jeff, and I were on our own again until one o'clock, when we would meet for lunch at the front of the park. Just as we were all about to take off again, Dad said, "Hey, does anyone want to go on 'Fire in the Hole' again as long as we're right here?"

Meg and Chelsea both jumped up and down at the thought. I glanced over at Danny, remembering how he'd reacted to the ride the day before.

"I'll stay outside with Daniel," Dad continued, "while the rest of you take the ride. The line's not too long right now."

We all agreed and headed for the entrance to the ride.

"Daniel, you're staying with me," Dad said as Danny started to scurry after us.

He stopped and turned halfway toward Dad and stared down at his feet. "I want to go, too!" he pouted.

"But you got all wet last time," Dad explained. "You said you didn't like it."

"I want to go, too!" he repeated, his lower lip sticking out almost as far as his nose.

"Is it okay if you get wet?" Dad asked him.

"Yes," Danny said emphatically.

"Are you sure?" Dad asked again.

"Yes!" Danny sounded almost insulted this time.

"Okay," Dad sighed, "let's go!"

The ride was great and ended with the same big splash it had the day before. We were all dripping wet once again and laughing as we got off. But Danny reacted exactly the same way he had the day before. I almost started laughing when I saw him standing on the platform, his hair matted down with water, and his shirt drenched.

"Was it fun?" Dad asked hopefully.

"No!" He sounded insulted again.

"What's the matter?" Jeff asked, trying not to laugh.

Separating the words for emphasis, just as he had done before, Danny blurted out, "It made me mad . . . *two times!*"

Not one of us could keep from laughing this time. In fact, I laughed every time I thought about it for the rest of the day.

Dad was still trying to comfort Danny as Shauna, Jeff, and I took off. We wanted to hit some more rides before it was time for the Nickelodeon Show. We had a great time. Dad was right—because we'd done everything the first day, we knew what we liked and just spent our time at those places the second day. It was great. I was expecting the Nickelodeon Show to be the same as the day before, but it had some different games and other stuff.

After the show Shauna said that she just *had* to have a funnel cake. They would put whatever you wanted on top, but our favorite was powdered sugar. We kept walking and talking as we ate the cake and started wandering around through some of the shops. There were lots of interesting things, and we each bought a couple of souvenirs, which I put into my backpack. *Somehow* we ended up not too far from the homestead area, and I thought about Hannah again. I headed over there to see if she was around now, but I had no intention of asking the nutso lady for any more information.

The porch was empty as I walked into the cabin, but the lady was inside sweeping up around the beds where some straw had fallen out of the mattresses. There was no sign of Hannah, so I continued right out into the back. Hannah wasn't anywhere to be seen, so I checked the barn. There were three or four people inside. One was a man dressed in old-fashioned clothes brushing down one of the horses, but no Hannah. I asked the man, but he had no "recollection of anyone" like Hannah.

I decided to check the other cabins and headed that direction. I glanced around for Shauna and Jeff as I approached one of the cabins but couldn't see them. The first cabin was empty. The second cabin seemed empty, too, at first, but then I heard something from the loft just as I was leaving. I stopped in the doorway and turned around and saw a man moving toward the edge of the loft where the ladder was. He was dressed pretty much like the man in the barn: leather boots, brown pants, and a long-sleeved, loose-fitting white shirt.

"Excuse me, sir," I asked as he was starting down the ladder. "Is there a girl named Hannah here somewhere today?"

"Let me think," he responded without turning his head or taking his eyes away from his feet as he carefully placed them on each rung of the ladder. From where I was standing, his face was mostly hidden by his shoulder and arm, but I could tell that he was wearing wire-framed glasses.

He was taking so long to inch down the ladder, and obviously he didn't have the ability to think about the ladder and my question at the same time, so my mind started to wander. I thought about the crazy dream I'd had twice now, and I realized almost immediately that this man reminded me a lot of Professor Anthon. It gave me a tingly feeling as I watched him step off the last rung of the ladder. He was even dressed just like Professor Anthon in my dream.

The man turned to face me and said, "Let's go see if this 'Hannah' is in the back, shall we?" He smiled a sick smile that I knew far too well.

My feet suddenly felt as though they were glued to the floor, and I could feel myself start to shake. *It was Anthony!* His smile melted quickly into a sneer when he saw the fear on my face and realized that I had recognized him.

"I was told I might find a boy matching your description around here," he sniffed. Then very slowly he almost whispered the words, "Give me my book, boy!" Neither of us moved. We just stood there facing each other about fifteen feet apart. I don't know how long we were staring before I noticed his smile start to reappear.

"Whatcha got in that backpack?" he asked, assuming he already knew the answer.

My eyes got even wider—if that was possible—and I started to lean backward and squeeze the sides of my backpack between my elbows. I felt my toes begin to lift off the floor as I rocked onto my heels. The sensation of being glued to the floor left as quickly as it had come, and I spun around and ran as fast as I could. I heard him scramble after me, but I didn't dare even turn to look. I just ran as far and as fast as possible. I'm sure I looked something like our cat does when that dog from down the street gets out.

I didn't even think about where I was going at first, I just ran for my life. Then I headed for the biggest crowds possible, hoping to make myself harder to see. Several people yelled at me as I went flying by; some because I startled them and some because I actually bumped into them. There was a little girl with a drippy ice cream cone who looked like she'd just barely learned to walk who suddenly turned right into my path. My only choices were to plow right through her or to try and jump over her head. I'm sure I would have set a new high jump record for a kid my age if there had been someone there to measure it. The little girl didn't even know what had happened. I did, however, notice a distinct scream coming from a woman who was obviously her mother.

I was getting tired and wanted someplace to hide and rest. As I got close to the Nickelodeon Show I saw that no one was lined up, which meant that there was probably a show going on. That seemed like a *great* place to hide. The main doors were guarded by a couple guys, so I charged toward one of the side doors. Just as I started to pull the handle, one of them yelled, "Hey, you can't go in there!"

"I won't be watching the show!" I called over my shoulder as I ripped through the door and headed into the auditorium. Now I had somebody else chasing me, but I was certainly much more concerned about Anthony. For a moment I even thought that getting caught by the guard might save me from Anthony, but then I realized that he would probably just claim that *I* had stolen *his* book. Then he'd get away while I was stuck trying to explain why I'd run into the show without a ticket.

There was music blaring and people yelling and shouting as I parted the curtain leading into the auditorium. They were in the middle of a volleyball game, so people were in the aisles, charging back and forth, trying to keep all the huge beach balls on the other side of the net. This was perfect. I headed straight for the biggest crowd I could see, then looked back to find the guard standing next to the curtain I had just come through. I didn't think he'd be able to spot me as long as the game was going, but I knew it wouldn't last for long. I quickly hid my backpack under a seat by the aisle and went and stood in an area where there were several empty seats, hoping that there would be at least one extra seat once everyone returned to their places.

Just as the game was ending another guard appeared at the curtain with Dr. Anthony right behind him. I was far enough away that I didn't think he'd be able to pick me out, though. I stood watching Anthony and the two guards out of the corner of my eye. They were gesturing in a way that made me think they were probably talking about my backpack, so I was glad that I had hidden it. Suddenly I realized that everyone in the auditorium was sitting now except for me. I looked at the row next to me and found that every seat had been filled. I scanned the area but I couldn't find an empty seat anywhere. I knew I had to do something fast or they'd spot me for sure. There were still a couple of employees taking down the volleyball net and gathering up the beach balls, but soon I would be the only person left standing.

I didn't dare go anywhere now, so I just sat in the aisle right next to one of the rows of seats. My head was low enough that I didn't think Anthony or the guards would be able to see me from where they were.

"Excuse me, but you can't sit here," came a voice from just behind me. It was one of the employees who had now finished putting the volleyball net away. I looked back over my shoulder and just stared at her. She smiled and said, "Did you lose your seat? Come with me, and I'll help you find another one."

This was the last thing I needed, but I didn't want to call any more attention to myself by refusing to go with her, so I stood up, trying to keep my back to where Anthony was. There weren't any empty seats close, so she started taking me toward the back of the auditorium. We'd gone about twenty feet when I heard some sort of yelp. I turned my head enough to see that Anthony had indeed spotted me and was on his way. It was time to run again, but my backpack was closer to Anthony than it was to me, and I didn't want to leave it behind.

Anthony and the guards were coming around the back of the auditorium, so I headed straight for the front. The guards quickly decided to split up and try to trap me. The girl who had been escorting me realized that I was no longer following her and decided to join in the chase. There were two different aisles that led to the front of the auditorium, and there were two people coming after me down each aisle. There was a guard and Anthony coming from one side and the guard and my escort coming from the other.

Just as I was about to be sandwiched between the four of them, I decided that jumping onto the three-and-a-half-foot-high stage was my only way out. I'm sure adrenaline was on my side once again. As I got to my feet I saw the announcer coming toward me.

"Hey, we're not quite ready for another contestant just yet!" he laughed. The guards scrambled onto the stage. I didn't think I had a chance of hiding backstage anywhere because I wouldn't know where I was going. So I decided to use what I *did* know.

The first thing I did was run straight for the announcer's control panel and start hitting buttons. I knew that somewhere was the control I needed: the green slime dumper. There were probably twelve buttons, and I had hit four or five before the announcer got to where I was and made a grab for me. But by then I'd already found the right button and could hear the "green slime sound" that always came before it dumped. I headed straight for the slime machine and ran right under the spout. The slime just barely missed me as I ran underneath. *Perfect!*

Close at my heels, though, were the announcer and the two guards. I couldn't have timed it better if I'd tried. The announcer and the first guard got it right on their heads. The second guard tried to avoid the mess but ended up sliding right through what had just landed on the floor. I could hear the audience screaming and laughing with pleasure.

I noticed that at least two other machines were making some noise, too, in preparation for launching their surprises. I looked out in the audience and saw more guards coming and quickly decided I still needed more confusion if I was going to be able to retrieve my backpack and make a clean getaway.

I returned to the control panel, smiling at the thought of the announcer experiencing green slime for the first time in his life. With him having inflicted the torture on so many others, it seemed fitting that he should have the pleasure at least once. The two guards were falling over each other trying to catch up with me. Before they could grab me, I hit just about every button on the panel at least twice. This set off every dumping, throwing, or whatever-else device they had on stage!

There was confetti being sprayed over the audience, there were streamers, there was fog, there was music. A couple of cream pies went flying across the stage. And the slime machine dumped another load. People were yelling and screaming and running around. Someone released the beach balls, and a free-for-all volley-ball game began. It was great! And it was *exactly* the kind of mess I needed!

I figured it was time to go, so I grabbed a cream pie that was sitting next to the control panel and headed straight for Anthony. He was trying to climb onto the stage and happened to look up just as I approached. The pie I was holding somehow landed right in his face as I repeated my high-jump stunt from earlier and landed on the floor behind him. I raced up the aisle, all the while dodging volley ball players jumping around and streamers shooting down from the ceiling. I pulled my backpack out from under the seat and escaped through a side door.

As I turned the corner and headed down a path, I could still hear the music and screams from the Nickelodeon theater. I didn't dare relax, though, because I could also hear footsteps and shouts not too far behind me.

I ran for at least half a minute at full speed. Then, as I turned another corner, I heard someone hiss my name. I stopped short and looked toward some bushes but didn't see anyone.

"Brandon!" came the voice again. Then I saw a head appear above the hedge.

"Hannah!" I exclaimed as I ran toward her.

"Come with me," she whispered. "I know a good place to hide!"

I followed her down a short walkway between a building and the hedge, then through a doorway at the back of the building. We were in a dark storage room of some kind. There was only one small window, and we found a place to sit on the floor right underneath it, where there was some pretty good light.

"Thanks!" I breathed. "You saved me!"

"Happy to help!" she answered.

"But how did you know I was in trouble?" I asked, my eyes starting to get used to the darker surroundings.

"I saw you running from the homestead with that man chasing you," she answered. "I knew you'd be clever enough to get away, so I just came here and waited until you came running around the corner. We'll be safe in here until your family comes." She smiled. "What did that man want?" she asked.

"He's been trying to steal a book from me," I answered, "but what makes you think my family will be able to find us here?"

"Is that what you have in the bag?" she asked, ignoring my question. "Why does he want it so badly?"

189

"Well, apparently he's a historian," I explained, "and this book is over 150 years old and for some reason he thinks there's a treasure map with the book, but I have no idea what he's talking about. The book was given to me by my great-aunt just a couple of weeks ago when we were visiting her on her farm in Iowa."

"Oh," she nodded.

"Would you like to see it?" I asked.

"Sure," she brightened.

I unzipped my bag and carefully pulled out the old copy of the Book of Mormon. I removed it from the plastic bag and held it out for her to take. She seemed a little hesitant.

"Are you sure it's all right if I hold it?" she asked.

"Sure," I smiled. "I know you'll be careful with it."

She removed the book from its pouch, turned it over carefully in her hands, and as she started to open the front cover, said, "You know, this is my favorite book in the whole world."

"W-w-what?" I stammered as she looked carefully at the title page. "Do you know what this is?" I asked.

"Sure," she said, without looking up. "It's an old copy of the Book of Mormon. I'm a member of the Church, just like you. I was baptized by my father in the Mississippi River when I was eight years old."

"Really?"

"Yes," she continued. "And I've always loved the Book of Mormon. My father read to me from this book from the time I was just tiny. It has so many wonderful stories in it, don't you agree?"

"Yeah," I said slowly. "I think it's great, too, but how did you know . . . I mean . . . I didn't know that you . . ." I couldn't decide what question to ask, so she just went ahead with what she had been saying.

"And heroes!" she exclaimed. "So many *great* heroes are in this book: Helaman and Alma and the brother of Jared! But Nephi is probably my favorite. He teaches so many wonderful things both by his actions and by his teachings, don't you agree? Do you know what my favorite quote from Nephi is?"

"Uh," I began. She was going too fast! I was still confused about how she knew that I was a member of the Church and that this was a copy of the Book of Mormon before she even opened it. And what made her think that my family would be able to find us here?

"It's in First Nephi, chapter 19," she smiled. "Of course you don't have chapters in this copy, but I think I can find it."

Not only could she find it, but it took her only about three seconds.

"Here it is," she said, pointing to the page. "It reads: 'I did liken all scriptures unto us, that it might be for our profit and learning.' That is the way I love to read the scriptures: reading each line as if it were written just for me. What's your favorite scripture from the Book of Mormon, Brandon?"

This girl was amazing! I was not about to let myself look any stupider than I already had. I needed to show her that I knew something about the Book of Mormon and that I could find scriptures in this copy without chapters or verses, just like she had!

"Alma 17:2," I said immediately. "Actually Alma 17, verses 2 through 4," I corrected myself. "I'm sure I can find it," I smiled, reaching for the book in her hands. I must admit that I didn't find it quite as fast as she had found her scripture, but I did my best to hide that fact by explaining the scripture as I was looking for it.

"It's where Alma the Younger finally sees his friends, the sons of Mosiah, after they've all been preaching to the Lamanites for fourteen years. He was excited that they were still being righteous, and the scripture explains all the good things they had been doing."

I had found the right page at this point, so I read the verses out loud.

"That's one of *my* favorites, too," she sighed. "How does it make you feel, Brandon, knowing that you'll be receiving the priesthood soon and be able to teach with the power and authority of God, just like they did?"

I just sat there with my mouth half open as I realized that I'd never even thought about this before. Aunt Ella and I had talked about becoming "strong in the knowledge of the truth," but I'd never thought about what it was for.

"That's what Nephi was saying in the verse that *I* read," she continued. "You need to liken this scripture to yourself! This is saying that if *you* search the scriptures and fast and pray, *you* will have the spirit of prophecy and revelation, and someday *you* will be able to teach with the power and authority of God!"

We both just stared at each other intently for a moment. Then, abruptly, she continued.

"I also love the writings of Isaiah. In that same verse that I read to you, Nephi states that he read the words of Isaiah to his people. Did you know that Jesus Christ commanded the people in America to specifically read the words of Isaiah?" she asked.

"He tells us to search the scriptures," I answered. "But I didn't know . . . or I don't remember . . ."

"Yes!" she beamed. "When he visited the people in America after his resurrection, he told them that all the words of Isaiah will be fulfilled, and they must search them. It's in 3 Nephi 20:11. The prophets in America obviously understood how important this was before Jesus ever said it because so many of them quoted from Isaiah. Whole chapters from the book of Isaiah are found in First and Second Nephi. And there are other quotes from Isaiah in the book of Mosiah and the book of Helaman. And even *Jesus* quoted an entire chapter of Isaiah after he told the people that they needed to search his writings. It was about the last days—our time—when stakes will be established and Israel will be gathered again."

"Wow," I breathed. "You know a lot about the Book of Mormon!"

She shook her head slightly. "It's just because my father loved the book—and I guess he taught me to love it, too," she said quietly. "There's something in the Book of Mormon to help you with *every* situation you'll ever find yourself in," she continued. "That's why I love it." She paused and then asked, "Shall we go see if your family has found us yet?"

"How are they going to find us?" I asked.

"Isaiah knows!" she smiled. "When you get a chance, you can read 2 Nephi 21:6. But let's go back outside now."

As I returned the book to my backpack, I made a mental note of the reference so I could look it up later and then followed Hannah out the door and around to the front of the building. When we came around the corner of the building, I couldn't believe what I saw. My whole family was there and some police officers, too.

"There he is," yelled Meg, pointing in my direction. "I told you he'd be here!" she giggled.

Everyone came rushing up to me and asked if I was all right and what had happened. Jeff and Shauna had apparently seen me being chased by Anthony. When they couldn't find us, they told some park officials what was going on, and so someone called the police. After finding Mom and Dad, everyone started searching for me and Dr. Anthony.

The police asked us all to come with them to the front of the park and fill out some reports about what everyone had seen. I turned to ask Hannah if she wanted to come with us, but she was gone!

"Hey," I said, "did anyone see where that girl went who was with me?"

"What girl?" Jeff asked.

"I didn't notice anyone," Dad said.

"It was the girl from the homestead!" I cried at Jeff. "The one I was telling you about. She was right here! She helped me hide."

"Sorry, Brandon," Mom said, looking around. "She must have left."

I was really confused! Where could she have gone?

"She knew you guys would find me here," I said when I remembered what she'd said. "So how did you know to come here?" I asked.

"Meg told us," Dad said slowly. "We just followed her."

"Meg?" I questioned; then I turned to look at her beaming face. "How did you know where I was?"

"I just followed the Liahona," she said.

"What Liahona?" I asked.

"Those," she said as she pointed over my shoulder.

I turned and saw a little plastic clock face mounted on the post in front of the building. This was a small theater. Each of the theaters and auditoriums in the park had one of these plastic clock faces on the front of the building. They weren't real clocks; they were just used to display the time of the next show. This one read 3:45.

"You used this clock?" I asked.

"Well," she explained, "you said in the car that a Liahona was kinda like a clock because it was a ball with two pointers."

"Okay," I said, confusion obvious on my face, "so you just saw this clock here and decided it must mean that I was around here somewhere?"

"No," she said again. "It was different before. Both the pointers were pointing straight at the ground. That's how I knew to wait here. And all the other ones we saw on the way kept pointing the way we should go."

I paused for a moment. "So you led everyone here?" I asked.

"That's right," Dad explained. "We were clear on the other side of the park when Meg suddenly called to us that she knew where you were. She brought us to this building, and we stood here for about thirty seconds before you came walking out."

"Except the Liahona was different before," Meg said again.

"Will you show us the other 'Liahonas' on the way back?" I asked. "We're supposed to go with the policemen now."

"Sure!" she said as she went skipping away. All the way to the front of the park, Meg kept showing us the plastic clocks she'd followed. And each time she explained that the hands had been different before; they'd both been pointing the same direction, and that's how she knew which way to go.

That night, after we'd finished the police reports, had dinner at the park, and finally made it back to the condo, I lay in my sleeping bag thinking about Hannah. I was sure I'd never see her again. We were planning to leave for Nauvoo first thing in the morning. I'm not sure how long I lay there before I remembered that she'd told me a scripture reference that I should read. I remembered immediately what it was: 2 Nephi 21:6.

I turned on the light and went to the kitchen table and opened my copy of the Book of Mormon with chapters and verses in it. The reference didn't mean much to me until I got to the very last line. Then I sat in amazement for a minute. Shaking my head, I took out my spiral notebook and added this entry:

Wednesday, May 21

Hannah told me how my family would be able to find me:

2 Nephi 21:6: "And a little child shall lead them."

CHAPTER 14

Trail of Tears

Thursday morning we packed up the van so we could go to Nauvoo. Branson turned out not to be such a bad place after all. I'd had a pretty good time all week—at least until Dr. Demented showed up. Most of the shows we saw were pretty okay, and Silver Dollar City was a lot of fun (especially the third time I hit the Nickelodeon Show). And then there was Hannah. I couldn't stop thinking about her. I thought she was really nice, but mostly I kept thinking about how weird everything was about her being there—and then *not* being there and how she seemed to know so much about me and my family and about my book and everything.

There was a call from the Branson police department just before we left, telling us that they had made no progress in tracking down Dr. Anthony. He had disappeared from the theme park, and no one had seen him since. Once everything was loaded in the van, we all came back into the condo for family prayer. Then Dad spread out the atlas on the kitchen table and showed us the route we were going to take to Nauvoo.

The plan was to go diagonally across Missouri from the south-west corner to the northeast corner of the state and then go north to Nauvoo. Dad said it would take most of the day.

"Are we going to stop and see any Church history sites along the way?" Shauna asked.

"I'd like to stop and see one place," Dad answered, "but it's not a Church history site."

"What is it?" asked Jeff.

"It's a little town called Hannibal, Missouri," Dad said, putting his finger on the map right next to the Mississippi River just below the Iowa border.

"I've heard of that," Shauna said, trying to remember what she'd heard about it.

"I haven't," I added.

"Are you sure?" Dad smiled.

"Oh-h-h!" Shauna blurted out. "Isn't Hannibal the place where Mark Twain lived or wrote about or something?"

"Both," replied Dad. "It's where he grew up, and it's the model he used for the town where Tom Sawyer lived."

"Cool!" Jeff and I responded in unison.

"But we'd better get going," Dad said, looking at his watch. "If we get there too late, the visitors' center may be closed."

We all tumbled into the van, waved to the police officer—who agreed to again make sure we weren't being followed—and then watched the Missouri countryside fly past the windows for the next six hours. We'd been going nonstop for the past week, so it was nice to just sit in one place and relax for a while. It was also good to be getting away from Anthony again. We couldn't figure out how he'd found out that we were in Branson. But once he got there, he probably just drove around the biggest parking lots in the area until he spotted our van. Branson isn't that big of a place, and there really aren't too many big, white, 12-seater MAVS around, especially with Utah license plates.

We were pretty sure that Anthony probably didn't know where we were staying, otherwise he likely would have trashed the condo just like he'd done at Aunt Ella's farm and our home in Utah. Dad intentionally avoided the main roads on the way out of Branson and waved at the police car when it pulled off the road behind us. On the way to Hannibal there weren't really any main highways or freeways to choose from since we were cutting across the middle of Missouri. We did see an awful lot of farms, though.

Jeff, Shauna, and I talked most of the day. The three of us were in the back bench of the van munching on some chips and cookies when the conversation changed.

"Tell us about this girl you met at the homestead," Shauna suggested.

"It's really weird," I responded after a short pause. "The more I think about her the more I'm convinced that something really . . . I don't know."

"What?" Shauna asked.

"Well, it's strange the way nobody but me ever seemed to notice her. The lady at the cabin said that she had been by herself the day before, and none of you said you saw her when I came out from around the building. It's just weird. And then I told you about when we were in the storage room. It was like she already knew all about me and my Book of Mormon. And then it turns out that she's a member of the Church? C'mon, how many members are there around here anyway? I don't know—it's just weird."

"It does seem pretty strange," Jeff agreed. "What did you say her name is?"

"Hannah," I responded. "And that's another thing," I continued, as I snapped my fingers. "Do you remember what Aunt Ella's grandmother's name was—the one who first got that Book of Mormon from her father in Nauvoo?"

"Oh," Shauna smiled, "it was Hannah, wasn't it? How funny!"

"That's right!" I agreed. "It's *almost* like she's . . ." I hesitated.

"Like she's what?" Shauna asked.

"Like she's the . . . like she's . . . the same . . ." I couldn't bring myself to say it. "Oh, never mind," I said finally.

"No, tell us," Shauna pressured.

"No," I said, partially with disgust. I couldn't believe that I was even thinking it. "No," I said again, "the whole thing's just weird, that's all. Let's talk about something else."

Jeff and Shauna both tried a couple more times to get me to say what I was thinking, but I was determined to keep it to myself. I couldn't stop thinking about it all the way to Hannibal, though.

Hannibal turned out to be a pretty neat place. There was a visitors' center right next to the house where Mark Twain had grown up. The people there said that this house was the model he had used for Tom Sawyer's house. Everything seemed to fit with the story Dad had read to us. We saw the kitchen and the sitting room and even the bedroom where Tom supposedly climbed out the window in the middle of the night. We also saw Becky Thatcher's house.

Next door to Tom Sawyer's house was a museum filled with all sorts of things that had belonged to Mark Twain. The museum had a big model of a riverboat and a real wooden steering wheel that was about four feet across. It was pretty great. Then we went and saw the famous cave. They were supposed to be closing it down for the day, but they let us go in just for a minute for a quick look. It was a lot smaller than I'd imagined from the story. A least the entrance wasn't very big; I have no idea how deep it went. This was where Tom and Becky supposedly got lost and all they had were a couple of candles for light and a little bit of food they'd taken from the picnic. They were also trying to avoid being caught by Injun Joe, who was in the cave, too. This had been one of my favorite parts of the book when Dad read it to us, but now it made me tense to be there.

We drove straight from Mark Twain's cave to Nauvoo and got there well after dinnertime. We were all starving, so we went to eat before we even took time to dump our stuff at the room where we were going to be staying. Some people Mom and Dad knew told them that the best place to eat in Nauvoo was a buffet in the Nauvoo Hotel, so we drove straight there. It was easy to find because Nauvoo's a pretty tiny place. There's the old section down by the river, where all the historical sites are, and then there's just one main street going a mile or so east to the newer section. The hotel is on this street.

We ate until we were stuffed, and we all had to agree it was the best meal we'd had since leaving Aunt Ella's farm. Just a couple blocks down from the hotel was what Dad called a "bed and breakfast" inn where we had reservations. It was a really old house that had been fixed up with separate rooms. There was a kitchen on the main floor that everyone in the house could use, and then we had a huge room upstairs that was as wide as the whole house. It had four huge beds in it, so it was perfect for our family.

Traveling all day then eating a huge dinner made me pretty sleepy. I lay on the bed that had been assigned to Jeff and me and started thinking about Dr. Anthony and my copy of the Book of Mormon and about Hannah. I'm sure I was zonked within about two minutes.

Sometime in the night I had another dream. Luckily it wasn't the same dream I'd had before because that one always made me wake up scared to death. This dream was completely mixed up with all sorts of different things in it (as if I ever had a dream that wasn't that way). It started out in Nauvoo, and I was with Hannah. But it was the old Nauvoo when it was just being built, around 1840, and Hannah suddenly turned into my great-great-grandmother Hannah, who got my Book of Mormon from her dad, Elias Franzen. Joseph Smith was in the dream, too, and Hannah and I watched and listened for a while as Hannah's dad and Joseph talked about some of the Nauvoo building projects that Hannah's dad was supervising for Joseph.

Then all of a sudden young Hannah and I were on a boat on the river with a bunch of other kids going to a picnic. Except now we were down by Hannibal instead of Nauvoo. After we'd been at the picnic for a while, Hannah gave me the old Book of Mormon and asked me to keep it safe. I put the book into my backpack along with some candles and some bread. Then she asked me to go for a walk with her. As we began walking in the direction of Mark Twain's cave, she started telling me all about her favorite parts of the Book of Mormon. The last thing I remember was standing at the mouth of the cave and listening to her say that the Book of Mormon had an answer for *every* situation that I would ever find myself in. I woke up with the words, "Don't ever forget to use your Liahona" echoing in my head.

I was still pretty groggy. It was obviously either very late or very early. The room was dark and completely silent. All I could hear were Hannah's words being repeated over and over in my head. I was still in my clothes on top of the covers, so I got undressed and crawled between the cool sheets. I was still thinking about the dream as I drifted back to sleep.

The next morning, as we were all getting ready to spend the day checking out Nauvoo, I did some things that I didn't really think about until later. Almost unconsciously, I began to put stuff into my backpack. I had both my regular set of scriptures and the old copy of the Book of Mormon in the bottom. The old book was still in the plastic bag, and I checked it to make sure it was tightly zipped. There was an unopened box of fruit snacks next to our cooler, which I placed on top of my scriptures. Next I found a plastic sack half full of dinner rolls, which I added to my bag. Then I asked my Dad if we had any candles.

"Candles?" he asked with a curious look. "What do you need candles for?"

I had to think for a minute because I hadn't really been thinking about what I was doing. Then the image of Tom and Becky lost in the cave came to mind.

"For light," I finally answered, not sounding too sure of myself.

"Oh," Dad replied, still looking puzzled. "How about a flashlight? There's one under the driver's seat in the van." He tossed me the keys from the little table next to his bed. I could tell by the way he was looking at me that he would have appreciated a little more explanation.

"That's great," I said, forcing a smile. I hurried out of the room so he wouldn't ask me what I was up to—mostly because I realized that I wasn't sure myself.

I found the flashlight and stared at it for a moment as I tried to figure out where my mind was. I started sifting through the other stuff I'd collected in my backpack as I sat in the driver's seat of our van with the door open.

"Dad wants you to come help us straighten up the room before we go," Jeff called from the edge of the parking lot. His voice seemed to wake me up a little bit.

"Coming!" I called. I dropped the flashlight into my backpack, zipped it closed, and turned and slid it under the first bench. I figured my book would be safe for a few minutes, but I locked the van door just to be sure.

Half an hour later we were driving toward old Nauvoo. The first place we stopped was the temple site. It's on the edge of the hill right between the new part of town and the old part. You can see all of the old section down the hill, as well as the Mississippi River and Iowa on the other side of the river. It's a beautiful place.

There was an older missionary couple from Idaho at the temple site who explained everything about the foundation stones that were still in place and the history of the temple until it was destroyed a few years after the Saints left for Utah. There were even some rocks outlining where the baptismal font had been. It was amazing.

Next we went to see the sites that are owned by the Reorganized LDS Church. This church was organized about twenty years after Joseph Smith died, by some people who didn't follow Brigham Young to Utah. The Reorganized Church owns a couple of different houses that Joseph Smith lived in, as well as some other buildings in Nauvoo. That church also owns the area where Joseph and Hyrum are buried. This was all down at the south end of the original city. We walked through the visitors' center, and then a guide took us out to some of the other historical sites. I kept my backpack strapped tightly to my back the whole time.

At one point our guide was explaining some of the early history of Nauvoo. He said that Joseph Smith had this idea of making a canal run right through the middle of the city since they were right next to a big loop in the river. He thought that they could build a straight canal that connected to the river at both ends, and then boats on the river could be directed right through the middle of the city for buying and selling and loading and unloading. The guide said that when the swamp was drained, though, it was discovered that there was a lot of rock under the area, and so they decided it would be too hard to do.

"Do you know who probably told Joseph that it would be too difficult?" Dad whispered to me as we followed our guide to the next location.

"Who?" I asked, not having a clue what he was talking about.

"Your triple-great-grandfather Elias Franzen," Dad said, matter-of-factly. "Don't you remember that he was one of the first ones here, and it was his job to make sure the swamp was drained so that building could begin? As I understand it, they dug a series of east-west ditches leading from the base of the hill to the river. I think they even dug a couple that ran north-south, the direction that Joseph wanted to build his big canal. Elias Franzen's journal states that some of the ditches were deep enough for a man to stand up in without being seen."

"Wow," I breathed.

"That gives you a pretty good idea of how he knew it would be too difficult to build a canal wide enough and deep enough to handle those big riverboats.

"So where are the ditches now?" I asked. "I haven't seen any."

"I don't know," Dad shrugged. "I guess they just filled them in again once the area was drained."

"But then wouldn't it just turn into a swamp again?" I asked. "Wouldn't it be better to just leave them or put something over the top and let the ditches keep draining underneath?"

"Well, I guess so," Dad said. "But what would they cover them up with that wouldn't cave in? It's not like they had any pipe to put in the ditches. They were using all the wood they could find for building. They even hauled lumber from Wisconsin to build the temple. I don't know, but maybe after the area had been drained once, they didn't have to worry about it anymore."

It didn't make sense to me. It seemed that if the area had been swampy once, then it could easily become a swamp again, especially in a place like this, where it rains so much and three sides of the city are next to the huge Mississippi River. I wanted to ask, but Dad was listening to the guide explaining the next building we were in, so we didn't talk about it anymore.

When the guide was finished with our tour, we walked a block to Parley Street, which runs east to west from the hill to the river. We were told that all the property from there to the north is owned by The Church of Jesus Christ of Latter-day Saints. There were a few houses and buildings scattered around the area, but most of the sites were along two main roads: Parley Street, which was named for Parley P. Pratt, and Main Street. Main Street runs north from Parley Street. There are restored buildings and shops all along this street, and a big LDS visitors' center has been built at the north end.

We decided to try to hit everything on Parley Street before lunch. It was really fun. Everywhere we stopped there was a senior missionary couple from the Church. The first place was a kiln where they were making bricks. The missionaries described how the bricks were made and then they gave our family a free brick with an imprint of the Nauvoo Temple on it. Next we went to the

204

blacksmith's shop, where they make horseshoes that they really use. The missionary here told us that the Saints had made hundreds of wagon wheels in this shop when they were preparing to leave Nauvoo for good. There were fifteen or twenty other visitors there at the same time we were, and we all got to watch the man actually make a small horseshoe that was about an inch long. He thought Chelsea was so cute sitting on the front bench that he handed her the horseshoe he'd just made and told her she could keep it. That was the most excited I'd seen her get in a month.

The last place Mom and Dad wanted to see before lunch was the Seventy's Hall. This was a big chapel with some museum stuff on the second floor above the chapel. After I'd pretty much seen everything in the museum, I walked over to a window and looked out toward the river. I could see where Parley Street ended at the river, and it looked really familiar for some reason. But I knew that I'd never been here before. It just gave me a really strange feeling.

"It looks like the road goes right into the river," I said out loud to myself, as I continued to stare out the window. The senior missionary who had talked to us downstairs in the chapel was wandering around not far from where I was standing. He heard what I had said and came and stood behind me.

"Do you know what they called this road?" he asked, looking out the window over my shoulder.

"It's Parley Street, isn't it?" I responded.

"Yes, that's its name," he answered, "but they called it the 'Trail of Tears.' Do you know why?"

"No," I said, turning to look up at him.

"Because this is the road the Saints took when they left Nauvoo for the last time to go west. The reason the road looks like it goes right into the river is that it does. The first wagons were ferried across in early February 1846. But by the end of the month it was so cold that the river froze and then they drove the wagons right across the ice. Now do you have an idea as to why they may have called it the 'Trail of Tears'?"

"Because they were sad to have to leave their homes again?" I asked.

"I believe that's correct, son," he sighed. He just stared out the window without saying anything else. After a moment I turned my face back to the window.

"What are you guys looking at?" Jeff asked as he walked toward us.

"Look how the road runs right into the river," I said. "That's the road that they took when they left Nauvoo and crossed the river to go west."

"Let's go see it," Jeff suggested.

We found Mom and Dad talking with the sister missionary downstairs in the chapel.

"Just don't get too close to the water," Mom warned.

"Okay!" we called as we ran out the door and down the road.

"That guy said they called this the 'Trail of Tears,'" I told Jeff after we were about halfway to the river and we'd slowed to a walk, "because they were sad to be leaving their homes again."

I told him about putting the wagons on ferry boats at first and then crossing on the ice after it got so cold that the river froze.

"Hey, Jeff," I called. "Look over there. There's an old car in the weeds."

Right next to the river was a car almost completely hidden by tall weeds. It looked like it used to be bright red, but now it was covered with rust and had dents all over it.

"What a piece of junk!" Jeff laughed. "I wonder how long it's been here!"

"I don't know," I laughed. Then more quietly I added, "Maybe not very long. Look at those muddy footprints."

We both stared at the mud for a minute and then started looking around. That's when I noticed a man walking down the road behind us. He was maybe thirty feet away.

"Not again!" I breathed. It was Anthony.

"Hold on, boys!" he sneered, quickening his step. "I'd like to see what you have in your backpack!"

"Follow me!" Jeff called as he started down the bank of the river. I did exactly what he suggested, and I could hear Anthony not far behind us. We'd only gone a little way when Jeff hissed, "Look at this, Bran!"

We'd stumbled onto about ten or twelve small logs that had been tied together to make a flat platform. It had been pulled up on the riverbank, but one corner of it was floating in the water.

"Help me," Jeff grunted as he began to push the platform away from the shore. It only took a couple of pushes before the platform swung free and floated out into the current. Visions of Tom Sawyer and Huck Finn floating down the river on a raft popped into my head. Jeff obviously had pretty much the same idea.

"Jump on!" Jeff yelled. We both jumped on the raft at the same time and almost knocked each other off in the process. My backpack thumped me hard on the back when I landed and took my breath away for a second. As we floated slowly away from the shore, Jeff and I turned to see Anthony dancing in frustration on the muddy riverbank, glaring at us.

"I'll get you!" he shouted, shaking his fist. Then he turned and scrambled back toward the road. The look on his face had made me shiver, and we watched in silence until he was out of sight.

"I wonder if Mom would think being on a raft is too close to the water," Jeff said softly. We both quietly watched the shore recede as the current carried us downstream and out toward the middle of the huge Mississippi River.

CHAPTER 15

Your Prayer Is in Vain

After we had been floating for a minute, Jeff said, "Look!" He was staring back toward the bank where we'd come from. I turned to see the rusty red car moving up Parley Street.

"That must have been Anthony's car hidden in the weeds," Jeff said.

"You're right," I agreed. "I wonder where he's going. He said he was going to *get* us, and I had the distinct impression he wasn't talking about waiting until sometime next week."

"But what can he do?" Jeff asked. His voice sounded like he thought it was entirely possible that Anthony had thought of something we hadn't yet.

Within two or three minutes we had the answer.

"There he is," Jeff yelled, pointing to the highway that ran parallel to the river on the Illinois side. Sure enough, I could see the rusty red car bouncing along the highway pretty much even with our position. A chill went through my body.

"I'm cold," I shuddered.

Looking up, Jeff said, "It looks like it's going to rain."

I hadn't noticed any clouds earlier, but now the sky was quickly darkening, and the wind was beginning to blow. The water had gotten rougher, too, more so as we got closer to the middle of the river.

"This is *bad*," Jeff breathed. Jeff has always been pretty quick with the obvious. I looked over at him, ready to ask him to tell me something I *didn't* know, but his expression showed that he already was. He was looking upstream over my shoulder, and his eyes were about as big as golf balls.

I spun on my hands and knees to find out what he was looking at, and I almost fell over once I saw it. About a half mile upstream and coming straight for us was a huge boat. We had seen a couple of boats like this on the river the night before, when we were driving up to Nauvoo. Dad called them "longboats." He told us that they were several hundred feet long and were used for carrying cargo up and down the river.

The boat's cabin was clear at the back of the boat, so it seemed hopeless to think that whoever was steering the thing would have any chance of noticing our tiny raft before the longboat smashed us to smithereens.

"What are we going to do?" I asked, doing my best not to sound nearly as frantic as I felt.

"I don't know," Jeff said flatly. "You're looking at the wrong guy for answers."

As soon as he said that, I thought about Hannah. I could even hear her voice saying, "The Book of Mormon has an answer for *every* situation." At first I thought I'd really heard her voice, but it must have just been in my head.

"The Book of Mormon has an answer for everything," I said, pulling my backpack off my back.

"What?!" Jeff asked in total astonishment.

"That's what Hannah told me to remember," I said, reaching into the bag for my triple combination.

"Who?" Jeff asked.

"Never mind," I said quickly. "Anyway, the Book of Mormon's my Liahona. Aunt Ella told me that; I've *got* to use it."

Jeff just stared at me like I was nuts.

"There's got to be something in here that will help us," I continued, opening the book.

"Like *what?!*" Jeff asked in exasperation. "You think there's something in there about being 'up a creek without a paddle', and there's a storm, and this huge boat's about to smash us, and we're going to die?"

"That's *it!*" I yelled. "You're brilliant!"

"Huh?" Jeff questioned.

"Don't you remember?" I asked, quickly turning to the first part of the book. "Nephi and everybody were on the ship in the storm, and they couldn't steer, and they all thought they were about to die!"

"You're kidding," Jeff said, throwing his hands in the air. "Bran, I hate to break this to you, but this isn't exactly the same kind of thing here."

"It's close enough!" I faked a smile through gritted teeth. "I want to read what they did." I flipped through the pages. "Here it is!"

I had found 1 Nephi 18:15, where Nephi's brothers finally untied him. Then I read verse 16 out loud: "Nevertheless, I did look unto my God, and I did praise him all the day long; and I did not murmur against the Lord because of mine afflictions."

"There we go," I said firmly. "We need to say a prayer."

Jeff blinked a couple of times and then said, "I think we probably could have thought of that on our own, Brandon."

"I know," I agreed, "but let's do it the way it says: Don't complain about our situation, just praise God."

Jeff just stared at me for a moment with his mouth half open. Then he closed it and nodded.

"I'll say it," I offered. Jeff closed his eyes and waited. Then I gave the most praising and thankful prayer I had ever given in my life. I talked about God's goodness and how grateful we were for everything he'd given us. I just kept thinking of blessings that our family enjoyed. I thanked him for things that I'd never even thought of before. I don't know how long I prayed, but all of a sudden I felt something nudge the raft and heard a soft thud. It seemed like a good time to close my prayer.

When I opened my eyes, I saw a board floating in the water right next to me. Jeff's eyes were open now, too, and he said, "Look at all this stuff!"

We were drifting in the middle of at least a dozen 1" x 6" boards of various lengths. I noticed the ragged ends of the boards and said, "Something must have gotten smashed!"

That comment made both of us immediately think about the longboat. We turned and saw that it was only a couple hundred feet away now.

"Grab something quick and start paddling!" Jeff called as he reached for a board. I did as he said, and we started paddling back toward the Illinois side of the river. Within a couple of minutes the longboat was alongside us and moving past, but by now we were probably fifty feet to the side, so we stopped working. We dropped the boards onto the raft and panted thankfully.

We continued to pant and watch until the longboat had completely passed by us. Then we braced ourselves for the wake. It rocked us a little but not too badly, not nearly as much as I had expected, anyway.

"Should we try to paddle over to the shore now?" I asked, once the rocking had pretty much stopped.

"I don't think so," Jeff replied, pointing to the shore.

I followed his gaze and saw that the rusty red car was still moving along the highway parallel to us. This area had quite a few trees along the bank, but the gaps were big enough that there was no mistaking the car on the highway.

"Well, we can't keep floating forever," I said.

"We shouldn't have to," Jeff answered. "I'm sure somebody will spot us and send help eventually."

"It's going to start raining really soon," I said, looking skyward. "And you remember how hard it rains around here. How about we paddle to the *other* side of the river and get some help ourselves."

Jeff agreed with my suggestion, and so we started for the other side of the river. It seemed harder now than before. I'm sure it took at least ten minutes before it looked like we were about in the middle of the river again. We rested for a couple of minutes. When there was a break in the trees we noticed that the red car was still staying even with our position. We decided to work harder.

When we were about three-quarters of the way across we rested again. Here there were no trees between the river and the highway on the Illinois side. We could see several cars but not the rusty red one. We continued to watch for several minutes.

"Maybe it wasn't Anthony after all," I suggested.

"It *had* to be!" Jeff replied.

"I guess so," I said, hoping he was wrong.

We rested and watched for another couple of minutes.

"Oh, no!" Jeff said suddenly.

"What?"

"There's a bridge up ahead! I'll bet Anthony took off down there and crossed the bridge once he saw that we were trying to get to the Iowa side of the river!"

My heart sank. Several miles ahead was a huge drawbridge. We could see that it was open, probably for the longboat that had nearly brought our Tom Sawyer adventure to an early end. The bridge stayed open for another minute or two and then began to close. We were still way too far away to see if any cars were waiting to cross the bridge, let alone spot Anthony's rusty red one.

"What do you think?" Jeff asked.

"I don't know. What do you think?"

"I think," Jeff answered, "that Dr. Anthony is crossing that bridge right now and he's going to be waiting for us. And the trees along here are so thick there's no way we'll be able to see him before he sees us."

I looked along the Iowa shore. Jeff was right about the trees: they were tall and thick all the way down to the drawbridge and beyond.

"So *now* what?" I asked, feeling completely defeated.

Jeff looked upstream. "Perfect!" he yelled.

I looked and saw another longboat coming down the middle of the river a couple of miles away.

"Now," Jeff smiled, "we get back over to the Illinois side as fast as we can! Let's go!"

"*What?*" I practically screamed. "You're nuts! We barely got out of the way of the *last* longboat, and now you want to play chicken with this one?"

"Brandon!" Jeff said with frustration. "Don't you see? That drawbridge is going to be down only long enough to let the cars cross, and then they'll open it again for the second boat. That means Anthony will be stuck on the *Iowa* side until the boat passes the bridge. If we can get over to the shore fast enough, then we should be able to get some help before Anthony can cross the bridge again!"

I stared at him for a second, then turned and looked at the boat. Then I grabbed my board and started paddling back toward Illinois as fast as I could.

I heard Jeff exclaim, "All right!" under his breath, and immediately he was paddling just as hard as I was.

We worked for several minutes without speaking.

"Don't look at the boat," Jeff cautioned quietly. "It's just like being up high—you know how they tell you not to look down."

As I paddled, I kept thinking about what he had just said. Before he said anything it never crossed my mind to look at the boat. I was just paddling as hard as I could to the other side of the river. But now the urge to look just wouldn't go away. I couldn't help it! I tried not to! But I looked at the boat anyway.

I'm happy to say that looking at the boat was the right thing to do. You see, when you're up high and look down, then you might get scared and nervous and lose your grip or freeze up or something. But when you're about to be smashed by a boat and you look at it, it has an incredibly effective way of motivating you to *move* a whole lot quicker. At least that's the effect it had on me.

"Whaaah!!" I yelled when I saw that the boat was only a hundred yards away and we were exactly in front of it. "Let's *move!*"

I began paddling at least twice as fast as I had been before. Looking at the boat was *definitely* the right thing to do.

"Did you look at the *boat?!*" Jeff asked.

"Of *course* I looked at the boat!" I said between strokes. "And you'd look too, if you knew what was good for you!"

"Aaaagh!" Jeff screamed. I didn't look at him, but I got the distinct impression that he had looked at the boat. I did notice that he also seemed to be paddling considerably faster now than before. The sound of the longboat kept growing steadily louder over the next few minutes. I decided it was time to look again. Without daring to stop paddling, I glanced backward over my shoulder. To my horror, all I could see was a huge wall of steel!

The longboat was less than ten feet away. I could have thrown my board and hit it, even with zero strength left in my arms. But it wasn't behind us anymore, it was passing *beside* us.

"We made it!" I yelled.

That's when the wake hit. Jeff and I discovered that the wake from a longboat is considerably bigger when you're ten feet away than when you're fifty feet away. I was sure we were going to be dumped right there, but somehow we managed to hang on and ride it out. Actually, it even gave us a pretty good push, so we ended up quite a bit closer to the shore once the boat was completely past us. Given the option, though, I still think I would have preferred to paddle the entire distance rather than catch the wake and genuinely fear for my life.

Once the longboat had passed and the wake had died, we sprawled out on the raft. My lungs were burning, and I could hear Jeff panting just as hard as I was. Neither of us moved or said a word for at least two minutes. Once my panting had slowed a little and my lungs weren't hurting quite so much, I propped myself up on my elbows and looked around. The longboat was just reaching the open bridge. There were cars lined up on both sides of the river, waiting for the bridge to close again. Then I watched the highway on our side of the river for a moment; there was no sign of the rusty red car.

"Let's get to the shore," Jeff said.

We were only about thirty yards away now, and we were able to cover that distance in less than a minute. Jeff grabbed the branch of a small tree and ran one corner of our raft onto the bank. It wasn't solid, but it was good enough for us to reach dry ground without getting any more wet than we already were. Actually, considering everything we'd been through for the past hour or so, I thought we'd done pretty well at keeping ourselves dry. I thought Mom ought to be pleased, but for some reason I had the feeling that wasn't very likely.

We climbed up the bank to the highway and saw that we were only a couple hundred feet from the bridge now. Only the middle section of the bridge actually opened and closed. The part that didn't open probably extended about a third of the way across the river from each side. Cars were lined up on the bridge waiting for it to close again so they could get to the other side. The line went clear back to the shore and onto the highway where we were standing.

"So how do we get back to Nauvoo?" I asked.

"I don't know," Jeff said. "I don't really want to hitchhike."

"I know, me, neither," I agreed, "but it's way too far to walk." I looked at the drawbridge.

"Well, we'd better decide fast," Jeff said, "before that bridge closes and Anthony gets back over here."

"I wonder what's taking them so long to close it," I said.

We watched for a moment and then noticed that another boat was coming upstream. The bridge was obviously going to stay open until this boat had passed also. That was good for us because it kept

Anthony away that much longer—at least if he had done what we *hoped* he had and was stuck on the other side of the river.

"Maybe I should check my Liahona again," I suggested, reaching for the zipper on my backpack.

"I don't think we have time, Bran," Jeff said. "Let's just say a prayer." As he spoke, he walked away and knelt down behind a large bush that shielded him from the road. I closed the zipper and joined him.

This time Jeff said the prayer. I was glad that he started out by making a big deal about our recent near-disaster with the longboat. I was convinced that we hadn't found those boards by accident. Then Jeff asked for help to get back to Nauvoo. He was even so specific as to ask Heavenly Father to send someone to pick us up so we wouldn't have to worry about Anthony finding us. When he was done he stood up and headed straight for the road. I followed until we reached the side of the highway.

"What do we do now?" I asked.

"We just wait for someone to come pick us up," Jeff said.

"Okay," I said, trying to sound as positive as I could. I certainly wasn't going to be the one to question Jeff's faith. I was actually pretty impressed that he seemed so confident. Jeff watched the cars down at the drawbridge, and I watched Jeff. Then I noticed his expression change, so I turned to see where he was looking.

It looked like the last car in the line for the drawbridge was backing up. It backed across the road and turned around, then headed in our direction. It was an old full-size truck with a camper on the back. If I'd been thinking about the fact that Anthony was around somewhere looking for us, I probably would have run for the trees, but instead I just stood next to Jeff by the side of the road as the truck drove past on the other side.

After the truck had gone by I turned to look at the bridge again. That's when I heard the brakes squeak softly as the truck came to a stop. Jeff and I both watched for a moment as the truck sat in the middle of the road about a hundred feet away. The brake lights were on but there was no other sign of life for at least a minute. Then slowly the truck began to back up until it was alongside us. The sky was dark enough from the clouds that it was hard to see through the windows, but I could make out what looked like an older couple sitting in the cab. The woman was rolling down the window as the truck came to a stop.

"You boys need a hand with something?" she asked, continuing to open the window. "My land, Steve!" she exclaimed, turning to her husband and then back to us again, "it's the Andrews boys! *What* in the *world* are you two doing out here in the middle of nowhere?"

"Hello, Sister Miller," Jeff said. "Hi, Brother Miller," we said in unison.

What a relief it was to see someone we knew! Brother and Sister Miller were really great people who lived in our ward in Orem. They didn't have any kids living at home anymore, and so we hadn't really even known who they were until Brother Miller had gotten sick a year or so earlier. I think he had an operation or something. Anyway, while he was stuck in bed for a few weeks, Dad would take Jeff or me, and we would go over and help Sister Miller with some things that needed to be done around the yard.

After Brother Miller got better, Jeff and I still kept going over every once in a while after school or on Saturdays. Brother Miller would let us help him with whatever he was working on, and we could generally count on Sister Miller to be dishing out plenty of high praise and good cookies in our direction as well.

We both started to explain what we were doing there, but Sister Miller barely took enough time to breathe before continuing.

"We don't *ever* pick up hitchhikers, you know, 'cause you just don't know who you can trust these days. But I just had the feelin', and I made Steve stop even though he didn't want to," she said as she whacked him on the arm. "That's why we were just sittin' up the road a piece for s'long. I was tryin' to get him to turn around and at least drive by and see what the story was with you two boys. And now look what we've found."

She beamed in our direction as she spoke. We knew from experience that there was no use trying to say anything yet. She'd be talking for at least another minute or two before we'd get a chance to respond.

"You know," she continued after a short breath, "we'd just come from Nauvoo, but while we were waitin' in that line down at the bridge—did you see that huge bridge down there? My land, that's an amazin' sight watching that whole thing open up and let those boats drift on through. Well, we were waitin' in the line, you know, and I seen that I didn't have my camera with me. Then I remembered settin' it down at the visitors' center in Nauvoo just before we left, and I just know that's where it's *got* to be!"

Jeff and I smiled at Brother Miller. He was smiling, too. His expression hadn't changed the entire time she'd been talking. He was always like that. It was as if someone hit the pause button, and he was just frozen with this pleasant look on his face until she was done with whatever she was talking about. Then she whacked him on the arm again. His expression still didn't change, though he did glance at her.

"Why it's *Providence*, Steven Miller," she said, using the whack on his arm as emphasis, "and you *know* it is. So now don't you *ever* say anything *ever* again about me forgettin' somethin' somewhere!"

His smile did droop just a little at that comment, and I had the feeling that he realized he'd be hearing about this one for the rest of his life.

"Thanks for stopping, Brother and Sister Miller," Jeff said. "We had just said a prayer asking for someone to stop and give us a ride back to Nauvoo. I'm sure our parents are worried about us."

"Well, my land, why don't you just hop in the back of the camper as fast as spring bunnies, and we'll go find your parents as quick as can be," Sister Miller said. "You can tell us all about it once your good folks know that you're safe and sound."

"That's great," Jeff said. "We last saw them at the Seventy's Hall an hour or two ago."

"Do they have that big white van of yours with 'em?" Brother Miller asked, his pause button now released.

"Yeah," Jeff and I both responded.

"That thing's easier to spot than a flare at midnight," Brother Miller said confidently. "Climb in the camper, and we'll go track 'em down."

Jeff and I climbed into the camper, and Brother Miller shut the door behind us "just to make sure it's tight." He also told us to lock the door from the inside, so we did. There was a short bench on either side of a table. We each sat on one as Brother Miller drove back toward Nauvoo. I opened my backpack on the table and made sure nothing inside was wet. There were a couple of good-sized water spots on the outside, so I was glad that I'd been keeping Aunt Ella's book in a plastic bag. The book was fine, and so was everything else inside my backpack.

"Boy, I'm glad to be in *here*," I said as the truck gained speed.

"Me, too," Jeff said. "Heavenly Father sure took care of us this time, didn't He?"

"Yeah," I agreed. "We should say another prayer."

We folded our arms and said a prayer of thanks as the camper rocked gently back and forth. Then we each sprawled out on the benches. It was great to be out of sight and out of Anthony's reach for a while. I started thinking about everything that had happened the last couple of hours.

"It's a good thing we found those boards that we could paddle with," I said, breaking the silence.

"Yeah," Jeff immediately agreed, as if he'd been thinking about the same thing.

"And it's a good thing we followed my Liahona, so we knew what to do," I added.

"You mean pray for help?" Jeff asked.

"No, not just that," I said defensively.

"Well that's what we did on the raft," Jeff continued. "And that's what we did before Brother and Sister Miller came along."

"I know," I said. "But it's *more* than that." I tried to think of a way to explain what I was thinking, but I couldn't. I guess praying was all that we had done, but it felt like more.

"I wonder what we would have found if we had tried to use the Book of Mormon before the Millers came," I said as I sat up and reached into my backpack. "Hannah said there's something for *every* situation."

"So what are you going to look for?" Jeff asked. "I don't think you'll find anything about being stranded next to a drawbridge, forty miles away from anyone you know, and with no way to get away from a fruitcake who wants to steal your copy of the Book of Mormon."

"That's the same thing you said about being almost smashed by a longboat," I reminded him. "Your problem is that you're trying to be too specific." I opened the index of my triple combination.

"It doesn't have anything about a *bridge*," I said, turning a few pages, "and it doesn't have the word *drawbridge*, either. But," I continued slowly, "it does have the word *draw*."

"Whatever!" Jeff laughed.

"I *just* want to see what I can find," I mumbled.

I looked up the first two references listed under "draw, drew, drawn," but they didn't seem to have anything to do with our situation. Then I read the third reference, which was Alma 34:27.

I couldn't help smiling. "Hey, Jeff," I said. "Listen to this one. It says, 'Let your hearts be full, drawn out in prayer unto him continually for your welfare, and also for the welfare of those who are around you.'"

"Brandon," Jeff laughed, "that's another prayer scripture! Every scripture you find says to pray, and then you act like it's all new stuff!"

"No!" I said emphatically. "There's more! Listen to the next verse: 'And now behold, my beloved brethren, I say unto you, do not suppose that this is all; for after ye have done all these things, if ye turn away the needy, and the naked, and visit not the sick and afflicted, and impart of your substance, if ye have, to those who stand in need—I say unto you, if ye do not any of these things, behold, your prayer is vain, and availeth you nothing, and ye are as hypocrites who do deny the faith.'"

I looked at Jeff, but he just stared back at me. I could tell his mind was spinning.

"Don't you get it?" I smiled. "How many times have we gone with Dad to help people? Remember when he went to a meeting at that one guy's house, and the doorbell wasn't working, so he made us go back with him the next Saturday, and we installed a new doorbell for him?"

"Oh, yeah!" Jeff smiled, remembering.

"And think how many times we went to help Brother and Sister Miller," I continued. "And now look who just happens to show up to help us."

Jeff was quiet for a moment, thinking. "You're right," he agreed.

"*That's* what this scripture is talking about," I went on. "It says to pray for your own welfare and for those around you, sure. But *then* it says if you're just praying and *not* doing what you can to help people who need your help, then your prayer is *vain!*"

"Okay!" Jeff smiled. "I said you were right!"

I just folded my arms across my chest and smiled confidently across the table at him. My head was bobbing slightly as I thought about it all.

"The scripture fits, huh?" I asked.

"Yes," Jeff answered, almost reluctantly.

"It's *not* just like all the others, is it?" I asked again.

"Yes!" Jeff replied, bugging his eyes out at me with a look that just dared me to try to make him say it one more time. It was enough, though. I just smiled back at him and raised my eyebrows a couple of times; then I sprawled out on the bench again. Neither of us spoke for a couple of minutes.

"You know," I said finally, "it's pretty cool how much help we seem to be getting taking care of this book."

"What do you mean?" Jeff asked. He was sprawled out, too, staring at the ceiling of the camper. "I mean, the Millers came to help," he continued, "but what else?"

"Well," I sighed, "the Millers are helping us now, but I was also thinking about Hannah."

Jeff didn't say anything.

"You know," I said, "the girl who helped me get away from Anthony when we were at Silver Dollar City."

"Yeah, I know," Jeff mumbled.

"Remember what I was telling you about her when we were driving to Nauvoo yesterday?"

"Don't you mean what you *wouldn't* tell me when we were driving to Nauvoo yesterday?" Jeff corrected me.

"Yeah, I guess," I answered. "Anyway, she seemed to know so much about me and our family and the book—it's just weird!"

"You told us that part yesterday," Jeff yawned.

"And our great-great-grandmother who first got this book from her dad was named Hannah, also," I continued.

"You told us *that* part yesterday, too," Jeff said.

"I know," I said slowly. "But what I didn't tell you was that it's like . . . I mean I'm almost *convinced* that . . . that she's . . . that she's the *same* . . ."

Just then the camper came to a stop, and we heard the truck engine turn off.

"They must have found Mom and Dad," I said as I hopped off the bench and threw my backpack over my shoulder.

"Wait," Jeff said. "Finish what you were saying. She's the same *what?*"

I hesitated with my hand on the doorknob. "I'll tell you later," I said.

CHAPTER 16

The Martyrs

I unlocked the door to the camper and climbed out. Jeff was right behind me. As I came around the side of the truck I heard Brother Miller say, "Hello, Craig. I think we found something that belongs to you."

We were parked in front of the Seventy's Hall. The van was right where Dad had parked it a couple of hours earlier, but now there was a police car next to it. Mom and Dad were standing next to the car talking to an officer. Another officer was sitting in the car filling out some paperwork.

"Actually we found *two* somethings," Sister Miller corrected.

"Brandon!" Mom exclaimed. "Jeff! Are you two all right?" She rushed over to us and squeezed as hard as possible in an effort to ensure that we were not just inflatable look-alikes.

"We're fine," we assured her.

"Where have you been?" Dad asked, in the middle of hugs of his own.

Mom and Dad both seemed a little frantic, and I guess that's not too surprising. After all, we'd been missing for a couple of hours, and the Mississippi River seemed to be the only place we could have gone. Normally I think I would have milked this situation for all it was worth. I can get pretty dramatic in my explanations, and I certainly enjoy telling a good story. And with Anthony around there was plenty to tell. But for some reason I felt strangely calm about the whole thing. We had definitely been protected and helped, and I didn't have any desire to make it seem otherwise.

Jeff seemed to be feeling the same way, so we both told the story as calmly as possible. We had to repeat things so the police could make their reports, and we had to pause every once in a while, long enough to allow Sister Miller to insert a couple of exclamations. She would add things like, "My land! I can't even *imagine* anything so harrowing!" or "Steve, are you hearing what these boys have been up to?" Brother Miller had the pause button on again.

As soon as Jeff and I said that Dr. Anthony had chased us down at the riverbank, Dad turned to the officer and added, "That's the crazy historian we were telling you about." Apparently, Mom and Dad already suspected that Anthony was involved, and so his description had already been radioed to all the local police departments and the highway patrol. Once we'd finished the story, the officer got back in the car and gave out a description of the rusty red car.

"Suspect last seen heading south on highway 96 a few miles north of Keokuk," the officer added. "It is believed that he may have crossed the bridge into Iowa. Car 12 out."

It probably took half an hour for the police to fill out all of the papers they wanted and for Sister Miller to stop saying, "My *land!*" every few seconds. Then Dad talked to the police for a minute about what we should do next. The police wanted to know if we thought we needed an escort or what else they could do to help us.

"Actually," Dad said, "we were thinking about going over to Carthage for the afternoon."

"Well," one of the officers replied, "if you do that, then don't take Highway 96 south. This Anthony character may be still hanging around down in that area. Sounds like he's been pretty persistent up to now. Instead," he suggested, pointing toward the new part of Nauvoo, "if you head east out of town on Mulholland Street, you can get to Carthage almost as fast. There are signs that will take you there easily enough, but it'll keep you off the main highway."

"Sounds great," Dad said. Then he added, "We've got tickets for a show over at the LDS visitors' center this evening at six. Do you think it's okay for us to go ahead and go to that?"

"I think so," the other officer reassured us. "We'll plan to have an officer at the visitors' center by 5:45 to let you know what we've been able to find out between now and then. The Carthage Police Department has already been notified to keep a lookout for the suspect's vehicle. We'll update the department on your plans for the afternoon."

"Okay," Dad said. "If we see any signs of him, then we'll contact you as soon as we can."

"Let me give you something that will make that a little easier," said the officer, leaning into his car. He pulled out a police walkie-talkie and said, "Keep this with you, and then you can let us know immediately if anything happens."

He showed us all which button to push when we wanted to talk into it and told us to use it if we saw anything at all that looked suspicious. Dad thanked him, and the officer climbed back into his car and started making notes on a clipboard. Then Mom and Dad started to discuss what to do next.

Granny and Shauna had taken Meg, Chelsea, and Daniel down Main Street to keep them occupied and distracted while Mom and Dad talked to the police. They weren't back yet, so the four of us climbed in the van to go find them. They were just coming out of the bakery as we drove slowly past, and Dad stopped in the middle of the road and rolled down his window.

"The boys are fine!" he called to them.

"Are they with you?" Granny asked.

"Yes, they're right here," Dad answered. "Come climb in, and they can tell you all about it."

They all scurried around the car and Granny opened the side door. "I was a little worried about you," she smiled. "Come give me hugs."

Granny hugged us long and hard, and then, of course, Chelsea and Daniel wanted hugs, too, just so they didn't feel like they were missing out on anything. They all climbed in and got their seatbelts on, and then Jeff and I told the whole story again. Granny just kept staring back and forth between Jeff and me with a look of shock and disbelief on her face. A couple of minutes into our explanation she started shaking her head slightly back and forth, emphasizing how incredible she thought the whole thing was. Shauna just kept saying, "Oh, *man!*" the whole time we were telling the story.

Once we were done, Granny wanted to know what the police were doing about the situation, so Dad explained everything they had talked about. We were just pulling into Carthage as he finished what he was saying.

"There's the visitors' center," Dad said. I looked and saw a large open area with walkways, grass, flowers, and benches. There was a statue in the middle and then two buildings back behind. One building looked pretty new, and the other was obviously quite old.

"Let's get something to eat before we go in," Mom suggested. "Anybody hungry?"

"Yes!" I panted. "I'm starving!"

"Me, too," agreed Jeff. I think all that energy we'd exerted earlier was catching up to us. I was really thirsty all of a sudden, too.

Everyone agreed that eating sounded better than anything else for the moment, so Dad drove around to see what he could find. What he found was that Carthage is a pretty small place. One or two blocks in any direction from the visitors' center put us right into residential areas. We could pretty much see the entire business district from one spot. After spending a total of about five minutes searching almost every street in town, Dad parked in front of a little diner right across the street from the visitors' center.

"Everybody out," Dad called back.

"Dad," Meg answered, "Danny's asleep. Do you want me to wake him up?"

"He walked around quite a bit this morning," Granny answered. "I think he can probably use the rest."

Mom and Dad agreed, so Dad unbuckled the seatbelt holding Danny's car seat in place and then carried Danny and the car seat into the diner. Danny didn't even stir as he was jostled back and forth. The diner was long and skinny inside and had booths all down one wall. There were some small tables in front and one large round table toward the back that looked like it might be big enough for our family. That's where we were seated. The table already had eight chairs around it, which was perfect for us, since Danny had come with his own chair.

"This is a great table," Dad said to the server when she came to take our order.

"Glad you like it," she smiled. "Nobody from around here uses it much, but the tourists that come in always seem to be in large groups. Not sure why that is."

We just smiled knowingly and then gave our order. Jeff and I had each emptied our own water glasses and were in the process of trying to guzzle down everyone else's by the time the server had finished taking orders. She returned after a moment with two pitchers of water and placed one directly in front of Jeff and me after refilling our glasses.

"Thanks," we chimed in unison. She just smiled.

I wasn't thirsty anymore by the time our food came, but I was more than ready to dig into the French dip sandwich I'd ordered.

"Wait," Meg said. "Shouldn't we say a blessing first?" She was facing Mom and Dad, but her eyes were on me. I stopped with my sandwich about two inches from my mouth and stared right back at her.

"We don't usually say a blessing when we're in a restaurant," Mom answered. I started to move my sandwich a little closer.

"Why not?" Meg asked, still with her eyes on me. I felt a little of the juice run down my thumb. I was trying to imagine it running down my throat.

"Well," Mom explained, "because there are other people around who can see and hear us, and praying is something special that we usually do only in places where everyone else is praying with us."

"Why?" she asked again. Then she looked around the restaurant. There was a lady standing behind the counter with her back to us and two couples sitting in booths toward the front. "Nobody's looking at us," she said as she shook her head, "and they're not close enough to hear what we're saying."

I could tell what was coming from the look on Dad's face. I put my sandwich down and wiped the drip from my thumb with my napkin. As I looked around I had to agree that she had a point, but I didn't bother to say anything.

"You're right," Dad said after a moment. "Would you like to ask a blessing on the food for us?"

"Okay," she smiled as she folded her arms and wriggled herself up a little taller in her seat.

"Softly," Dad instructed.

When Meg finished her short, soft prayer, I glanced around to see if anyone in the restaurant had noticed what we were doing. I didn't think so. I sat quietly staring at my sandwich for a moment before picking it up again.

"Wow," said Jeff with a grin, "that didn't hurt at all!"

Dad chuckled a little, and I began to eat.

After lunch we walked across the street to the visitors' center. Danny had slept soundly the entire meal, not waking until Dad pulled his car seat out from under the table. Dad held Danny on his shoulder and asked Jeff and me to put his car seat in the van. Everyone was approaching the statue in the middle of the small park when Jeff and I caught up to them.

"Who are those men?" Meg asked.

"Isn't it Joseph Smith and Hyrum?" Shauna asked.

"Yes, it is," Dad answered.

Chelsea was standing right in front of the statue, staring up into the faces.

"Why did they put a statue here?" Meg asked.

"Because this is where they were killed," Mom answered.

"It *is*?" Meg responded with wide eyes. "When?"

"A long time ago," Mom said. "It's been more than one hundred and fifty years."

"Oh," Meg breathed with a very serious look on her face. She turned to look at the statues again.

"I want to get down," Daniel said to Dad as he wriggled in his arms. As soon as his feet hit the ground he scampered over and stood next to Chelsea, staring up into the same faces. The bronze statue was life-sized and very real looking. We all just stood for a few moments without saying anything. I had a strange feeling.

"Let's go inside," Dad suggested, and we all followed. There were some nice senior missionaries ready to greet us as we entered the newer of the two buildings. They asked us if we'd been to Carthage or to the visitors' center before and what we knew about it. Then they showed us some stuff, and we watched a short film. They talked to us for quite a while and told us all about everything that led up to Joseph Smith being arrested in Nauvoo and being brought to Carthage and locked up in the jail. I found out that the old building next door was Carthage Jail. The missionaries led us outside and over to the old jail. They stopped us next to a small well and pointed up to a second-story window.

"That's the window that Joseph fell out of when he was killed," the man said. "He landed on the ground here. This well didn't exist at the time—it was dug sometime later. Let's go inside, and I'll show you the room on the other side of that window."

We followed in silence. Inside there was a long, narrow staircase leading up to a small landing with two doors. The missionary stopped on the landing and turned around to talk to us as we were still standing on the stairs.

"Joseph and Hyrum and several others were in this room when the mob entered," he said, pointing at the door right at the top of the staircase. "Earlier Joseph had been locked in the cell in the other room, but by this time the jailer, who lived on the main floor, allowed Joseph his freedom to move about. The jailer even allowed the group with Joseph to keep a small gun with them. When the mob came up the stairs," he continued, "Hyrum tried to hold the door shut but was killed when a ball came through the door. After seeing that Hyrum was dead, Joseph retrieved the gun and shot back into the hallway a couple of times. One or two of the men in the mob were killed. Joseph was killed at the far window when he tried to escape through it and was shot from both inside and outside simultaneously."

The missionary explained more about who else was there and what happened to them, and then he let our family go into the room and look around. I was surprised at how big the hole in the door was. A large marble could have fit through it. Then I went over and looked out the window that Joseph had fallen from. I had a sick, sad feeling as I looked down to the ground.

I also looked in the other room. This one actually had a jail cell in it with bars, and there were chains and shackles inside the cell. I didn't like this place at all, so I took Danny with me and went back outside by the well. I was only inside for a few minutes, but that was enough for me. After a while, everyone else wandered out to where we were. I sat on a bench and watched Danny run in circles around the statue. Shauna and Jeff came and sat next to me without saying anything.

"I'm glad we came here," Shauna said after a few minutes. Jeff and I both looked at her, but nobody said anything else for a couple of minutes. I still had a sick feeling, but I didn't feel like trying to explain it to them.

Finally Shauna continued, "Being here makes Joseph Smith seem so *real*," she said. "I know that what happened here was terrible, and it's awful the way he died, but I can't stop thinking about *why* he died. His commitment was so strong that he was willing to die for the Lord and for what he believed in. He gave everything he had. And that book you got from Aunt Ella was made possible by him, too." She paused before adding softly, "What an amazing man. I will *never* forget this place."

Shauna made me think about all this a little differently. I took Danny's hand and walked slowly over to the jail again as I thought about Joseph Smith and the Book of Mormon. I had a different feeling this time as I stared up at the window. I heard the breeze rustle in the trees behind me and felt very calm and peaceful.

A few minutes later we were on our way back toward Nauvoo, being careful to avoid the main highway again. Dad stopped at a small store to pick up some groceries, and then we went back to the bed and breakfast place where we were staying.

"Jeff and Bran," Dad said as he was climbing out of the car, "come help me put the groceries away."

As I was handing Dad the last carton of milk for the fridge, Jeff said, "Hey, Brandon, do you want to go out and play soccer for a while?"

I turned and saw him leaning over the kitchen table and looking between the curtains out the back of the house.

"Sure," I answered. "Can we, Dad?"

Dad looked at his watch as he closed the refrigerator door. "We've got a couple of hours until we need to leave for the show at the visitors' center," he said. "It's fine with me."

"I'll go upstairs and get the ball," Jeff offered, turning away from the window.

"Here," I said, holding up my backpack. "Take this with you."

Jeff grabbed my bag and ran upstairs to get the soccer ball. Shauna and Meg saw what he was up to and followed him back downstairs. There was a huge grassy area behind the house, surrounded by tall trees that kept it all pretty well shaded even in the middle of the afternoon. It turned out that all this grass belonged to an elementary school. We could see the back of the school straight across the field as we came out the back of the house. Shauna, Jeff, and I immediately started kicking the ball to each other, forming a triangle that grew in size with each kick.

"Can I go play over there?" Meg asked. She was standing not far from the back door, pointing past us. We all turned to see what she was talking about. Next to the elementary school was a playground with slides, swings, and some other stuff.

"Sure," Shauna said, kicking the ball toward the playground. "C'mon, guys, let's move over there so we can be close to Meg." Turning to Meg she added, "C'mon Meg, we'll go with you."

Meg took off running as fast as an eight-year-old can. She zoomed past us, and we followed, kicking the ball back and forth as we went. I noticed her go straight to the tallest slide she could find and head for the top; then I turned my full attention back to the soccer ball.

"What's the matter, Meg?" Jeff asked about sixty seconds later. Meg was standing right at the edge of the playground area with her head slightly bowed and her lower lip slightly forward.

Meg tilted her head sideways as she answered as pitifully as she could, "I need someone to push me."

We tried desperately to get her to play on some of the other stuff that was there, but I guess she was kind of tired from all the walking she'd done. She really just wanted to sit on the swing and be pushed. So the three of us took turns pushing her as the other two kicked the ball back and forth. We must have been there for at least an hour before Meg decided she wanted to go back inside.

"I'm kind of tired, too," Shauna said. "I'll go with you." She grabbed Meg's hand and headed for the house. "See you guys later," she called over her shoulder.

After they had been gone for a while, Jeff and I started swinging and trying out the other stuff on the playground. It was a pretty nice place, and the ground was all covered with what looked like bark chips, except they were really soft and spongy. I decided it must have come from some kind of tree that I'd never seen before. I was in the middle of digging to see how deep it went when Jeff said, "Looks like it's time to go, Bran."

"Jeff! Brandon!" Dad called. He was standing in the parking area next to the back of the house. "Let's go!"

We jogged over to where he was standing, kicking the soccer ball in front of us as we went. Everyone else was climbing into the van, and Dad turned in that direction as we approached.

"Do we have to go?" Jeff asked. "Can't we just stay here and play soccer or something?"

Dad stopped and turned back. "I don't know if that's such a good idea," he answered thoughtfully. "We don't know if Dr. Anthony's still around here or not."

"We can keep the police walkie-talkie with us," I said. "We can use it if we see him or anything."

"Well, we're supposed to meet with the police right now," Dad said, looking at his watch. "I guess we're still a little early, and the visitors' center is only about five minutes away. Okay, I'll take everyone else down to the show and find out from the officer if they've made any progress finding this guy yet. Now, if they haven't found him, then I'm coming straight back to get you. I'm not going to leave you two alone here for the next two hours if Dr. Anthony is still roaming around looking for you, okay?"

"Great!" Jeff and I agreed. "We'll be over there," Jeff added, pointing toward the playground.

"Okay," Dad said, reaching into his pocket. "Here's one of the room keys. Please don't lose it—I don't want to have to pay for it."

"We'll be careful," Jeff assured him as he put the key in his pocket. "Thanks, Dad."

"Yeah, thanks!" I agreed.

Dad opened the van door and handed the walkie-talkie to Jeff.

"Do you know how to use it?" Dad asked.

After giving us both a quick walkie-talkie refresher course, Dad shut the van door and backed out.

"Jeff, come with me to get my backpack," I said, once they were out of sight. "I don't want to leave it up in the room with nobody there."

Jeff followed me up the stairs and unlocked the door. I grabbed my bag and went back down the stairs as he locked the door again. We walked across the field and climbed up on this wooden play structure that was probably ten feet high. Jeff had brought the soccer ball, but left it at the edge of the grass. I had my backpack strapped to my back as Jeff and I sat on top of the structure, talking to each other. We sat facing the house so that we could see the van pull up if Dad decided to come back for us. Jeff was holding the walkie-talkie.

"Do you think they've found Dr. Anthony yet?" I asked.

"I don't know," Jeff answered, sounding a little bit discouraged. "Doesn't seem like anybody can find him. Those guys in Iowa had him once, but they couldn't even hang on to him."

"I know," I agreed. "I'm getting really tired of it."

We both jumped when we heard a voice coming from right behind us: "If you will simply give me what I want I'll be happy to leave you alone!"

When Jeff jumped, he lost hold of the walkie-talkie. We both grabbed at it, but it slipped out of his hands and fell to the ground with a thud. Slowly, we turned to see Dr. Anthony standing on the ground right next to the play structure where we were sitting.

CHAPTER 17

The Cavity of a Rock

I started shaking so much, I almost fell.

"You'll not be getting away this time," Anthony sneered. "I've chased you across three states now, and I'm getting *extremely* tired of it!" He was slowly climbing up the side of the play structure as he spoke. "Third time's the charm, though," he smiled sickeningly.

"No way!" Jeff growled back at him. "Don't give it to him, Brandon!"

I looked around frantically, and suddenly I had an idea.

"Go over to that side," I told Jeff, pointing past him as I started to move backward. "But stay on top."

I moved over to one side and climbed down just far enough so that my waist was against the top bar of the play structure. Anthony was about halfway up the front side when he saw what I was doing and started moving around toward me. I took the backpack off my back and held the straps in one hand as I held onto the top bar with the other.

Just when Anthony got to the corner of the side I was on, I yelled, "You want my bag? Go and get it!" Then with all the strength I could manage I threw the pack across the top of the play structure to the side where Jeff was. I was planning on it landing on the soft ground behind Jeff, but somehow he managed to reach out and catch it with one hand as it went flying past his head. He almost lost his balance in the process.

"Good catch!" I yelled to Jeff.

"Whoa!" Jeff gasped. His eyes were huge. He was holding the backpack by the bottom of one strap.

Anthony now started hurrying back across the front toward the side that Jeff was on.

I wanted to jump to the ground, but I didn't dare. This was almost as high as jumping off the roof of our house in our backyard, and I knew from experience that you can get hurt pretty badly doing that. So as quickly as I could I climbed down a couple of bars and then jumped the rest of the way. I looked up and saw that Anthony was almost at the corner. Jeff was just staring at him. I ran for the soccer ball.

"Let it drop!" I yelled at Jeff.

"Gladly!" he responded. Immediately the backpack fell to the ground beneath.

"I've got it now!" Anthony called, jumping to the ground and landing about five feet from the bag. He landed first on his feet and then sort of rolled onto his side, letting out a huge grunt. I don't think he realized how high up he had been. He had a look on his face that reminded me of how I felt the time I jumped off our roof, but he was already staggering to his feet.

"Hey, Dr. *Demented!*" I yelled. He was on his feet now, with his hands on his knees. He looked up at me at the same time I kicked the soccer ball. And I kicked it as hard as I could. It's amazing how when you're shooting a soccer ball in a game and the only person in front of you is the goalkeeper, most of the time the ball just seems to go right straight at the goalkeeper. At this moment I was imagining that Anthony was the goalkeeper.

To his credit, Anthony tried to get his hands up to block the ball, but all he managed to accomplish was to stand up straight enough for the full force of the ball to hit him right in the stomach. I thought his eyes were going to pop right out of his head. He looked like he was gagging or coughing or something, but no sound came out. He stumbled backward until he tripped over a seesaw and landed on his back.

"Nice *shot!*" Jeff called as he climbed down.

"*Gooaal-l-l-l!*" I yelled as I ran over and scooped up the backpack.

"Let's get out of here," Jeff said as he jumped down and landed next to me.

We took off running like two scared rabbits. I looked over my shoulder a couple of times and saw Anthony get up on one elbow as we were about halfway across the grass toward the house.

"I think we'd better not go in there," Jeff panted, so we headed through the parking lot and stopped at the sidewalk. There was no sign of anyone, not even Dad with the van. We turned and saw Anthony stumbling across the lawn in our direction.

"Let's go," I said and started jogging down the sidewalk in the direction of old Nauvoo. Jeff followed. There weren't too many buildings along here, and so we were in full view of Anthony as we ran. He angled toward us when he saw where we were going.

We had run a block or two when Jeff suggested, "We'd better hide somewhere, Bran." We looked into a couple of stores, but they were closed. We didn't see anyone walking or driving down the street, either. It was strange how there didn't seem to be anybody around.

There were several buildings close together on the other side of the street, and we crossed over, slipping in-between a couple of the buildings and running to the back. At this point we both were so out of breath that we stopped for a couple of minutes to rest, carefully watching for Anthony. I was bending over with my hands on my knees staring down the alley we had just come through. The alley was about fifty feet long, and I could see just a little of the sidewalk and street at the other end. I was hoping to see him run by.

I saw him all right, but he didn't run by. He must have seen us come into the alley, and he came straight in. I was standing in full view, and Anthony started running as soon as he saw me.

"There he is!" I screamed as I turned to run and almost knocked Jeff over in the process. We'd obviously had enough rest at this point because we both ran for all we were worth. There was a group of buildings on the edge of the hill overlooking the south end of old Nauvoo.

"That way!" Jeff pointed. We headed off in that direction as I glanced over my shoulder to see what Anthony was up to. He wasn't getting any closer, but he was definitely keeping up with us.

My lungs were burning by the time we reached the buildings. Again we slipped in-between a couple of them and ran down the alley to the back. This looked like a shipping yard. There were a couple of old flatbed trucks and a whole bunch of beat-up, wooden crates and other piles of boards stacked everywhere.

"We've got to hide!" I hissed at Jeff. My pack was getting heavy, and I didn't think I could run much farther. We checked the doors on the trucks and the building, but everything was locked.

"Let's try this," I said to Jeff. At the back corner of the building on the ground at the bottom of the wall were two wooden doors. They looked like they might lead to a storm cellar. I pulled up on one of the doors, and it opened easily. I could see steps leading down into the blackness. "In here," I said as I quickly stepped inside. Jeff followed, and we closed the door gently over the top of us.

"We need to find a light switch," Jeff whispered.

"Hold on," I answered. "I've got Dad's flashlight in here." I carefully pulled the pack from my shoulders and unzipped it, fumbling around inside for the flashlight.

"I hope it didn't get broken when I dropped it," Jeff said while I was searching through the bag. "Point it away from the doors when you try it," he suggested, "in case they don't close tight and he can see the light from outside."

I turned my back to where Jeff's voice was coming from, pointed the flashlight at my feet, and switched it on. It seemed really bright after standing in the darkness for a minute. I put my hand partway over the light to make it dimmer. We looked around and found that we really were in a cellar.

"Let's get away from the door," Jeff whispered as he moved down the stairs. We hurried around a corner at the bottom. I moved the light around so we could get an idea of where we were. The room was filled with stacks of wooden crates. They were all stacked so high we couldn't see much, and it was hard to tell how big the room was or if there were any other ways to get in or out. We started wandering up and down the aisles between the stacks of crates.

"What's in all these boxes?" Jeff asked. I shined the flashlight on the crates so we could read what was stamped on the side. It said "The Finest Winery in Illinois, Established 1852."

"These are boxes of wine!" I said.

"You're right," Jeff answered. "Remember the tour guide told us that after Brigham Young and most of the Saints left, the area became famous for wine and cheese?"

"Oh, yeah," I answered.

Just then we heard one of the cellar doors swing open. I switched the light off as fast as I could. We were two or three rows away from the doors, so I didn't think he would have seen the light. My ears were pounding, and I could feel myself starting to shake. We stood there for a few moments before we heard anything else. Then Anthony started to talk.

"Well, what do you know," we heard him call into the blackness. It sounded like he was still over by the cellar doors. "I think I see a couple of sets of wet footprints on the stairs here."

"Oh, great," Jeff whispered.

We heard the other door open. "Yes, indeed," Anthony called. "I definitely see some footprints. Now I just need a light switch."

"If he finds the light," Jeff whispered, "let's move to the back and see if we can find another way out of here."

I nodded in the darkness, forgetting that he couldn't see me.

"Brandon," Jeff whispered again, "did you hear me?"

"Yeah," I answered as quietly as I could. We stood in the dark for probably two or three minutes listening to Anthony shuffle around. There was also an occasional bump or grunt. Then all of a sudden a light switched on, but it wasn't bright enough to make much difference. I could see where each end of our row was, and I could make out Jeff's outline, but that was about all.

Without saying anything, Jeff pointed toward the end of the row away from the doors. I moved as quietly as possible down the row. It's amazing how loud everything sounds when you're scared to death and trying to be quiet. Jeff was pushing me from behind, so I moved a little faster.

We came to a concrete wall and looked both ways. There was nothing but row after row of crates in each direction. We listened intently for a moment, but Anthony hadn't made a sound since the light had come on. Jeff pointed to the right, and I started that way, skimming my hand along the back wall of the cellar. We were moving farther away from the door and from the light.

As we came to each new row of crates, I carefully peeked around the corner and down the row to see if Anthony was around anywhere. The deeper we went into the wine cellar, the darker it got. We finally reached the corner. There was a much wider aisle here between the last row of crates and the other wall. About ten feet down this wall was a door.

"Try the doorknob," Jeff whispered as we came to the door. He spoke so quietly I could barely make out what he said. I turned the knob slowly and found that it moved easily. I pushed gently on the door and breathed a soft sigh of relief when I found that it swung open without a sound. We were met by a cool breeze. Jeff and I quickly moved through the doorway and closed it behind us. It was pitch black.

"Turn on the flashlight for a sec," Jeff whispered, "but point it away from the door."

I put my hand over the end of the flashlight and switched it on. Again we squinted until our eyes became used to the new light. We were in another storage room, but instead of being filled with crates, this one was wall-to-wall wine racks filled with bottles.

As quickly as possible we moved along all the walls of the room, hoping to find another door. This room wasn't as big as the first, and we quickly discovered that there were no windows and that the only door was the one we'd just come through.

"Hey," I said after a moment, snapping my fingers. "Wasn't there a time when the Nephites were slaves to the Lamanites, and they gave the guards wine so they got drunk, and then the Nephites were able to get away?"

"What are you suggesting?" Jeff asked with obvious disbelief in his voice. "That we try to offer him some wine instead of the book? Somehow I don't think that would work too well."

"Well, maybe he'll just get tired and decide to start drinking," I offered.

Jeff didn't say anything.

"Okay, so it's a bad idea. What do *you* suggest?" I asked. We were standing in the corner of the room about ten feet from the door.

Just then we heard a noise from the other room. I wasn't sure what the noise was, but there was no doubt that Anthony was right on the other side of the door. Jeff quickly moved to the back of the room. I covered most of the light and followed. When he stopped, I stood next to him and turned off the flashlight. I could hear his shallow breathing in the dark.

We stood in silence for about ten seconds; then a light suddenly came on. Anthony had found the light switch. I looked over at Jeff, and he stared back with wide eyes. I could feel myself starting to shake again when Jeff reached over and touched my hand. Then he inched slowly down the aisle, staring at the floor as he moved. After we'd gone a few feet he looked back at me and pointed to the ground. I looked down and saw a large drain. The metal cover was at least two feet across. There was a trickle of water running down the aisle and into this drain. I looked back to where we'd come from and figured Jeff must have seen the trail of water and followed it.

I looked back at Jeff, who had a huge smile on his face. I shrugged to show him I didn't understand. In answer to my shrug he touched his chest, pointed at me, and then pointed at the drain. My shrug turned into a look of shock and fear. Just to make sure I'd understood what he was suggesting, I quickly pointed at myself, then at him, and then at the drain.

Jeff began nodding his head as he continued to smile. Although I was now sure about what he was trying to tell me, I wanted to make it very clear how I felt about his idea. I emphatically pointed to myself and then at the drain, all the while shaking my head vigorously back and forth. I had absolutely no intention of climbing down into a drain, and I wanted him to know it. He stopped smiling but kept nodding his head and pointing at the drain. I responded by acting like I was going to crack him over the head with the flashlight.

"I know you're in here," Anthony's voice came suddenly. It sounded like he was over at the door. Jeff's face got hard now, and he thrust his finger toward the drain. I stared at him for a moment and then slowly started to nod. I couldn't see any other choice.

The holes in the metal drain cover were big enough that neither one of us had any trouble getting our fingers through. Luckily, the cover wasn't too heavy, and we were able to lift it and set it down next to the hole with hardly a sound. I held the flashlight down in the opening and turned it on. The hole went almost straight down for about ten feet and was much wider than I expected. It looked like there was easily enough room for the two of us at the bottom.

Jeff immediately started to climb in. The sides of the hole were lined with rocks, reminding me of an old stone wall or well or something. The stones made for easy handholds, and Jeff had no trouble moving quickly down to the bottom, where it was flat. He looked up and motioned for me to give him the flashlight, so I let it drop into his hands.

With Jeff shining the light back toward me, I made my way down into the drain. When my head was about level with the floor, I found two footholds on either side so I could keep my balance without holding on. With Jeff steadying my legs, I reached for the drain cover and carefully lifted it back into place. I was able to do it without making hardly any noise. It sort of looked like one side wasn't down all the way, but in the dim light it was hard to be sure.

My legs were beginning to shake, so I decided I'd better quickly climb down to where Jeff was. Just as I looked down I found out that the drain cover had not been down all the way because it fell into place, making a clanking noise that echoed in the room above me. I cringed for a moment, but there was nothing I could do about it at that point, so I climbed down and stood next to Jeff on the damp stone floor. He turned off the flashlight as soon as I was next to him. The hole was wider at the bottom, giving us plenty of room to stand side by side. There was an opening on one side at the bottom of the shaft that came up about to our knees, and the ground where we stood seemed to slope slightly downward toward this opening.

I was still shaking as I looked up to watch the drain cover. The light from the room was shining through the holes. Probably sixty seconds had gone by when a shadow fell over the drain, blocking most of the light.

"What do we have here?" Anthony asked himself, just loud enough for us to hear. He lifted the drain cover and moved it to the side. He leaned over the edge and peered down toward us. His head was only about five feet away. I could tell that he was straining to see down where we were, but there just wasn't enough light. Jeff and I both held our breath.

"Okay, boys," Anthony yelled down at us. We both jumped because his voice was so loud. I'm sure he had no idea how close we were. "I know you're in here," he shouted. "You've got two choices.

Just give me the book, and I'll leave you alone for the rest of your lives." He paused. "Or," he continued after a moment, "I'll trap you boys in here and be back with a flashlight in just a bit."

Neither of us moved.

"Fine!" he yelled in frustration as he stood up. We heard the drain cover drop back into place and then listened quietly for a couple of minutes to the sound of something heavy being dragged across the floor above us. Then the little bit of light shining through the holes in the drain disappeared.

When he spoke again, his voice was muffled. "There's now a wine rack positioned right on top of the drain, boys." He paused, probably trying to catch his breath. Then he said, "I'll be back soon, so have fun." We heard him walking away, and a moment later the door slammed.

"We're in trouble," Jeff whispered. "Do you think he really left?"

"I don't know," I responded. "Let's wait a couple of minutes before we turn on the flashlight."

"Okay," Jeff said.

I don't know how long we listened to the silence, but after a while, Jeff turned the flashlight on. We both squinted for a minute.

"Do you think we're really trapped in here?" I asked.

"I don't know," Jeff answered, handing me the light, "but I'm going to find out."

He climbed up and pushed on the drain cover a couple of times. It didn't budge.

"Hand me the light," Jeff said, reaching down.

I climbed partway up and handed it to him. After shining the flashlight around through the holes for a few seconds he said, "Yeah, there's something up there all right. And I can't move the cover at all."

He dropped the flashlight into my hands and then climbed back down.

"Well," Jeff sighed, "I think it's Liahona time again, Bran."

"What do you mean?" I asked. "Time to pray or time to look something up in the index?"

"Don't look anything up anymore," Jeff replied. "Let's just say a prayer."

We each took a turn saying a prayer and then stood quietly in our cramped quarters. After a moment Jeff said, "This hole has to go somewhere. Here, let me see the flashlight for a sec. Can you climb up out of the way real quick?"

I handed him the light and then climbed up the walls a couple of feet. I saw him crouch down the best he could and shine the light down where the hole angled off. He adjusted himself a couple of times as he moved the light around.

"I think we might be able to fit through here," Jeff called up, still leaning over. "You might have a little trouble with the back-pack on, but if you took it off . . ."

"Jeff!" I practically yelled. "You're crazy! I'm not climbing any farther down this hole. We have no idea where it goes. What if we get stuck?"

"We're already stuck," Jeff answered, standing up again. "I guess our other choice is to take our chances with Mr. Loony Tunes."

I thought about this for a moment and then quietly said, "I'll follow you. Are you going to go head first or feet first?"

"I don't know," he sighed. "I think I'll try head first until I can get a better look at what's down there."

"Okay," I replied. "I'll stay here."

From my perch on the wall of the hole, I watched as Jeff twisted himself this way and that way until he finally managed to get his head into the hole. Slowly the rest of his body followed, and the light disappeared. After a moment, I heard him say something that was too muffled to understand.

"What?" I called down. "I can't hear you!"

He didn't answer, and in the total darkness, I panicked. I climbed down as fast as I dared, then leaned over to get my face down by the hole so I could call to him again. Just as I got myself in position, the flashlight blazed right in my eyes. It was less than ten feet away.

"What did you find?" I called, squinting against the light.

"It opens up down here," Jeff called back. "There's a lot more room. It's like a passageway or tunnel or something."

"Can I fit?" I asked.

"Easy," he answered. "It gets kind of tight in the middle before you get to where I am, so take your backpack off before you crawl through. Do you want me to keep shining the light at you?"

"Yes! But not in my eyes," I answered emphatically. "I want to see where I'm going."

I pushed my backpack into the hole, then I twisted myself around until I could get in a good position to follow Jeff. He was bigger than me, and I had no idea how he managed to get in because it took everything I had. I was finally able to get in the right position and started sliding down the hole, pushing my backpack in front of me.

The passageway was damp and a little bit slippery, and I couldn't see where I was going because of my backpack, but I could see the light shining around it, and it continued to get brighter as I moved forward.

"I've got it!" Jeff said as he pulled the backpack from my hands.

It was easier to crawl the rest of the way without having to push the backpack in front of me.

"Be careful of the drop," Jeff said when I reached the bottom. He pointed the light down so I could see the ground about two feet below. I pulled myself forward and out of the hole.

Getting to my feet, I said, "How big is this place?"

"It's pretty big," Jeff replied as he moved the light around. The tunnel was about three feet wide. Jeff was a little taller than me, and he was able to stand up straight with a few inches to spare. He held the light toward the tunnel, showing that it sloped downward at a pretty steep angle for as far as we could see. The passageway seemed to stay pretty much the same size and be perfectly square.

"I wonder where it goes," I said as I tried to rub some of the mud off of my hands and knees. Jeff and I were both pretty dirty, but it could have been a lot worse, considering we'd come through a drain with water running into it.

"I don't know," Jeff said. "Do you think we should go down there? I'm not sure what the best thing to do is." He sounded a little discouraged.

I didn't answer for a minute. "You know," I finally said, "I've been thinking about what you said about it being 'Liahona time.' Remember when Anthony said this is his third try to get the book?"

"Yeah," Jeff answered.

"Well, I was thinking about when Nephi and his brothers went to get the brass plates from Laban. Do you remember how many times they tried before they finally got the plates away from the evil guy?"

"I think I see what you're getting at," Jeff replied. "They didn't succeed until the third time, huh?"

"That's right," I continued. "They were really discouraged, and they went and hid in a cave, and that's when Laman and Lemuel starting beating on Nephi and Sam. But then the angel came and told them that Laban would be delivered into their hands and they would be able to get the plates."

"You're right," Jeff said. "So what do you think we should do?"

"I don't know," I confessed. "Nephi said he was led by the Spirit, not knowing what he was going to do. If a prophet doesn't always know what to do, then how should I know? But we can't get back out the way we came, so how about we explore the tunnel and see what happens?"

Jeff agreed, so we took off down the tunnel.

"Which direction do you think we're going?" I asked as I followed Jeff deeper down the slope.

Jeff stopped and thought for a moment before answering. "It seems like we're going toward the river, doesn't it?" He paused before adding, "Think about where we were in the storage room. The drain was on the back wall, and we've been moving away from the building ever since we climbed down."

"You're right," I agreed as Jeff started to move again. "I guess that explains why we're going downhill. That building was right on the edge of the hill above the old part of Nauvoo."

"Oh, yeah," Jeff said.

We continued in silence for a few minutes, and then the tunnel suddenly leveled off.

"We must be at the bottom of the hill," Jeff said. It was hard to tell for sure in the dim light, but it felt like the tunnel was very straight. Once it leveled off we seemed to be stepping on a lot more rocks.

"There are more rocks on the ground," I commented.

"Yeah," Jeff agreed, "and along the walls, too."

I hadn't noticed that before. I started thinking about the tunnel at Aunt Ella's farm. It was only about half as wide as this one, and there were wood planks all along the walls that supported a wood ceiling.

"Hey, Jeff," I said, "what's the ceiling made out of?"

"I don't know," he answered as he stopped and shined the flashlight upward. He moved it slowly along the ceiling.

"It's rock!" I exclaimed. "It's covered by big, flat rocks."

It looked like a stone walkway, only the stones were huge. They were all big enough to reach all the way across the tunnel so they were supported by the sides. There were places where I could see some dirt in-between the rocks, but it was mostly just rock.

"Whoa," Jeff breathed. "Somebody went to a lot of work to build this thing."

We looked around for another moment before Jeff said, "C'mon, Bran, we've got to find our way out of here."

We had walked just a little farther when we came to another tunnel that went off to the right. We debated which way we should go before deciding to keep going the same direction.

"Let's leave a mark, though," Jeff suggested. He used the handle of the flashlight to scratch a mark in the dirt on the wall opposite the new tunnel. At about eye level he made a six-inch arrow that pointed back the way we had come.

We continued forward for a little while before coming to another tunnel that went off to the right. Again Jeff put a mark on the wall pointing backwards, and then we continued on. After walking for another few minutes Jeff stopped suddenly and said, "Uh-oh, Bran, look at this."

He moved to the side, still shining the light down the tunnel. We'd mostly been walking on rocks, but now there was some mud around the rocks for the first few feet, and then there was water after that. We went forward a little way to see if it got any better, but we could see water for as far as the light would shine, and it was getting deeper and deeper.

"Better try one of those other tunnels," I suggested. We sloshed our way back and tried to stomp the mud and water from our shoes.

As we went back the way we had come, I noticed that it seemed like it was a lot harder.

"Are we going uphill?" I asked Jeff.

"It feels like it, huh?" he replied. "We must have been going gradually downhill before without noticing."

"Oh," I said, "that's probably where all that water came from, huh? We were probably getting close to the river!"

"You're right," Jeff said. "It felt like we were going pretty much straight the whole time. And I'm sure we've come far enough to reach the river by now. I guess that makes sense because this is supposed to be a drain, right?"

"But why would someone make such a huge long tunnel just for a drain for that building?" I asked.

"I don't know," Jeff sighed.

We decided to explore the first tunnel we came to on the way back. Jeff shined the flashlight on the wall to make sure we could still see his arrow. It was pointing in the same direction we were now going. Seeing something familiar seemed to make me just a little more comfortable.

We walked down the side tunnel for a few minutes before we came to a place where tunnels went both left and right. Here we scratched arrows on the walls on both sides, pointing back toward the first tunnel. We started calling the tunnels by number. The first tunnel being "Tunnel 1." The two tunnels going off to the right from Tunnel 1 we called "Tunnel 2" and "Tunnel 3" in the order we found them, so the tunnel we were in now became Tunnel 3.

We continued down Tunnel 3 for a long way, but every few minutes we came to a place where other tunnels went both left and right again. At each place Jeff used the flashlight handle to scratch arrows on the wall.

"How far can this go?" I finally asked. "If it's straight, then it will have to hit the river again sometime soon."

"I don't know," Jeff said. He sounded tired. "I think I can see the end up ahead, but I'm dead. I need to rest." He stopped and leaned against the side of the tunnel.

"Me, too," I said as I stopped to take the backpack off my shoulders. "Do you want something to eat? I've got some food in here."

"No way! Really?" Jeff exclaimed. "What do you have?" He rushed over and shined the flashlight into my backpack to examine its contents.

A few minutes later we were both feeling much better. I could have used something to drink, but under the circumstances neither of us complained.

"Did you say you saw the end of the tunnel up ahead?" I asked.

"Yeah," Jeff said, pointing the flashlight in that direction. "I don't see anything now, but I thought I saw a wooden wall down there before."

"*What?*" I yelled, jumping to my feet. "You never said anything about a wood wall! C'mon, maybe it's a door!"

We made our way down the tunnel and soon found a dead end that was indeed made of wood. In fact the last few feet of one side of the tunnel were also lined with wood. There were several sections, and we tried frantically to determine if any of them might be a door. We pushed for all we were worth and then looked around for any way to pull them open.

I took the flashlight from Jeff and was going around the edges of one of the panels looking for anything hopeful when something caught my eye.

"Look at this," I said with excitement. "It looks like a word."

I could hardly believe it, but carved in the stone just above one of the panels was the word *Bountiful*. We soon discovered that there was something written above each of the panels. One stated *Valley of Lemuel*, another had the word *Jerusalem*, and still another said *Mount Zerin*. We also found one that said *Lamanites* with something else after it. It looked like the number 3 and then a couple more letters, but we couldn't make it out.

"Whoever did this believed in the Book of Mormon," I said, "because these are all places from the book. But why would they put all these names here?"

"I don't know," Jeff replied quietly, "but I think we have a bigger problem."

"What?" I asked quickly. I was sure that I didn't really want to hear what he had to say.

"Look at the flashlight," he said. "The batteries are going dead."

He pointed it down the tunnel, and it lit up only about three feet in front of us. We debated for several minutes about what we should do. Finally we agreed to go back to the top of Tunnel 1 to see if we could get back out through the drain. Maybe someone else had come and moved the wine rack off the drain cover. Or maybe Anthony had come back with his flashlight and couldn't find us and then left it off. In any case it seemed better to be close to where someone might hear us or see us than to be lost down in this crazy maze of tunnels.

As fast as we could, we headed back for Tunnel 1, with the light growing dimmer and dimmer as we went. Jeff began to jog when we started back up the tunnel, and I was sure to keep up with him. We passed Tunnel 2 without slowing down and were soon hiking up the hill to where we'd first come in.

My lungs were burning by the time we made it to the top of the hill and were back to the tiny crawl space that led to the drain under the building. The light was almost completely gone.

"I've got to rest a minute before we crawl back through there," I panted.

"Okay," Jeff agreed between deep breaths of his own.

A couple of minutes later Jeff crawled through the narrow space back to the drain, taking what was left of the light with him. I followed right behind because I was not liking the dark very much. When Jeff reached the bottom of the drain he pulled the backpack through and then stood up. He left the flashlight on the floor where I could see the dim light as I crawled the last couple of feet.

"C'mon, Bran," he said. "Maybe with both of us, we can get the lid off."

Suddenly a light shined down on us from above.

"The lid's already off," came the voice that I was getting way too sick of. "And I'm happy to see that I was successful in keeping you right where I wanted you."

CHAPTER 18

Led by the Spirit

"Go, Brandon!" Jeff yelled. Pushing the backpack ahead of me, I dove headfirst into the crawl space and slithered down. Behind me, I could hear Jeff scrambling to get into position to follow me. I shot out of the slimy passageway into the tunnel, but before I could get to my feet, Jeff came sliding down on top of me.

"Sorry, Bran!" he whispered.

"It's okay," I whispered back, scrambling to my feet. "What's he doing?"

"He was climbing down the drain," Jeff answered, "but I don't know if he's coming through the crawl space or not."

Just then we saw a light shining through the crawl space.

"Do you think he can get through there?" I whispered.

"I don't know," Jeff said softly between short breaths. "He's tall, but he is pretty skinny." He paused before adding, "And desperate."

We watched as the light moved around sporadically and listened to Anthony gasping and squirming around for about a minute. Then the light became more steady. It looked like it was getting closer.

"I have an idea," Jeff whispered. "You go down the tunnel a little way until you can't see the opening anymore. That way Anthony won't be able to see you. I'll catch up with you in just a minute. Point the flashlight back toward me so I'll know where you are when I get close."

"What are you going to do?" I hissed.

"I'm going to try to slow him down a little," Jeff answered. "Go, hurry!"

I made my way down the dim tunnel, dragging my hand along one wall. I was at least thirty feet from the opening, but Anthony's flashlight was still bright enough to reach me. I looked back to see what Jeff was up to, but I couldn't see him anywhere. Squinting frantically, I tried to see where he had gone, but it was like he had just disappeared. Nervously, I continued quickly down the tunnel until I couldn't see the opening anymore because of the slope. I was amazed at how much stronger Anthony's flashlight was than Dad's had been, even when the batteries were still fresh. I could easily make out details on the ceiling above me.

I stopped with my hand on the wall and pointed our dismal light back toward the top of the tunnel where I had left Jeff. "Where could he be?" I whispered to myself. Not knowing where Jeff was made me really nervous. I did *not* want to be down here alone.

Suddenly the light was gone from the ceiling. I could see it moving around wildly at the top of the tunnel; then it went out.

"Hey!" I heard Anthony grunt. "Get back here!"

I listened intently but couldn't hear anything else. It was completely dark, so I looked down at the flashlight I was holding to make sure it was still putting out a little light. I kept hoping Jeff was coming because I was getting really scared. I waited for at least two minutes, seeing nothing and hearing nothing but my own heartbeat.

I jumped when I suddenly thought I saw something moving right in front of me.

"It's okay," Jeff whispered. "It's just me. Turn the light off now."

"What happened?" I asked softly as I switched off the light. "Where were you?"

"I crouched down right in front of the opening," Jeff answered, "and then I grabbed his flashlight when it was right above me. I turned it off and moved away as quietly as I could."

"Is that when he yelled?"

"Yeah," Jeff answered with a little laugh.

"Then what did he do?" I asked.

"He didn't make any noise for a minute or so," Jeff whispered. "I think he was listening for me. But then it sounded like he was feeling around the opening trying to figure out where he was or something."

"Did he say anything else?" I asked.

"Finally he just mumbled that he would be back, and I heard him going back through the crawl space. That's when I came down here to find you. I thought he might try to chase us. That's why I told you to wait down here, but I guess he didn't dare come after us in the dark."

"I don't blame him," I said.

"I know," Jeff agreed. Neither of us said anything for a moment.

"Should we go see if he's gone?" Jeff asked.

"You're kidding, right?" I couldn't believe what he was suggesting.

"I'm serious," he whispered. "This flashlight is really bright, so we can just shine it ahead of us. If he's still there, we can turn it off and head down the tunnel. He doesn't know what to expect, so there's no way he could keep up with us in the dark."

"Whatever," I replied.

Jeff turned the flashlight on, and it lit up the tunnel as far as we could see. I followed him as he made his way back toward the opening. There was no sign of Anthony anywhere. He had obviously gone all the way back out. And there was no light coming down through the drain.

"There's got to be another way out of here," Jeff said. "Let's go find it."

"It should be easier with *this* flashlight," I commented as I followed Jeff back down the tunnel, "because we can see everything a lot better now."

When we got to the bottom of the hill we decided to explore

Tunnel 2. I had wanted to go back to the wood panels, but Jeff said that was too far and would be a waste of time unless we explored other tunnels on the way. Tunnel 2 turned out to be pretty much exactly like Tunnel 3. It was really long and had five or six other tunnels intersecting it. We made arrows next to these intersections just as we had done in the other tunnels. Really, the only difference we could tell was that there were no wooden panels at the end. It just sort of ended.

"Do you think all these side tunnels connect to the other tunnel?" I asked.

"I don't know," Jeff answered. "Probably. Let's find out."

We went down the very first tunnel we came to after turning around at the dead end of Tunnel 2. It seemed a little narrower than the other tunnels had been. We walked for about five minutes before coming to an intersection.

"Look at that," Jeff said over his shoulder. He was shining the light right onto one of his arrow marks on the wall. "I think we found Tunnel 3," he concluded.

"That means the wood panels should be down this way," I said. "Let's go see."

"I don't want to try to break through there anymore," Jeff said.

"I know," I answered. "I just want to go see, so we can be sure how everything fits together."

Jeff finally agreed, and we headed for the end of the tunnel. We found the wooden panels, all right. I felt a little better seeing something familiar.

"I still wonder what these words are here for," I said, trying to get Jeff interested and to maybe help me.

"Not now, Bran. We've got to see if we can find an *easy* way out of here."

"Maybe this *is* the easy way," I argued.

"The last time we were here," Jeff said, "we stayed so long that the batteries ran out. We need to see what else we can find before that happens again."

I could see his point, so we left. We spent what must have been a couple of hours searching up and down all the tunnels we could find. It was totally amazing. What we discovered was a huge grid. There were the two long tunnels that we figured had to be going north-south and then there were seven shorter tunnels going east-west. The tunnel leading to the winery was the east-west tunnel that was farthest south.

All the east-west tunnels ended in water just like the first one. They weren't all the same length, but the longer ones all went uphill just like Tunnel 1. Unfortunately, none of the other tunnels connected with anything; they all just sort of died out or came to a dead end.

"It looks to me like there's no way out of here except the way we came in," Jeff said finally as he leaned against a wall in the east-west tunnel closest to Tunnel 1.

"We could go try the wood panels again," I suggested.

Jeff didn't answer right away. Finally he sighed, "I guess. But let's rest for a minute, first. I'm really tired."

"Okay," I agreed, slumping to the ground. Jeff sat down also. He was still holding the flashlight, but it was pointed straight up.

"Do you want something to eat?" I offered.

"No, thanks," Jeff muttered. After a moment he said, "I can't even imagine how frantic Mom must be by now, wondering where we are."

We sat in silence for a couple of minutes before I looked up where the light was shining and something caught my attention.

"What's that?" I asked, standing up to get a closer look.

"What's what?" Jeff replied without much interest.

"It's another rock with something carved in it!" I said as I stood closer.

"No way," Jeff responded, rising to his feet to see for himself.

It was kind of hard to make out, but finally we decided it said "Skins of Beasts."

"What does that mean?" Jeff asked. "I mean, all those other things were places. There's no place in the Book of Mormon called 'Skins of Beasts,' is there?"

"I don't know," I admitted. "But I don't think so." I unzipped my backpack, pulled out my triple combination, and looked up "skin" in the index. The very first reference was 1 Nephi 17:11, and it said: "Nephi makes bellows of skins of beasts."

"What are bellows?" I asked.

"It's one of those big accordion things they use to blow fires," Jeff answered.

I looked through the rest of the references under "skin," but I couldn't find anything else about "skins of beasts."

"So why would anyone write 'Skins of Beasts' up there?" I asked.

"I have no clue," Jeff responded, slowly shaking his head back and forth. "Why did they write 'Valley of Lemuel' and 'Jerusalem' down at the other place? I couldn't tell you that, either."

"I wonder if there are more of these things around, but we just haven't seen them," I said. "Let me see the flashlight for a minute."

Jeff handed me the flashlight, and I made my way down the tunnel searching the ceiling for more engravings.

"Here's another one!" I called over my shoulder after I'd gone about thirty or forty feet.

Jeff had followed me. "What does it say?" he asked.

"It looks like 'Noah—Life as Garment,'" I said slowly. "What does that mean?"

"Better look in the index," Jeff suggested.

I handed the flashlight back to Jeff and opened my book. I looked up "Noah" first, but there were three different Noahs and a ton of references. Then I looked up "garment." About halfway through the listing I found this: "Mosiah 12:3 life of Noah to be valued as a garment in a hot furnace."

I read it to Jeff.

"Those are both about fires," Jeff offered. "The first one was a bellows for a fire, and now this one is about a furnace. I don't get it."

Suddenly it hit me. "Oh, no!" I said. "This is like . . . ! No, where are we? Yes, it is! I don't believe it! Do you get it?"

"What?" Jeff asked, exasperated. "Do I get what?"

"This is like a map," I said excitedly. "This tunnel is under that street we were on this morning, whatever it was. Parley Street, I think, wasn't it?"

"I don't know," Jeff said. He looked confused. "What about Parley Street? W-what makes you think . . . ?" He paused. "What are you *talking* about?"

"Don't you get it?" I asked again. "Where did we see a bellows in Nauvoo? It was at the blacksmith's shop, right? And where was there a furnace? At the brick-making place! They called it a kiln or something like that!"

"Yeah, . . ." Jeff said slowly. "So?"

"So think about where we are in the tunnels," I said, smiling. "I think we're right under Parley Street, and this sign is telling us that we're under the kiln, and back there is where the blacksmith's shop is."

"Oh, cool!" Jeff said.

"Hey, Jeff, do you still have that little booklet with the map of Nauvoo in it?"

"I think I stuck it in my pocket," Jeff said as he started searching for the map.

"Maybe we can find some more of these things, and we can figure out better where we are."

Jeff found the map, and we started searching through the tunnels with new energy. We found a bunch more stones that had words engraved in them. Some of them we couldn't read well enough to figure out what they were saying, but a lot of them were quite clear.

We found that every one of the tunnels leading down to the river had the word "Irreantum" at the last intersection. We read in 1 Nephi 17:5 that *Irreantum* means "many waters."

At the top of the east-west tunnel that was farthest north there was a dead end, but here we found the words "Manner of Solomon" engraved. There were only four references under "manner" in the index, but they didn't have anything to do with Solomon. But the very first reference I found under "Solomon" was 2 Nephi 5:16, which says: "Nephi builds temple after manner of temple of Solomon."

The only thing on the map even close to where we were was the Nauvoo Temple site. We decided there was no doubt what this was referring to.

We found a stone under Main Street that had "Mormon and Lamanite King" engraved on it. I looked up "Mormon" in the index and found a reference to Mormon 6:2 that talks about Mormon sending an epistle to the Lamanite king. According to Jeff's map, we were right under the post office.

North of the post office a little way we found the words "Remember His Body." It didn't take us long to find Moroni 4:3, which is the sacrament prayer for the bread. The bread in the sacrament is supposed to remind us of Jesus' body. We figured from the map that we must be under the bakery.

"Hey, look at this!" Jeff said, pointing at the map. "There's supposed to be a well right behind the bakery."

We were right next to one of the "Irreantum" tunnels, so we followed it about as far as where we thought the well should be. We found a place in the ceiling that opened upward a little bit and looked sort of like the drain we'd come through under the winery. But just a foot or so up into the shaft there were lots of rocks crammed into the opening.

"Looks like it used to be a well," Jeff muttered, "but it's closed off now."

We talked about maybe trying to pull some of the rocks loose, but then decided we didn't want to die in a cave-in. We slumped to the ground and sat in silence for a few minutes. I had no idea how long we'd been down here or how in the world we were going to get out, and I was cold, hungry, and worn out. I wondered what Anthony was up to but didn't feel like bringing up the subject. Jeff was still pointing the flashlight up into what used to be the well, just sort of staring into space.

"Is there any place we haven't been yet?" I asked, glancing back down the tunnel toward where we had found the bakery. I saw something that excited me and scared me at the same time.

"Jeff!" I hissed. "Turn it off!"

He quickly snapped back from wherever he was, and everything went black. Everything, that is, except the tunnel we'd just come from. We could see a faint light at the last intersection. Neither of us made a sound as the light continued to get brighter.

My heart began to race. I was sure it was Anthony. He must have found another flashlight somewhere and had crawled through the drain after us.

"Let's move," Jeff whispered. "We're too close to the other tunnel. If he shines his light down here, he'll see us."

I stood quickly and felt my way farther back into the tunnel. We kept going until the ground felt muddy under our feet, constantly checking to see the light getting brighter behind us.

"Think we're far enough?" Jeff asked.

"Yeah," I answered softly, "but let's crouch down just in case."

About ten seconds later Anthony reached the intersection. We watched fearfully as he shined the light first down to the right and then to the left. We couldn't tell if the light was reaching us or not, but there was no doubt he would have seen us if we'd stayed where we were at first.

The light seemed to linger just a little longer when it was pointed toward us than it had for the other tunnel. But then Anthony continued past the intersection, and the light quickly dimmed. Jeff and I both released our breath at the same time.

"That was close," Jeff hissed. "He had us!"

"I know," I breathed.

Jeff took a couple of swallows. "If we can get to that intersection, then we can beat him to the first tunnel and get out of here the way we came in."

"Okay," I said, "I want to get out of here."

We made our way back to the intersection as quickly as we could in the dark. There was no more sign of Anthony's light, so it was hard to tell how close we were getting. I was in front dragging my hand along the wall when all of a sudden the wall ended. It surprised me, and I stumbled a bit, kicking a loose rock in the dark that skipped through the tunnel and seemed to echo forever. Before the last echo had died, a light switched on only about ten feet away. Anthony had been waiting for us!

"R-r-run!" Jeff yelled from behind me. He sort of halfway picked me up as he went by. He switched on his flashlight and headed for Tunnel 1. I was right behind him, and I could see Anthony's light bouncing past me. We had adrenaline on our side for now, but I could tell from the light that Anthony was definitely keeping pretty close to us.

We turned the corner and started toward the winery.

"I don't think we can make it," I called to Jeff. "He's too close! He'll catch us before we can crawl through and get out!"

"So what do you want to do?" Jeff called back over his shoulder.

"Go down Tunnel 2 when you get there!" I called back.

"Okay!"

A couple of minutes later Jeff turned the corner, and I followed right behind. I glanced back one more time just to see how far behind Anthony was.

Jeff slowed down and asked, "Now what? Did he see us come this way?"

"Yeah," I panted. We were getting close to the place where three of the tunnels intersected. "Keep going," I said. "I think we can make it to the next intersection before he gets around this corner."

We both took off running again. I kept a close watch over my shoulder to see how close Anthony's light was getting.

"Jeff!" I called. "Get ready to turn off the flashlight! I think we can stay away from him in the dark! I'll tell you when it looks like he's close to the corner!"

"Okay!" Jeff called back, continuing to run.

Just when Anthony's light looked like it was about to reach the corner, I yelled, "Now!" and Jeff immediately turned off the light. We weren't quite to the intersection yet, but Anthony's new flashlight wasn't bright enough to reach us from where he was. We could tell that he was still running in our direction, though.

"We're almost to the corner," Jeff panted. "Hurry!"

We stumbled along in the dark for just a few seconds before we reached the next intersection. We knew this tunnel pretty well because it was the Parley Street tunnel. We kept moving as fast as we could in the dark until we thought we were far enough away that Anthony's light wouldn't be able to reach us from the intersection. Together we watched his light grow brighter.

Anthony stopped and pointed the flashlight down each of the three tunnels. We watched for two or three minutes as he kept shining the light in different directions. Then he turned and went back the way he had come. We didn't want to get caught the way we had before, so we decided to stay close enough that we could still see his flashlight. We moved closer and closer back to the intersection as the light dimmed.

This time the light dimmed much slower than before. When we peeked around the corner, we found out why. Instead of pointing the flashlight the direction he was going, this time he was shining the light behind him as he made his way back to Tunnel 1.

He was moving pretty slowly, so we watched for several minutes until he came to a stop. When he got back to the intersection of Tunnel 1, he just stood there shining the light back and forth in each direction.

"What's he doing?" Jeff whispered after a few moments. "We won't be able to get back to the drain as long as he's standing there."

"That's probably why he's doing it," I said. "He may not know his way around all these tunnels the way we do, but he probably knows that the only way to get back is the way we came in."

We watched for several more minutes. At one point it looked like he was moving, but then we decided he had just sat down. He just keep alternating between the two tunnels with his flashlight.

"There's *got* to be another way out!" Jeff hissed with frustration.

"I've been thinking about that," I said quietly.

"You're not going to suggest the wood panels again, are you?" Jeff asked.

"Well, wait," I defended myself. "You know how we looked up scriptures for all those engravings we found and they gave us clues? Well, we never looked up anything about what was above the panels."

"They were just *places*," Jeff replied. "There are probably a ton of scriptures about Jerusalem and—what was the other one—Bountiful, right? There are probably just as many about Bountiful, too."

"What about the other ones, though?" I asked. "I was thinking about those. Remember one said 'Valley of Lemuel,' right? I think the Book of Mormon talks about that maybe only one or two times. So we can look at that one. But the other one . . . do you remember what it was?"

"I don't know. It was a mountain or something, I think."

"It was Mount Zerin," I said. "Remember? I said that I had seen that name somewhere before but couldn't figure out where."

"No. But you've probably read it in the Book of Mormon before."

"No! I mean someplace *else!* Don't you remember me saying that?"

"No," Jeff replied.

"Well, I said it. And I finally figured out *where* I'd seen it before!" I waited for Jeff to respond.

"Where?" Jeff asked finally, acting extremely uninterested.

I glanced toward Anthony's light before I answered.

"It's written on Hannah's old bookmark that's in Aunt Ella's Book of Mormon! And do you know what else? I think it said something about the Valley of Lemuel and the Lamanite king on that bookmark, too!"

"Really?" Jeff asked, slightly more interested now.

"Yeah," I whispered. "But do you know what that means?" I didn't wait for him to answer. "It means that Elias Franzen probably built these tunnels! And he was using clues from his Book of Mormon to mark where things were!"

"So?" Jeff said.

"Let's go back down this tunnel a little way and look up 'Valley of Lemuel' and 'Mount Zerin' and see what we find," I suggested.

Jeff hesitated. "You go," he said after a moment. "I'll stay here and keep an eye on the guard dog."

"Okay," I said. "Give me the flashlight."

I made my way down the tunnel until I thought I was far enough that Anthony wouldn't be able to see the light from around the corner. Then I switched it on. I'd forgotten how bright it was and quickly put it inside my backpack, letting just a little bit of light seep out. Then I pulled out my triple combination and opened up the index. I looked up "valley" and found 1 Nephi 2:10. It states: "And he also spake unto Lemuel: O that thou mightest be like unto this valley, firm and steadfast, and immovable in keeping the commandments of the Lord!"

There were a whole bunch of references under "mount" and I didn't want to search through all those. I wasn't sure how to spell *Zerin*, so I pulled out the old Book of Mormon and looked at Hannah's bookmark. Here's what I found under "Zerin" in the index: "Ether 12:30 brother of Jared said to mountain Zerin, Remove, and it was removed."

I started to get excited. Were these clues supposed to be telling me which panel was "immovable" and which one could be "removed"? The thought made me shake with hope. Then I glanced at the bookmark to see what else was written there. It had "Mormon and Lamanite king" just as I had remembered. But the one I hadn't remembered was "Lamanites, A.D. 30."

I thought about this one for a minute, before remembering that one of the panels had "Lamanites" above it and there was something else with it.

"It must have said 'A.D. 30,'" I whispered to myself.

Quickly I looked up "Lamanite" in the index. The list of references was huge. I was trying to remember when A.D. 30, was, thinking that might help. Then I remembered that the entire Book of Mormon has the date at the bottom of each page. Frantically I turned through the book until I found a page that had A.D. 30, at the bottom. It was printed on the pages for 3 Nephi, chapters 6 and 7. Turning to the index again, I looked for a reference under "Lamanite" that was in 3 Nephi, chapter 6 or 7.

"Yes!" I said out loud when I found 3 Nephi 6:14 in the listing. I read the whole verse. It talks about "Lamanites who were converted unto the true faith." And then it says that "they were firm, and steadfast, and immovable" in keeping the commandments.

As fast as I could, I put the books away, switched off the flashlight, and made my way back to where Jeff was watching Anthony.

"Jeff!" I whispered in the dark. "Where are you?"

"I'm right here," he answered quietly. "Anthony's still down there."

"I found it!" I hissed. "Every one of the scriptures says something about being immovable except one: the one about Mount Zerin! Mount Zerin was moved by the brother of Jared! That's the way out! I *know* it!"

I could tell Jeff was hopeful, but he asked for a few more details before deciding to go with me to try to get out through the "Mount Zerin" panel. Finally he agreed. We decided it was safe to turn on the flashlight again but only after we were two tunnels away from where Anthony had set up his stakeout.

Once we had light, we ran all the way to the wood panels. I think Jeff was just as excited as I was. When we got there we both started throwing ourselves against the panel as hard as we could. After about the third try it felt like it budged. Jeff felt it, too, and so without a word we both kept hitting it harder and harder. Within five minutes we had one side of the panel moved back about a foot.

"Can you see around it?" I asked Jeff, who was standing on the side that was moving. He picked up the flashlight and shined it around the side of the panel.

"Yes!" he exclaimed. "It's another tunnel."

With just a few more hits we had it open far enough that we could squeeze through. Once inside, we decided to push it back into place so Anthony wouldn't be able to see where we'd gone. We also found a couple of small, loose rocks to put up against it. It probably wasn't enough to make much difference, but it made us feel just a little safer.

"Let's get out of here!" Jeff hissed, and with the flashlight beam dancing in front of us, the two of us took off exploring the new tunnel.

CHAPTER 19

The Promised Land

This tunnel behind the "Mount Zerin" panel went east for only a few feet and then turned north. The walls, floor, and ceiling all looked pretty much like the other tunnels. We had gone about fifty feet when we noticed that the ceiling was quickly getting lower and lower.

"Oh, no!" I moaned to Jeff, who was in front. "Don't tell me this is another dead end!"

"I don't think so," Jeff said hopefully. "Can't you feel that breeze?"

"Yeah!" I said, realizing that he was right. "Hey, Jeff, turn off the flashlight for a minute!"

"Why?"

"Just do it, okay?"

The tunnel went dark.

"Yes!" I yelled. "Do you see what I see?"

"No way!" Jeff answered. "It's light up ahead! Let's go."

We had to crawl the last twenty feet, but the tunnel came to an end in some thick bushes about fifty feet from the Mississippi River. We could see the sun was just above the hill to the east when we staggered to our feet. We both squinted and covered our eyes. I think I'd almost forgotten what daylight was and what fresh air smells like.

"Brandon!" Jeff said after a moment. "We were in there all night!"

"I know!" I responded. "I can't believe we're finally out! Do you think Dr. Dopey is still down there guarding the tunnel?"

"I hope so!" Jeff laughed. "We better go find somebody so they know we're safe. Maybe the police can go down the drain and catch him."

I was genuinely ecstatic over that thought, and the two of us took off running for help. We could see the LDS visitors' center a few hundred yards south of us, and we headed in that direction. Our exhaustion caught up with us, though, and our running soon turned into a determined walk. Just as we hit the visitors' center parking lot we saw a police car heading our direction. Waving our arms, we flagged it down.

"Are you the Andrews boys?" the officer asked as he rolled down the window.

"Yes!" we panted in unison.

"Are you okay?"

"We're fine." Jeff answered. "But there was a guy chasing us, and we think we know where he probably still is, and you could catch him!"

"Is that the Anthony fellow you're talking about?" asked the officer, jumping out to let us into the backseat of his car. We were muddy and wet, and I'm not so sure he was happy about having us climb into his clean car.

"Yes!" I answered. "There's a building up on the top of the hill over there." I pointed in the direction of the winery. "And there's a drain in the cellar that leads into a tunnel and . . ."

"Hold on a minute, boys!" the officer pleaded. "First things first! We've got to let your folks know that you're all right before anything else. They've been real upset."

We waited impatiently in the backseat as he got on the radio and told the radio dispatcher that we had been found and to please notify our mom and dad. I didn't understand why he didn't just turn on his siren and drive as fast as possible to the winery. In fact, he didn't even put the car into gear until he knew exactly which building we were talking about and had gotten on the radio one more time to ask for some other officers to meet him there. I have no idea what this guy's problem was, but he not only didn't use his siren, he didn't commit even one single traffic violation on the way to the winery. He obviously had no appreciation for what we'd been through.

There were already two other police cars in front of the building when we pulled up, and we saw Anthony wearing handcuffs and being helped into the back of one of the cars. It turned out that the other officers had seen him coming out from around the back of the winery just as they arrived.

Anthony was taken off to jail as soon as Jeff and I identified him. He didn't seem to really notice anything else—he just kept muttering softly about almost getting his hands on the treasure map. We could see him through the car window still muttering as he was driven away. As soon as he was gone, we were taken to the bed and breakfast place, where we had a pretty happy reunion with the whole family. There were lots of hugs, tears, and smiles—even from Shauna.

Everyone was totally amazed as Jeff and I recounted the story of where we had been for the last fifteen hours. When the police officers heard about the drain under the winery, they immediately sent someone to investigate. When we got to the part about how we finally got out, they sent someone else to check that out, too.

Jeff and I were exhausted and hungry, so once the storytelling was over we had a few bites and then each fell into a deep sleep. It was late Saturday afternoon by the time I woke up. Jeff was still sleeping.

"Did Anthony escape yet?" I asked, only half joking.

"No," Dad laughed, "not that I know of, anyway. The FBI has him now, so I think he'll be well taken care of."

"The FBI?" I asked, surprised by the thought. "Whoa."

"Well," Dad explained, "I think as soon as a criminal moves from one state to another, the FBI takes charge."

"Oh," I nodded. "So what did the police think about the tunnel?" I asked.

Dad's smile turned into a hesitant look. "Well," he sighed, "they—they can't find it."

"What do you mean?" I asked in total shock.

"You've *got* to be kidding!" Jeff mumbled, just waking up.

"Well," Dad explained, "they went to the winery and talked to the owner, but he said he didn't want them going down there unless it was completely necessary. He said he was too busy and didn't want to deal with it. The police agreed that they didn't really have any reason to require him to let them in, so they dropped it."

"What about where we came out?" Jeff asked.

Dad shrugged. "The police said they conducted a thorough search and could never find anything."

Neither Jeff nor I could believe what we were hearing. We made Mom and Dad drive us down past the visitors' center so we could show them the exit from the tunnel, but *we* couldn't find it, either. All the bushes and rocks looked the same. We searched for at least half an hour before Dad finally convinced us to quit.

"It's okay," Dad said. "It would have been fun for us to see it, but it's obviously just not going to happen. We're all tired and hungry. Let's go get something to eat."

Of course Jeff and I both argued, but it didn't make any difference. I have no idea how many times during the rest of the evening Jeff and I would look at each other and just shake our heads in disbelief. The whole thing was quickly starting to feel like a complete dream.

Dad had originally intended to stay in Nauvoo only two nights and then drive back to Aunt Ella's farm, but Anthony had effectively ruined that plan. We ended up staying two extra nights: Saturday and Sunday. Sunday we went to church and saw a couple of shows at the LDS visitors' center. The rest of the day we spent relaxing at the bed and breakfast.

That evening Dad started asking Jeff and me more details about the tunnels under old Nauvoo. I got out my Book of Mormon and showed him the bookmark with Elias Franzen's handwriting on it, explaining how we used the clues to figure out which panel was moveable. I think he was pretty impressed that we knew how to use the index. I smiled over at Shauna, and she smiled back.

As I was putting the book away, I was surprised that I had a little trouble getting the book back into the pouch. It had always slipped in easily before, but this time it felt like something was in the way. I slid my hand in and discovered an extra little slot halfway down the inside cover of the pouch. The edge of the book had gotten caught on this slot as I was trying to slide it back in place.

Inside the slot I found a single piece of paper, which had been folded several times. It looked really wrinkled and old and had a couple of corners torn away. It was covered with faded handwriting, which looked different from the writing on the bookmark. The paper had obviously been written by somebody other than Elias Franzen.

"What do you have there?" Dad asked.

"I don't know," I said, handing the paper to him. "I've never seen this before."

He spent a few moments looking it over and then began to laugh.

"What is it?" Jeff asked.

"I think Brandon just found the treasure map that Anthony was looking for!" he chuckled.

"That doesn't look like a treasure map," Shauna said.

"It's not!" Dad replied. "I think it's Elias Franzen's patriarchal blessing! Right here it says that this will be a 'map' for the rest of his life and that it's a 'treasure' equal to the Book of Mormon and other scriptures!"

"Ha!" Jeff laughed. "That's why the letter in the plastic cover said something about a map and a treasure! Do you think we should break the news to Dr. Anthony?"

"I don't know if this would make him feel better or *worse*." Dad smiled. "But look at this," he continued, "it's signed by Joseph Smith, *Senior*. That makes sense, because he was the patriarch of the Church. So the letter from Elias wasn't to Joseph Smith, *Junior*, the Prophet, it was to Joseph Smith, *Senior*, the patriarch!"

We all had a good laugh. Dad suggested that I might want to donate the paper to the Church. It seemed like a good idea, so I let him keep it. For the rest of the evening, I smiled every time I thought about Anthony's "treasure map."

Monday morning we made the four-hour drive to Aunt Ella's farm. It was good to see her again, and she was very interested in all that had happened since we had last seen her. I could hardly believe it had been less than two weeks; it seemed like years. I kept a glass of Aunt Ella's lemonade with me all afternoon.

Shauna found something to keep with her all afternoon, too. It was a letter from Tom saying that he still wanted to go out with her and that she now had two guaranteed dates with him. One was for dinner and a movie whenever we finally made it back to Utah, and the other was for the first school dance the next year. She just smiled at everyone and every*thing* the whole rest of the day.

I had some mail waiting for me, too. Gabe sent me a postcard that said our team had taken first place in the tournament. I was happy for them, but somehow it didn't get me nearly as excited as I thought it would.

I spent some time Tuesday morning trying to remember all the clues and scriptures that Jeff and I had found in the Nauvoo tunnels, writing each one in my spiral notebook. I also drew a map of the tunnels and marked all the places where we found clues carved in the stones. I had Jeff look it over to make sure I hadn't missed anything.

After putting my notebook away I began wandering around the

farmhouse just looking at things and remembering everything that had happened over the last six weeks. I knew I was definitely going to miss this place. I couldn't even remember the last time I'd had such a great time.

As I was walking past the bookcases in the sitting room, something caught my eye that I hadn't noticed before. It was a very old brown and white picture of a young girl in a checkered dress. My mouth fell open when I saw it. I snatched it from the bookshelf and went to find Aunt Ella.

"Who is this girl?" I asked, showing Aunt Ella the picture.

"Why, this is a photograph my father took of me when I was ten or eleven years old," Aunt Ella smiled. "Dad always said it was one of his favorites because the photo reminded him so much of his own mother. All the relatives said that I looked a lot like my grandmother."

"Really?" I smiled. "That's fun."

"Would you like to have it?" she asked.

"Yes!" I couldn't believe she was offering. "Are you sure it's all right?"

"Certainly!" Her eyes twinkled. "I would love for you to have it."

Carefully, I removed the Book of Mormon from the plastic bag and the pouch and placed Aunt Ella's picture inside the front cover. I don't have any idea how long I held it before putting it away again.

The next day we each gave Aunt Ella one last hug before climbing into the MAV. As we drove away I had the feeling I would never see her again. I knew I would miss her terribly. I turned my head to the window, hoping no one would notice me wiping my eyes.

We stopped at the Winter Quarters visitors' center in Omaha. Just as Mom had promised, there were some pretty neat displays of mud huts, cabins, and wagons and ox carts. The missionaries let

Danny lift the handle of a handcart to show how perfectly balanced it was. We were told the Saints stayed here just one winter on their way to Utah. It made me think about Elias Franzen and the fact that he had never made it this far.

Winter Quarters was the last place we stopped for sightseeing. We spent the next day and a half just trying to get home. Meg asked Dad if her bedroom was going to be all fixed before we got there, and he said that he thought it would be. Somewhere in Wyoming, I pulled out my spiral notebook to check over the bets. Granny's was the only one that I couldn't be sure of yet. Here's what I wrote:

Thursday, May 29. More Andrews Family Betting Results:

DAD: (Won) He got everything worked out just like he said he would.

MOM: (Lost) Dad won (see above).

ME: (Lost) Again, Dad won (see above).

I was only slightly disgusted at the thought that so far Dad was the only one who had been right. I was getting anxious to get home and see how Granny's house-sitter had done. We were all numb from the long drive, and we had been gone so long it didn't even seem like our own house when we first drove up. To stretch our legs, the first thing Jeff and I did was go to the backyard and kick a few goals. It was great to be home. I turned to look at the back door when I heard it swing open.

"Brandon!" Meg giggled. "Have you seen your room?"

"No, . . ." I answered slowly. "Why?"

She was still giggling as she said, "You'd better come see!"

"*What!?*" I asked, feeling a little uneasy.

"You'd better come, too, Jeff!" she smiled. "It's your room, too!"

We both took off running, being careful not to knock Meg over as we flew by. I suddenly had a terrible feeling about what I might find.

I got to the doorway of our room and froze in horror. Dad was standing in the middle of the room with half a smile on his face.

"Oh, *no!*" I groaned.

Jeff pushed his way past me into our room. "No way!" he yelled. "It's *pink!*"

"Sorry!" Dad grimaced. "It looks like the painters switched the colors when they painted the bedrooms. The girls got your color, and you got theirs."

I tried for about twenty seconds to think of something to say as I looked from one wall to the next. My mouth was hanging open the entire time just ready for me to say whatever I thought of, but nothing ever came out. Finally I just turned around and marched out to the MAV. I don't think I could even begin to count how many times I heard Jeff say, "No way!" before the front door slammed behind me. I climbed into the van, pulled out my spiral notebook, and made this entry:

Thursday, May 29. Final Andrews Family Betting Results:

GRANNY: (LOST!!!!) *Her friend did a LOUSY job taking care of the house.*

Dad was the only one who had been right, but at the moment I was far more upset about the color of my bedroom. We had to sleep in it only one night, though, because Dad went with us the very next morning to buy some new paint. Of course, Jeff tried to talk Dad into getting Dodge Ram red, but that was way too close to pink, in my opinion. We finally agreed on some generic off-white stuff with a fancy name that wouldn't make anybody imagine the color it really was. By lunchtime the pink walls were nothing more than a horrible memory.

Later that evening when the paint was dry, Jeff came up with an idea that I liked. We agreed that it would be a fun reminder of our trip. We spent an hour or so looking up stuff in the index of our triple combinations and hanging scripture references around our room. We hung a sign by the window that read "3 Nephi 24:10." That references states: "Bring ye all the tithes into the storehouse, that there may be meat in my house; and prove me now herewith, saith the Lord of Hosts, if I will not open you the windows of heaven, and pour you out a blessing that there shall not be room enough to receive it."

We had two references on our closet. Alma 33:7 says this: "And when I did turn unto my closet, O Lord, and prayed unto thee, thou didst hear me."

And 3 Nephi 13:6 reads: "But thou, when thou prayest, enter into thy closet, and when thou hast shut thy door, pray to thy Father who is in secret; and thy Father, who seeth in secret, shall reward thee openly."

On the post of our bunk bed we had "Alma 37:37," which reads: "Counsel with the Lord in all thy doings, and he will direct thee for good; yea, when thou liest down at night lie down unto the Lord, that he may watch over you in your sleep; and when thou risest in the morning let thy heart be full of thanks unto God; and if ye do these things, ye shall be lifted up at the last day."

That night as I lay in bed smelling the fresh paint, I started thinking about everything that had happened the last couple of months. I sincerely hoped that Dr. Anthony was out of my life for good, now that he was in the hands of the FBI. Thinking of him quickly reminded me of the incredible gift I had received from Aunt Ella. I switched on my reading light and picked up the old Book of Mormon from my nightstand. I had left it there with my other set of scriptures. After turning it over slowly in my hands for a moment, I carefully untied the straps and removed the book from its pouch. I still felt reverent every time I touched it.

I spent a few minutes rereading all the scriptures that had been marked by Elias Franzen and looking over the bookmark that was still between the pages in Third Nephi. I smiled as I thought about the words on the bookmark. My smile quickly turned into a yawn, though, and I realized how tired I was. It was definitely time to put the book away and go to sleep.

Just then Jeff called to me from the upper bunk.

"Hey, Brandon!" he said softly.

"Yeah?" I answered.

"Do you think Shauna's asleep yet?"

"I don't know. Why?"

"Well," Jeff paused, "you know that 'No Trespassing' sign she has on her bedroom door?"

"What about it?"

"I found a scripture to go with it," he snickered. "It's 3 Nephi 13:14."

"What does it say?" I asked.

"Look it up!" he answered. "Tell me what you think."

I got my regular triple combination from my nightstand and looked up the scripture. After reading it I immediately let out a laugh and said, "Let's do it! I'll bet she's asleep!"

We found a black, permanent marker and sneaked down the hall to Shauna's bedroom. Just as I finished adding the reference to Shauna's sign, she ripped open the door.

"What did you do?" she demanded, staring at her sign. Jeff and I both turned and ran for our lives. She was right behind us.

"Stop!" I yelled as she came charging into our room. Both my hands were out in front of me, ready to protect myself against her attack. "Before you do anything else, you have to read the scripture!"

She stared at me for a minute before turning around and going back to her room.

"Do you think she'll be back after she reads it?" Jeff asked.

"I don't know," I said as I crawled into bed.

We both waited silently in the dark, listening for any sound that might warn us that Shauna was coming back. I thought I heard her laugh, but she didn't come back or say anything. After a while, Jeff's breathing sounded like he'd fallen asleep, and I began to relax, too. The last thing I remember thinking was how lucky I was to have such a cool Book of Mormon.

About the Author

Carl Blaine Andersen holds a bachelor of science degree and a master's degree in mechanical engineering from Brigham Young University and is a software engineer at Novell. A former member of the Mormon Youth Symphony, Carl enjoys music and teaches cello. He has served in The Church of Jesus Christ of Latter-day Saints as an elders quorum president, a ward executive secretary, a Primary teacher, and as a counselor in the bishopric of a single adult ward. Brother Andersen is married to Shari Lynn Tillery Andersen. They are the parents of six children and reside in Orem, Utah. Evolving from a story he originally wrote to read to his children, *The Book of Mormon Sleuth* is Brother Andersen's first published novel.